PAST GRIEF

A NOVEL BY

EDWARD J. LEAHY

Black Rose Writing | Texas

ISBN: 978-1-68433-652-4
PUBLISHED BY BLACK ROSE WRITING
www.blackrosewriting.com

Printed in the United States of America
Suggested Retail Price (SRP) $21.95

Past Grief is printed in Baskerville

*As a planet-friendly publisher, Black Rose Writing does its best to eliminate
unnecessary waste to reduce paper usage and energy costs, while never
compromising the reading experience. As a result, the final word count vs. page count
may not meet common expectations.

PAST GRIEF

PAST GRIEF

CHAPTER ONE

Thursday, February 23rd, 8:35 PM

Detective Kim Brady stared at the shot-up front of The Cove, a bar on Gansevoort Street in New York City's Meatpacking District. Three bullet-riddled men lay sprawled on the sidewalk in front of the vacant storefront next door.

Her partner, Mike Resnick, pointed toward the bar's entrance. "Crime Scene guys say it's gruesome as hell inside. You sure you're up for this?"

"Are you?" Damn, she shouldn't snap at him. But his pat on her shoulder told her no harm, no foul. She took a deep cleansing breath, pushing her still raw emotions to the farthest corner of her mental closet. "Sorry, Mike, yes, I'm fine." Toughen up, girl, because if Mike says it's bad... "Let's see what we've got."

Ambulances crowded both ends of the street beyond the yellow-tape perimeter CSU had already established. Two emergency medical technicians—EMTs—barged past her bearing a young Chinese woman on a stretcher as blood seeped through the pressure bandage wrapped around her head. A third EMT followed close behind, keeping pace and holding an IV bag aloft.

Inside, shards of glass from the shot-up front window crunched under Kim's flats. She stiffened at the coppery odor of blood mixed with the smell of alcohol from a dozen shattered bottles behind the bar. A woman in her twenties, her eyes vacant, lay at an angle away from the bar. A halo of blood surrounded her head, her white satin blouse turned crimson. Her right foot was shoeless, the reinforced toe of her hose pointing upward. Under the bar rail, a high-heeled pump lay on its side.

Closer to the bar, a second woman with skin like cinnamon lay sprawled on her back. One slug had shattered the back of her head, leaving her tight, black curls matted with crimson red. Next to her, a guy about thirty lay lifeless, having sustained shots to the back, neck and head.

Mike turned away, more shaken than she would have expected. "They never knew what hit them. I miss the old days, slaughterhouses handled Meatpacking District killing."

Kim refused to turn away because this was her job, damn it.

A sudden flash made her flinch. A guy she remembered from the Medical Examiner's Office snapped a photo of the woman with the shattered skull. "Sorry about your dad, Kim." He resumed snapping photos.

"Thanks." She shook herself. Get the facts, analyze, and solve the case.

Mike stared at the woman being photographed, saying nothing. Unusual for him.

Wood splinters and fresh gouges from bullet strikes ran the length of the ornate bar, set along the right side of the building. Shattered pieces of cocktail glasses and beer bottles littered the bar and the floor. Scarred tables and old bentwood chairs occupied the left side, many of them overturned or shoved aside by people rushing to escape the carnage.

She turned back to Mike. "The shooter fired high, shattering the front window and splintering the main door."

Other than a slight nod, he didn't answer.

They stepped back outside, where Kim gulped the cold, fresh air. The crowd gawking from CSU's yellow-tape perimeter at the dead bodies on the ground was growing, despite the deepening cold. Kyle Dobson, a detective from the Sixth Precinct, was waiting. "Hey, Kim. Sorry about your dad. EMTs already took out the ones who were still breathing. Five females and two males in critical condition and three females and three males with moderate-to-severe injuries."

Mike stirred himself. "What else you got?" At forty-seven, he had twenty-four years on the job. The weariness in his voice alarmed her, but his uncharacteristic lack of leadership even more.

Dobson nodded toward the three bodies. "One of them had a SIG Sauer P224 with six rounds still in the magazine. CSU recovered five nine-millimeter shell casings, so he came with a full one."

That didn't add up. "There were sixteen victims in here."

"Yeah," Dobson replied, "and he didn't pop any of them. He was returning the attacker's fire, but no signs yet he hit anybody."

Kim nodded her thanks for Dobson's condolences. "Which one was the shooter?"

Dobson's partner, Chris Ryba, spoke up. "The SIG Sauer was found closest to the tall one. According to his driver's license, he's..."

She stopped him. He was holding something behind his back. "What are you hiding?"

Ryba turned sheepish. "Oh. This." He held up an evidence bag. Inside was a pair of women's shoes. "CSU had them tabbed on the sidewalk up the block, about two hundred feet from Washington Street. They were just sitting there."

And he should have left them there. "How? In what position?"

"Each lying sideways, a few feet apart. I left the marker tabs where they were."

She inspected the shoes. Nine West black pumps, size eight-and-a-half, three-inch spike heel. Looked brand new except for heavy scuffing on the bottom of the heels. She waited for Mike to say something, but he stared off into space. "This investigation is now being run by Manhattan South Homicide. Any decisions about what evidence we keep and what we discard, Detective Resnick or I will make. Do you understand?"

Dobson and Ryba both nodded with vigor.

Deep breath. "Okay, tell me about the tall guy laying near the weapon."

Ryba relaxed a little. "Malcolm Drake, age twenty-two, home address in Parkchester, up in the Bronx. Way taller than your usual street dealer." He hesitated before adding, "Sorry about your father, Kim."

"Thank you. Don't place the shoes where you found them, return them to CSU so they can record the chain of evidence."

Mike's head snapped up as Ryba walked away. "Wasn't there a kid named Malcolm Drake, blew through the city public high school playoffs a few years back?"

"I remember him." Kim jammed her hands into her jacket pockets against the biting wind. "He played college ball for a year, came out, but no one drafted him." Dobson stared at her, mouth agape. "My boyfriend works for the Nets." Dobson failed to hide his dismay at the mention of a boyfriend.

Enough chatter of boyfriends and hoops. "What about his two associates?"

Dobson, after consulting his cell, said, "The Latino had four big ones in cash on him. The other black kid had four glassine envelopes on him containing white powder, which CSU already has."

They must have stashed more, somewhere. "Where's the rest of it?"

"I checked around," Dobson replied. "Found nothing."

Most buildings on the block showed various stages of renovation. A large dumpster stood fifty feet east of the Cove. Kim donned latex gloves. "Got a flashlight? I left mine in the car."

Dobson offered his, and she made her way around the dumpster, probing every nook and crevice. At the far end, her light glinted off something shiny, a zippered plastic bag of glassine envelopes. "Let's bag it."

Mike stared first at the Cove, then at the dumpster. "Stupid, dealing in the open with no pathway for quick getaways."

He just noticed now? She turned back to Dobson. "Where are the witnesses?"

4

"No one saw much of anything. Everybody kept down, out of the line of fire. You saw the shape of the bar."

She glanced around. "Where are they, now? I need to question them."

Dobson blushed, casting nervous glances for his partner, who still hadn't returned. "We thought..."

"You let them go?" Not what she wanted to hear.

"Shit," Dobson said, "there's no place warm for them out here. We couldn't keep them inside with the stiffs. But I got twenty names and addresses of folks willing to talk to us, and we detained Tracy, the waitress, and one guy. A girl he'd been chatting with ran out moments before the shooting started. I figured you'd want to locate her, learn what she saw."

Well, if either provided a lead, not a total loss. "Where?"

"He's sitting in the patrol car over there. Pretty freaked out, though. Tracy's in the first ambulance. She got cut by some flying glass."

As she walked away, Dobson said to Mike, "Must be a major distraction to your workday." He'd kept his voice low but not low enough. "Those eyes, hair in pigtails, nice tight ass..."

She hated when anyone referred to her "low dog ears" style as "pigtails".

Mike barked at him. "Cut the shit." The big brother she'd never had.

CHAPTER TWO

Thursday, February 23rd, 9:22 PM

The witness, Matt Berringer, sat in the parked squad car, a thousand-yard stare in his eyes, as Kim introduced herself. "Thanks for waiting. I understand you spoke with a woman who left moments before the shooting."

"Yeah." His voice quivered, and he struggled to focus. "She left right before the shooting. Ran out. Her name was Leanne, a likeable girl. Shy. Sweet." A momentary smile vanished.

"Why did she run?" Kim kept her voice low and gentle, trying to calm him.

"Don't know. I bought her a glass of wine. Is she okay?"

"We found no female victims outside. What happened before she left?"

"I offered to take her to dinner, because the crowd was getting loud... she was wearing this cross... such a likeable girl..."

"What happened when you invited her to dinner?"

"She... Leanne... didn't want to go. Gave me her number... jumped up and ran out... right before..."

Nice-looking guy. Kind of like her boyfriend. Not a self-styled stud, not a creep, or a guy who'd make a girl run. But then, she hadn't seen him in target acquisition mode. "What did she look like?"

"Tall, I think. About five-nine. Her name was Leanne."

She had to refocus him. "Did you notice if she was wearing heels?"

His eyes met hers. "I don't know. I didn't look."

"What about her hair; her eyes…"

He took a deep breath and focused. "Brown hair, straight; short in back, much longer in front; hazel eyes." He paused, his brows furrowed. "Lips were thin." He reached for the door handle.

She didn't blame him for wanting out, but she needed more. "What was she wearing?"

"A black or dark blue dress with tiny white dots." He pulled on the door handle.

"I need a little more, Mr. Berringer. What about jewelry? You mentioned a cross."

He slumped back. "Yeah, she had a pendant, a cross, on a neck chain. I never saw one like it."

"How do you mean?" Unusual often meant easier to identify.

"It was gold, very delicate, not your basic cross. Had a circle around the middle…" He glanced at his watch. "It's getting late."

"I know. You seem to have an excellent picture of her in your mind. I'd like you to give a full description to a police artist for a sketch in the next day or so."

He frowned. "You think she's mixed up in this?"

Her gut told her no. "I need to learn what she saw. May I have the phone number she gave you?" She copied it into her Notes app and gave him her card. "I'll call you as soon as I get hold of an artist. If you think of anything else, please let me know."

He sighed. "Okay."

Tracy, the waitress, was sitting in the ambulance, its rear doors ajar, the heat inside blasting. She had a gauze dressing on her left temple and a few scratches on her face. "Yeah, I saw the girl as soon as she came in, a shy kid, kind of cute, but way out of her league. She made a beeline for a corner table and didn't so much as open a mouth. I told her to watch out for the sharks, but when this one guy bought her a drink, I told her he wasn't one of them. Decent guy."

"How long did he sit with her? And what made her run out?"

"I'd say he was with her about twenty minutes, thirty at most. I didn't see her leave; some asshole was blocking the front door. I was on my way to tell him to get out when she bolted past me, looking scared shitless. How she got past the asshole, I'll never know. But she did."

"Did you see him? The guy at the door?"

Tracy rolled her eyes. "I saw him, all right. He'd spent the last hour ducking in and out, taking cash and handing out little plastic envelopes."

"You saw the cash and the envelopes?"

Tracy snorted. "Oh, yeah, had to happen. Mario—he's the owner—loves his badass rep. He isn't badass, he just likes the vibe, but over the last few months, it's been turning into the genuine thing."

"You've seen this guy in here, before?"

"Not him. Others. I told Mario to crack down, because if it keeps up, I'm gone."

"What did he look like?" Kim was already making entries to her Notes app. "The guy at the door."

"About five-ten, weighed about one-eighty or one-ninety. White guy, with short, dark brown hair. Scruffy. Either starting on a beard or too lazy to shave. Wore a gray suit, white shirt open at the collar, red striped tie, loose. Smelled like he hadn't showered in a week."

Kim took Tracy's contact info. "I'd like you to meet with a police sketch artist."

Tracy shrugged. "Sure. I don't think I'll be working for a while."

Dobson was waiting as she stepped down from the ambulance. "Mike's questioning witnesses around Gansevoort Plaza at the east end of the block. Chris isn't back, yet. What can I do?"

"Canvass the apartments facing Washington Street and any of the boutiques still open." They passed two yellow markers on the sidewalk which she assumed were for the shoes Ryba was returning to CSU. "Meet me in front of the bar when you finish." She crossed the street and entered Bubby's, the restaurant on the corner of Washington.

A waiter there had seen a vehicle, possibly an SUV, turn onto Gansevoort a few moments before the shooting but hadn't thought much of it. "I saw a woman dive into a cab on Washington as the shooting started. But I couldn't see her face."

"A yellow cab?" They were easier to track down than car services.

"No. Car service. Small van. Ugly paint job, red, gray roof, I think." Okay, something useful. Mike kept a book on car services. "Drove south on Washington." He reflected a moment. "One weird thing. She was barefoot."

"Did you see her take off her shoes?"

He shook his head, and she thanked him.

A small Chinese man was stacking packs of cigarettes into a display behind the counter of the deli on Gansevoort Street. As Kim entered, she flashed her gold badge.

"Coffee?" he asked.

The strong, bitter aroma suggested it had aged several hours since brewing, like convenience store coffee. "Sure. Light and sweet." On the other hand, Mike drank convenience store coffee all the time. "And please give me one black, no sugar." She placed a five on the counter. "Can you tell me anything about the shooting earlier this evening?"

"Don't see nothing. Loading stock. Nephew supposed to work tonight, but..." He shook his head. "No respect."

"I'm sorry about your inconvenience." Perhaps sympathizing would encourage him to cooperate. "You heard the shots, though?"

"Yeah. Bringing box in from sidewalk. Lazy driver dumped it and ran off. Things hard enough already. Neighborhood changing fast. Getting fancy. Can't afford rent. And then nephew not come."

"I'm so sorry," she said. "But about the shots?"

"I hide behind counter. Stay till everything quiet again."

"Did you notice anyone out on the street before the shooting?"

"No, too mad about delivery." He brightened. "Yes, lady across street was running. Didn't see good. Heard loud shoes."

An unfamiliar expression to her. "Excuse me? Loud shoes?"

"When she walk, make noise, clip-clop."

She had still been wearing the heels, fitting with where CSU had left their two markers. "Any cars pass your store?" She took a sip of the coffee and suppressed the urge to gag. It was even worse than she'd expected.

"Couldn't see street good, too dark. Sorry, wish I could help."

She picked up the second cup of dark swill. "Thank you. Excellent coffee." She walked back toward the Cove, stopping to empty her cup in the gutter.

Several TV vans now crowded the outer perimeter, while officers kept news reporters at bay. No sign of Dobson or Ryba, which she found a considerable relief. She gave Mike his coffee.

"Thanks." He took a sip. "Hey, this is good."

She shook her head in sorrow and recapped what she'd learned.

"Spoke to a barmaid at Bagatelle," Mike said, "over on Ninth and Little West Twelfth Street. She saw what looked like a Chevy Blazer haul ass out of Gansevoort and up Ninth."

"The Blazer was going the wrong way. Gansevoort is a one-way street going west."

Dad's first step in investigating: what appears out of place?

"Good. When we nail the bastards, we can tack on a moving violation."

Dobson and Ryba met them near the entrance to the bar. "No one saw anything," Dobson said.

They'd have to wait for the reports from CSU and the Medical Examiner. "I guess we're done for tonight. We'll regroup in the morning and see what we've got."

The door to the bar opened and teams from the ME's office brought out the three dead victims. Mike froze, staring at the woman who'd suffered the head injury.

"You got the skull fragments?" one attendant asked.

"In the bag," said the other.

Her cell buzzed on the way to the car. It was their lieutenant, John Kiley. She ignored it.

Mike stared after the ME teams. His square jaw was now less firm, his broad shoulders sagged, and flecks of gray were visible in the black hair above his ears. "I'm getting too old for this shit."

CHAPTER THREE

Friday, February 24th, 1:45 AM

"This station is Clark Street." The computerized voice jolted Kim from her thoughts. The Two train was almost empty. Almost an hour after end-of-tour on the 4:00 PM to 1:00 AM shift, Kim was still struggling to rid herself of the image of the dead Latina's blood-soaked hair. Also haunting her were memories of the blouse of the woman missing her shoe.

Standing relieved the pressure of her second piece, kept tucked in the waistband of her slacks, against her lower back. It was a vintage 1950 Smith and Wesson "Chief's Special", a long-nose thirty-eight with a five-round cylinder. It had belonged to her grandfather, Detective Daniel Patrick Brady, a native of Dublin who'd emigrated to New York in 1928 and later died in the line of duty. Dad had given it to her when she graduated from the Academy. When anyone asked, she said she carried it because an ankle holster was too cumbersome.

Until her parents divorced when she was ten, a portrait of Grandad in his dress blue uniform laden with ribbons sat on the mantel over the fireplace. Unlike Dad, a hero in life and in death.

She trudged up the stairs and entered the waiting elevator, wary. A twenty-something guy, his overcoat open, his navy-blue Joseph A. Bank suit rumpled, leaned against the far side of the car, exhausted. He reminded her of the guy lying next to the dark-skinned girl in the bar. No threat there.

They rode in silence up to the lobby of the old Hotel St. George, which now served as housing for students from NYU and New York Law School. A few were arguing in murmured voices. "Wait, you'll see. Today, it's Muslims; tomorrow, it'll be Jews, and then..."

Once on the street, she smelled weed, common of late given the mayor's determination to relax enforcement of laws against it. On the two-block walk home, she called the number Leanne had given to Matt Berringer, but it wasn't a working number.

She and her boyfriend, Jake, shared the first-floor apartment of a brownstone on Monroe Place. Brooklyn Heights, yuppie heaven, and for the past year, hers, too. Jake's father owned the building and Jake managed it in return for living there rent-free.

Light from two high front windows illuminated the magnolia sapling in their modest garden, including its first buds. She climbed the front steps. Flower boxes would be a pleasant touch, and she'd see if they could add them this spring.

Jake took her in his arms. "I heard about a big shooting downtown. Had me worried."

"Mike and I caught the case."

He held her. "Your first case back? Not what I'd call easing into it. It's all over the news."

"I saw the vans. Last thing we need." Media cases were always hard—so many expectations; all decisions second-guessed. The crime scene came back to her. She could almost smell the blood. She'd seen plenty in her eight years on the job, but nothing like this. "And Mike's off his game."

"You sure you're ready for this?" A former backup point guard at Brooklyn College, he still worked out and played in a rec league. His arms were firm, muscular, and protective, holding her as they had when she'd come home that awful night she'd stopped to check in on Dad.

She stroked his cheek, lingering on the black stubble, her way of chiding him for not having shaved, and tried to bury the memory. "Sorry I couldn't be here on your night off."

"Hey, we can deal. I was fine watching hoops."

Her eyes met his, large, brown, soulful. "A busman's holiday." They'd met at a party where she'd felt overwhelmed and slipped away to watch a televised Knick game. He'd followed her. They'd talked basketball all night. Those gorgeous eyes.

"Cavs beat the Knicks by fifteen," he said. "They're sinking to Brooklyn's level."

"Did LeBron get fifty points?"

"No, he was up for best supporting tonight. Eighteen, I think. Cavs are looking good for the title."

Despite her exhaustion, she laughed. "Golden State might disagree."

The microwave beeped. Jake waved her into the dining area. "Leftover lasagna, salad and a glass of wine is the best I could do, I'm afraid."

"Thanks." She took a bite, and then a sip of wine, but struggled to get it down. "Hell of a first case back."

"The grief counselor said it might be too soon to…"

"He was wrong." She popped out of her seat. "Yes, it's bad right now. 'Joe Brady's poor daughter; imagine a thing like that'. They drown me in condolences while avoiding the word 'suicide'. But staying away from the job isn't the answer." She shrugged. "They mean well."

He took her back into his arms. "Then, what is the answer?"

She didn't resist, clinging to him for a long moment. "I think it's getting back on the horse and solving this case. And I'm concerned about Mike. He was a step behind all night. Yes, the crime scene was terrible— horrific—but he's seen plenty of those."

"So, you're leading?"

"He's a first-grade detective, I'm third." Besides, Kiley would have to approve it.

Jake broke into a grin. "You getting on the horse or not? Who took charge tonight?"

"I did."

He continued to hold her. "So, where will you start?"

Three amateurs dealing in the open with no escape. Stash right there on the street, also in the open.

Car going the wrong way. The gray suit guy at the door.

The bar shot up with an automatic weapon.

Leanne giving Berringer a phony number; running out for no reason; ditching her shoes.

She broke the embrace and shook her head. "I can't decide because everything is out of place."

CHAPTER FOUR

Friday, February 24th, 2:25 AM

He liked to think of himself as the mastermind of a very lucrative operation. But he wanted more, and tonight had done more than eliminate a careless street dealer whom they never should have allowed in. He'd sent a message to everyone in the organization, such as it was, saying they were now working for him. He'd sent a warning to anyone who dared think they could get a piece.

But his jubilation at the appointed hour, when he'd poured a cognac to celebrate the assignment going off exactly as he'd planned with computer-like efficiency, had vanished. The local cable news station flashed its "breaking news" alerts. Horrific images of innocent victims and heart-tugging tales of woe and loss had followed.

Who the fuck told that idiot to shoot up an entire bar? Those were *customers*.

Neither the idiot shooter nor his fool of a driver had called in to report. No doubt they were scared, as they should be.

Tired of waiting, he punched up the number of a prepaid cell, a burner phone, in the Bronx. "Where are they?"

The voice on the other end, his closest advisor, the man he called his "aide-de-camp", was soft but concerned. "They haven't reported in."

"Find them and instruct them. They're now over budget on fuck ups."

His aide-de-camp had advised against tonight's operation. "You calling the captain?"

But a brilliant commander did not second-guess his decisions. He needed to control events from now on.

He allowed himself a smile. "No. You call him. Taking orders from someone of lower rank reminds him of his place. I want him to report which detectives Manhattan South Homicide assigns to the case, and to provide the information no later than first thing in the morning."

"Understood."

"One other thing we need is damage control."

Ten minutes later, his cell buzzed. It was the captain. "Mike Resnick and Kim Brady are the assigned detectives."

Obedient dog. "Excellent. Isn't Kim Brady…"?

"Joe Brady's daughter."

"Keep me informed." Joe Brady's daughter, returning to work after her daddy offed himself. He raised the snifter of cognac. "I must live right."

CHAPTER FIVE

Friday, February 24th, 8:05 AM
The TV in the squad room at Patrol Borough Manhattan South—PBMS—on East Twenty-First Street, was always on. This morning, *New York One* was blaring the news of the shooting. The officers on duty paid no attention. It was the same news they'd been hearing for hours.

Kim hated going in super early while on the four-to-one shift. Home by two, up at six, and at her desk at PBMS by eight. Groan. But she wanted Sheila Gregg of the NYPD's Forensic Artist Unit on this one. Sheila picked up on the first ring. "You're in bright and early." An excellent omen to start the day.

"Rape last night in Chelsea," Sheila replied. "They're bringing the victim here straight from the ER. I understand you caught the Cove case."

Word was getting around fast. "Yeah, I need you to see someone."

"They suspect this guy is a serial rapist. Someone got a look at your shooter?"

She explained about Matt Berringer and Leanne.

"You think she's involved?"

"No, but she might've seen the shooter. I need to find her."

Sheila lapsed into momentary silence. "A sketch of a witness is definitely outside the box. You might catch some shit from upstairs about…"

"I'll worry about catching any shit. Can you see my guy today? I also have a waitress from the bar who saw someone working with the dealers."

"Get one down to One Police Plaza at ten, the other at eleven, I can squeeze them in."

"Thanks." She called Berringer and Tracy to firm up the arrangements.

Kiley walked in, casting a quick glance at the TV screen and muttering "Fuck" under his breath. "Where's Mike?"

"Not in yet. He's on the four-to-one."

"So are you. And why the hell didn't either of you answer my calls last night? The Chief of Detectives has been on my ass since the news broke."

"We were kind of busy, Lieu."

He studied her. "You sure you're ready to come back?"

She swallowed her irritation. Be positive. "No question. Besides, with the media swarming, we'll need everyone available full time. True?"

Kiley scowled at her mention of media. "Got that right." He turned thoughtful. "Something's up with Mike. He's moody and unfocused. Even muttered something about dropping his papers the other day. He'll need all the help he can get. Are you're up to it? You sure you didn't come back too soon?"

This pity party was getting ridiculous. But she couldn't snap back at him. "I can handle whatever you need me to do. Anything, no limitations."

Dobson and Ryba walked in.

"Our lieu told us to report to you until you don't need us," Dobson said. "I spoke with the CSU sergeant last night before I left. He said the shell casings they recovered from the street looked like they might be from an AR-15, but Ballistics will tell us today for sure. They also recovered two slugs from the SIG Sauer; they're searching for the others."

"Thanks." She turned to Kiley. "We should set up an information board." She glanced around for an appropriate place.

Kiley's irritation receded as he focused on tasks. "Put it in my office."

She was skeptical. Kiley's office looked like a hoarder's paradise, with files stacked everywhere. "Not much space."

"We'll manage. There's a marker board and easel already in there, jammed in next to the file cabinet." He led them inside. Dobson and Ryba extracted the marker board while Kiley grabbed a bunch of files and shoved them onto a teetering stack. Dobson began making entries on the board.

"There's a drug angle, here," she said, "so we'll need help from Narcotics. Mike has a contact there."

Kiley nodded. "Bob Nolan. They were partners back in the day. Should be an excellent starting point."

She turned back to Dobson. "As we get any information from CSU, the crime lab, Ballistics or the ME's office, note it here."

"Yes, ma'am."

"What's your plan until Mike gets here?" Kiley dug into the closest pile of papers on his desk, trying to multitask.

The noise level in the squad room was rising. "I'm meeting Sheila Gregg this morning…"

He brightened, shoving the pile aside. "You have a lead on the shooter? Amazing, fan—"

"No. I'm getting a sketch of a woman who may have seen him." She braced herself for Kiley to tell her to clear it with Mike, first.

But he didn't. "Okay. A sketch will help if she becomes a suspect. What else?"

She told him about the gray suit guy and Tracy seeing Sheila. "We'll check for any recent thefts of small SUVs. Ryba, check the three mopes who were dealing outside for priors." She was gaining confidence as she put a plan into words. "We'll get leads. There are no perfect crimes."

"Better not be. Not in my command."

Mike walked in, looking like he hadn't slept. "What's up?" He read as Dobson posted on the marker board. "Wow. Excellent job, Kim."

Two minutes passed as Kiley said nothing. "Okay, listen up, all of you. Kim, I want you as lead detective on this case. Keep me posted on your progress. When I call you, either answer or call me right back." He shook his head. "Fucking media cases."

Back outside, Kim studied Mike's expression for signs of resentment but saw something more like relief.

"Tell me what you need," he said.

"Please monitor those two and check out any SUVs stolen in the past couple of days for a potential match. And we need to meet with your pal, Bob Nolan."

.   .   .

Matt Berringer was waiting for Kim outside of One-PP, his pleasant features creased with disappointment. "I tried to call Leanne. Not a working number."

"I know. I tried, too." Once inside, she introduced Sheila to Matt and pulled up another chair. "What kind of work do you do?"

"I'm a tax attorney for an insurance company." He appeared calm and focused this morning.

"Does Leanne work for the same company?"

"No, she works at one of the major banks as an accountant. She didn't say which one."

Matt repeated the description he had given to Kim the night before, with some additional details. Sheila showed him templates of face shapes, nose shapes, eyes, and mouths. As Matt made his selections, she sketched, pausing only to ask for additional details.

Sheila sketched in details of Leanne's dress, with its low Peter Pan collar. Next came her hair, a pixie with long side bangs, and her glasses with wide tortoiseshell frames. They spent a lot of time on her pendant, a Celtic cross.

"I feel like I saw it myself," Sheila said as she sketched. "How is it you remember it in such detail?"

"I'd never seen one like it. Delicate. Classy. I was studying it when she got up to leave."

Sheila returned to the face, asking specific questions about Leanne's makeup. The details emerged—eye liner and shadow, long, thick lashes, blush and lipstick.

She showed them the finished product, and Matt smiled. "Yeah. Wow, you captured her."

He grew sheepish. "I know. She's not..."

Kim's first thought was of a nerdy accountant—plain but sweet. "I'm not one of the guys. I think it's great when a guy pays attention to a girl who's not a supermodel. What if she'd accepted your dinner invitation?"

"I'd have taken her to a great little restaurant on Bleecker, then home in a cab, and I'd have asked to see her again."

"And perhaps she'd invite you up when you got to her place?" She hoped she'd said it with tact.

"Not this girl. Never even occurred to me. Why?"

"I'm trying to figure out why she bolted."

He stared at the floor. "If you find her, could you please tell her I'm worried about her?"

"Sure will. Thanks for coming in."

Sheila scanned the sketch into the system. "I'll e-mail it to you with the second one."

Tracy arrived a few minutes later.

CHAPTER SIX

Friday, February 24th, 11:55 AM

When Kim showed the Leanne sketch to Mike back at PBMS, he shrugged. "Not much, if you ask me. Looks like a likeable kid, but I don't see what this guy went all gaga over."

"He wasn't looking for a party. He was looking for someone to love."

"I guess there's worse."

She tossed the sketch onto her desk. "Why would she run? She'd already given him a phony number."

"She was afraid he wasn't taking no for an answer?"

"Don't think so. This guy oozes sincerity." Like Jake. "A girl would pick up on that."

"Maybe she wasn't looking for love."

"Look at her, Mike—her dress, those glasses, her Celtic cross. She wasn't looking for a party, either."

"Maybe she was in on it."

Dobson and Ryba came over. Ryba handed Kim a printout. "The guy with the cash had two low-level busts on his sheet. No priors on the other two."

"Ballistics confirms the killer used an AR-15 on the three guys outside and the sixteen victims inside," Dobson said. "CSU found a bunch of shell casings on the street several feet east of the Cove matching the slugs they found inside. Forty-eight slugs altogether, and CSU is still working."

"He continued shooting up the Cove after hitting the dealers." Kim made additional notes.

Mike sat back. "He had to be packing a hundred-round drum. I think the firing into the bar was suppression fire to keep the curious from coming out."

But an AR-15 was a semi-automatic weapon. "Someone must've converted it to full auto."

"Easy to do. And ballistics don't lie." Mike sat back. "But shooting up the bar when the targets were outside? It's like something out of an old Edward G. Robinson movie."

"Don't forget the gray suit guy at the door," Kim said.

Dobson exchanged glances with Ryba. "What gray suit guy?"

This was ridiculous. "Didn't you guys take a statement from Tracy, the waitress?"

Ryba shrank back, leaving Dobson to explain. "No. We had her wait for you."

Okay, they were precinct detectives and trying not to step on any toes. "The three guys outside were dealing. The gray suit guy was their runner. But then, according to Tracy, he blocked people from leaving when the shooting started." The deeper she dug, the less sense it made. "And Leanne must have run smack into him."

"Makes me wonder if she's not as sweet and innocent as you think," Mike said, his voice low.

She remembered the heels. "Any word from the lab on those shoes CSU tabbed on the street?"

"They haven't reported back yet," Dobson said. "I'll follow up."

"Yes, please do. Text me as soon as you learn what they found. In the meantime, you and Ryba search the mug shots for a match with this sketch of the gray suit guy. Keep on it until you either find him or run out of mugshots."

"Got it," Dobson replied.

She turned to Mike. "Time to check out our three venture capitalists. Which guy held the cash?"

Mike checked his notes. "Diego Paredes, twenty-eight, address in the South Bronx. Mott Haven, to be exact. The guy with the glassine envelopes in his possession was Luke Wilson, twenty-three, of Washington Heights."

"Looks like Paredes was the ringleader. And Drake lived in Parkchester. So, let's start in the Bronx."

.   .   .

Kim caught the street sign as Mike turned off Brook Avenue onto 140th Street. "This doesn't look like public housing. I thought we were looking for 141st."

"I got assigned here to the Four-Oh straight out of the Academy in 1993," Mike said. "Armpit of the city, sink or swim. A memorial stood in one of these doorways to a guy they called Moondog. A twenty-year-old kid who died shielding a pregnant woman during a wild shootout."

"These buildings are lovely. Look at those polished wood doors."

"Gentrification. Back then, they were all boarded up. Windows, too." He pointed toward the school across the street. "My ex taught there. Every kid qualified for free breakfast and lunch. When schools were closed, some of those kids didn't eat." He picked up speed until turning onto Willis Avenue. He parked in front of the public housing project on 141st Street.

Kim buzzed for the super, and a few moments later, a rotund, greasy-haired workman in a dirty shirt came to the door. The stark fluorescent lighting inside highlighted the cracks in the wall, the missing chips of plaster, the unreadable scrawl of graffiti. The hallways had the familiar odor of stale urine. Not much different from Kim's first tour, the Seven-Three in Brooklyn.

"Paredes' apartment is 1-E," the super said. "Don't you cops talk to each other? There's already somebody in there."

"Thanks, we'll find it ourselves." Kim exchanged glances with Mike. No one else should have been there.

The studio apartment's door was ajar. Dirty laundry lay in a pile on the floor next to the unmade bed. The living room reeked of stale beer and empty cans were everywhere. The odor of garbage hung heavy in the kitchen. Roaches skittered along the baseboards.

A young black police officer in uniform was rummaging through Paredes' dresser drawers.

Kim cleared her throat. "What are you doing here?"

He jumped and turned around. "I'm a cop." His collar bore the number fifty-one. "Police Officer Ken Ames."

She flashed her badge. "Detective Kim Brady, Manhattan South Homicide, and this is Detective Resnick. Why are you here, far from the Five-One?"

"My sergeant asked me to check it out."

She put her badge away. "Are you aware Mr. Paredes, who lived in this apartment, was murdered last night? The Cove shooting."

The young officer appeared shocked. "That was him? No, I didn't know. I guess you're here investigating his murder."

"Ya think? Now, why are you here? What are you looking for?"

"We're involved in an informal borough-wide investigation of a burglary ring. There's been a rash of break-ins in several neighborhoods in the North Bronx. We think it's being directed from down here. My sergeant wants us to get the Four-Oh off the dime."

"Who's your sergeant?" she asked.

"Sergeant Henry Phillips. But I don't think you want to push him on this, Detective. I'll be on my way, now." He stormed out.

She turned to Mike. "A threat?"

"Not a total loss." Mike held up a ripped zip-lock plastic bag with a hanger. "Officer Ames forgot something. Got an evidence bag?"

Not an answer to her question. She gave him an evidence bag. "Let's get CSU in here. Then, on to Malcolm Drake's place."

.   .   .

Kim stared out the passenger window as Mike pulled onto the soon-to-be-decommissioned Sheridan Expressway. Traffic on the Bruckner had slowed to a crawl.

The Bronx reminded her of Dad, Detective Joseph Francis Xavier Brady.

The first time she'd asked him about the job, she was eight and he was cleaning the Chief's Special she now carried as her second piece. He worked in the Bronx, back when Mom was still making excuses for his lengthy absences. Later, Mom would say Kim had caught on to Dad's cheating before Mom did. And Dad claimed it proved Kim was a talented detective, on a par with him and Grandad.

"Metropolitan Oval, right?" Mike asked.

She snapped back to the present. Mike had reached the end of the Sheridan and was following East 177th Street to the service road of the Cross Bronx Expressway. "Huh?"

Mike chuckled. "Malcolm Drake's address?"

She checked her notes app. "Um... yeah, Metropolitan. Oval."

He cast a sidelong glance at her. "You okay?"

"Does it make any sense to you Paredes might've been dealing and in a burglary ring?"

"No." He took a deep breath. "To tell you the truth, I'm glad Kiley put you in charge of this case instead of me."

CHAPTER SEVEN

Friday, February 24th, 1:40 PM

Malcolm Drake had lived with his grandmother and younger brother. The apartment was tidy, with decades-old furniture.

The grandmother was sobbing. "It was all that Paredes boy's fault. He struck me as bad news the first time I laid eyes on him."

Kim sat next to her on the floral print sofa. "When did you first meet him?"

"A few months ago. A rude and arrogant young man."

"We found Malcolm with a handgun in his possession," Mike said. "Did you know…"

"Any gun had to belong to Paredes." The old woman sobbed. Kim caught Mike's eye and shook her head.

The brother had remained sullen and quiet until then. "Hey, man, why don't you go pick on someone else for a while?"

Kim took the grandmother's hands in hers. "I'm so sorry for your loss. I promise you we will do everything we can to bring your grandson's killers to justice. We're asking these questions because we need to piece together what happened."

The woman nodded.

"You want to go, now?" The brother's hostility was mounting.

28

The grandmother dabbed at her tears with a tissue. "Be nice, Ethan."

Kim stood. "Ethan, why don't you walk us out? We'll let your grandma be."

They walked down the stairs, the boy glancing from Mike to Kim.

"It had to be hard for Malcolm," Kim said. "What did he do when he couldn't hook on with an NBA team?"

"Stayed fucking inside. Everywhere he went, everyone asked the same fucking thing. 'What happened? Why ain't you in the NBA? Why not give the Knicks a call?' Drove him crazy."

Don't challenge or threaten him. "So, what happened?"

Ethan stopped on the landing. "He and Luke were teammates from high school. Luke invited him to hang in the Heights, where Luke made sure they didn't give Malcolm no shit."

"What about Paredes?" Kim asked.

"What about him?"

Mike snapped. "How'd Malcolm hook up with him, genius?"

"Please tell us." Kim shot a warning scowl at Mike.

"Luke introduced him, but I ain't sure when." Ethan slouched against the wall. "Like, one day, he was there."

She looked him up and down. He couldn't be over fourteen, and he was hurting, trying to protect his brother's memory. "You were aware he had the gun."

He broke eye contact.

She softened. "We're not after you and we're not trying to smear your brother. But the more we know, the better the chances we'll catch his killers."

"You think there's more than one?"

"They needed at least two," she replied. "One to drive, one to shoot."

The boy remained sullen. "Yeah, I was aware of it."

"And…?" she asked, playing good cop as Mike snarled disapproval.

Ethan heaved an enormous sigh. "They argued Tuesday night. Kept real quiet. Didn't want to wake up my grandmother. I overheard Luke say, 'I don't want it'."

"When was this?" Kim asked.

"Tuesday. When Luke gave Malcolm the gun."

"Any idea where Luke got it?" Mike asked.

"No. We done?" Ethan stomped back up the stairs.

As Mike drove back into Manhattan, Kim said, "I'll bet he's not an awful kid underneath."

Mike snorted. "Yeah, I know, you hope you have one like him."

She shuddered at the mention of having children, one of several topics she tried not to think about. But she'd never told Mike, so she changed the subject. "Next up, Luke Wilson."

．　　　．　　　．

On the way to Luke's apartment in Washington Heights, she got a text from Jake. *You need a break and we need to be us. Denver's in tonight, seven o'clock tip-off. I got you the usual courtside seat. The security folks will meet you at the VIP entrance. From the scorer's table, I'll see if you don't show up.*

She broke into a grin. *I'm on three hours of sleep.*

No excuse, you've worked double shifts on as little.

He had her there. And although she was on the four-to-one shift, she'd signed in before eight. Kiley would let her sign out at four, a full tour. *Okay, you've got a date.*

Mike parked the car on West 149th.

One more text from Jake. *Wear something nice and take a cab. Special night.*

There wasn't anything special about another Nets' loss, but she got it—Jake wanted her more in his world.

Luke's apartment belonged to Sylvia Walters, a light-skinned black woman in her early thirties. Kim took it in with a glance—decent size and well kept, not the typical abode for a street dealer. "Very sorry for your loss."

"Thanks." But her posture said, "Go away."

"How long ago did Luke move in with you?"

"About a year."

"So, you and he were long term, huh? Where did he work?"

"Didn't have no regular job."

"Nice place," Mike said. "What's the rent go for here?"

Sylvia scowled. "Seventeen fifty, but I'll let you sublet for nineteen hundred."

"Kind of rich for a guy with no job," he said.

"I got two jobs, waiting tables. Apollo Diner on Columbus and Manhattan Soul over on Lenox."

Kim glanced down at Sylvia's shoes—Manolo Blahnik zebra-print pumps with spike heels. She'd seen a pair in a boutique in SoHo. "A lot of time on your feet." And high-quality cotton-twill slacks.

"Got that right."

Kim softened her tone. "How well did you know Diego Paredes and Malcolm Drake?"

"Malcolm came around a few times. Likeable kid. Had a bit of a temper." Sylvia was relaxing. "Paredes? Only here once. Last November."

"What was the occasion?" Mike asked.

Sylvia shook her head. "No occasion. Came to hang with us."

"Was Malcolm Drake here, too?" Kim asked.

"I don't remember." Sylvia crossed her arms. "Luke never mentioned what he be doing with Paredes." Sylvia took a deep breath. "He mentioned a opportunity, but no details."

Mike jumped back in. "No mention of how he, Malcolm and Paredes were slinging?"

Sylvia glared at him. "Luke never talked about nothing involving drugs."

"Were you aware Luke had given Malcolm a handgun?"

"No."

Kim gave Sylvia her card. "We found Luke with several envelopes of cocaine in his possession. We suspect their dealing got the three of them killed. Please call if you think of anything else."

Mike pressed the elevator button for one. "Not quite overcome with grief."

"Did you notice her shoes?"

"They seemed unusual for a waitress; spends all day on her feet."

She chuckled. "She doesn't wear them for work, she wears them to party. And they go for thirteen-hundred dollars a pair. We need to talk to your pal, Nolan, to see if these mopes were on his radar."

CHAPTER EIGHT

Friday, February 24th, 6:20 PM

She checked the mirror, patting her chestnut hair, now in a bump. Not bad, she had to admit. Jake would hope for a skirt, but he liked her in leggings, too, when she wore them with heels.

Kiley had been okay with her signing out early, since she'd updated the case board before she left. Mike had assured her he'd be fine.

She paused at the framed photograph of Michael Jordan driving to the hoop which always made her smile. She'd fallen in love with basketball in 1993, watching the Knicks on television with Dad, before all the family turmoil. But when the Knicks faced the Bulls in the Eastern Conference finals, a magician in red and black wearing Number twenty-three had won her heart. Dad never held a grudge. He'd even bought a Bulls jersey with the number twenty-three for her birthday. Back before... everything.

Best not to go there. She turned back for her jacket and good purse and stopped.

The day's mail sat on the table, including a plain white envelope with her name and address printed with care by hand. No return address, no stamp, and no postmark. So, not sent by mail.

She donned latex gloves and opened it. Inside she found a flyer for a suicide hotline. Behind that she found a printout of an article on OxyContin overdoses from drug-overdose.com. Bringing up the rear was a clipping from a neighborhood newspaper on Dad's funeral.

She texted Jake. *I'm sorry, but I can't make it tonight. I've got a situation.*

Two minutes later, he responded. *Are you okay?*

Fine. She couldn't put her fears into words. *Talk later.*

Mike called. "A friend of mine in the Four-Oh is looking into the burglary ring Ames mentioned, but he's heard nothing about it. Dobson found the car service in Woodside Leanne took home. They dropped her at the corner of Fifty-First and Vernon in Hunters Point. Also, I matched the sketch of the gray suit guy to a mugshot. Pierre Duval. Three busts on his sheet, two for possession, one buy-and-bust. Has a last-known in Brownsville."

She told him about the envelope. "It's a crank."

A lengthy silence. "A crank who knows your dad killed himself? With OxyContin?"

"OxyContin's been in the news quite a lot. Could be a lucky guess. Please don't mention it to Kiley."

Mike considered Kim's request. "Okay, but if this keeps up..."

"I know, Mike. Anything else?"

"I've got a list of SUVs reported stolen this week. The usual Escalades, Navigators, and other beasts of the road, but one Blazer and one Escape."

Kim updated her Notes app. "Let's have Dobson and Ryba check out Duval first thing."

"What do you want me to do?" Voice flat, devoid of his customary spark.

Time to address it. "Mike, what's going on with you? This is your partner asking."

"I can't get the dead girl with the long black hair and part of her skull missing out of my mind. I got less than a year until I can drop my papers. If I could do it tomorrow, I would."

"You've seen awful shit before. What makes this one different?"

After a long and almost painful silence, he answered, his voice low, almost hopeless. "That girl reminded me of my sister's oldest, Hannah. Same long, curly black hair. She's been having a lot of headaches. And then there were bouts of nausea. Blurred vision. Started with doctors two weeks ago, and the results of her CAT scan came back two days ago. Brain tumor. They're seeing a surgeon on Monday."

"You should take time off to support your sister. Kiley would understand."

He was there, breathing. "No, thanks, Kim. Now we've caught this case and you're leading, I'm better off working, keeping my mind busy. Tell me what you need."

"Run down the Blazer and the Escape owners. See if either could be the vehicle. Meantime, I'll go back to the crime scene tomorrow. I want to talk to your barmaid from Bagatelle."

"The French place? Betty Robson. Look for a woman with a linebacker's build and pink hair."

"Got it. Also, see if you can establish a range of addresses for Leanne after they dropped her off. And check with the lab about Leanne's shoes."

.　　　　.　　　　.

The cognac that had lost its flavor the night before now warmed him once again. Ms. Brady had received the little greeting. And it had upset her enough to skip her evening out. One thing he'd learned was every cop, no matter how tough or brave, had a soft underbelly, an emotional weak spot, a vulnerability. Some had several. He only needed to find one, stick the knife in, and twist.

His burner phone buzzed. "Yes?"

"They know about Duval."

He'd known they would. It hadn't bothered him. But subsequent developments transformed Duval into a greater risk. "Take care of it."

"We can't find him."

The cognac lost its flavor again. "I have a severe dislike for the word 'can't'."

CHAPTER NINE

Saturday, February 25th, 12:30 AM

There was no way to quell Jake's anger when he arrived home after the game. "You used the code phrase. 'I have a situation'. We agreed it has a specific meaning—you or we are in immediate danger. I don't see any."

She showed him what she'd received.

He stared at each sheet in turn. "I don't get it. The article says nothing about what he used."

"Correct. The department made no information public."

"I deal with the media. Stuff gets leaked all the time. You're overreacting." He turned away to the bedroom.

Overreacting? The very word galled her. It wasn't enough that Mike was dealing with a family crisis, Dobson and Ryba were spotty and their key witness was nowhere in sight. Now, Jake was... she took a deep breath. Stop. Analyze.

This was the man she loved. He'd wanted tonight to be special. The mailing had ruined whatever he'd planned.

He was sitting on the bed. She sat next to him, ready to explain suspicion was part of what she did. But first, "I'm sorry I ruined your special night."

"I'd planned to ask you to marry me. I had a message ready to go up on the big scoreboard during a timeout."

The room blurred; Jake faded to the background. She was ten years old, huddling at the top of the stairs in the middle of the night, her nightgown tucked around her knees. Mom was shouting at Dad in the living room. "Who is she this time? A bar maid? A hooker? Or are you rolling out your old 'I was working a case' bullshit on me?"

Then the shattering of a living room lamp, causing Kim to draw back in fear. Mom screaming, "Get out. Get the fuck out of my house, cheating bastard."

Kim's attention snapped back to the here-and-now, in the bedroom with Jake, heart pounding. "You know I love you. But what I do for a living... Seventy percent of married police officers wind up divorced."

"I do statistics for a living; they don't determine outcomes; they reflect them. It's not about the seventy percent. It's about the thirty percent who stay married. They're the ones who stay committed. A hundred percent."

She turned away, but he turned her face toward his again. "I'm committed to you, Kim. I will be true to you for the rest of my life. And I trust you'll always be true to me."

"Jake, if we love each other so much, can't we leave it alone?" Her voice cracked. She couldn't bear the notion of them failing.

"Because we each deserve a full commitment. Till death do us part is a lot more substantial than let's see how it goes."

"But... what I do for a living..." The job had killed Grandad. Dad, too, in a way.

Jake didn't waver. "Scares the shit out of me. I pray for you every time you walk out that door and I say a brief prayer of thanks every time you come back home. I won't change."

She let him pull her close. Images flashed through her mind... the woman with one shoe... the OxyContin article... the cop at Paredes' apartment... Mom screaming at her she couldn't date until she was seventeen...

"You will not end up like your mother." Jake's uncanny ability to guess what she was thinking. "She wound up bitter and alone, resentful of everyone and everything. She poisoned her own life until she didn't want to live it anymore. You're so different from her."

Deep breath. "You don't understand; I'm the lead detective on this case, now. Mike's not up to it. It has to be my focus."

"I don't see any connection between your case and us getting married."

Someone might fuck with the case? What if he somehow became a target? No, she couldn't go there. "I have to do this my way."

"And what happens when the next case comes along? And the one after? Your dad's marriage failed, but your grandad stayed true."

Until he died in the line of duty. No, she bit her tongue. And although Dad had disillusioned her many times, she wasn't Dad in a relationship, nor as a cop. "Let's talk about it after we solve the case. Okay?"

"A genuine talk about it? Not putting it off?"

"Yes."

He kissed her. "I need a shower."

She slipped back out to stare at the contents of the envelope.

Someone was fucking with her case.

CHAPTER TEN

Saturday, February 25th, 10:35 AM

Kiley was staring at the case board when she arrived. Mike had added the information about Duval and Leanne, and the lab had confirmed the cache under the dumpster was "girl", street slang for cocaine. Dad had used it, too. "Boy" was heroin.

She sidled up to him. "Dobson and Ryba are after Duval. I'm on Leanne."

Kiley chuckled and muttered, "I'd pay to see that."

"What did you say, Lieutenant?"

He cleared his throat. "I said, 'Good luck with that.' Keep me posted."

.　　.　　.

The shops around Gansevoort Plaza were already buzzing. There were already spring ensembles in the windows. Bagatelle wouldn't open for another half hour, so she strolled along Gansevoort Street, which was still closed to traffic. Sounds of hammering and power tools echoed from nearby storefronts undergoing renovations.

Mario Gallo, owner of the Cove, was arguing with a detective from CSU in front of the boarded-up window. Curious pedestrians gaped from the space beyond the yellow tape marking the outer perimeter. Gallo brightened as Kim ducked under the tape. "Ah, Detective, could you resolve this?"

The CSU detective rolled his eyes.

"I got contractors waiting to get inside," Gallo said. "But these guys won't even let me near it."

She adopted her most soothing manner. "Standard procedure, I'm afraid. CSU assures no one fouls the crime scene. They're still gathering evidence."

"You don't understand," he said. "I got to hustle to stay in business. I opened this place after the meatpackers had booked and the neighborhood had gone to hell. The city was shutting down the bathhouses, crack houses, and sex clubs. Rents were dirt cheap. Kids could come and feel badass. Look around, now. Cafés, restaurants? Geez, frigging boutiques. Rents are through the roof. I catch a break, a hook, I gotta cash in on it."

Using a mass shooting for a marketing tool. Lovely. "Aren't you afraid the shooting will dampen business?"

"Are you kidding? We're badass. The contractors will leave all the bullet marks in place. Can I get the shell casings when you people finish with them? And a slug? The kids will love that shit."

She had to laugh, because no doubt they would. She pulled out the sketch of Duval. "Do you recognize this guy?"

"Yeah, he was in here Thursday night. Kept coming and going." He lowered his voice. "Tracy thought he was dealing."

"Ever see him in your place before?"

He frowned over the sketch. "Yeah, twice. But less obvious than on Thursday."

Kim thanked him and walked back to Bagatelle. Women strolled in leather sneakers and canvas slip-ons along clean Belgian Block streets. Thirty years earlier, these streets would have been slick with filmy meat sludge.

Betty Robson stood behind the bar, stocky, her light pink hair in a short-cropped shag. "Yeah, right after the shots I saw a dark Blazer—boxy look from the late nineties—tear ass around the corner and zoom up Ninth. Can I get you something?"

"No, thanks. You into cars?"

"Kind of, yeah. I'm into lots of things." She looked Kim up and down. "You got a much softer look than other women cops I see."

"Did you see where the Blazer went after it turned onto Ninth?"

"No, I didn't." A sly smile. "Bet the guys hit on you a lot."

Kim remained serious. "Where were you standing?"

Robson pointed to a corner table. "Some guy was giving one of our servers a hard time. Claimed I'd given him blended scotch instead of single malt. I was straightening him out."

"And you didn't see how far they might have gone?"

"No, I lost sight of them right away."

Kim made an entry on her notes app. "Notice anything unusual about the vehicle?"

"It'd been tail-ended. Damage to the rear bumper and tailgate. Can I get you anything?"

"No, thanks. But I appreciate your help."

·   ·   ·

"Police have made little progress with the massive shooting that took place Thursday night outside a bar in the Meatpacking District. Anyone with information should call..."

Kim strode past the TV set in the squad room to Kiley's office, which for the moment was empty. She corrected the "Blazer or Escape" note and added the information Betty Robson had given her.

Mike walked in as she finished. "The Blazer on the Stolen Vehicles report was a 1999, stolen from Washington Heights. Luke Wilson's neighborhood. How about that, sports fans?" He grabbed a marker and noted the plate number—BDY-139—on the board, along with the VIN.

"What else did Pinky have to say?"

"They drove up Ninth." No need to mention Pinky's extracurricular interest.

Kim took the marker and listed the shooter's escape options—Holland Tunnel to Jersey, Hugh Carey Tunnel to Long Island, or back up through midtown.

Someone opened the door to one of the interrogation rooms, and protestations of innocence echoed in the hallway for a moment. The door slammed shut.

Mike scratched his head. "I have to tell you, it bothers me the girl was the only one able to get out. It also bothers me the Blazer drove north on Ninth while the girl's cab drove south on Washington."

It bothered her, too. Reality wasn't a hundred percent symmetrical. Unless it was. "Based on what Tracy said, Leanne did nothing we could connect with the shooting."

"Maybe she was part of the plan and got scared at the last minute," Mike replied. "She should have come forward and given us a statement."

Find her first. "Please issue a BOLO for the Blazer. Any word from Dobson and Ryba on Duval?"

"They said they'd get to it right after they tracked down Leanne."

"God damn it, I said I wanted them on Duval. Didn't you relay those instructions to them?" Okay, Mike was off his game, but this made no sense.

"Yes. But when they mentioned going after Leanne first, I had to assume you changed your mind. Sorry, Kim."

Deep breath. Stay calm. "Mike, I can see you're struggling, but I need you as a reliable second. For the record, if I change my mind about any decision I've made, you'll be the first to know. What about Nolan?"

"We're set for eight tomorrow morning at Tal Bagels. I figured it'd be quiet enough so early on a Sunday. You want me to call Dobson?"

"No. I'll call him." But when she called, she got voicemail without the phone ringing.

42

She tried Ryba. It rang three times, then voicemail. She tried again. Same thing.

This time she left a message. "This is Brady. If I don't get a call back from one of you within the next three minutes, I'm getting Kiley to throw your asses off this case."

One minute; two minutes...

Her cell buzzed. It was Dobson. "Sorry, Kim..."

"Okay, in order. One, what the fuck is your phone doing off? Two, what the fuck is Ryba doing ducking my calls? Three, who the fuck gave you permission to ignore my instructions?" Heads turned in the squad room. She lowered her voice. "In order."

"Okay." Dobson was keeping his voice down, as if he didn't want Ryba to hear. "First, I wasn't aware my phone was off. No idea how that happened, but I won't let it happen again. Two, Ryba's ringer was off. He felt it vibrate on the second call but couldn't get the phone out before you left your message. Regarding Leanne, we figured it made sense."

"Listen to me, Dobson. You two are precinct detectives. This is a homicide case. You take instructions from me, or you stay the hell back at the Sixth. Any bright ideas either of you have, you ask me. Not Mike. Me. Am I clear?"

"Crystal."

"Good. Now get the fuck over to Duval's last known and track him down. Keep me informed."

CHAPTER ELEVEN

Saturday, February 25th, 2:17 PM
He answered the burner phone on the first ring. "Yes?"

"They're still trying to track down Duval."

"May they have the same luck we've had. Any genuine news to report?"

"The cab dropped the woman off in Hunters Point near the Midtown Tunnel. No address yet. Also, Brady's leading the investigation. Not Resnick."

Now, that was news. Excellent news. "He sick or something?"

"Not sure if there's a personal problem or if he's just feeling his age."

"Report to me if they locate the woman. In the meantime, we may require the services of our old friend, Mr. Garner. Any idea where he may be?"

"My most recent reports showed he'd downgraded from coke to crack and gotten himself evicted."

Good. He'd be nice and hungry. "Find him."

CHAPTER TWELVE

Saturday, February 25th, 3:25 PM

Kim was about to leave for Hunters Point when Kiley rushed out of his office. "What's this about you two interfering with a local investigation in the Bronx? I got a call this morning from a Sergeant Phillips in the Bronx on behalf of his captain, complaining you two have been snooping around into things not concerning you in the Four-Oh."

Kim told him about the uniform at Paredes' apartment and his story about a burglary ring. "Mike checked with someone he knows in the Four-Oh, and they had nothing on it. Since this uniform was stomping around a crime scene fouling evidence, I thought we should look into his story."

Mike spoke up. "Admit it, John, it's weird, some uniform from the North Bronx mucking around Paredes' apartment the morning after he got killed. Makes me wonder…"

Kiley set his jaw. "Listen, both of you. I don't care if Paredes had a Ted Bundy scrapbook. Your job is to solve this fucking shooting, not investigate cops doing shit you don't understand. Your Bronx inquiry stops now."

Kim watched him walk back into his office. "I wonder what else he won't let us do."

•   •   •

Kim had walked from Borden Avenue to Forty-Sixth, from Eleventh Street to the river, showing Leanne's sketch to store owners and pedestrians. Someone at a convenience store next to the Vernon-Jackson subway stop and a waitress at the little café across the street both said she looked somewhat familiar, but not so much as a glimmer of recognition from anyone else.

There was no sign of Kiley back at PBMS, but Dobson and Ryba were in his office at the case board. Mike joined her as she called an impromptu team meeting.

"No one around Duval's place has seen him in several days," Dobson said. "His landlord says he's three months behind on the rent. He let me into the apartment—a furnished hellhole—and it looks like he booked."

"Find anything of interest?" Although without a warrant they couldn't use it.

"Not a thing. No trace he was ever there." He made a brief notation on the board.

Mike had already added to the information about the SIG Sauer. Registered to Donald Breen in Yonkers. Reported it stolen on the Twenty-First.

"Two days before the shooting." The run of news was depressing her. "I've gotten nothing on Leanne,"

Kiley materialized in the doorway. "She could have gotten out of the cab and walked down into the subway." He didn't sound like he was joking.

"Except it wouldn't jibe with everything we've learned about Leanne."

"Which is what?"

She couldn't argue. They didn't have any information on her, other than her shyness. Best to change the subject. "Check out Duval. We need to track him down."

"Isn't he a dead end?" Dobson asked.

He couldn't be serious. "The guy who was selling inside and then blocking the door a dead end? Are you fucking kidding me?"

"Sounds important to me," Mike said, not quite grinning.

"Yeah," Ryba said. "But isn't Leanne more important?"

She would solve this right now. "Who's running this investigation, Ryba?"

He cast a sidelong glance at Kiley, who said nothing. "You are."

"Correct. This is the second time you've tried to put finding Leanne ahead of our need for you to find Duval. I guess I didn't make myself clear the last time. I'm directing this investigation, not you. One more fuck-up, and you're off the case." She turned to Kiley. "Right?"

"We need everyone on the same page, Ryba. Kim, I need to speak to you about something else."

Not the endorsement she'd expected. She closed the door as the others walked out.

"You realize," he said, "if we send him back, we have no one to replace him."

"What about Jimmy Stephenson?" He was another Manhattan South Homicide detective.

"His wife went into labor this morning. Pat Holloran has a pool going on the baby's weight. You can still get in. Part of leading is working with others."

"Even the incompetent ones?" She wasn't backing down.

"If need be, yes." He reached for a sheet of paper on his desk. "Got this from the crime lab, a report on an envelope you send them to check for prints. An envelope found at your home address." He glared at her. "Is this something I should know about?"

She described the contents.

"So, let me understand this," Kiley said. "You don't tolerate insubordination from someone on your team, but it's okay to be insubordinate with me?"

"I haven't been insubordinate. Given the contents, I didn't see an immediate threat to me or this investigation. I referred it to the crime lab as a precaution. Had the lab come back with anything, I'd have reported it to you." She scanned the lab report. "But they found nothing."

"So, you think this means it's nothing?"

"I think it means if I get anything further like this, I will evaluate it for plausible threats and submit it to the crime lab. After informing you."

.   .   .

Another hand-printed plain envelope, again with no return address and no postmark, was sitting on the dining area table when she got home. As with the first one, she donned latex gloves before opening it, although she was sure the sender had been as careful to leave no fingerprints as he'd been the first time.

Inside was a single sheet of white paper with letters cut from various newspapers, like the archetypal ransom note. "What signs did Daddy give he wanted to die? Plenty. And how did you miss them? How it must hurt."

Jake watched her the whole time. "What's going on, Kim?"

Someone was fucking with her. "Where did you find this?"

"In the mailbox." He leaned over to read it. "Holy shit."

"Must be a crank." But she lacked the conviction she'd felt with the first note. One note could be a crank. A second, with a specific reference, wasn't so easy to shrug off. Whoever had sent it already had her address and had slipped it unseen into the mail carrier's pouch. They could also have information on Jake.

"Shouldn't you be calling someone?" he asked.

She'd send it off to the lab, and she'd tell Kiley. "In the morning. And, starting tomorrow, I want you to check in with me by text, and I'll respond. I'm sure it's nothing, but better safe than sorry."

CHAPTER THIRTEEN

Sunday, February 26th, 2:10 AM

Kim couldn't sleep. Jake was snoring, but he wasn't the reason.

In six hours, they'd be meeting with Nolan. That wasn't the reason, either.

She did her best to force the latest mailing from her mind. But every time she tried to drop off to sleep, the conversation with Dad kept coming back to her. After eighteen months in the Seven-Three with an excellent arrest record and her first medal, a Commendation—Community Service, she'd had options, including transfer to a new anti-drug task force in Brooklyn South. She'd assumed Dad, as a former narcotics detective, would approve.

Even now, laying still with Jake snoring beside her, she could still see Dad's expression, like someone had punched him in the stomach. She could still hear the agony in his voice. "I blurred the lines, then wiped them out. Ripped-off drug dealers and used the drugs to buy information. Allowed dealers to continue to do business so I could trade up. The system trades up all the time, but I didn't bother with them. Figured I'd clean up the city on my own terms."

Her stomach churned at the memory. "In Narcotics, the law gets hard. It's an easy trap to fall into, and I did. Lucky for me, the old Internal Affairs

49

Division couldn't find their butts with both hands. Some of those cheese-eating rats were as crooked as we were. I got out of Narcotics right after the incident with your friend and the dress. Figured I'd lost all sense of judgment."

He'd served another twelve years before retiring with no disciplinary action ever taken against him. "I dropped my papers when I did because you were entering the Academy. There's always talk. I didn't want to take any chances my reputation might hurt your career. I don't, now. There's a spot opening at Manhattan South Homicide. Please, as a last favor to me..."

She couldn't stop the flood of mental images. The night she'd driven over to his apartment, the hallway echoed with snatches of television dramas. She'd pressed the buzzer several times with the sense of dread growing stronger, until she'd let herself in with her own key, calling his name, getting no answer. She'd ignored the sloppy apartment, the dirty dishes in the sink and several old newspapers lying about.

Dad lying on the bed with a dreadful pallor, no pulse, his skin cold to the touch. Then she saw an envelope of pills—more than a hundred of them—on the nightstand, some crushed, and the empty glass, smelling of cheap scotch.

Numb, she called 9-1-1.

She'd snatched up the envelope on the night table with her name on it before she could change her mind.

"Dear Kim, I always said you were a bright kid, and you are. Bright enough to have been right—about your Mom and me, your friend, the job, the law. I could have learned more from you than you did from me. There's one way out for me, one way to salvage some self-respect, and to keep your record in the Department above reproach, like Grandad's. At least the cheese-eating rats never got their teeth into me. I realize this will hurt you, and I'm sorry, but it's the best thing for both of us. I hope you'll forgive me someday. Goodbye. Dad."

She'd taken the note into the kitchen, turned on a burner on the gas stove, and touched the corner of the note to the flame. By the time the police and ambulance arrived, nothing of the note remained except a trace of ash and her agony.

If only she'd recognized the "last favor" remark for what it was, caught the other, similar comments, and recognized the furtive glances when she was in his apartment with him.

She could have checked on him a day earlier.

"They look like warning signs after it's too late," the grief counselor had said.

Warm milk. Mom's cure-all for insomnia. She slipped out of bed, padded into the kitchen, poured some milk into a mug, and slipped it into the microwave. Her thoughts turned back to the mailings. They weren't from a sick crank. This was a deliberate campaign to throw her off her game.

In a few hours they'd have some answers. Duval had to be on Nolan's radar, whether he'd been working with Paredes or with someone else looking to take Paredes down. With any luck, Paredes had been on his radar, too.

Time to get some sleep. She washed out the mug and put it in the dish drain. Jake was still snoring and didn't stir as she slipped back under the covers. She had almost drifted off to sleep when the whoop-whoop of a dashing patrol car on Clark Street jolted her back to wide awake.

The guilt was still there. So was the resentment. But no way was she going to allow some motherfucker to use it against her.

CHAPTER FOURTEEN

Sunday, February 26th, 8:05 AM

Kim spotted Nolan as soon as she and Mike entered Tal Bagels: late forties, dark brown hair without a trace of gray; black-rimmed glasses, bulbous nose, pock-marked skin, sitting at the last table on the left of the narrow seating area with his back against the wall. "I guess he takes no chances."

"No one in Narcotics does." Mike looked around. "I wonder where his partner is."

They both placed their orders at the counter, then joined Nolan. Mike introduced him to Kim. *New York One* droned on from the television mounted above them, with the same speculations about the Cove shooting they'd been spouting since Thursday night. At least no one would overhear them.

"Pleasure," Nolan said to her. "I worked with your dad. Real sorry about what happened. No cop deserves to die that way, buried under a pile of pills. Damned shame. What can I do for you?"

Kim managed a tight smile. "Thanks." No one in the NYPD ever mentioned Dad's suicide. Not even Mike. A warning shot. Or worse. She needed information for the case, but Dad took precedence. "How do you know how my father died?"

Nolan looked surprised. "I don't. There's been a lot of talk he killed himself. Rumors are he OD'd on something. In Narcotics, guys have access to all kinds of shit—boy, girl, OxyContin. It's available, and we remember how to get it. Who knows, maybe he built up a cache. Some guys do if they have plans."

OxyContin. Now, he was two for two. She was trying to decide how to attack this when Mike said, "There's a drug angle to the Cove shooting."

She let it go. For now. "The three guys outside were dealing girl. Have you ever heard the names Diego Paredes or Pierre Duval?"

Nolan snorted. "Why would you care about a mope like Duval?"

She laid the sketch in front of him. "A witness gave us that." Nolan's eyes flickered, but he said nothing. A commercial for maintaining perfect skin droned on overhead. "A witness puts him at the scene, and he booked before anyone from the department arrived."

"His game has improved," Nolan said.

"Improved from what?" If one person could be allergic to another, she was breaking out in a rash.

Nolan peered for a moment at Mike, who remained quiet. "Duval was in Jordy Hill's crew back in the day. Never amounted to much—a very dim bulb with delusions of grandeur."

"Who is Jordy Hill?" she asked.

"Jordy was the Number Two to a big dealer named Ice Williams. We collared them both three years ago. After they both got sent up, Duval dropped out of sight."

Had Mike believed this guy could help? "Where are Williams and Hill, now?"

"Someone killed Hill in Dannemora a few months after they got there. Ice is a suspect, but they don't have any hard evidence. He's also proven to be an incorrigible prisoner, so he's been in and out of solitary."

Move along, folks, there's nothing to see, here. "Anyone left from Williams' operation who might carry on the business?"

"The only one of Williams' lieutenants we missed was one Thomas Kincaid. Street name of Viper. But as far as we can tell, he hasn't stepped up. No dealing activities at all. None of my sources have even mentioned his name."

"Got a regular job? Working at Home Depot?" This was feeling like pulling teeth. "So, Duval wouldn't be working for Kincaid?"

"Shit, no. Word is Kincaid blamed him for Ice and Jordy getting sent up."

"Was he right?" she asked. "I mean, Williams was your collar, wasn't he?"

"My collar but not my rat." Nolan took a sip of coffee. "So, what's the drug angle?"

Either Mike hadn't told him, or he was playing dumb. She played it straight and told him what they'd found. "They were slinging with enough girl stashed nearby for a Two-A felony."

"Sounds like Duval might have been working with the dealers," Nolan said.

Good for you. "An eyewitness also identified Duval as the guy who was jamming the exit, keeping people from getting out. Doesn't add up. We need to talk to him, but he's no longer at his last known. Any idea where he might be?"

"None. Sorry."

Time to change directions. "What about Diego Paredes?"

Nolan looked puzzled. "Who?"

Now, he was pissing her off. "The guy dealing under your nose with Duval Thursday night."

Nolan turned to Mike. "Is there a problem, here?"

Mike grinned. "Course not, Bob. But you know how it is. Big shooting, media all over it like flies on shit. We're getting heat."

"Doesn't mean you have to turn it on me."

She leaned forward. "Is that what you think I'm doing?"

Nolan's jaw tightened.

Mike tried to keep it light. "Hey, we're all friends, here. Look, Bob, we need to learn whatever you've got, who Paredes might have been working with, who Duval was working with."

"Even if you don't think it's relevant," she added.

"Sorry," Nolan replied. "I told you what little I can about Duval, and I draw a complete blank on Paredes. Sorry if none of it helps your case."

Mike stood. "Okay, thanks. We'll be in touch if we need anything else."

Kim stood, too. "Nice meeting you." But she hadn't finished. yet. "One other question. You said Ice Williams was your collar, but the rat wasn't yours. Whose was he?"

Nolan blinked. "I can't tell you."

Time to force the issue. "If he wasn't yours, he must have been your partner's. What's his name?"

Nolan sprang to his feet, legs apart, like a man about to jump into a bar fight. Not too tall, but muscular. "George Barlowe was my partner until the Williams arrest, but not anymore." He struggled to control his temper. "And he can't risk compromising a Confidential Informant any more than I can."

She took a step toward him. "Ever hear the name Sylvia Walters?" No way was she going to let him intimidate her.

"Can't say I have."

Not backing down. "Or, you won't."

Mike stepped into the shrinking space between her and Nolan. "It's important you give us whatever you can. We got to get this one right."

She decided not to give Nolan time to respond. "And you guys had nothing on Paredes, Luke Wilson or Malcolm Drake?"

"Sorry."

She flashed an insincere smile. "Thanks. It's been such a pleasure." Mike was right behind her as she stalked out, leaving Nolan behind.

CHAPTER FIFTEEN

Sunday, February 26th, 8:55 AM

So Nolan was clueless. And had no interest in learning anything. Mike hadn't helped. Bad enough his old pal had stonewalled them. Mike hadn't given him a single prod.

Twice, she started to say something to Mike while walking back to PBMS but decided against it. What good would it do, now?

Back at their desks, she took out her phone to scan her notes from the night of the shooting.

"Okay," Mike said at last. "The silence is deafening. What's the matter?"

She didn't look up. "Nolan wasn't very helpful."

Mike shrugged. "Narcotics guys always keep things close to the vest. Bob…"

"I'm aware of what Narcotics guys do, and how much shit goes down when they do it. So, please, no tutorial on working Narcotics."

Mike gave her a quizzical look. "Is that the problem? Bob isn't your father."

No, but he sure had plenty of information about him. She didn't say it.

56

"He's an old pro," Mike continued. "Patient as hell. When he sends them up, they stay sent up. He listened to us, who we're looking at, and decided he couldn't help. Might've saved us chasing down some blind alleys."

Her cell pinged. It was Jake. *Checking in, like you asked. You okay?*

She tapped out a reply. *I'm safe. Stay safe and keep checking in.*

Kiley wasn't in his office, so she entered and made a note on the case board about Duval's connection with Jordy Hill. Kiley walked in behind her, reading over her shoulder. She hesitated before making a note about the mailings. But since she was almost certain they related to the case, she couldn't hold back.

"Another one?" Kiley asked. "This isn't a crank. Send it to the lab."

"I did, first thing this morning."

"Think this might qualify as a threat?"

She decided not to tell him the content. "No. I have to assume it's harassment."

"Meaning it's someone who knows you're on this case."

She looked him in the eye. "Yes."

He held her gaze. "So, what are you saying?"

"You and I expect the report will come back from the lab stating they found no prints, no traces of DNA, suggesting this person is no amateur. There's always a vacuum created when a dealer like Ice Williams goes down and it gets filled. Who? And a mope like Duval doesn't vanish. I've got to nail down his role in this."

Back at her desk, she opened her laptop and checked Duval's records. He'd moved around a lot—Brownsville, East New York, Mott Haven, South Jamaica, and back to Brownsville. Twice in the Seven-Three. Her first patrol partner had remained and risen to sergeant. She called him.

"Hi, Kim. Good to hear from you. Sorry about your dad. Word is you caught the Cove case."

She explained about Duval.

"Sounds familiar. I'll check into it and get back to you."

Pat Holloran, the desk sergeant, came up to them. "False alarm on the Stephenson kid. Turned out to be a false labor. You guys can still get in on the weight pool. Five bucks. If nobody gets it, the kitty goes to Jimmy and his wife."

Kim fished a five out of her purse. "Anybody take six pounds, ten ounces?"

Pat checked his clipboard. "Nope."

"I'll take it."

The sergeant turned to Mike. "You want in?"

He pulled out his wallet. "Eight pounds, even?"

Kim laughed. "Gee, Mike, give Jimmy's poor wife a break."

Mike handed over a five. "I'm betting the over."

Holloran laughed and walked away.

"Sorry I dragged you in today for a meeting yielding nothing," Mike said to Kim. "Ruined a day off for both of us."

"Might not be a total loss. Let's head up to Yonkers and find out who separated Mr. Donald Breen from his SIG Sauer."

．　　　　　　．　　　　　　．

The store, on New Main Street, had been a combination stationery store and luncheonette decades earlier. Now, it was a place to buy assorted cheap items. A bell hanging from the top of the door clanged announcing their arrival. Donald Breen, lanky, with ebony skin and white hair, snapped his head up at the sound. "Help you folks?"

Kim flashed her badge. Mike did the same.

Breen grew cautious. "Want some coffee?"

"No, thanks." It smelled worse than the coffee from the deli the night of the shooting. "We need to ask you some questions about a gun you reported stolen on February Twenty-first. A SIG Sauer?"

Breen didn't relax at all. "Yes, ma'am. I did. Had a license for it and everything."

"We know. What were the circumstances of the theft?"

Breen stared and said nothing.

She gave a thin smile. "Were you burglarized, or was it taken when the store was open?"

He thought a moment. "There wasn't no break in. I was in the back."

"Do you often leave the store front during business hours?"

"Try not to. Kids come in and steal things."

"Why did you this time?"

"I was getting some... I mean, I'd just gotten a delivery. Office supplies. I do my paperwork in the back, after the store closes."

She glanced around at his stock. Much of it was dingy and faded. Not much had been moving. "What else did they take?"

"Nothing. At least nothing I could spot."

"Where was the gun before the robbery?"

A deer caught in the headlights.

"Mr. Breen? Where was the gun?"

He pointed toward the cash register which sat atop a glass display case. "Behind there."

Kim walked around behind the register. There were sliding wooden doors giving access to the display case.

"No," Breen said. "Behind you."

She turned around to find a rack of several brands of cigarettes. Beneath it sat a long, flat set of shelves with old items scattered along them. One item was a snow globe. "You kept the gun here?" She walked back around to the front. The shelves were in plain view. "Where anyone could see it?"

"No. Not in the open. Hidden behind that snow-globe. Scared of holdups. I kept it for protection."

"Had you ever fired it?" Kim asked.

"Yes, ma'am. Over at the Yonkers Rifle and Pistol Range."

"Fired it there in recent weeks? And can we verify if you have?"

His face clouded over at "verify". "Well, no, ma'am. Business ain't been so good. My membership ran out."

Time to change direction. "So, you kept the gun here, out of sight?" Breen nodded. "How much did you lose from the cash register?"

"About forty dollars."

"Did you report the cash theft to the police at the same time you reported the gun stolen?"

"Yes… Er, no. Sorry. No, I didn't. I was too upset about the gun."

"Tell me, Mr. Breen, how would someone open the register?"

"Push down the black key."

She did. The cash drawer opened, the coins inside rattling. "Sounded loud enough to bring you running."

"No, I didn't realize what had happened until I came out and saw the register drawer hanging open and the snow globe moved."

She walked back around to the front of the display case. "Did anyone know you kept the gun there?"

"I doubt it, although I might've mentioned it to some friends. Don't recall."

"How long were you in the back before you discovered the open register drawer?"

Breen thought a moment. "I'd say five minutes or a little longer. I'd like to hire someone to help, but I can't afford nobody."

The door to the street opened, setting the bell to clanging. A customer bought a newspaper and left.

Kim turned back to Breen. "Loud bell on your door. You mean to say you didn't hear it in the back the day of the robbery? Isn't that why it's there?"

"Why are you asking me all these questions? I reported the gun stolen, like the law says to. Am I in trouble?"

She looked him in the eye. "Not if someone stole it, as you say it was. We found your gun on the body of a dead drug dealer. We're trying to learn how and why it got there."

Breen brightened. "Whoever stole it must have sold it to him."

She nodded. "One possibility. We're trying to discover who sold it—or gave it—to him, which is why we're here." She pulled out photos of Diego Paredes, Luke Wilson, and Malcolm Drake. "Ever see any of them before?"

Breen shook his head. "Sorry. Afraid I can't tell you no more."

CHAPTER SIXTEEN

Monday, February 27th, 12:02 PM

"Police remain stymied in their investigation of the shooting outside the Cove last Thursday night," blared the report from *New York One* on the squad room TV. "Meanwhile, a seventh victim has died. Dale Keegan, who had been in critical condition, died overnight at Mount Sinai-Beth Israel Hospital. Police are asking anyone with information about the shooting to call the Crime Stoppers Hotline."

Kim plopped down her second cup of coffee, popping off the top and sloshing a significant amount of light-and-sweet over her desk. "Bollocks." As Dad would have said. She hastened to mop it up. The dinner with Jake the night before at the charming little French restaurant in Hunters Point, Tournesol, was already a distant memory.

Mike brought her a fresh supply of paper towels. "Out of sorts, I see."

"Breen was lying. I'd stake my badge on it. He didn't hear his bell? A stranger spots the hidden gun in thirty seconds? We need to press him." She finished mopping up the mess and tossed the sodden paper towels in the trash.

He cleared his throat and stared over her shoulder. "Incoming."

Dobson dashed through the squad room. "Got something on the Cove case."

Mike coughed and grimaced. "Great."

"Got these from my old sergeant at the Fifteen." Dobson offered a large manila envelope to Kim. "I figured you'd want to see them right away."

"Thanks." She sliced open the envelope and slid out two enlarged photos of a dark Blazer, plate number BDY-139. She slid them over to Mike. "Damaged rear bumper and tailgate. We have a timestamp?"

"7:48, the night of the twenty-third." Dobson said. "Thirty-Fourth Street camera between Lex and Third. Eastbound. I realize you want me on Duval, but this was on my way in."

"Thanks." She turned to Mike. "They blended into traffic and then got out as fast as possible."

Mike cleared his throat again, louder this time. "He drove up Third and cut over the Queensborough Bridge. No toll, no cameras. I'll make some calls to the Queens precincts."

"Dobson, you stick with Mike and give him a hand. Then you and Mike get back on Duval's trail. Ryba, too, when he gets here."

Kim pulled out the drawing of Leanne. What made her flee?

Mike had said something. "Kim? You with us?"

She shook herself. "Berringer was definite—he'd only been admiring her cross." No other marks on her throat. No beauty marks, scars, or blemishes. Nothing a girl would hide from a guy she just met.

Mike cleared his throat once again and rubbed it with his fingers. "Aw, hell."

She glanced up. "What's wrong?"

"Throat's been getting worse all morning. This'll be my third cold this winter."

She squirted from the small bottle of Purell on her desk and rubbed her hands with it. "Bad?"

"Horrible. Like someone took a blowtorch to my Adam's Apple."

A childhood friend she remembered as Chrissy flashed through her mind. Could Leanne be...? It would explain a lot. She rummaged through a desk drawer, pulled out a bottle of aspirin, and slid it over to Mike. "Help yourself."

Then she called Sheila Gregg. "Remember the sketch you made of the witness to the Cove shooting? Can you take some things out?"

"Like what?"

"Start with the glasses."

There was a pause as Sheila worked. "Give me a minute to scan this and send it. The glasses kind of help her look."

As others have done. "Eliminate everything below the neck."

Another pause while Sheila worked, then scanned and e-mailed the image. "The dress helps her look, too."

Kim studied the image for a few moments. "The earrings next." They wouldn't change much, but she wanted a clean image. "Then the cosmetics. Eyes, blush, lips, everything."

Sheila said nothing until she finished. "Holy shit. You won't believe this."

Kim studied the finished sketch on screen as it printed out. "Oh, yes, I do."

CHAPTER SEVENTEEN

Monday, February 27th, 5:15 PM
Several blocks north of the Vernon-Jackson station in Hunters Point, Kim found a Sushi takeout place displaying the same phone number Leanne had given Matt Berringer. Only the area code differed.

A delivery girl inside took one look at the revised sketch and blurted, "Oh, my God. That's Mr. Sweetie." She blushed. "My private name for him. His name is Andy Mallory. He's the nicest, sweetest guy. He's not in any trouble, is he?"

"I need to ask him about something he might have seen."

"Oh, good. I'd hate to get him into trouble. He lives on Fifty-First, off Vernon." She gave Kim the address.

It was a charming old three-story walkup. She picked up the intercom receiver in the vestibule and pushed the button labeled "A. Mallory—1-A".

The receiver speaker crackled in her ear. "Yes?"

"Mr. Mallory? Detective Kim Brady, New York City Police. I need to speak to you about something you may have seen last Thursday evening in the Meatpacking District."

The pause was excruciating.

"I'm sorry. I wasn't in the Meatpacking District Thursday night."

A soft click. She pushed the buzzer again.

"Yes?" His voice dripped with impatience.

"What about Leanne?"

Silence. But no click.

Kim lowered her voice. "My focus isn't you. Or Leanne. It's what you—or she—saw."

Another minute passed. No click. He was still there, as if weighing his options.

The buzzing of the door lock startled her, but she opened the vestibule door. His was the front apartment. He opened the door wearing skinny jeans and a teal tee shirt. No glasses, fresh scrubbed face, and the side bangs were damp. She caught the faint aroma of moisturizing soap.

Standing in his bare feet, he was only an inch taller than she. His features were delicate, as in the sketch. Hair in a pixie, short in back, long bangs sweeping across the forehead. Matt Berringer's description had been perfect.

"I'm very glad to meet you at last," she said. He hesitated before he took her hand. His touch was soft. "Mr. Mallory, you're not a suspect or anything, but you may be the only eyewitness to a heinous crime. Seven people have died and twelve more injured from the shooting outside the Cove on Gansevoort Street last Thursday."

They sat down at his kitchen table.

"What makes you think I was there?" he asked.

"This," she said, showing him the revised sketch. "A police artist sketched that from a description given by a man named Matt Berringer of a woman he met at the Cove."

"Not possible..."

"This isn't the original sketch." She pulled out a copy of the initial sketch Sheila had done. "This is."

He paled but said nothing.

"Leanne made a powerful impression on Mr. Berringer," she said. "I talked to him an hour after the shooting. He was anxious to learn if you were all right."

"I'm not gay."

"Yes, I understand the difference between gay and transgender."

He lapsed into silence and she decided not to press him. Already, she felt obligated to protect Leanne beyond what any cop owed a witness. Leanne would not share Chrissy's fate.

"How did you find me?" he asked. Not like banter. Almost pained.

"One of the delivery girls at the Sushi place recognized you from the first sketch I showed you." She glanced around the apartment. Not a thing out of place. "When did you first dress?"

He glared at her. "What difference does it make?"

"I'm just interested."

His glare faded. "I can't remember a time when I didn't wish I'd been born a girl. My sister, Allison, is two years older than me. She was always my best friend, my guardian angel. I'd play with her and her friends on rainy days. She thought it was cute." He grimaced. "Then I got caught. My father and two older brothers didn't think it was cute."

She could almost feel pain radiating from him. The sense of obligation was growing stronger. "So, about Thursday…"

"I can't help you. Sorry."

Obligation or no, she needed Leanne's cooperation. "I realize this is uncomfortable for you…"

He snorted. "You have no clue what you're asking. If I had any information for you—and I don't—I'd have to admit that I, a guy, dressed as a woman and got picked up in a bar. They'd splash me across the front page of every tabloid in this city. And the cable news shows. My life is shitty enough now, thanks."

She wouldn't convince him tonight. Too much pain in his eyes, a pain she'd seen before. She wondered if he had a good heart.

"And don't think you can scare me. Show my picture—me, Andy Mallory—to anyone there, and they might say, 'I think there was a girl there who looked something like him'. But nothing more concrete. You can't prove I was there, period. People jammed into the place. And people on the street. Somebody saw something."

"There were ninety-six people in the bar, none of whom saw anything because the shooter sprayed the windows with gunfire. Someone blocked the exit, and we think he might have had a role in the shooting."

He couldn't hide the momentary flicker in his expression.

"Let me tell you about a woman who's in critical condition, clinging to her life by a thread. Her name is Theresa Santos. She's twenty-two, a recent college grad working her first job and trying to pay off her student loans. A guy from her office had invited her out for a drink. A bullet caught her behind her ear. They are struggling to keep her alive. If she lives, the doctors expect it will be in a vegetative state."

He stared at the table.

Kim pressed on. "Jenna Guarnaccia is twenty. She's also in critical condition. She'd gotten engaged."

His jaw tightened.

"Leanne, whatever pain may lay ahead for you is nothing compared to what the families of these victims are going through right now. You can help their families by helping me nail their killers."

He sat motionless, eyes starting to glisten. Even now, they were his best feature.

"Not to mention," she added, "what your conscience will do to you if you say nothing."

"Don't be so sure."

She stood and looked him in the eye. "I am sure. I'm an excellent judge of people. It helps in my line of work. You're a wonderful person who is very frightened now. I understand and sympathize. And if you can help me, I will do whatever I can to help you."

He laughed. "Like what?"

But she'd never had a situation like this before, and she didn't want to make promises she couldn't keep. She gave him her card. "Please call me when you change your mind." The usual tactics used to force a reluctant witness to come forward would not work here. Leanne would have to volunteer her information. Kim had to convince her to volunteer it.

CHAPTER EIGHTEEN

Tuesday, February 28th, 8:15 AM

"Wow," Mike said between coughing fits, making heads turn at PBMS. "I can't believe it. Not only were you right, you tracked him down."

Kim glanced in at Kiley. She needed to update the board. "Means nothing. He isn't coming forward." She paused before adding, "Although I don't blame him."

"Well, I blame him," Mike said. "If playing dress-up is a higher priority than helping to put some murderers in jail, fuck him. Excuse my French."

"This isn't 'playing dress-up'." She glanced around to make sure they weren't being overheard, pulled out the first sketch and placed it in front of him. "Look, Mike. A conscious decision stemming from a deep-seated need to be a different gender than..." She stopped, glimpsing Kiley standing at his desk. She had to make Mike understand before she took this to her lieutenant.

Mike caught it and waited until Kiley turned away before responding. "So, you're saying nature makes mistakes?"

"All kinds of them. But I'll bet when Andy is being Leanne, he doesn't feel like a mistake." She saw in her mind's eye that magical Saturday afternoon when she was ten, with Chrissy, her new best friend.

68

Mike leaned forward and dropped his voice, pulling her back to the present. "So, what if you arrived home tonight and found Jake wearing your best dress? You'd be copacetic?"

She laughed. "We'll leave aside one point: my best dress would be way too small for him and he'd tear it to shreds. It'd be a shock because he's mentioned nothing about being transgender. I'd need time to get used to it. But he'd still be the love of my life."

"Fair enough." He turned away as he coughed, not yet sounding convinced.

She tried to be inconspicuous as she spritzed Purell on her hands.

But he caught it. "Sorry. First full day is always the worst."

Kiley, in his office, snatched up his phone on the first ring. "Homicide."

Mike turned back to his notes. "I found nothing unusual about Sylvia Walters' finances. Her cash deposits were about what they would expect for a waitress working two jobs. Sufficient to live on but forget designer shoes and clothes."

"So, Luke's dealing couldn't have been a secret."

Kiley slammed down the phone and called them in. "Four bystanders are dead. Two more are fading fast. So, where the fuck are we? The media's putting us on a fucking spit."

Kim, regretting she'd done her hair in the low dog ears today, told him about Leanne.

"Great," Kiley said. "Let's bring him in."

"She's not a suspect," Kim said.

"Hey," Kiley snapped, "he's not cooperating. Doesn't it make him a suspect? Jesus, we got seven stiffs and counting. Force his hand."

"Like how?" Mike asked.

Kiley glared at Kim. "Threaten to 'out' him."

Like Dad had outed Chrissy to her parents? She choked down her rising anger. No way. Leanne already feared it. Kim had to keep control of events. Leanne was a sweet person; even Matt Berringer had seen it. She'd come around.

Kiley was still glaring. "You have a problem, Ms. Brady?"

"She needs…"

"What's all this 'she' and 'her' bullshit? This is a guy we're talking about, right? One who likes to wear dresses."

"No. This is a guy living as the wrong gender. He sees himself as 'she', and if we have any hope of getting anything useful, I advise both of you to think of her as a woman. Because her emotional responses will be feminine. Bludgeon her and she'll clam up."

"He left the bar right before the shooting and nothing happened to him," Kiley said. "Shouldn't we consider him at least a person of interest?"

"You can't even put him in the bar." Stay calm. Rational. "If you ever get to trial and you put Andy Mallory on the stand, regardless of what he says, the defense can get ninety-six witnesses. They'll show each witness his photo and ask, 'Did you see this man in the Cove the night of February twenty-third?'. And ninety-six will reply in the negative. We only get Leanne Mallory on the stand if she volunteers to take it, and we won't win her over with threats."

Kiley sat back, struggling to hold his temper. She'd addressed him as an equal and he still didn't see her as one.

Mike spoke up, his voice soft. "John, we go back a long way. Back to our days in OCCB. I'm saying this as a friend. Kim's right. She's been right about this case all along. I never would have figured the transgender angle. Even now, I can't even guess how she thought of it."

Kim's voice dropped to little more than a whisper. "Berringer had paid her the highest compliment possible, asking for her number and inviting her to dinner. She had passed. She ran out because she thought he'd realized she wasn't cis, a genetic girl."

Kiley was impassive. "And you know this, how?"

If she told him, he'd accuse her of being emotional. "Let's accept that I understand, okay?"

70

"I trust Kim's judgment," Mike said. "I'm experienced enough to realize when someone else has a better handle on a case than I do. Let's just do it her way, okay?"

Kiley threw up his hands. "All right, Brady. Handle it as you see fit. But I want progress reports and I'd better see some fucking progress. Get this... person to cooperate."

They returned to their desks. Mike took a call on his cell, and Kim focused on her notes so as not to listen in. Her habit had served her well with partners.

"That was my sister," Mike said as he ended the call. "The surgeon wants another MRI before they decide on surgery."

"How's Hannah holding up?"

"Scared shitless." He sat back. "And I feel so fucking useless. I wish I could do something, anything, to make her feel better. Or at least not so scared."

"What do they think of her chances?"

"They're not saying, yet."

"You can't make her feel less frightened. All you can do is keep showing her she's loved." She patted his hand. "And it's obvious she is."

Back to the case. She needed to find Duval and convince Leanne Mallory to come forward; everything would fall into place.

Time to check the case file on Ice Williams and see what surprises awaited her there.

CHAPTER NINETEEN

Tuesday, February 28th, 11:30 AM
Kim sat at the same table where they'd had their chat with Nolan. As she took a bite out of her chicken salad on sesame bagel, a tall, attractive guy waiting for his order was checking her out. He had wavy sandy-colored hair, buzz-cut back and sides. She tried to focus on her notes from the Ice Williams file, but the guy at the counter was a distraction. An attractive distraction. A stab of guilt forced her to turn away. No man had caught her absolute attention since she'd met Jake.

A chunk of chicken slid out of her bagel and plopped down on the paper plate. She caught another one as the nice-looking guy approached. She added blue eyes to his inventory, and a dimpled chin. And he wore a sharp red striped tie, a crisp white shirt, trousers with knife-edge creases and high-glossed shoes. It was impossible not to look twice.

"Are you Kim Brady?" His voice was just loud enough over the droning of CNN from the television mounted above her.

She took a moment to swallow. "Have we met?"

"George Barlowe. Narcotics." He extended his hand, and she took it. He held it a moment longer than necessary.

Her cheeks warmed. "Who told you who I am?"

"The PBMS desk sergeant advised me I'd find you here, and no other women are present." His grin returned. It was infectious. "His description didn't do you justice."

"Thank you." She hoped she didn't sound rude. "Why were you looking for me?"

"I understand you met with my former partner yesterday. Detective Nolan."

"You understand, or is this a fishing expedition?"

"I overheard him on the phone in our office when he got back." A sly grin. "I wish you'd tell me how you did it."

"Did what?"

"Freaked him out. He was ranting, trying to keep his voice down. I heard something about Joe Brady's bitch daughter—sorry, his words, not mine—poking her nose into his business, all because she couldn't solve the Cove case. I take it he didn't give you anything you could use. Can I get you another cup of coffee?"

"No, thanks. He didn't give me anything, period." Her eyes met his. "When did you split as partners?"

"After Ice Williams took up residence at Dannemora. Nolan had written his report and left my name out of it. You can verify by reading the file."

This was getting interesting. "I have."

"Talk about a W-T-F. I decided I couldn't trust him and asked our lieu to assign me to another partner. Can I get you a dessert? The brownies look incredible."

"No, thanks. I'm good." She took a sip of coffee. "Doesn't seem right. Weren't you the reason they could take Ice down?"

He gave her a quizzical look.

"Wasn't the CI your guy?" she asked.

His charm vanished. "He had the balls to say that?"

"He said it was his collar but not his rat. I assumed it had to be his partner's. Which would have been you."

Barlowe studied the surroundings. When he spoke, his voice was much lower. "He never told me."

She put down the sandwich, picked up a napkin, and wiped a trace of dressing away from the corner of her mouth. "You mean Nolan didn't tell his own partner where the information came from leading to such a huge bust?"

He leaned forward. "Look, I would love to help you, if I can. I have some command aspirations, myself, and I'd hate to see a big case like this fall on its ass because my unit didn't do its job."

His frankness touched her. "I need to learn who might have taken over for Ice Williams. The name Kincaid has popped up. Also…"

"Wait a second." He put down his own sandwich and pulled out his cell. He started making notes. "You want to share a brownie?"

"Nothing for me, thank you. Also, I need anything you have on Diego Paredes, Sylvia Walters, or Pierre Duval."

"Duval? Haven't heard his name in ages. How does he fit in?"

If Nolan was dirty, and it was looking like he was, she needed Barlowe. She told him.

He grinned at her. "Wow. You're good. Where'd the eyewitness come from?"

"She's a waitress at the Cove. She was about to tell him to move when the shooting started."

"I remember Kincaid's name. I think our unit has been looking at him."

And Nolan had said he'd dropped off their radar. "Can you tell me what you have on him?"

"I'll check. Duval was a low-level stooge; Jordy Hill gave him a pity job. Sylvia Walters? No idea who she might be."

"We're trying to locate Duval. We need to bring him in for questioning." Best not to mention her old partner, even if Barlowe was looking to help. Always best to keep some hole cards, Dad used to say.

Barlowe nodded. "I'll poke around, see what I can learn about Duval or Kincaid. Or both. Let's exchange cell numbers and keep in touch on this."

CHAPTER TWENTY

Tuesday, February 28th, 5:20 PM

Kim stopped by both the Apollo Diner and Manhattan Soul, but Sylvia Walters hadn't been to work at either of them for the past five days. Next stop was Sylvia's apartment. Once in the vestibule, she pressed the buzzer for the apartment. No answer.

An older man came in, and while he was fumbling for his key, she tried again, but still no answer.

"You looking for Svetlana in 9-B?" he asked. "She ain't around much these days. Works."

"Svetlana? I thought her name was Sylvia."

He laughed. "Yeah, it is. I liked her better when she was dancing. She was something at a pole."

Kim blinked. "She was a pole dancer?"

"Yeah. At Exotica, on West Fifty-Fourth Street. Hot as hell with her hair all blonde." He sighed, as if savoring the memory. "Svetlana." He unlocked the door and held it for her.

Once outside Sylvia's apartment, she pressed her ear to the door. Sounds of movement inside. She knocked twice. The sounds stopped. "Ms. Walters?"

Steps approaching the door. A thin sound of scraping metal: the cover of the small round glass lens being moved. "I'm alone," Kim said.

The door opened. Sylvia stood before her wearing her waitress uniform and a pair of black Reeboks. "I guess I'll take your word."

"May I come in? Or were you going to work? I looked for you at the Apollo diner. They're eager for you to return to work."

"Thanks." Sylvia gestured for her to come in. "I ain't working today. Just not ready to go back, I guess." She'd left the kitchen sink jammed with dirty dishes and newspapers scattered around the living room. She'd draped a hot pink dress dripping with sequins across the back of an easy chair. "I bought the dress today. No idea why. I don't got anywhere to go in it." She picked up the dress. "I'll end up taking it back."

"The last time we spoke, you said Luke never told you he was dealing. But you were aware he was, weren't you?"

Sylvia pulled the dress closer to her, pressing it against her breasts. "What makes you think I was?"

"Because you're a hardworking woman who likes pleasurable things, and you've acquired some—expensive clothes, well-furnished apartment—while waiting tables. And an additional source of income."

"So, you figure my man with no job had to be slinging."

"He was. There's no question." Kim glanced around the apartment. "And it's obvious he shared the proceeds with you. So, you had to know, even if you didn't ask questions. If you tell me who he and Paredes did business with, we might discover who killed them and why."

Sylvia clutched the dress. "Told you, he never said nothing."

It would take more to shake her loose. For a moment, she considered asking her about her Svetlana alias, but decided she would only make her more defensive. "Thanks. Sorry to have bothered you."

Sylvia shrugged but said nothing. Kim turned back at the door, pulling out a copy of Duval's mug shot. "Ever see this man before?"

Sylvia faltered. "No."

"You sure? Because he was working with Luke and the others last Thursday night." Sylvia remained sullen, shaking her head. "Regardless of the facts, you'll be far better off telling me yourself than waiting until I find out on my own."

But Sylvia remained silent.

CHAPTER TWENTY-ONE

Tuesday, February 28th, 6:50 PM
When Kim walked in, the squad room was empty except for the desk sergeant and two uniforms. Mike had takeout containers on his desk. "Where have you been? I got enough for two."

"I ate at the Apollo Diner. The food wasn't bad. Dropped by Sylvia Walters' place for a chat."

"And...?"

She plopped down into her chair. "I don't know. She'd bought a designer dress."

"So much for the grief-stricken lover."

"People grieve in distinct ways, Mike."

He picked up a white container. "I got some dim sum for you."

"Thanks, but no, thanks." The tailored slacks she wore on the job had gotten a little tight since catching this case. Time to watch the diet. "Guilt could be part of it." She picked out a dumpling. She'd eat one, and then she'd watch the diet. "But she looked scared."

Out front, Pat Holloran was giving a uniform hell about supplies.

"We still don't have a lead on the shooter." She plucked another dumpling. "What about Duval? Dobson and Ryba haven't checked in once today."

Mike stopped eating. "They're still coming up empty. It's on the board."

Her cell pinged. Text from Jake. *My check-in. Rec league game tonight. See you later.*

Mike's phone rang. "Resnick." He listened, paled, and mumbled, "Thanks" and hung up.

Uh oh. "Theresa Santos?"

"An hour ago."

Kiley would be in an uproar. Leanne stared at her from the sketch on her desk. How do I reach her? She's a sweet person, like Chrissy was. Make it human. Make it about others' suffering. Two more victims had now died since the shooting. She must be hurting.

A cold call might work as a change of approach. "Hi, Leanne, this is Detective Brady. Could you look through mug shots? Tell me if any of them ring a bell?"

"That wouldn't be the end, and you know it." Her voice sounded morose. She had to be stewing about it.

"You remember the two youthful women I told you about who were critical? One of them died an hour ago. The other is clinging to life. Dale Keegan died Monday." No response. "You're an honorable person, Leanne. How can you live with yourself?"

Two beeps. She glanced at the screen on her phone. The call had dropped. "I guess that could have gone better."

"I take it she wasn't too receptive." Mike's tone was soft.

Kim tucked her cell in her hip pocket. "No, but at least we're making a little progress."

"How you figure?"

"You said 'she'."

•   •   •

To: allison91_<Alli>
From: mallgirl_<Leanne>
Alli,

Sorry Mom is worse. Wish I could help. I owe you so much. Rod and Sean should help you. She's their mom, too.

And, yes, I'm spending a lot of time en femme. Almost all the time, other than work. Can we hook up, soon? I need to talk to you about something in person.
Love, Leanne.

.   .   .

He had Garner meet him in a strip club near the Long Island Expressway. "You look a little ragged around the edges, Harold." An intentional understatement. Garner looked like he'd been on the street for a year and smelled like he hadn't showered in as long.

Garner's eye twitched, and he made little grimaces with his mouth every few seconds. "Been sleeping in my car."

"You have any money left at all?"

Garner shook his head, tiny shakes.

Time to give him the lecture he's expecting along with the pleasant news he's desperate to hear. "You've made some awful choices, rent money going for coke, food money going for rocks. So far on this job, you've done well. I want to expand it. Surveillance for now. Later, we'll see. I'll advance you enough to make you presentable and keep your car going." He slipped him a glassine envelope. "A sufficient amount to rid you of those hideous twitches. Someone will re-supply you daily, unless you go through it too soon." He dropped his voice. "Then, you're fucked."

Garner couldn't stop nodding.

Desperation was so pathetic, and yet he enjoyed watching. Exercising his power over others was always enjoyable.

He slipped Garner a wad of cash. "Buy yourself some decent clothes and something you can use to get you inside places you don't belong." He placed a prepaid cell on the table. "Use this to contact me when you have something to report. I want you to track a woman in her twenties, lives at this address in Hunters Point." He provided Garner with a slip of paper.

80

"Tell me where she goes, where she works, what she does. Then, I want you to track an old friend at this address." Another slip of paper. Garner's eyes grew wider. "You remember? Excellent. And if you see Pierre Duval, you're to inform me at once."

CHAPTER TWENTY-TWO

Wednesday, March 1st, 11:30 AM

No matter where Andy Mallory looked, no matter how he concentrated, he saw the eyes that had caught his as soon as he walked into the Cove. The guy had been standing at the corner of the bar nearest the entrance. He'd grinned as if to say, "Sorry, I'm waiting for someone else."

But Monday morning, "the guy" had acquired a name. Dale Keegan. And for the second day in a row, every newspaper in town had his smiling, confident face on the front page, along with a fresh face, Theresa Santos. She was young and pretty, with long dark hair. On the subway. In the office. Even passers-by in the street. From all angles, their engaging smiles damned him.

Coward.

"Hey, you okay?" Joyce Kendall, coworker and best friend, was working on a project with him. They were to clear hundreds of entries in a suspense account.

"Yeah. Let's clear these entries." He resumed scanning the stack of printed pages.

But Dale's eyes kept at him. His date had entered the Cove a few minutes later, wearing the prettiest white satin blouse. She was killed outright in the shooting. The news reports said she was Dale's wife, and she was pregnant. Dale's eyes haunted him now on behalf of her and the child who would never be.

Coward. Pathetic loser.

Rod, Sean, and their father had called him those names for years.

"Andy?" Joyce touched his hand, glancing around to make sure they weren't being watched. "Did you get a critical review, too? Is that what's been bothering you?"

"Yeah." He'd taken off last Thursday because of it; all forgotten in the shooting's wake. "Let's finish this."

They cleared an entry. Then a second. He forced himself to concentrate enough to accomplish something for a change.

Rick Meagher, their manager, stuck his head over the wall of the group cubicle everyone called the bullpen. "Hey, what do you two think you're doing?" Earlier, he'd kicked them out of a conference room.

Sometimes, Meagher was like an extension of the tyranny of Andy's father and brothers. "We're doing the job you gave us to do."

"Which requires us to be together," Joyce added.

"Shut up, Slim." Meagher was always shaming her about her weight. "You'll work how and where I tell you to work, or we'll have another run at your evaluation." He raised his voice. "But no afternoon delights on company time." He stalked away while stifled snorts drifted out from behind cubicle walls.

Joyce stared at the floor, red-faced. "Let's break for lunch."

They found a table in the company cafeteria together, by a window looking out at the harbor. Andy poked at a salad but only ate a few bites.

Joyce broke the silence. "I got a 'well below standard' rating on my review."

"Me, too." Which made the "pathetic loser" label official.

"I'm scared. If we don't finish this project and get it right, they could fire us. Meagher's already gotten rid of people."

For a moment, Dale's eyes faded from his attention. He always felt better helping Joyce. "I know."

"Something's bothering you," she said. "Something other than this crap. You've been miserable all week. Please tell me."

He glanced up. The day before the Cove shooting, the day they'd gotten their reviews, she'd given him the Celtic cross, signaling acceptance of his secret.

Her eyes were on his. "Was I right to give you the gift?"

With Joyce, it wasn't so dire. "How did you know?"

She reached across the table and laid her hand on his. "A guy who knows which colors suit a girl best? How her hairstyle can make her face appear thinner? How makeup can help her looks?" Her smile radiated genuine warmth. "But, when you started tweezing your eyebrows and using a little eyeliner and mascara, I realized you were serious."

He pulled back in alarm. "You think anyone else has noticed?"

"None of the Neanderthals. If any girls noticed, they've kept quiet about it. You don't overdo it."

He relaxed. "Last Thursday, when I took off, I treated myself to a little outing. I was so upset about the review. I needed space."

"How did it go?"

"Awesome. It wasn't the first time I've gone out dressed."

"I wouldn't think so."

"I did some shopping, and then I decided to, you know, take it to the next level."

"Did you wear the cross?" It was an excited whisper.

He nodded. "And the dress and shoes I'd bought. I went to a trendy bar, one where professionals go after work."

"And did you..."

The more he told her, the easier it became. "Pass? Yes."

She grinned at him. "Get picked up?"

He dropped to a hoarse whisper. "I wasn't trying."

"But...?"

He blushed. "A guy bought me a drink. But it was at the Cove."

She covered her mouth with both hands.

"I didn't see it happen, but if I say what I saw, it means..." He struggled to keep from crying. "People died. Gunned down." He put his fork down. "I can't eat anything."

"Me neither." But she made no move to leave. "I'll bet you went to the Cove to prove something to yourself. You're much happier as Andrea or Annie than Andy."

He stared at the floor. Groups at nearby tables got up to return to work, replaced by other groups.

"It's not Andrea or Annie, is it?" Joyce asked at last. "Please tell me my best friend's proper name."

He met her gaze. "Leanne." Wonderful to say it, regardless of whatever followed.

.   .   .

Dobson grew defensive as they gathered in Kiley's office for a status meeting. "We tried, Kim. We pounded every likely lead from every prior location, and the Brownsville lead was the best we got."

"Maybe," Ryba said, "he's fled the jurisdiction. In which case, we're wasting our time on Duval."

Typical Ryba, taking the route of least effort. But there was something in his expression, his body language. Like he had something riding on backing off Duval.

She glanced at Mike. "You might be right." Her cell buzzed. A text from Jake. *All good here.* "I have to return this. You guys go ahead, we'll catch up later. Mike, can you hang back?"

As soon as Dobson and Ryba left, Mike nodded toward her phone. "Who was it?"

"Text from Jake." She nodded toward the hallway. "I need your take on those two. Is it possible they're so incompetent?"

Mike considered it. "Anything's possible, but Dobson's been helpful, getting the photo of the Blazer from the Fifteen. Ryba, I admit, seems lazy. We'll monitor him."

Dobson poked his head in. "Queens South Traffic Enforcement called. They found the Blazer."

CHAPTER TWENTY-THREE

Wednesday, March 1ˢᵗ, 4:55 PM

Kim stepped around the Blazer, its front grill, wheels, and engine submerged in a murky creek at the edge of Jamaica Bay. The water reached the driver's door window. The setting sun was a spotlight on the damaged tailgate and rear bumper, and the license plate—BDY-139. Two bullet holes in the rear passenger-side door and one in the quarter panel caught her attention. Drake had shot three-for-five.

Ryba had already signed out when they left PBMS, but Dobson had come along. "Whoever drove it in here had the right idea."

"What do you mean?" Kim asked.

A police department flatbed truck backed up and halted well before the ground turned muddy. The driver hooked up chains, preparing to drag the Blazer out.

Dobson pointed across the creek. "I grew up over there in Howard Beach. This stretch is the deepest channel this close to land. Used to poke around these inlets in a little motorboat. The driver wanted to sink it. Either he panicked at the shock of hitting the water or he was afraid he wouldn't get out."

Mike joined them. He'd been talking with CSU. "I asked about the AR-15." He gestured to a group of officers in the water wearing waders. "No sign of it in the Blazer, but they found some shell casings. They're looking."

Kim peered inside. Someone had ripped out all the back-seat upholstery. "What the...?"

"Yeah," Mike said. "Rugs, too."

"Blood." She and Dobson said it together.

Mike nodded. "Most likely. I'm hoping we'll catch a break and there'll be some spatter on the seat backs."

The tow truck winch ground away as it dragged the Blazer out. Chains banged against the metal bed of the truck as the driver locked it down.

The CSU Sergeant approached. "We'll get this to the shop and notify you right away if we find any slugs. The holes are consistent with nine-millimeter shells."

Kim leaned in closer to examine the holes. "Sergeant, assuming an average-sized male was sitting in the back seat, where might a shot have hit him?"

The sergeant scratched his head. "Couldn't say which one hit when, or the perp's position for either shot. We'll compare the exit hole to the entrance hole which will provide us with the bullet's trajectory. Then I can answer your question."

"But at least one shot might have hit?" she asked.

"For now, I'd say if the low one hit, it would be in the leg area. Second one? Could have hit his ribs, lower back or abdomen."

"Okay, thanks. Whatever you can expedite for us, we appreciate it." The clock was ticking.

"I get it." The sergeant held up the tabloid tucked in his jacket pocket. Its banner headline, "DEATH TOLL RISING", appeared superimposed on a montage of the eight fatalities. Photos of Dale Keegan and Theresa Santos now joined the three inside the bar and the dealers.

Kim slid into the front passenger seat beside Mike, while Dobson climbed in the back. They pulled onto the access road leading back to the Belt Parkway. Kiley would be breathing fire by tomorrow morning.

Her cell buzzed. She pressed the phone against her ear so the other side of the conversation couldn't be overheard.

It was her old partner from the Seven-Three. "I checked some old notes of mine, not in case files. Back when we were working a lot with OCCB on drug enforcement, I tried to recruit Duval as a Confidential Informant, but he was too unreliable. Most of his residences appear in his file—he's always moved around a lot—but I found one not in the file. It's an address in the South Bronx, someone he claimed was his cousin, although I doubt they're related. I'll text it to you."

"Thanks." She ended the call. "We'll drop you off at the Sixth," she said to Dobson. "Then, Mike and I have an errand to run."

CHAPTER TWENTY-FOUR

Wednesday, March 1st, 11:54 PM

Mike and Kim pulled in behind the patrol car from the Four-Oh parked on the corner of East 136th and Willow in the Port Morris section of the South Bronx.

A sergeant greeted them. "He's in there."

Kim studied the building. "Cover the fire escapes and the windows on his side of the building. Have two men come with us."

It was a three-floor tenement. The front door was ajar, impossible to shut. Kim jiggled the handle on the inner door, and it popped open. Duval's apartment was on the second floor toward the rear.

Mike pounded on the door. "Con Ed. Got a report of a gas leak."

The door lock clicked, the knob turned, and Mike and the two uniforms slammed against it with their shoulders, forcing it open and knocking Duval back.

Kim pulled her main piece, a Glock. "Freeze, Duval. Hands on your head."

Duval stood shaking in grimy, stained boxer shorts, a yellowed tee shirt, torn robe and tattered socks. "I did nothing…"

Mike turned him around and cuffed him. "Your customers say otherwise."

Kim read Duval his rights. Once they cuffed him, they searched the apartment.

"No drugs, no weapons," Mike said.

"Look at this." Kim held up a gray suit in dry cleaner's plastic. "It matches the description given by everyone who saw him in the club." She pulled the plastic to the hanger, laid the suit on the bed, and studied the inside of the jacket. Then she pulled the trousers inside out and studied the inseams. "Someone's done some heavy alterations."

Mike chuckled. "Hey, some suits don't fit off the rack."

"Yeah, but do you ever buy a size fifty suit when you need a forty-four?"

"I never wanted any suit that bad. Serious weight loss?"

"Or hand-me-downs."

As soon as they got Duval into the car, he announced he wanted a lawyer and he couldn't afford one. "I ain't saying anything till I get one."

"Spoken like a veteran of the system," Mike said. He turned to Kim. "I'll drop you off at PBMS, then take him to Central Booking. You get some sleep." He pulled an evidence bag out of his pocket containing a cell phone. "Found this in his apartment."

.　　　.　　　.

To: <Leanne>

From: <Alli>

I wish we could get together, but it's impossible right now. Mom's back in the hospital, killing my day. The kids and Bart take the rest. Can't you just tell me?

Please tell me you're not going back on your promise. I couldn't bear losing you.

Love, Alli.

CHAPTER TWENTY-FIVE

Thursday, March 2nd, 8:32 AM

Everywhere Andy turned, he saw the faces of the dead victims. As the Two train crawled downtown, he tried not to look at them.

"HOW MANY MORE WILL DIE?" one headline blared.

His stomach wrenched. When the train reached the Park Place stop, he pushed his way off and through the crowd jamming the platform because of delays. By the time he reached the street, perspiration soaked his collar and under his arms, and he was gasping for breath.

The chilly air refreshed him, and he calmed down. But then he passed a newsstand on Vesey Street. More headlines. More glimpses of Theresa Santos. It looked like her college yearbook picture.

Coward.

Maybe Joyce was right, and he should let the chips fall where they may. But then Meagher's ridicule and humiliation would be relentless, endless. He'd have less than nothing.

He couldn't think about it. Not about Dale Keegan or Theresa Santos. He couldn't handle one more thing.

He stepped out of the elevator onto his floor. The light over Joyce's section of the bullpen was out, even though she'd been looking forward to wrapping up their project.

Rick Meagher was joking with two other guys and started laughing when he saw Andy. But he came no closer.

Celia Coravos, one of the other accountants, stood in whispered conversation with two other women, but they scattered when Andy approached. Celia dashed into the break room. Andy followed her.

They were alone. Celia tried to leave, but Andy blocked her way. "What's going on?"

"What do you mean?"

"Joyce said she'd meet me here this morning, but she's not here. What happened?"

Celia trembled, close to tears. "I don't think I should…"

"Do you hate Joyce?"

She looked like he'd slapped her. "Of course not. She and I are friends."

"Then tell me what happened. Now."

She glanced toward the door; it was closed. "Joyce came in for a muffin from the vending machine. When she left, Rick Meagher yelled, loud enough to carry the entire floor, 'Way to go, Tubby. Got to make weight.' He made some other disgusting comments I won't repeat. Most of the guys laughed. Joyce ran out crying."

For a moment, rage washed over him. He half turned to the door. But what could he do to Rick Meagher, who dwarfed Andy in size and strength? He scanned the room for a potential weapon.

A roll of brown paper towel hung over the sink. Andy tore off a length of the paper, slapped it down on a table and took a pen from his shirt pocket. "Write it down, Celia. All of it, please, including the disgusting comments you wouldn't tell me."

"Andy, please…"

"Don't argue." He had to stay calm, for Joyce's sake. "We draw the line, stand for what's decent. You could be next."

She took the pen, her trembling giving way to a sudden determination. She wrote her account and signed and dated it.

Andy folded the paper. "Thank you."

He strode back to the bullpen, stuffed the stack of paper from the suspense account project into an extensive accordion file, then slipped Celia's statement in with it.

Meagher was sitting in his manager's cubicle, looking smug.

"I've had something personal come up," Andy said. "So, I'm taking a personal day."

"Wait a second," Meagher replied. "Personal days are subject to managerial approval."

"Try to dock me if you think you can get away with it." He left without waiting for an answer. And it felt so good.

Once he was on Vesey Street, he called Joyce's home number, but it went to voicemail. "Joyce, it's Andy. Please call my cell as soon as you get this message." But something told him she wouldn't go home.

Before entering the subway station, he called her cell. Voicemail. He left the same message and grabbed a Two train uptown.

At Times Square, he tried again. "Joyce, it's Andy. Please call me right back. I'm out looking for you."

Five minutes passed. Ten. He tried a text. *Out looking for you. Scared shit. Know what went down. Please call. Love, Leanne.* He hesitated a moment, then sent it.

A minute later, his phone rang. Joyce.

He answered. "Where are you?"

"Museum of Natural History. Opens at ten."

"Kind of cold to wait, isn't it?"

Her laugh was bitter. "The Joyce bear carries several protective layers of fat, rendering it impervious to low temperatures."

He softened his voice, the way he'd been practicing for months. Leanne's voice. "Hey, come on, Joyce."

"Sorry." She was crying.

"Wait for me? Be there in about twenty minutes."

"Okay." She hesitated. "Thanks, Leanne."

He took the C train to Eighty-First Street. There she was, pacing in front of the main entrance. A few others were waiting with her.

As soon as he reached the top step, she collapsed in his embrace. "Thank you so much. But please don't talk about it. Please?"

He grinned at her. "Hey, it's your day."

"What's in the folder?" she asked, nodding at the accordion file.

"My stamp collection." He reached into the file and pulled out the length of brown paper towel as they entered the main lobby. "Celia Coravos wrote this statement describing the incident this morning. I'm taking it to HR tomorrow."

Her body stiffened. "You promised not to mention this."

"You asked me not to talk about what happened this morning, and I'm not. I won't show you what Celia wrote, either." He put Celia's statement back in the file. "I'm going to HR, and I hope you join me. I'm doing it because you are my BFF, like a sister to me. This has to end."

She stared at the floor.

"I hope you come with me." He swallowed hard against the rising tide of emotion. "Because it'll be better for you. They'll keep ruining our lives if we let them. Meagher. My brothers. I refuse to let them ruin mine anymore."

She dabbed at her eyes with a tissue. "How does this involve your brothers?" She offered him the tissue. "Your mascara is running."

He snatched it and dabbed at his eyes. "They're all bullies. When I got beaten up in school for being a 'sissy faggot', they told me I deserved it." He took out his cell and punched up a number. "Human Resources, please… yes, my name is Andrew Mallory, I'm an employee, and I'd like to make an appointment for tomorrow morning to file a harassment complaint."

She tugged at his arm. "I'll go with you."

•   •   •

He listened as Garner gave him the latest. Sylvia Walters was staying in her apartment, except for the occasional quick run to the bodega and one shopping trip.

No surprise there. She couldn't help herself. Although money must be getting tight. "Has Duval visited?" Unlikely, but Duval was unpredictable. Best to be certain.

"No."

Where the hell was Duval? Perhaps he was learning a few things. "And what about the girl?"

"I haven't seen her."

"Are you sure about the address?"

Garner got defensive. "It's the one you gave me. Are you sure it's the one?"

He wasn't taking any shit from Garner. His voice was like ice. "I got it from a most reliable source."

"Well, I haven't seen the girl. Only her brother. At least I think it's her brother. He looks a lot like the sketch you gave me."

He'd heard she was the shy, quiet type. It made sense she might have gone to her brother's place instead of hers. Or perhaps they shared an apartment. "Follow the brother. See where it leads."

CHAPTER TWENTY-SIX

Thursday, March 2nd, 10:05 AM

As soon as Kim reached the top of the subway stairs at Twenty-Second Street and Park Avenue South, she spotted Barlowe. He was leaning against the stately old building on the corner. "Unusual spot to be hanging out, isn't it?"

He gestured to the building. "My dear woman, this is an excellent example of Flemish Renaissance architecture. Although there doesn't seem to have been any part of the Renaissance specifically identified as Flemish." He paused while she bought coffee from the nearby cart. "I have some information for you. First, Kincaid. I can't imagine what Nolan was thinking, telling you he'd dropped out of sight. He's on our radar. But locating him has become difficult. Several of my sources have dried up. You can arrive at your own conclusions."

"Protection. Nolan?" She wondered if she shouldn't have been so direct.

Barlowe looked uncomfortable for a moment. "I, um, didn't mention any names. You don't want me making any accusations without evidence. Checked on Kincaid's last known, but he's no longer there. Same with Duval."

"We collared Duval last night in the South Bronx. Port Morris section."

His grin returned. "Fantastic. I'm mad impressed. How did you find...? No, don't tell me. Have you talked to him, yet?"

"No. He lawyered up when we arrested him. Later today."

"Okay. If he gives you anything about who he was working with, please keep me informed. It'll help me focus my efforts. In the meantime, I'll do my best to locate Kincaid for you."

A Narcotics guy who was a help. Things were looking up.

·   ·   ·

"Morning, Kim," Sergeant Holloran said as she entered PBMS. "Stephenson's wife had the baby at last. The poor woman was in labor for sixteen hours. It's a girl, six pounds, eleven ounces."

Missed it by an ounce. "Who won the pool?"

"No one. The money goes to Mom."

Kim laughed. "She's more than earned it." She placed her coffee cup on her desk and joined Mike and Dobson at the case board. No sign of Kiley.

"You collared Duval?" Dobson asked. "How did you track him down? Where was he?"

"Police work." She decided not to tell him where. If Barlowe didn't need to know, neither did Dobson.

Mike was updating. "The VIN on the Blazer is a match for the one reported stolen. They also found two slugs, one buried in the back of the passenger front seat, the other in the trunk. Both look like nine millimeters, but they're messed up. Ballistics may not tell us much. The lab's working up trajectory diagrams."

A third slug should've been in the interior. With luck, it hit the shooter. "Dobson, I want you and Ryba to check for any reports from any medical providers on gunshot wounds treated since Thursday night.

Focus on Queens and the east side of Manhattan." She looked around. "Where's Ryba?"

"He called and said he was running late," Dobson replied. "But I'll get started on the reported gunshot wounds."

The reference on the board to the shoes Leanne had ditched caught her eye. "Still nothing back from the lab. Find out what the holdup is."

CHAPTER TWENTY-SEVEN

Thursday, March 2nd, 1:09 PM

Kim introduced herself to ADA Yvette Driscoll, forty, tall and thin and a fitness fanatic. Her tailored skirt suits lent her a no-nonsense air, and her ash blonde hair, worn in a long shag, did nothing to soften it. Kim briefed her on what they had so far.

Duval's Legal Aid attorney was waiting with him in the consultation room at Rikers. He had receding jet black hair, and a bald spot already showing. Heavy on the hair dye? Wire-rimmed glasses. His gray suit—genuine JC Penney—had a shine in spots and his wing tips had come from a discount outlet. Either he was a genuine believer, or just another C-student lawyer who lacked the chops for a better paying job.

The attorney's grip was firm, his manner calm. Duval sat next to him, sullen.

Kim started things off. "Mr. Duval, you were at a bar called The Cove on the evening of Thursday, February twenty-third, selling cocaine to patrons. Correct?"

Duval stared at the table.

She turned to the attorney. "Your client has three priors, one for dealing, so he'll do serious time. A witness spotted him dealing at the bar. Silence is not his best option."

"What options are you offering?"

So, he was a genuine believer. "This same eyewitness will testify your client blocked patrons from leaving. We found his suppliers gunned down right outside with over four thousand dollars in their possession and a sizable stash of cocaine. We'll make this easy for you. Your client is not our target. We're interested in who hired him, what his instructions were and any other details he can give us."

"Unless," Mike added, "he was a conspirator in the shooting."

The attorney was getting agitated. "You don't have anywhere near that."

Yvette spoke up. "I've got him cold on the dealing charge and enough on the shooting to support an indictment."

"We're still collecting evidence," Kim added. "For example, the cell phone we snagged when we arrested you, Mr. Duval. You received a call at five after seven. Who from, and about what?"

The attorney turned to Duval. "Not a word. This conference is over."

Back outside, Kim turned to Yvette. "Can you do me a favor? About two years ago, there was a trial of two dealers named Isaac Williams and Jordy Hill. Can I get a transcript?"

.   .   .

Kiley was waiting when they got back. "Brady, Resnick, Dobson, Ryba, in my office, now." He waited until Kim closed the door. "Another critical victim, Jenna Guarnaccia, is back on the table for emergency surgery. Not looking good." He sat back. "So, Ms. Brady, how's the investigation going?"

Oh, no. He would not force her on the defensive. "Ignoring, for the moment, your habit of referring to my gender every time you criticize my work, I'd say not as smoothly as we'd like. Duval didn't give us anything."

Kiley pressed her. "And our dress-wearing star eyewitness?"

"You mean Leanne?" Dobson asked.

"Or whatever his actual name is," Kiley said.

Kim glowered at him. "I'm working on her. As I explained, she needs to come forward voluntarily."

Kiley gave a curt nod. "So, we should have this all wrapped by, oh, St. Swiggin's Day? What do you think, Detective Brady?"

"We're doing our best, Mr. Kiley." She walked out. Dobson and Ryba returned to their places. No one closed the door behind them.

"John, remember a certain summer night in Red Hook?" Mike's voice.

"If you're about to remind me of your timely shooting on my behalf," Kiley replied, "you're out of line."

"Remember the guy who bought it?"

"Yeah. Best goddamned detective I ever met. What's your point?"

"She's better. Smarter. And a better shot. Get off her case." Mike returned to his desk.

Kim didn't look up from the search she was doing on her laptop. "Please don't do that."

"Do what?"

"Stick up for me. I realize you mean well, and I appreciate your support more than you can know, but please don't do it. It only reinforces his notion I'm a weak female who needs a man's protection."

"Okay, what can I do?"

She nodded toward Dobson and Ryba. "Stay on top of them."

.   .   .

Garner's voice was tinny on the speaker, but his panic came through. "I don't understand it. The brother leaves every morning and returns every evening, but no sign of his sister."

"Calm, Harold." He tried not to snicker. Even a brilliant planner like himself never would have guessed this one. "I learned the reason a short while ago, and it's an intriguing one. They're the same person. She's a tranny. A shemale. A chick with a dick. So, a change of plan. Over the weekend, I want you to tail her wherever she goes, whether as a guy or girl. I want no more surprises popping up."

"What about the other one?"

Good question. Circumstances had changed. Brady would soon learn of her connection. "Shadow her tomorrow."

He ended the call and turned back to his visitor, his aide-de-camp who had brought the latest news, and asked, "Our source is sure the tranny isn't talking?"

"Positive. She, or he, or whatever, must be afraid of being 'outed'. Kiley's pissed about it. But we have another problem. Brady has Ryba and Dobson scanning reports for treated gunshot wounds. She knows the nigger hit the vehicle and figures he might have hit our guy."

This was why he was his aide-de-camp: he worried about details. "But our guy convinced the doc not to report it, correct? So, they won't to find anything."

"It's a lead I would have preferred they not find."

He couldn't argue with his trusted advisor. His plan had been for them to ditch the vehicle out of state and slip back into the city, undetected. Who'd expect the kid would pack a piece? Or hit anyone with it? "Agreed. But it's all good. Is there anything else?"

"Duval remains among the missing."

Still living right. But Brady still hadn't lost steam. He needed something to adjust her priorities.

CHAPTER TWENTY-EIGHT

Friday, March 3rd, 8:07 AM

"The death toll in the horrific Cove shooting has now reached nine, as young Jenna Guarnaccia died last night after emergency surgery failed to stop internal bleeding. *New York One* has learned police have someone in custody in connection with the shooting but who is not the shooter himself."

Sergeant Holloran caught Kim's grimace as she passed the squad room TV. "Sorry the news isn't better, Kim."

She could only shrug. "It is what it is."

He came out from behind the desk. "We're getting up a bracket pool for the NCAA tourney in two weeks. You want in? Only, you can't have Jake help you."

She stifled a laugh. "Last year, my guesses were better than his. Offer rescinded?"

"Nah. We'll take our chances."

Her smile faded as she crossed to her desk. The Master Roll Call showed Kiley as having the day off, but with the news of Jenna Guarnaccia, all bets were off. Mike was sitting at his desk, ashen-faced. "Uh oh. Grim news?"

"Hannah needs the surgery. Next Thursday. I saw her last night. She's trying so hard to be brave."

"Waiting has got to be the worst."

"That's what my sister said. So, yesterday, after end-of-tour, I drove out to North Shore Animal League and I got Hannah a dog, a ten-month-old cocker spaniel named Sonny. It felt right. And Hannah fell in love with him."

"How'd your sister feel about it?" She bit her lip to keep from grinning.

"At first, not great. But, Kim, this little guy, he's the friendliest little pooch, ever. Loves when we pet him and scratch him behind the ears. His little stubby tail goes a mile-a-minute when you pay any attention to him at all. He won my sister over in nanoseconds."

"A beautiful thing to do. No wonder you're her favorite uncle." She decided not to mention Sonny would be therapeutic for Mike, too.

She spread the crime lab's trajectory diagram on her desk and waved Mike over. "The exit hole of the fragment they found in the front seat was further forward than the entrance hole. It either grazed the shooter or missed him altogether. The Blazer had already passed Malcolm. Another shot exited the interior of the door a little forward of where it entered; might've hit the shooter, because they didn't find the slug."

Mike showed her the Ballistics report. "They couldn't use the fragments in the trunk from the slug piercing the quarter panel." He checked the crime scene diagram. "They dug the two missed shots out of the construction near the Ninth Avenue end of the block."

"Shots four and five, after Malcolm went down. The slug in the trunk traveled from the front toward the rear. Shot number one. The one we can't find was number two, and the one buried in the seat was number three."

At the front desk, Sgt. Holloran pointed a messenger toward Kim and Mike.

"Detective Brady?" the messenger asked. "From ADA Driscoll." He laid a huge binder, bristling with post-it notes, on her desk. There was a note from Yvette. "Here's your transcript. The yellow sticky is where you'll find the witness lists, and my assistant used pink stickies to tag the pages where each one's testimony begins. Hope you find what you're looking for."

"I'm digging into the Ice Williams case," she said to Mike. "And please don't offer to do it for me, because when Nolan finds out, he'll make it all about how you were partners and the good old days. Shrug and say, 'Hey, my partner's a bitch'."

Mike looked stunned.

She broke into a grin. "It's okay, Mike. I know you won't mean it."

· · ·

Andy met Joyce in front of the building and joined her in the Human Resources Department on the second floor. After checking in with the receptionist, they sat and waited. A television, its sound off, flashed images from a local news station. Jenna Guarnaccia's lovely youthful face appeared on the screen, with a graphic underneath reading, "Cove shooting claims ninth fatality".

"Oh, my God," he said in a whisper.

"What is it?" Joyce asked. But then she saw the screen. "Oh, no. Andy, should we do this another time?"

"No." He needed something to keep him from thinking.

Abigail Donner, an austere woman, tall and thin, with short white hair, wearing a gray wool skirt suit and black oxfords, waved them into her office. Together, they laid out the pattern of bullying and harassment they'd been enduring for over a year. Donner took copious notes.

As Joyce relaxed, she described incidents Andy hadn't known about. He sank back into his own thoughts. He snapped out of it when Joyce said, "I have a coworker friend who's transgender. Would the company protect her if she transitioned?"

Ms. Donner's eyes locked on Joyce. "Our anti-harassment policy would cover her. She should contact our Employee Assistance Program for a confidential referral to a professional who can help her through the transition process."

He said nothing to Joyce when they left HR. At lunch time, he slipped out on his own. Wherever he went, Dale, Theresa and Jenna followed, their ghostly eyes damning him.

.   .   .

It was slow going as Kim plodded through the transcript, double checking the evidence submitted against what was in Williams' file. No sign of Kiley, so she worked in relative peace.

Mike broke her train of thought shortly before two. "How's it going?"

"Outstanding, considering I don't know what I'm looking for, might not recognize it when I find it, and may not know what to do about it when I do." She closed the binder. "I need a break. How about lunch?"

"I'd love to, but the owner of the Blazer is coming in. My advice is to head down to Tal's and eat there. Decompress. I'll join you after the Blazer owner leaves."

CHAPTER TWENTY-NINE

Friday, March 3rd, 3:30 PM

"He saw two guys snatch the vehicle," Mike said when she returned. "He described the one who got in the passenger's side as a 'rough looking Chinese guy, thirty or a little older', but nothing more. The driver he saw from the back. Black guy, not too tall."

"Narrows it down. Any luck with mug shots?"

"He paged through all our binders, but no luck. He ranted at me about the lousy work we do before he left."

Kiley stormed in and flung the late edition of the *New York Post* down on Kim's desk, with "COVE COPS FLOUNDERING" in bold, two-inch type. "You're in overtime, Brady. The Chief of Detectives just had me on the carpet. The commissioner's all over his ass about this. Guess where the chief puts us."

"It's a bitch of a case, John," Mike said.

Kiley wheeled around on him. "Which we've been making worse. But that's over."

Kim struggled to keep calm. "Meaning what?"

"I no longer buy your theory of Mallory's role," Kiley replied. "Minutes before the shooting, a bunch of people try to leave. Duval's blocking the exit, but Mallory gets out. The only one. Walks away unscathed. Which I'd say is impossible unless he's part of the attack."

Kim exploded. "What?"

Kiley shrugged. "I'm thinking he was part of the plan to jam up the exit. It's enough to name him a suspect. Before the right judge, it's enough to get us a search warrant."

"Except," Mike said, "as Kim has already pointed out, you can't even put him in the bar."

"Sure, I can." Kiley became smug. "He's as much as admitted it to Brady. Plus, we have 'him' and 'her' sketches. One witness has identified Mallory from the 'him' sketch, and another has already put the subject of the 'her' sketch in the bar. The 'him' sketch is a mere alteration of the 'her'. A search of Mallory's apartment will no doubt reveal a wardrobe to rival Detective Brady's."

"Doesn't make him a party to the shooting," Kim said.

Kiley remained smug. "Nope. But, with his fleeing the scene and lying to police when questioned, it's a decent shot at probable cause. At the very least, being outed will force Mallory to tell us what he knows."

Kim sprang to her feet. "You want me to threaten him with an arrest I know is false?"

Kiley sneered at her. "You don't know any such thing. But it no longer matters because I'm considering taking you off this case. You're emotional about this witness, ignoring the few snippets of genuine evidence he's given you. On Monday, Judge Castellano gets back from vacation, and by Tuesday we will ask him for a search warrant based on our theory. I make Tuesday morning Mallory's deadline to come forward voluntarily."

·   ·   ·

Kim didn't say a word to Mike. She walked down to the Union Square station and grabbed the packed Five train. She wedged herself into the car and spent the entire ride plastered against an old man who reeked of garlic. But since there were extensive delays on the Two and Three trains, she decided not to change at Fulton Street. When the train reached Borough Hall, a longer walk home for her than from the Clark Street station, she shoved her way past the garlic man.

On the walk home, it occurred to her she'd been rude to the garlic man. But fuck it.

She'd been right every step of the way on this case except betting Leanne would come forward. She'd doubled down by challenging Kiley, which was now threatening her career. Because if Kiley took her off this high-profile case, she'd be a marked woman. There wouldn't be anything official, nothing in her file. But word would get around. It always did. It had with Dad, despite her grandfather's heroic legacy.

She had to act before Kiley did.

Did Jake have a game tonight? The two front windows were lit, so no, he didn't.

She wished he had a game. Because she didn't want to talk about it. Any of it.

Jake slumped in the easy chair. The Nets pregame show from the Barclays Center was on television. He pulled an ice pack away from his swollen jaw. "Root canal today, remember?"

Right. He'd texted her he was taking the night off—long ago, before her world had crashed.

"Hey," he said, sitting up. "What's wrong? You look upset."

"No, I'm fine."

"You don't sound fine."

She didn't meet his gaze. "This is as fine as I can sound after a week on a shitty case." She turned into the bedroom, hoping he'd take the hint.

He followed her as far as the doorway. "Hey, don't shut me out."

Why couldn't this most sensitive of men read the tea leaves the one time she was desperate for him to leave her alone? "I don't want to talk about it."

But she couldn't put him off and she told him about Kiley's threat to "out" Andy Mallory if he didn't cooperate. "He'll take me off the case if I don't."

Jake shrugged. "He might be right. I'm sorry Mallory's being forced into the open, but a killer is going scot free because this guy is embarrassed to admit he enjoys wearing dresses. Doesn't get any sympathy from me."

She pushed passed him, grabbed her jacket, snatched her purse off the mantel and stormed out. Time faded to the background as she walked, not conscious of direction, and the memories flooded in.

After she'd forgiven Dad for Chrissy, she'd spent weekends at his place throughout her teen years because Mom wouldn't allow her to date. She'd had to meet Dad at a restaurant the day after high school graduation because Mom wouldn't allow him at the ceremony. And he'd greeted her announcement of going to John Jay and then the Police Academy with a mixture of pride and dismay.

She stopped at a corner and checked the street signs. Saratoga Avenue and Bergen Street. Brownsville. The Seven-Three, her first post of duty. Still struggling to gentrify, but better than when she patrolled these streets.

Her cell buzzed. Text from Jake. *Please call me. Please!* There were also nine missed calls. And two missed calls from Mike. She didn't want to talk to either of them. But as she put her cell away, a familiar dark blue Honda Civic pulled up from behind her.

It was Mike. "You're exhausted. Please get in the car before you fall down."

Surrender. It was a relief. "How did you find me?"

Mike turned onto Prospect Place. "Jake's been tracking you on Family Map, whatever that is. He called me and I got in the car. He updated me on your location every few minutes. Hail to the tech gods."

Mike needed a haircut. The thickening growth, sprouting streaks of silver, was creeping down over his ears. "Thanks. You'll always be my friend, Mike, no matter what else happens."

"Agreed." He stopped at the light at Ralph Avenue. "Any specific 'what else' you'd care to discuss?"

Loyalty pre-empted everything else. "I'm considering putting in for a transfer. I can't let Kiley take me off this case and I can't let him force me to do something so reprehensible."

Mike said nothing.

"You think he's right, don't you?" she asked at last.

"He's flat out wrong thinking you're willing to risk blowing the case to protect Mallory." He got as far as the light at Atlantic Avenue, now choked with taxi traffic.

"Nets game must have ended," she said.

"Traffic's too heavy."

At another time, she would have laughed.

The light changed. "But you are emotional about Mallory." He drove in silence until they were turning onto Monroe Place. "I never asked how you learned about transgender people. But whatever the reason is, it's driving your thinking on Mallory. That's both good and bad."

"Is that what you told Kiley after I walked out?"

"No. I told him he was the biggest fucking asshole in fifty states."

No argument, there.

He pulled up in front of the house and put it in park. "What good will transferring do you?" He held up a hand. "Not arguing. Just asking."

"So much of what drives decisions in this department is unofficial, undocumented. Word of mouth. If he takes me off this case, it will always hang around my neck. But if I put in for a transfer, then unofficial departmental memory turns on Kiley. People still remember Susan Bentner, the detective who filed a discrimination claim against Kiley, even though she withdrew it and took a transfer."

"So, this is revenge? For one case?"

"Not one case. The case."

"Do yourself a favor," he said. "Take the weekend off. Go make up with your worried-sick, throbbing-mouthed boyfriend and forget this shit. We'll talk Monday and see what we want to do. Who knows? Maybe I'll enjoy working in Brooklyn."

Now, there was support. "Thanks, partner." As she got out of the car, Jake's silhouette was in the front window. She couldn't tell Mike the story because he'd say it was clouding her judgment. But it was time to tell Jake.

.   .   .

"You okay?" Jake asked as she entered the apartment. The swelling had gone down a little. She walked past him and into the bedroom.

He followed her. "Kim, I'm sorry. I was only trying to help." He'd mussed his hair, running his fingers through it, a sure sign of worry.

She retreated behind the closed bathroom door to collect herself. When she came out, he was sitting on the bed.

"Kim, I suspect there is something about Mallory keeping you torqued up and…"

"Oh, so it's my fault?" Damn. This wasn't how she'd envisioned this.

He took a deep breath. "I don't think it's anyone's fault. Something unhealthy about Mallory's situation locks you in. I suspect it goes beyond your belief in everyone living however they want as long as they don't bother anyone else."

She pulled off the sweater she'd worn all day. Although she needed a shower, this took priority and she pulled on an old sweatshirt.

"I love you," Jake said. "Help me understand so I'm offended by the same things offending you."

She sat next to him and stared at the floor. What to tell? What to hold back? Would it offend him?

He reached over and brushed stray strands of her hair from her face the way she loved.

But not now. "Fifth grade."

"The year your parents split."

"Yes. In school, we got a new classmate. Chris. He was shorter than the other boys, slight, with delicate features. The boys pounced on him, a pack of jackals."

"Why?"

She tried not to show her annoyance. She needed to get this out. "They sensed his weakness. And hated when he answered in class, showing he was smarter than they were. One afternoon, on my way home, I found him in a playground, sobbing. His nose was bleeding."

She took a moment to keep her emotions under control. Stick to the facts. Get it out there. "Mom forbade me from bringing anyone into the house when she wasn't home. I left him on the front steps while I fetched the first aid kit from our apartment upstairs. He calmed down as I cleaned him up."

Jake slipped his arm around her.

She resisted the urge to rest her head against him. "Chris walked me home every day afterward, rushing away from school before the boys could bully him and meeting me on the way. He was always telling me how pretty I looked in my school uniform."

Jake grinned at her. "I'll bet you did."

"He started coming over for play-days on Saturdays. We'd play board games and watch television in my room. He'd always ask me about whatever clothes were out. One rainy Saturday, my mother got a frantic call to go to my grandmother's after Chris arrived and she went, leaving us alone. One of my dresses was hanging from the door, and he was staring at it. As a joke, I asked if he wanted to try it on. But he admitted he did. So, I let him, and the change was astonishing. I started calling him Chrissy, which he loved. He told me how he sometimes tried on his mother's clothes when he was alone. We lost track of time, chattering and giggling the afternoon away. And then my father walked in. He'd come by to pick up some things he'd left behind, and seeing the car gone, assumed no one was home."

She choked down the rising tide of anger. He tried to hold her, to comfort her, but she pulled away, stood up and forced herself to go on. "He totally freaked. Outed Chrissy to his parents."

"Jesus," Jake muttered.

"They transferred him to a private school and moved to another town. We kept in touch, even though his parents and mine did their best to prevent it. At fourteen, after entering a military academy, all crew cuts and harsh discipline, he started cutting himself. The school said he was mentally ill and expelled him. He left one night, never returned home. They found his body two days later. He'd gone out dressed as a girl."

She sprang up and paced until the rage passed. "I'd stopped seeing Dad after the dress incident. When I learned of Chrissy's murder, I called him and said I never again wanted anything to do with him. Six months passed with no news about Chrissy's case. One day, I came out of school and Dad was waiting in his car. He told me he'd pulled a favor from a sergeant in the county police department and had some information for me if I'd talk to him. We made a deal—I'd forgive him, and he'd tell me what he'd learned."

"Sounds rather cold."

"Prepared me for being a cop. Anyway, the police had closed the case at the request of the parents." Her voice cracked. "The consensus was he'd been asking for trouble going out wearing a dress."

She leaned over and kissed Jake on the cheek, then retreated to the bathroom to calm herself and wash her face.

He was wiping his eyes when she came back.

"Once I started using the internet, I researched anything I could find about trans people. I can't explain why." The old anger welled up, white hot. "What awful crime did he commit? He didn't hurt anyone. He wasn't dangerous, he was different. And so sweet."

He wrapped his arms around her. This time, she let him, but her mind kept working. What Kiley wanted to do sickened Kim, but she couldn't stop him. All she could do was warn Leanne, even if it meant losing her trust.

And it was time Leanne learned the cost of her silence.

CHAPTER THIRTY

Saturday, March 4th, 10:04 AM

This time, Kim had called first, telling Leanne she had some recent developments she needed to discuss with her. The resentment pouring from the phone was palpable.

Mallory answered the door wearing skinny jeans and a lightweight white sweatshirt, and the apartment bore the odor of acetone. They sat at the little table in the kitchen.

"I realize I'm intruding on your personal time," Kim said, she hoped with tact. "But my lieutenant is threatening to take me off the Cove case. He doesn't think I've been aggressive enough. He wants to name you as a suspect and get a search warrant."

"For what?"

"Women's clothing. There'd be no mention on the warrant, but we can both guess they'd find your wardrobe."

It didn't take long. "So, your lieutenant threatens you, and you come and threaten me."

Just as she'd expected. "No. I came to explain what you are facing. I'm not above threatening an uncooperative witness. People want justice to be easy, leave the dirty work to someone else. You think you're the only one who's scared? But justice requires someone to stand up in court, point the finger, and say what they saw and when and how they saw it. And take all the shit sleazebag defense lawyers throw at them. I've tried from the beginning to make this easier for you because I understand the cost."

"And how have you gained this understanding?"

She was all in, now. No other way. She told her about Chrissy. Everything. "The bottom line, Leanne? You are the one person in this entire city who saw the shooter."

"What makes you so sure I did?"

"A cab picked you up at Washington and Gansevoort as the shooting started. The shooter's vehicle sped up Ninth, so it entered Gansevoort from Washington Street. It had to pass you. Had to. I expect it scared you since you had already freaked out."

"What makes you think I did?"

"Matt Berringer had been staring at your cross. I think you were afraid he'd realize you weren't a cis girl. Since you'd already passed, that had to terrify you. So, you bolted, and broke free from someone blocking the doorway, keeping others from leaving. His name is Pierre Duval, and he's in custody but he's not talking. If he pushed back or restrained you, it's an important fact to know."

Mallory sat back, stunned. "He was staring at my pendant?"

Kim smiled for the first time. "Yes, Leanne."

"I ran for nothing."

"One interpretation. Another is you're the one person who can solve this crime."

"So, I'm trapped." Fear wrenched his delicate features.

She had to get this right; there wouldn't be another chance. "I'm sorry you feel trapped. And I'm sorry this happened after what had to be one of the most thrilling and satisfying moments of your life. Proper question is, what course do you steer now?"

No answer.

"I will not force you to come forward. I'll request a transfer rather than do that. But once I'm off the case, someone else will. I've done everything possible to protect you for as long as I could, but the stakes are too high. The city needs this crime solved. It doesn't give a shit about your privacy or my ethics."

"I'm trapped," he said again.

"So am I." She glanced around the apartment. On the coffee table sat a fine wooden chess set, the pieces arrayed in starting position on a polished wooden board. "You play chess, Leanne?"

"Yes. Why?"

"Me, too. Sometimes, the best response to a trap is a gambit." Kim fished her card out of her purse and wrote on the back. "This is my cell number. You can call me anytime, day or night. If I don't answer, I will get back to you as soon as I can. If I'm taken off this case, it will be sometime on Tuesday, so I'm afraid you have little time to decide." She got up to leave. "What do you want most, Leanne?"

.　　　.　　　.

Andy sat for a long while after Detective Brady left. His gaze fell on the chessboard. It was obvious what kind of gambit she had in mind. Joyce had hinted the same thing.

The detective had also said she couldn't protect him anymore. He hadn't considered she was protecting him, or her protecting him might cost her something. Joyce protected his secret at the office, but with the complaint, he was now at risk. Although Donner would keep it confidential. She'd been adamant and even suggested he go to Employee Assistance.

No way out.

Or was there?

Couldn't he purge? Get rid of all the offending clothes? Leave nothing for the cops to find? Yes, he could solve it.

Excellent gambit.

Deny his true identity, as his father and brothers demanded.

Devastated, he sank back into the couch.

What do you want most, Leanne?

. . .

Garner's news was both unexpected and unwelcome. Brady had again visited the tranny. Either she was getting desperate, or she'd drawn an ace to play.

"Has he come out since?"

"No," Garner said. "It's been an hour since Brady left, and no sign of him."

"What was her manner when she left? How did she look?"

"I'd say she wasn't happy."

Which meant she didn't get the information she wanted. But was she getting close? "Stick to him like glue."

CHAPTER THIRTY-ONE

Saturday, March 4th, 11:02 AM

Kim entered PBMS with her completed transfer request form, signed but not dated, in her purse. She'd pulled her hair into a chignon, avoiding any appearance of "the girl next door".

Mike greeted her with a grin. "I see you decided against taking my advice."

"Good morning to you, too, Detective Resnick."

"Back to the salt mine?"

"For now." She took the transfer request out of her purse, held it up, and returned it.

Mike's face fell. "You're going through with your plan?"

"If he pushes me, yes. I'm an excellent cop, Mike. Qualified to lead this investigation. I worked damned hard to get here. When my lieutenant treats me like a perp, I have to fight back."

He sighed but didn't argue. "Well, I pulled Sylvia Walters' LUDs and rechecked her for priors. Nothing. No contacts with any known dealer or even anyone with priors. She's back at the Apollo Diner today, and no other activity."

Dobson sat at a nearby desk, pecking away at his laptop. No sign of Ryba. She remembered the missing shoes and asked him.

He paled. "I checked. The lab never got them. So, I called the Property Clerk. No one ever turned in any shoes on our case."

"So, Ryba was insubordinate? Never turned them in?"

Dobson swallowed. "Looks like it. I asked the CSU sergeant on duty."

She leaned over. "How long have you worked with Ryba? Is this his usual quality of work?"

"We've been partners about eighteen months, and, no, he's always been sharper than this. I can't understand what the..."

Kiley came in, looking grim. Kim grabbed her purse and Mike followed her into Kiley's office, closing the door.

Kiley tossed the *New York Daily News* on his desk, with its blaring headline: "COPS' COVE CONFUSION". "Okay, Detective Brady, will your prissy boy come forward?"

"You mean the witness who the Patrol Guide mandates us to treat and address as the gender with which she identifies?" Kiley lost a little bluster. Good. "We spoke this morning. I explained the situation to her and advised her my lieutenant was considering designating her as a 'person of interest' to pressure her into coming forward. As I expected, she accused me of threatening her and I lost her trust. I did my best to win it back."

"Did you succeed?"

For the first time in her dealings with Kiley, she was in the driver's seat. "I don't know, yet. Funny thing about trust. If you piss it away, it's difficult to get back."

"Answer me straight, Detective. Did he agree to cooperate?"

Don't show even a hint of conciliation. "She neither agreed nor disagreed. She said she'd think about it. I hinted it might be easier for her if she were to come out as trans." She pulled the transfer request out of her purse. "Now, given your stated intention to take me off the case..."

Kiley glanced at the folded form. "I said I was considering it. Nothing more. Until I say otherwise, you remain on the case."

Time to press her advantage. "Are you declaring Mallory a person of interest or suspect? Are you ordering me to get a search warrant?"

Kiley didn't meet her glare. "Not at the present time."

Too squishy. "Lieutenant, tell me where I stand, and when, under what conditions, and on what basis you would proceed with declaring Mallory a suspect."

He looked her in the eye. "We could bring him in as a material witness."

"Yes, we could. But she'll be much more helpful, and more effective as a witness, if she comes in of her own free will."

"How long do you propose we wait?"

With each passing day, the trail was getting colder. How much more time did Leanne deserve? "I told her she had until Tuesday before anyone would take any action against her."

A hint of a smile. Relief? "Then we'll leave it there."

"What about my standing on this case?"

Kiley's manner turned sheepish. "I see no reason to go there."

She put the transfer request back in her purse. "Good. Now, I have a request." She recounted the issue with the shoes. "Please take Ryba off this case."

"What about Dobson?"

Dobson had been getting better and had dug as deep as he could on the shoe issue. "The jury's still out on him. Let's keep him for now."

Kiley scanned the squad room. "Ryba's still out. Let's see how he responds to an ass-ripping from the both of us when he gets back."

●　　　●　　　●

Back at her desk, Kim dove back into the trial transcript. She had started on the case for the defense when she stopped cold at, "Testimony of defense witness Svetlana Bolshoi."

Svetlana. The name Sylvia Walters' neighbor had used. She hated coincidences.

She read on. Ms. Bolshoi testified she'd been Jordy Hill's lover for about a year. She also provided an alibi for various dates and times at which prosecutors had already proved major drug transactions had occurred.

Kim moved on to the cross-examination. The ADA's first question was, "Ms. Bolshoi, how did you and Mr. Hill first become acquainted?"

And her response was, "He came into the club where I worked."

"And what club was that?"

"Exotica, on West Fifty-Fourth Street."

"In what capacity were you employed at this club?"

"I was a pole dancer."

"And did Mr. Hill take any action to attract your attention?"

"He stuffed a fifty-dollar bill down my g-string and said he loved black women with blond hair."

Kim read through her testimony, then through the cross which tore her to shreds. She flipped back to the yellow sticky, the list of prosecution witnesses. Nolan was there, but not Barlowe. She slammed the binder shut. "Mike, let's get a car and head uptown."

.   .   .

The crowd at Exotica was sparse. Two lithe dancers were at a pole while a third was giving a middle-aged guy a lap dance. Mike stayed at the door, a bemused expression on his face. The music was deafening. The pounding of the bass rattled the pit of her stomach.

"Where's the manager?" she shouted to the bartender. He nodded to a guy in chinos and a Polo sports shirt.

The manager took his time checking her out. "You're a bit older than most of our girls, but I like your look. We can arrange an audition..."

"I'm not a dancer. I'm a detective." She flashed her badge.

He glanced around and grimaced. "Let's go to my office. A lot less noise."

She followed him to a spacious office in the back. The thumping bass penetrated the walls. "Do you remember a dancer you had here a few years ago? A black woman with blond hair and a Russian name?"

He grinned. "You must mean Svetlana. Yeah, I remember her. Actual name was Sylvia Walters. Worked longer than most dancers. She was terrific." He frowned. "Most of these girls are working their way through college, figuring it's a simple way to make money. Sylvia, though, she hated it. Booked when she hooked some guy. She was glad to get out. A shame, you know? You always lose the best ones. She in trouble?"

"Have you heard from her?"

"No, not since she left." He looked her over one last time. "You sure you couldn't use extra cash on the side?"

CHAPTER THIRTY-TWO

Saturday, March 4th, 1:16 PM

Breen wasn't in the store's front as the door closed behind Kim and Mike. The jangle of the bell brought him rushing out from the back.

"You heard the bell, I see," she said.

Breen's manner became guarded. "Can I help you?"

Kim strolled about, browsing. "I'll let you know." Mike circled around in the opposite direction.

"Are you looking for something in particular?" The pitch of Breen's voice rose an octave.

Kim shrugged. "No." As she browsed the shelves, most stocked with items yellowing with age, Breen sidled back behind the counter. Like he had something to hide.

She paused when she reached the entrance to the rear. Two enormous cardboard boxes stood stacked on the floor, behind a curtain. "Mind if I look back there?"

"Don't you need a warrant?"

Now, there was an interesting response. "Not if you give me permission. Do you?"

"What if I say no?"

"Then I'm restricted to what's in plain sight." Emblazoned on the boxes were cigarette brands.

Breen crossed his arms across his chest. "Then, no, I don't." He leaned back against the cigarette display, casting furtive glances at the door to the back.

She walked over to the counter. "Mr. Breen, please hand me a pack of cigarettes from the chute at the far left." She flipped the pack to the bottom. The tax stamp was missing. "May I have one from the next chute, please?" Another with no tax stamp. She had him pull three more. None of them had stamps. And none of the packs in the boxes she'd seen would, either. "Mr. Breen, you are selling cigarettes on which no one's paid taxes. You realize selling them is illegal."

"I sell what the distributor…"

She held up a hand. "You're paying well below full price. Any idea why?"

He was panicking. "I got to stay afloat, here. It's all I have."

"Well," she said, "I'm duty-bound to report this to the Yonkers police. However, if you can tell me what I need to know, I won't intrude on their jurisdiction. No one stole your gun, correct?"

Breen hesitated until she cast a meaningful glance at the packs of cigarettes on the counter. "No. I gave it to a woman. She begged me, said she was in trouble, someone was threatening her man, and she needed protection. I'd told her not to give up dancing or get into that life, but she wouldn't listen."

"What life?"

"I traveled to New York to watch her. She was a pole dancer. Black with blond hair. I was her biggest fan. But she got involved with some shady character so she could quit dancing."

"And her name?"

"Svetlana."

From Breen to Sylvia to Luke to Malcolm, all in one neat, unbroken line.

CHAPTER THIRTY-THREE

Saturday, March 4th, 5:22 PM

She'd arranged to meet Nolan at Tal's, this time without Mike. He was waiting in the back when she walked in.

She decided against any niceties. "Do you remember a woman named Svetlana Bolshoi?"

"Sorry, Russian ballerinas aren't much in my line."

"She wasn't Russian, she was black. Not a ballerina, but a pole dancer. She was Jordy Hill's girlfriend. Testified at his trial. Fell apart on cross."

Recognition dawned. "Hill's alibi witness."

"In her testimony, she mentioned being arrested with him. But there's nothing about her in the case file. No mention at all. Was anyone with Hill when you collared him?"

He paused, as if thinking about it. "I grabbed Williams. My partner back then, George Barlowe, collared Hill. He'd be the one to ask."

"According to the case file, you collared Hill, not Barlowe."

"Can't be. I wrote his arrest report, myself. Hill was his collar."

She had no time for this shit. "Look for yourself. Barlowe's name doesn't even appear in the file, other than being listed as your partner. So, I'm asking you, as the arresting officer, if anyone was with Hill."

"I remember a woman being with him. And, yeah, she was black with blond hair. She was all but naked, and I recall Barlowe saying she was gone on boy. He said he handed her over to someone, but he never said who."

She'd already pissed him off by calling him out on the case file. Best not to mention her talk with Barlowe. "Why isn't she mentioned in the case file?"

Nolan blinked. "You expect me to remember an old arrest report?"

"One of the biggest collars of your career. Don't sit there and claim you don't remember."

His composure slipped, and he got huffy. "I'm not sure why, but it's obvious we don't get along. Fine. But I don't like your insinuations about me, so you tell me what your problem is."

Bluster, the next step after move along, folks. "I don't enjoy getting evasive answers to direct questions."

"Fine. If her name doesn't appear in the report, it's because we let her go when she had nothing to tell us. Why does any of this matter?"

"Because Sylvia Walters, one name I ran past you at our last chat, is Svetlana Bolshoi. Which means there's a connection between Paredes and Ice Williams, which suggests many possibilities in this case in which you've been no help at all."

He set his jaw. "I want to help you. I'm trying to find sources for you. It's taking time."

She wasn't about to hold her breath waiting.

. . .

The light faded out. Andy turned on the lamp. Almost against his will, he slid open the drawer in the coffee table. He extracted the front page photos from three newspapers—one with Dale Keegan, one with Theresa Santos, and one with Jenna Guarnaccia.

Yes, he could purge. But he'd be taking an active step to conceal who he was, an active step to protect the animal who'd slaughtered nine people. He stared at the three untroubled faces gazing up at him. He would become complicit.

We draw the line, stand for what's decent. He'd said so to Celia Coravos, meaning every word. His own fear of reprisal had remained dormant as he pressed forward—Celia's statement, pushing Joyce, going to Ms. Donner.

It was dark beyond his window. Dale Keegan still grinned at him. And somewhere, a police lieutenant he'd never met, whose name he didn't know, was preparing to flush him into the open, ready or not.

The phone rang. He let the machine get it.

"It's Joyce. I was hoping you'd call today, and I'm kind of upset you haven't. I'm so sorry about yesterday, but…"

He picked up the phone. "I'm here, Joyce."

"Are you okay?"

"Yeah, I'm…" But his shoulders were already heaving.

"Hey," she said. "You're not okay. Let me come over."

He took some time to compose himself. "No, I'll be okay. I'm working through something."

Joyce paused before speaking. "Not alone, you're not. I want to take you to dinner at the Dorian Café tonight."

He couldn't go on alone. "Okay. What time?"

"I'm inviting Leanne. Seven o'clock okay?"

CHAPTER THIRTY-FOUR

Saturday, March 4th, 6:55 PM

Leanne checked herself one last time in the full-length mirror on the inside of her closet door: skirt, blouse, hose, dress flats, pendant, makeup. Better, and way more convincing, than when she'd ventured out alone in college. But did Joyce have to pick the Dorian, where they often ate? Another gambit.

She locked up the apartment and slipped out the front door, walking past the line outside Tournesol. Saturday night dinner out. No one stared. No one looked twice.

As she crossed Vernon Boulevard, Joyce, waiting on the other side, broke into a wide grin. "You look fantastic."

Leanne muttered her thanks as they hugged. Inside, a waitress she didn't recognize led them to a booth along the interior wall and gave them each a menu. "Can I get you ladies something to drink?" Her commercial smile grew warm as her eyes locked on Leanne's.

Clocked. Sure didn't take long.

"Chardonnay for me," Joyce said.

The initial spike of panic faded. "Same for me."

"Sure thing, honey," the waitress said.

Joyce waited until after the waitress brought their wine and took their orders. "You okay? You sounded awful on the phone."

"I guess." But Leanne was thinking about the waitress' smile. No trace of "look at the freak". More like acceptance.

Joyce lowered her voice. "Are you still mad at me about yesterday?"

Yesterday. A hundred years ago. "Donner could guess you were talking about me."

"I'm sorry if I embarrassed you. But I owed you something huge for helping me do this. Celia Coravos called me today. Mr. Franco, the assistant controller, has been hitting on her, and she's coming forward. Some other girls, too. We'll win."

The waitress returned with their salads. "Love your blouse, honey."

Leanne blinked. "Thank you."

The waitress smiled and walked away.

Leanne stabbed at a slice of cucumber. "I have bigger problems at the moment." She described the visit from Detective Brady.

Joyce brightened. "Perfect time to transition. You want to. Look at you, now." She dropped her voice. "Even being nervous someone might clock you, you're still way more relaxed than I've ever seen you. Face it: you're cute."

Matt Berringer had thought so.

"The company will support you," Joyce continued, "and the harassment complaint will make coming out much easier."

Leanne had to work hard to keep her voice soft. "How do you figure?"

"The entire atmosphere will change. The guys are all covering their asses. They won't dare say anything about you."

She would never have expected work to become her haven.

"You'll have me and the girls." Joyce dropped her voice again. "I don't even mind you're prettier than I am."

A guy in his thirties walked into the café. The waitress led him past their booth. For a moment, his eyes met Leanne's, and he flashed a flirtatious grin.

Her cheeks warmed, which was nice. But her course would not be easy.

.   .   .

Kim checked her watch. The manager of the Apollo Diner had told her Sylvia Walters would get off work at ten. It was now five after.

"There she is," Mike said. Walters was coming through the door. "You want to do this together?"

Kim chuckled. "She's finished working a double shift. If she runs, it won't be for long. But yeah, let's take the precaution."

Sylvia came down the diner steps, her waitress uniform stained in two places, with circles under her eyes, and a wary expression. "Here for a late dinner?"

Kim approached her from the front while Mike removed any avenue of escape from behind. "We need to talk, Ms. Bolshoi. We traced Malcolm Drake's gun back to a convenience store owner in Yonkers. He gave it to a former pole dancer named Svetlana—a black woman who used to have blonde hair. A witness has identified you as Svetlana. Another witness saw Luke Wilson give the gun to Malcolm Drake two days before the shooting, the same day you got it from the owner."

Sylvia's shoulders slumped. The "oh, shit!" look.

"Malcolm shot at the man who killed him, Luke, and Paredes. He must have expected a threat. You provided the gun. So, you expected the threat, too."

Sylvia looked away. "All right. I was afraid for Luke. I wanted him protected."

Kim waited, but Sylvia said nothing else. "Who from?"

"He was slinging. Lotsa shit on the street."

At last, an admission. "How long had they been dealing?"

"About four months," Sylvia replied.

Now, they were getting somewhere. "And yet, it wasn't until two days before the shooting you acquired a weapon, an action precipitating some kind of serious disagreement among the three of them."

"I can't tell you no more," Sylvia said.

"We're taking you into custody as a material witness."

Sylvia folded her arms. "I won't be no witness."

The time for nice was over. "You no longer have a choice."

.   .   .

The sight of his aide-de-camp at his door was unsettling. It meant the worst kind of news. At least he wasn't in uniform. "Come in. Something to drink?"

"No, thank you. One of our Corrections people at Rikers saw Duval in the exercise yard this afternoon. According to the visitors' log, he met with Brady, Resnick, Yvette Driscoll from the DA's office, and his Legal Aid attorney on Thursday."

At least forty-eight hours in custody, and he was only receiving a report on it now. Someone was falling down on the job. "Quite an ensemble. Did he sing?"

"Brady, Resnick and Driscoll signed in at 1:10 and signed out at 1:20. The Legal Aid guy's a haggler. They didn't take anywhere near enough time for a song."

He could have Duval shanked, but he didn't wish to place certain parties under a magnifying glass, which could prove inconvenient. Even if Duval sang, he wouldn't be credible. And the odds were he'd be too scared to sing. "Keep your eyes and ears on him. Let's see if he says anything." They always had shanking him as a fallback position. "Why didn't our source report these latest developments?"

"I'm still looking into the details."

CHAPTER THIRTY-FIVE

Sunday, March 5th, 9:05 AM

Kim returned from a run to Tal's. Mike was awake.

"Sylvia's still asleep in Room Two," he said.

As expected, she'd asked for a lawyer the minute they stepped foot into PBMS. Kim had informed Yvette after midnight. It would be awhile. The wheels of justice were slower on the weekends. By the time they got counsel assigned, it would be late afternoon, at least, before they could begin questioning Sylvia. Kim had to determine whether she was a witness or another perp.

Her cell buzzed. Leanne Mallory. She turned to Mike. "I have to take this."

"I'm sorry to call you so early on a Sunday, but..."

·   ·   ·

Mike peered out at the main desk. "Is that her?"

Kim followed his gaze. "Yes. Leanne." Dressed in a denim skirt, pink knit top and black ankle boots, she showed no trace of Andy. Sergeant Holloran addressed her with his best Sunday manners and gestured back toward the detective squad's desks,

134

Kim waved her over and introduced her to Mike.

"Nice to meet you." He colored taking Leanne's hand. "I hate to say it, but the one room available is an interrogation room."

Kim patted Leanne's arm. "Relax. You're not being interrogated. You look great. Even charmed our salty old desk sergeant." She gestured for Leanne to sit at the table in Room One, noticing the Celtic cross for the first time. "Just tell us what happened at the Cove a week ago Thursday."

Leanne's version matched Matt Berringer's.

"Why did you leave?" Kim asked.

Leanne sighed. "You were right. I thought the guy—Matt—had noticed something I feared would give me away, a gender cue."

"What happened when you tried to leave?" Mike asked.

She took a deep breath. "It got jammed, much worse than when I'd first arrived. Most of the crowd looked buzzed, which scared me. Near the door, I hit a crowd. Halfway through it, I came face to face with a guy I had noticed earlier. He was wearing a gray suit, red tie, very dapper, but it didn't fit."

"The suit didn't fit him?" Mike asked.

"No, I mean the guy wearing it looked out-of-place in it—sweating like a pig, not well shaven, had two or three day's growth. His eyes appeared wild, like he was on something."

Kim gestured for Leanne to continue.

"He said I should stay and have some fun. He tried to slip his arm around my waist but couldn't manage it in the crowd. Instead, he reached down and squeezed my backside hard. I stomped as hard as I could on his foot with my left heel. He muttered a curse and let go of me, and I pushed past him."

Mike was incredulous. "Sounds too easy."

"Well, I was wearing spike heels."

The Nine West pumps.

Leanne relaxed a bit. "Once out on the street, I walked as fast as I could. Three men were standing outside, arguing. They made me even more nervous, so I walked the other way. I was about fifty feet from the corner when I saw a small, dark SUV make a left turn from Washington Street onto Gansevoort."

"About how fast was it going?" Kim asked.

"It took the turn fast but slowed down right after. The rear window was down. I walked as fast as I could, trying not to look, but I couldn't help myself. I checked if he was stopping to chase me. A guy sat in the back seat holding a weapon. It looked like an M-16. I could see…"

A group passed the room, their voices audible but indecipherable with the door closed. Leanne glanced at the two-way mirror.

Kim patted her hand. "Don't worry, it's off. Please describe the guy with the weapon"

"Scary. Asian, dark complexion, with hard features. He had a mustache and a goatee."

Didn't ring a bell. Kim glanced at Mike, but there was no glimmer of recognition there, either.

"Can you describe any others with him?" Mike asked.

"Too frightened. I glimpsed the driver's head. I was so scared. Didn't notice anyone else. I panicked and ran." She took a deep breath, collecting herself. "I saw a livery van parked at the corner and ran for it. Someone fired the first shots as I was getting in."

Please, Mike, not a word. "What did you hear?" Kim kept her voice soft and calm, but her heart was racing. Leanne had been present for the shooting itself. Go slow. Get it all. Get it right. "Tell me verbatim as you remember it."

Leanne closed her eyes. "Three single shots—one, two, three. Then a burst of shots, like a submachine gun—the M16, I guess. There were two more single shots, then an extended burst, and the cab driver yelled at me to get in. Thank God he came from Queens; no way could I have given him directions. I was shaking all the way home. He dropped me off at the end of my block. I was still shaking the next morning. Called in sick to work. I hadn't slept a wink all night."

"Were you still wearing the heels when you got in the cab?" Everything had to match.

136

"No. I couldn't run in them, so I kicked them off and left them on the sidewalk. Shredded the soles of my pantyhose."

"Okay," Kim said. "Detective Resnick will show you some photos. Tell us if anyone looks familiar."

Mike opened the first binder in front of her. "Can I get you anything?"

"No, thanks." Leanne started turning pages, taking her time. She was a few pages into the second binder when she stopped and gasped. She pointed at a photo of Duval. "He's the guy who grabbed me inside the bar."

"The guy in the gray suit?" Kim asked. "You're positive?"

Leanne shuddered. "He had a look in his eye. It was disgusting."

She continued paging through the binders and was well into the third one when she stopped cold. "Oh, my God. He's the guy in the SUV."

"You're sure?" Kim checked the name. "Jack Choo."

Leanne was shaking. "He killed all those people."

Kim placed a hand on her shoulder. "Anything else you can tell us?"

"No."

Mike stood. "You sure I can't get you something, honey? A glass of water?"

Leanne nodded. "Please."

He ducked out of the room and soon returned with a plastic cup of lukewarm water. "Just take your time. You don't understand how big a help you've been."

CHAPTER THIRTY-SIX

Sunday, March 5th, 11:04 AM

Kim stayed with Leanne until she calmed down. "Since we've identified the shooter, we can focus on bringing him in. That could take time. I'll call you when we get to the next step." At the entrance, she gave Leanne's hand a gentle squeeze. "Thank you so much. I'll be in touch."

Mike was talking with Kiley in his office. She joined them.

"Come to gloat, Detective Brady?" Kiley asked.

"I wouldn't do that, Lieutenant."

"She gave us the shooter," Mike said as they sat down.

Kiley scowled. "So, now you're calling him 'she', too?"

Mike leaned forward. "She also verified the vehicle, verified Duval as the guy in the gray suit. Even told us who fired when. I'll call her Princess Kate if she wants."

"How sure is… she…" Kiley grimaced. "The shooter was Jack Choo?"

Kim grinned at him. "No doubt. None. Picked out his mugshot without hesitation. Plus, the owner of the Blazer described one thief as 'a rough looking Chinese guy'. Choo matches his description."

"She got past Pierre Duval?" Kiley asked. "Pretty big guy."

"He tried to keep her from getting out," Kim said. "She stomped his foot with a spike heel." And how helpful it would be to have her shoe as evidence.

"The problem is," Mike said, "we still can't figure out what his role here was. Was he there as someone's observer, or was he working with Paredes?"

"There's also the question of who else took part in this," Kiley said. "What do you think, Detective Brady?"

Kim didn't hesitate. "We'll interrogate Sylvia Walters once counsel gets here. Mike, why don't you call Nolan, see if Choo's name rings a bell. Meanwhile, I'll check Choo for priors."

Kiley agreed. "I'll get his mug shot over to DCPI and they'll get it to the news outlets with the Crime Stoppers hotline number."

"Could generate a lot of false leads," Mike said. "Is that what we want to do?"

Outside the office, Sergeant Holloran's voice all but rattled the walls. "Who the hell left the fucking copy machine with no paper?"

Kiley closed the door to his office, looking sheepish. "Can't be helped. We've been checking with emergency rooms and urgent care centers, right? But no one will admit they failed to report treating a gunshot wound. People see Choo, somebody might call the hotline. And it'll get the Commissioner off my case for a while."

Dobson knocked on the office door.

"Come." Kiley peered out at Holloran, who was back at the front desk, rant over.

"Where's Ryba?" Kim asked.

"He called out sick."

She turned to Kiley. "We can't."

Kiley nodded in agreement. "He's off the Cove case. I'll call the Sixth. Jimmy Stephenson is taking a week's paternity leave. He's back on Wednesday and he'll join your team then."

"Thanks." Kim turned back to Dobson. "Our eyewitness came in a little while ago and picked out the shooter's mug shot. We'll make it public. I'll want you to ride herd on the call center and alert me the minute you get anything credible."

"Will do," he said.

"Good," Kiley said. "Meeting over."

Back at their desks, she grinned at Mike until he looked up.

"What?" he asked at last.

"I love it. You called her 'honey'." She chuckled as he turned crimson. "It's okay. She's much cuter in person than the sketch."

Mike shuffled papers as he struggled to regain his composure. "I'll call Nolan about Choo and see if he has something for us."

Nolan having information she could use would be a first. Meanwhile, Kim made notes about Choo's priors: three arrests for assault and one for weapons possession.

·   ·   ·

"Where are you now, Harold?"

"Across the street from her building. She was at PBMS about an hour, then she stopped to do some shopping at the Manhattan Mall on Thirty-Third. Got home a few minutes ago."

"He's a guy, Harold." Time to explain the facts of life. "And he's got a gun pointed right at our collective head. You fucked up."

There was panic in his voice. "No, I stuck with her, um, him, following your orders."

"You watched while he waltzed into Manhattan Fucking South Fucking Homicide and told whatever he knows and didn't do a fucking thing about it. You've committed a major fuckup."

"I didn't think you'd want me to just…"

"Shut up. You must decide if you are with us or against us. Tireless friend or sworn enemy. No going back, no second chances. You agree to complete your mission and reap the rewards, or we part company now, with all appropriate implications. Which is it?"

"Take it easy. You know I'm with you."

Nice and fast. "All right. You have a week to shadow him and pick your shot."

"Shot?"

"Eliminate him, Harold." Silence. "Or are you backing out already?"

"No. I'm on it."

Better. He ended the call. His aide-de-camp hadn't checked in. Another call. "Any idea what information the tranny provided to the cops?"

His aide-de-camp's voice dripped with gloom. "No. I haven't been able to track down our contact."

Backup systems were everything. "Do what you have to do. Make sure he's in or out."

CHAPTER THIRTY-SEVEN

Sunday, March 5th, 12:53 PM

Kim sat next to Yvette Driscoll, while Mike and Kiley stood behind them. Across the table sat a sullen Sylvia Walters alongside the attorney who'd caught her case. The radiators were hissing with steam despite the mild temperature outside, and the room was stifling. Twenty minutes of legal fencing between Yvette and the attorney didn't help.

The attorney exchanged whispered comments with Sylvia. "My client is afraid her knowledge may not satisfy you, placing her in jeopardy."

"If she tells us what we need to know, we can protect her." Yvette gestured to Kim to proceed.

"Who ran the operation with Luke, Paredes, and Drake?" Kim asked. "Who was supplying them?" Sylvia's expression remained blank. A veteran of the system for sure. "You had a more than casual connection to this drug operation. Before he was arrested, you were Jordy Hill's girlfriend, and you later testified for him at trial. And you got Luke the gun he gave to Malcolm Drake."

The attorney held up a hand. "She says nothing without a specific, comprehensive offer on the table."

"We won't use anything she says now against her," Yvette replied. "Protective custody now, witness protection later. But she must tell us everything now and hold up at trial."

"She can't tell what she doesn't know. It's up to you to connect the dots."

Kim took over. "Let's start with your drug business."

Sylvia took a deep breath. "When Jordy got sent up, I had fifty thousand stashed at my apartment. I took a waitressing job because the money wouldn't last, and I swore I'd never go back to pole dancing. Once I hooked up with Luke, it got more expensive and I took a second job. Luke was hanging out with Malcolm, not doing jack."

"Where did the fifty thousand come from?" Kim asked. "Jordy's share of the profits?"

"No. After they busted Jordy, this narc comes around; says they need me to testify."

"But you were high on boy when they arrested you," Kim said. "How could you..."

Sylvia sat up, her back rigid. "Who says? I ain't touched no kinda shit in my life." She pulled up her sleeve. "See? No tracks. They let me go hoping I'd rat out Jordy and Ice. This narc said I'd get sent up if I didn't testify. Scared the shit out of me. How could I do such a thing? Jordy had got me off the pole..." She froze.

Kim waited, giving her space.

Sylvia took a deep breath. "The narc came back. Couple days later. Said, 'Don't testify against him. Testify for him, give him an alibi, but make it a poor one. Don't mention being arrested with him. It's a dog thing.'"

"What did he mean?" Kim asked.

"I didn't know." She shuddered. "But the night before I testified, I came home and found an envelope with fifty thousand on my kitchen table. Inside, there was a note saying, 'if we have to come back for a refund, you'll end up like the dog'."

"What dog?" Kim asked.

"In my apartment, I found a dead dog on my kitchen floor."

"Your dog?" Yvette asked.

"No. A stray I'd seen around the neighborhood, but it fucking freaked me out. So, the next day, I said what I'd told the defense attorney I'd say, then took it all back when the DA grilled me. After I testified, the narc caught up to me on the street and said, 'Enjoy life'."

Kim needed more. "What did he look like?"

"White. Tall. Thin. I ain't too good at describing faces."

Too vague to be of any use. "If you saw him again, do you think you would recognize him?"

"Yeah. He scared the shit out of me. Real cold."

Well, at least she remembered something. "What about the new drug business?"

"Last November, I was worrying about the money running out. Pierre came into the diner. He used to work for Jordy."

"Pierre Duval?" Had to make sure everything was clear.

"Yeah. Jordy had always looked out for him. He wanted to catch on with Viper Kincaid."

"A member of Ice Williams' operation who didn't get sent up," Kim said.

"He said Viper needed help on the street. I hooked him up with Diego Paredes. I'd seen him around the neighborhood. He took on Luke and Malcolm as runners. We bought girl from Viper. When Diego wanted to expand downtown, Viper told him, 'be cool'. When he wasn't, the cops were all over Diego."

Cops? From Narcotics? "Were they arrested?" There'd been nothing in the system.

"No, just roughed up and ripped off. Seemed like anywhere they went, they got hassled." Sylvia wiped gathering sweat from her brow with her sleeve.

Kim lost her focus for a moment. Dad had shaken down dealers; it was so easy to threaten arrest and take the drugs instead. He allowed dealers to remain on the street and traded the drugs for information. Nothing ever got into the system.

The attorney shucked off his jacket. "Is the excess heat necessary?"

"I'll see what I can do." Kiley ducked out.

Nolan had downplayed Kincaid. A street dealer supplied by Kincaid had moved into fresh territory. Undercovers hassled the street dealer. "Timeframe?"

"Month ago. I got nervous, Pierre went to Viper, hoping to chill the situation. Viper said, 'these things work themselves out'. Nothing more. I paid Don a visit."

Another loose end. "Why him?"

"He was hot for me when I danced. Said if I ever needed protection, he had a gun."

"Any contact with Viper or detectives since the shooting?" Kim asked.

"Haven't heard from Viper. The only detectives I seen are you guys, and the guy who sometimes follows me around."

"What guy? What does he look like?"

"White. Kind of heavy, about thirty-five. Brown hair, kind of bald on top. Figured he's undercover since he always wears work clothes, dark blue pants and shirt, but I ain't never seen him do no work. He sits in his little white car, watching."

This was their case, and they hadn't asked for an uncle—an undercover—to keep tabs on Sylvia. Had Nolan taken an interest on his own? There was the uniform they'd seen at Paredes' apartment— Ames—but he was a skinny black kid in his twenties. "After Duval came back from seeing Viper, how was he with you and Paredes?" At least the radiator had stopped hissing.

"Insisted we do everything his way. Diego, Luke and Malcolm were to stay outside the Cove while he shuttled back and forth with the stuff."

"Excuse me," Mike said, "but wasn't he rather, you know, stupid?"

Sylvia showed some spark. "Right? And he hated grunt work, but he insisted on acting as the runner. Insisted. Wore the suit I gave him so's he'd blend in."

Kim's eyes met Mike's for a moment. The suit had been Jordy Hill's. "What did Diego think of Duval's plan?"

"Hated it. But Viper insisted." She turned somber. "Had a terrible feeling. Couldn't do nothing about it."

Leanne's description provided specific details—the three single shots had come first. Drake had been waiting for a threat. Kim nodded to Yvette, who stood. "As of now, we will file no charges against your client, protective custody until the trial, witness protection after. She recants on one thing, all deals are off. Are we clear?"

"Okay", Sylvia said.

Yvette, Kim and Mike returned to Kiley's office.

"Let's head out to Rikers this afternoon to confront Duval with what we've learned," Yvette said.

Kim turned to Mike. "Anything from Nolan?"

"Yeah. He wants to meet us at Tal's."

．　　　．　　　．

To: <Leanne>
From: <Alli>

Mom is still in the hospital. Had another stroke, a bad one. Not sure if she'll make it. I was a little stunned by your news. I understand how you feel, but I was hoping being on your own would allow you to deal with it. Not trying to talk you out of it, but I worry. It's such a radical step. I mean, there's surgery involved, isn't there? You can't take surgery back. I love you always. Alli.

．　　　．　　　．

To: <Alli>
From: <Leanne>

146

I'm sorry we couldn't talk in person, but I understand you have your hands full.

Please don't worry about me. I'll be fine. I feel a genuine sense of direction and fulfillment.

Love, Leanne.

CHAPTER THIRTY-EIGHT

Sunday, March 5th, 2:38 PM

Kim would've preferred Mike not be there, since he would try to be a peacemaker, and she believed a little conflict often stirred the truth to the surface. Nolan appeared pensive, suggesting conciliation might not be the best way to go.

"We've discovered the identity of the shooter," she said as she sat down.

Nolan nodded toward Mike, sitting next to her. "He told me. Jack Choo."

"Now," she said, "it's your turn to tell me everything you've got on him."

"Not much, I'm afraid. He was muscle for Ice Williams for a while. Roughed up rival dealers and served as Williams' bodyguard. But he dropped out of sight long before we collared Williams."

"What was the reason?" When Nolan remained silent, staring at her, she pressed. "Change of scenery? Lover's quarrel? Better opportunity elsewhere?"

Nolan pushed back from the table. "Jesus!"

Mike jumped in. "Bob, it's like we told you before. It's all hands on deck for this one. No holding back. We got an eyewitness to come forward..."

"Who took her time, by all accounts."

Kim stood and leaned over the desk. "What accounts? Who from? We're not talking idle gossip at the water cooler here, Nolan. You're edging damned close to the textbook definition of obstruction."

Mike tugged on her arm. They were drawing attention.

Nolan signaled a thank you to Mike. "Look, Kim, I know you're pissed. Nobody enjoys getting stonewalled..."

"So, you admit I'm being stonewalled."

"I'm not admitting it, I'm saying it."

She kept her voice low. "By someone who knows whose operation this is."

"Right. And you think that someone is me, and you're dead wrong."

"Then tell me who it is."

Nolan sat back. "I don't know, yet. And I won't say anything until I know."

She stood. "Sounds very convenient."

Nolan stood, too. "Somebody changed my write-up of the Williams case. Someone whose name doesn't appear on the access log."

Even more convenient. And very unlikely.

CHAPTER THIRTY-NINE

Sunday, March 5th, 4:37 PM

Duval and his lawyer were waiting for them in the consultation room at Rikers. Duval had circles under his eyes, one eyelid twitched, and he squirmed in his seat. Three days inside could render serious changes in a man.

The attorney wore a smug expression, as if he held the upper hand. "I hope this means you've come to your senses about my client's role in all this."

"Let's say we've clarified our thinking," Yvette replied as they all sat at the table.

Kim didn't wait for anyone's approval to start. "We've discovered the identity of the individual who shot up the Cove while you prevented bystanders leaving by causing a logjam at the exit. One woman got out by stomping on your foot."

Duval fumed. "Who told you that fairy tale?"

"The woman who stomped you."

"Makes your client an accessory," Yvette said to the attorney. "Nine dead, ten injured."

The color drained from Duval's face and he turned on his counsel. "You got to stop this. You can't let them do this to me."

"A moment, please." The attorney and Duval whispered back and forth. Duval was growing agitated. The attorney nodded. "What can you do for him?"

"Depends on what information he provides and the accuracy of his information," Yvette replied, "and if he holds up on the stand."

Kim leaned forward. "Let's start by who he was working for."

Duval waited for a nod of approval. "Diego Paredes. He had big ideas about slinging, and I had some experience, so he asked if I'd like to work with him. I didn't have much going, so I said okay."

"Who else was working with him?" Kim asked.

"Just Luke Wilson and Malcolm Drake. Both were big on attitude, short on smarts."

"Unlike you," Mike said. "Who was Paredes buying from?"

The radiator clanged as the heat came up, making Duval jump a little. Not the first hoopster uncomfortable with being double-teamed. "I don't know. Once we got started, Diego clammed up. Wouldn't tell me a fucking thing."

"What about Sylvia Walters?"

Duval hesitated. "Luke was doing her, and it looked like she was getting more of his share than he was. I mean, she wore designer everything. But I never saw her around."

More pressure. "Didn't Walters introduce you to Paredes? After you approached her about going into business at the Apollo Diner?"

Duval looked alarmed but said nothing.

Kim pressed harder. "Wasn't Kincaid supplying Paredes? With you as the go-between?"

The attorney cut in. "Where did you get this?"

"Sorry, Counselor." She wasn't about to let him set a screen. "We ask the questions. Your client can guess from the accuracy where I got it. Well, Mr. Duval?"

Duval took a deep breath. "I ran into Sylvia at the diner, but it was her idea to go into business. We agreed Viper would be the best bet as a supplier. Heard he expanded Williams' operation. So, I contacted him."

"What happened the night of the shooting?"

"Around seven, my cell goes off. This guy tells me, 'Don't let anyone out of there until I tell you or you're a dead man.'"

"Who?" Mike asked.

"Don't know. Didn't recognize the voice."

"But you complied," Kim said.

"Shit, man, this guy sounded like he meant business. I mean, at first, I wanted to get out of there. But then I figured I'm a big enough guy, and the place was getting wild and crazy, so best to do what he said. Once the shooting started, it was raining shattered glass all over the fucking place. As soon as it stopped, I ran out the back."

It smelled like week-old fish. "What can you tell us about Jack Choo?"

Duval blinked. "Who?"

Yvette broke in again. "Your client has given us nothing useful, and his actions abetted the shooter. As of now, we're looking at nine counts of accessory and one on conspiracy, plus the drug charge. If he wants a deal, he has to cut the bullshit and talk to us straight."

"What's his straight talk worth? He needs specifics."

Yvette leaned on the table and glared at Duval. "Convince me you were a minor player and give me names I can use. If you do, and hold up at trial, I'll arrange for protective custody before the trial and witness protection afterward."

The attorney nodded to Duval. "Deal."

Kim resumed with a conversational tone. "The Cove on the night in question, according to several witnesses, was quite loud. You agree?"

"Yeah."

She pressed him. "How loud? Right before the shooting started?"

"Crazy loud. I mean, you couldn't hear yourself think."

Kim leaned forward. "All the noise must have made it impossible to hear your cell going off."

Duval sat back. "No, no. Had it on vibrate and in my shirt pocket so I'd…"

"You were expecting the call. And you were wearing a suit formerly owned by Jordy Hill, to help you blend in." Kim stood and leaned on the table. Full court press. "So, who... called... you?"

Echoes of shouting suggested rising tempers in a conflict nearby. Duval held his head in his hands but said nothing.

Kim remained standing. "Last chance: who called you?" Press long enough...

Duval coughed up the ball. "A guy named Cal Lewis. A go-fer for Viper. The one I first called about doing business. He called to tell me they were on their way. Him and Jack Choo. Cal was driving."

Now they were rolling. "What was the reason for Kincaid's falling out with Paredes?"

A shout echoed in the hallway and Duval looked panicked. "Viper's got a bigger network than Ice had. He made sure he didn't fuck up like Ice done, trusting the wrong people. Viper said the cops brought Ice down because of poor security."

"He told you this?" Kim asked.

More echoed shouts. Beads of sweat appeared on Duval's forehead. "Yeah. When I first approached him about Sylvia's offer."

"Word is Viper blamed you for Ice getting taken down," Mike said.

"Ain't no secret about him blaming me. Even told me I was on probation with him. I told him we'd do everything his way, no bullshit." More beads of sweat. "I meant it."

Mike sneered. "How nice."

Duval's temper flared. "Yeah? Well, check this: whoever sold Ice out was way higher in his setup than I was."

Kim glanced over at Mike, wondering if Viper himself had been Nolan's snitch. Mike stared at the table. His wheels had to be turning in the same direction. "So, what happened?"

"Fucking Paredes. He started dealing at some downtown clubs. Viper said the cops had already made him."

"How did he know?" She wasn't ready to believe him.

Duval snorted. "Like, he'd tell me? Anyway, Paredes got pissed about it. 'I ain't no delivery boy', he kept saying. Viper got cold every time he saw me. Then Paredes and the boys got stopped a bunch of times by guys claiming to be cops..."

Kim caught it. "Claiming to be?"

"Weren't in uniform. Flashed badges too fast to read."

"But they never arrested anyone?"

"No, just roughed them up and ripped them off."

Hearing it the second time didn't rattle her as much. "Did you get 'roughed up', too?"

"No. It was always one of them. I saw Viper. Sylvia was sure he was behind it. He said. 'These things work themselves out. If anyone calls, do what they say.' Four days before the shooting, Cal came to my apartment and told me to have them selling at the Cove on Thursday night. He ordered me to put Paredes, Wilson, and Drake outside and make certain nobody left after he called me. Said if I didn't follow instructions, Viper's 'security' would come see me."

An interesting term. And he'd used it twice. "Did Kincaid talk about his 'security' any other time?"

"When I first met with him about Sylvia, he said never forget he had better security than Ice Williams ever had." Duval slumped back down in his seat, spent.

One last opening to nail shut. "Did you inform Sylvia about this?"

Duval didn't look up. "Just Viper's comment about things working themselves out."

Duval's attorney spoke up. "So, my client has met your expectations, Ms. Driscoll?"

Yvette stood. "So long as he testifies as to everything he said today, no alterations."

"Can you move him?" Duval's attorney asked. "He won't be safe in here once you arrest Kincaid."

"I'll have him released into protective custody within the hour. In the meantime, keep him here with you."

.　　　　.　　　　.

Kim was dozing in the passenger's seat when her cell jolted her awake. Mike headed toward the RFK Bridge.

It was Dobson. "Where are you?"

"Somewhere in Northwestern Queens." She forced back the fog of sleep. "Why?"

"Got an anonymous tip on the Crime Stoppers line. A guy who matches Choo's mugshot got treatment the night of the shooting at the Mission Health Clinic in Ravenswood, Queens. Said he needed help walking and his leg was bleeding a lot around the right knee."

Kim had him repeat the address three times.

"It's across the street from the Ravenswood Public Houses."

"Any description of the helper?" she asked.

"Just a black guy, not too tall."

Kim chuckled. "Okay, we got something, anyway. Any idea who the caller was?"

"I serve you up a turkey with all the trimmings, and you ask for pie. Nice. Caller was a female, heavy accent. Sounded Oriental. I'm guessing patient, not worker."

"Thanks, Kyle. This is big."

Mike hit the accelerator. "Ravenswood, by the river. I'll stay on Astoria Boulevard all the way to Twenty-First Street."

.　　　　.　　　　.

"Duval talked."

"Are you sure?" Although his aide-de-camp was always sure before he reported.

"Heard the recording myself."

He'd miscalculated, expecting Duval to be too petrified to talk. What could be more terrifying than death? "What did they threaten him with?"

"They'd charge him as a conspirator."

Hilarious. Duval couldn't conspire to put one foot in front of the other. Which, he realized, made him vulnerable to such threats. "Where is he now?"

"They're placing him in protective custody. It'll take time to discover where. The captain may provide assistance."

"Do they also have Walters?"

"Listen to the recording."

He did. There was no mention of Walters telling them anything, but Brady's questions were so pointed, the source was obvious. "Proceed on the assumption she, too, is in protective custody. Order the captain to obtain the list and we'll establish surveillance on the most feasible places, the ones beyond city limits."

"Got it. I've also discovered the reason our source didn't report any of this. It seems they have removed him from the case."

"See he's rewarded for his contribution. In trade, not cash. Garner will take care of the tranny." He ended the call. Now, about Detective Brady...

•   •   •

Mission Health was away from Manhattan, where the shooting had occurred, but close enough for Choo to receive medical attention as soon as possible after getting out. It was also small enough to appear vulnerable to threats from a thug.

The director brought them into his office. "What can I do for you?"

Kim told him of the anonymous tip. "Did this clinic treat anyone for a gunshot wound on the night of February twenty-third?"

A few rapid keystrokes on his desktop. "We treated someone named John Lee."

"You never reported it," Kim replied. "We checked."

The doctor who had treated him came as soon as the director summoned him. "We were busy after eleven o'clock. A gang fight nearby."

Kim showed him Choo's mugshot. "Did you treat this man?"

The doctor paled. "We were deciding who needed the most urgent help when a friend brought him in saying he'd shot himself by accident. I took him right away. He'd suffered a gunshot wound in the right knee."

"You're aware the law requires you to report treating a victim of a gunshot wound," the director said. "They can arrest you right now and shut this clinic down."

Kim held up a hand. "I'm sure the doctor had his reasons for not reporting it." She turned to him. "And we're willing to listen."

"The man who'd been shot told me he had friends in the NYPD, and if I reported treating him, he'd find out and kill me and my family. I was afraid not to believe him." He reached into his pocket and pulled out a small plastic bag with a bullet in it. "This is what I extracted from his knee."

Kim stared at the slug. It looked like a nine-millimeter. Ballistics might establish the weapon firing it if piercing the door didn't obliterate the striations.

The doctor shifted his stance. "Does the bullet help you?"

The striations were distinguishable from other marks on the slug. "Yes, you can relax."

"What's the recommended aftercare?" Mike asked.

"Prescribed an antibiotic and a painkiller and told him he'd need follow-up care. Two days later, I called the number his friend had given to make sure he saw a doctor, but it was a nonworking number."

"Figures." Mike gestured toward the hallway. "Saw cameras outside. They work? Or for show?"

"They work," the director said. "Have to around here."

"Please show us the video you recorded the evening of February twenty-third," Kim said. "How bad was the damage to his knee?"

The doctor brought them back to his office and pulled the file. "I'm sure you're familiar with doctor-patient privilege."

She wanted to tell him nine people were dead and to go fuck his privilege, but her training won out. "We're trying to determine if he's a flight risk."

"He's not going anywhere. He needs crutches to walk, and even then, it would be very painful. The video room is in the back."

The technician ran the file as she'd requested.

"There's Choo," Kim said. "Freeze it." A stocky black man was all but carrying him. "You recognize him, Mike?"

"No. We'll need to take it with us." He took a flash drive from the technician.

CHAPTER FOURTY

Sunday, March 5th, 9:22 PM

After taking a long time to think matters through and analyze, he called his aide-de-camp back. "What about Lewis and Choo? We should move them if possible."

"I need not remind you we'd need an ambulance crew to move Choo. And where would we move him to?"

"Somewhere out of the city. Duval has already given them Lewis. They'll be knocking at his door at any moment. How long will it take you to assemble a medical team and an ambulance?"

"If we take the usual precautions, I'd say a week."

"We can't afford to take the usual precautions. I want them moved by dawn tomorrow."

.   .   .

The message indicator on the phone was blinking. Joyce asking how the interview with the detective had gone? It was such a relief to have done it.

But it wasn't Joyce.

159

It was Allison. "Hi, Andy. Sorry, Leanne." Her voice was heavy with melancholy. "Please call me as soon as you can. It's about Mom."

She hit the key to delete the message. If Alli had told Mom about her decision to transition, Mom might have told Rod. Perhaps they'd all made a scene there in the hospital.

A sense of dread gripped her as she called Alli back.

"Mom died a little while ago," Alli said.

"How are the kids taking it?"

"Not well. And Bart isn't helping."

"I'm sure your husband is being a model father."

Alli changed the subject. "The wake will be on Tuesday, the funeral on Wednesday at our church here in Northport. It'll be a madhouse, I'm afraid, and since you don't have a car..."

"It's okay, I'll rent one. What time on Tuesday?"

"Two to five, then seven to nine." Alli hesitated. "I'm sorry we haven't been able to talk about your, you know, but..."

"Not your fault, Alli. You've got more on your plate than anyone deserves. We'll talk after the funeral. A lunch together, just us girls?" Alli had always used that phrase when they played together as children.

Dead silence. Oh, no.

"Um, yeah, okay."

"What's wrong, Alli?"

Another pause. "You have every right to live as you wish, and I'm not hassling you, but at the wake and funeral..."

It took a moment to tamp down the rising tide of anger, but it wasn't Alli's fault, and she was most important, the one reason to even go. "Don't worry. My best jacket and tie."

"You don't mind?"

"I won't even wear mascara. See you Tuesday."

Next, she called Joyce to tell her she wouldn't be at work on Tuesday and Wednesday.

160

"Pick you up at your place at one," Joyce said. "No way in hell I'm letting you face your family alone. I'll drive you for the funeral, too."

·   ·   ·

Kim dozed on the drive returning to PBMS. She was still in a fog when they walked in.

Dobson was still there. "Figured you'd need some help when you got back."

Mike gave him the flash drive and a slip of paper. "Load this and forward to this location."

They crowded around a desktop. Dobson brought up the first frame with Choo. "Whoa. Our guy. Who's with him?"

Kim accepted a bottle of Red Bull from Mike and took a long gulp. "If Duval was telling us the truth this afternoon, Cal Lewis, the driver the night of the shooting."

"Hang on." Dobson opened a new window and brought up Calvin Lewis' mugshot. Then he split the screen so they could compare the frame from the video.

Mike shook his head. "How do you do that so fast?"

Kim had to laugh. "Easy when you know how." As Dad used to say. "Looks like Lewis is our guy. Kyle, since you're already in, check him for priors, please."

A quick riff of tippy taps. "Two counts of possession, one weapons charge."

He was quicker than she'd thought. "And?"

"Both substance charges were CPCS Seven, both tossed. They pled the weapons charge down to Menacing Three."

"Two A Misdemeanors and a B. Any jail time on the Menacing?" Didn't sound like a big operator.

Dobson shook his head. "Nope. Paid a fine. Wouldn't mind having his luck."

"I suspect it was more than luck, Kyle." She glanced at Mike, who stared at the screen. "What's his last known?"

Kiley came out of his office. "Hey, good to see you both back. How did..."

Dobson read off the address. "It's in the Ravenswood Housing Project."

Mike smacked his forehead. "Holy shit."

"We were there," Kim said. The thought of having to dash back made her groan.

Kiley took charge. "Okay, first things first. Kim, when did you sleep last? Not napping, a full night?"

"Friday."

He turned to Mike.

"Two hours in the early hours this morning."

"Not good enough. You two..."

No. She wouldn't allow him to sub her out at this point. "Lieutenant, we have to hurry. If Lewis and Choo move, we might not find them again."

"Based on the doctor's info," Mike put in, "Choo isn't going anywhere soon."

Line in the sand time. "With all due respect, Lieutenant, I'm not risking it. I'm grabbing a few hours of sleep here and then, with your permission, we'll call in an ESU team to back us up and go make the collar."

Kiley cast a side-long glance at Mike.

"I find her very convincing these days," Mike said.

CHAPTER FORTY-ONE

Monday, March 6th, 3:55 AM

Insomnia stalked him, still brooding, still calculating. One could manipulate any humans to a predetermined course of action so long as one could discover their motivations and weaknesses. The plan in this case had been perfect, a model of logical simplicity. His plan depending on the illogic of certain manipulated parties was an amusing paradox.

His aide-de-camp called. "I've assembled a team. The leader is a trusted member, Volnick, but the others are untested newcomers. Is this the wisest decision?"

It was his way of urging him not to execute. And if a better option were available, he'd take it. But he was in the uncomfortable position of not having much choice. "What is the plan?"

"They expect to grab an ambulance in about an hour, but no guarantees. They'll make it look like a 9-1-1 call."

• • •

Kim started as Kiley shook her awake. "What time..."

"Four in the morning. ESU suggests we go in around dawn to avoid having too many bystanders. They're on the way. You sure you're up for this?"

She was at full alert. "We?"

"Dobson and I will ride shotgun, assuming you don't object."

Not her first choice, but she couldn't refuse. "Sure."

"I've asked the One-Fourteen to keep you informed of any other emergency activity in the area. Lots of gang problems over there. We don't want anyone to get in our way."

"Thanks." Okay, so having Kiley along wasn't a terrible idea. She turned to Dobson. "No lights or sirens unless we hit traffic."

The roads in Manhattan were empty. They had already crossed the Queensborough Bridge when the radio crackled. It was ESU. "Mobile One, this is Team One. We are en route. What is your ETA?"

"Ten minutes or less," Dobson said.

Kim keyed the mic. "Team One, this is Mobile One. ETA in ten minutes or less. Out."

"Copy ten minutes. Our ETA is same or less. Team One out."

As they sped along a deserted Twenty-First Street in Queens, Kim called the precinct to check on any emergencies. "None reported."

"No traffic on 9-1-1, either," Kiley said from the back seat.

As Dobson approached the turn into the complex, an FDNY ambulance pulled out and raced northward on Twenty-First Street. Kim grabbed the mic. "Team One, this is Mobile One. FDNY bus just exited scene."

"Mobile One, this is Team One. FDNY bus entered the complex, turned around, and exited."

Dobson pulled up next to the ESU truck. The ESU sergeant greeted Kim as they got out. "They were southbound on Twenty-First before they turned in."

"So," Kim said, "they reversed course when they left." She glanced around the parking area. "No patrol cars."

The ESU sergeant followed her gaze. "No."

"Must've had the wrong address," Kiley said. "How many deployed, Sergeant?"

"One's covering the south stairwell, three toward the building's rear, two holding the main stairway, and two EMTs waiting in the truck. You should leave someone in the main stairwell when you take my guys in with you."

Kiley turned to Kim. "I'll take the stairwell."

Kim called the sergeant's cell. "Let's keep this open."

They climbed the stairs, except for Mike, who took the elevator to make certain no one else could use it. Introductions to the ESU officers were brief. When they got to the fourth floor, Kim pulled her Glock.

The ESU officers forced the apartment door open. She stepped into a narrow foyer. Cal Lewis was pulling out a piece.

Kim leveled hers. "Police. Drop the weapon."

Lewis dropped it. Dobson swooped in to cuff him and read him his rights. Mike picked up the gym bag at Jackson's feet.

Kim opened the bedroom door and holstered the Glock. Jack Choo was lying on the bed, damp with sweat, his blood staining the dirty sheets. She placed him under arrest and read him his rights, then stepped back and let the EMTs take over.

One of the EMTs gestured to Choo. "His knee's infected and he's running a high fever. We're taking him to Bellevue, stat."

Kim turned to Dobson. "You go with Choo. If he shows signs of becoming lucid, Mirandize him again. Once he's getting treatment, let me know." She led Lewis down to the car and slid into the back seat next to him.

Mike slid into the passenger seat in the front with the gym bag. "Few days' changes of clothes in there, Calvin. Planning a trip?"

"Yeah," Kim said. "Like, in an ambulance?"

"What ambulance?" Lewis asked.

She ignored the dagger look from Kiley in the driver's seat. "The one you were waiting for. It pulled into the parking lot, saw the ESU team and took off."

CHAPTER FORTY-TWO

Monday, March 6th, 2:52 PM

Kiley went home exhausted. His last comment to her, "Don't waste your time on any conspiracy theories", still rankled.

Dobson walked in, soaking wet. "It's started raining. Like a monsoon out there. They've admitted Choo to Bellevue. The infection's bad, but they don't think he'll lose the leg."

Mike rolled his eyes. "There's a relief."

"Thanks, Kyle." Legal Aid wouldn't get a lawyer appointed for Lewis until sometime tomorrow. "One more thing: please take Lewis to Central Booking."

"Sure." He looked her up and down. "Sounds like we've hit a lull. Go home and sleep."

"Out of the mouths of babes," Mike intoned. "Done."

She had to agree. "Thank you, Detective Dobson. We'll pick it up tomorrow."

·   ·   ·

She found the apartment unlocked when she arrived home. "Jake?"

"Be out in a minute."

His voice didn't sound right. "Everything okay?" She found him in the bathroom.

He was staring at his face in the mirror. There was white tape across the bridge of his nose, a gauze dressing on his left temple, and his left eye showed some swelling. "I would have texted you, but they took my cell."

"Who did? What happened?"

"A little after one, I braved the heavy rain and ventured out for lunch at my favorite little place on Fifth and Dean. When I came out, someone grabbed me by the hair from behind, turned me around, and started beating me up. They dragged me into the parking lot next door and worked me over. Took my cell, but nothing else."

"What did they look like?"

He started to smile, but the gash in his lower lip stopped him. "I already told the police. I didn't get a close look at either of them. Think there were two."

"Did they say anything?"

"When they first grabbed me, one said, 'Pig fucker.' They mumbled some other things I didn't catch. The last thing I remember is one of them saying, 'We be back.' I wasn't aware they'd taken my phone until the ambulance came."

First, she called the precinct and spoke to the detective on the case. No one had seen anything because of the heavy rain. The parking lot attendant had found Jake when he came back from lunch and called 9-1-1. Police couldn't understand why the muggers had taken Jake's cell phone but not his wallet, which held over a hundred dollars, or the Breitling watch she'd given him for Christmas.

Next, she called Kiley, who did not appreciate being awakened from a sound sleep. "This is no longer a crank. It's a campaign. I want police protection for Jake."

A groan. "I'll tend to it."

·   ·   ·

"Good news and bad news," his aide-de-camp said. "The boyfriend has received the message."

Excellent. "I'm sure Brady's next step will be to request police protection for him. Do we have a way around them?"

"It's the Eight-Four. We don't have anyone inside there."

"There are other ways. What's the bad news?" He would have preferred the bad first.

"ESU was already at Lewis' place when our team got there. We couldn't get them out."

"So, let's summarize. Volnick failed, and Choo and Lewis are in custody."

"Correct." At least his aide-de-camp never wavered in the truth's face.

But this was bad. "We may have no choice but to turn to more extreme measures."

"We might do better to consider circling the wagons."

While it was his aide-de-camp's function to advise and suggest, to keep uncomfortable truths in view, he did not appreciate it here. "As I recall, 'circling the wagons' in popular lore always preceded a massacre. I'm not about to walk away from what I've built merely because a few peons couldn't do their jobs."

"It was a thought." His aide-de-camp ended the call.

It didn't end his ruminations, though. He hadn't come all this way so the fuckups of some troglodytes could derail his brilliant plan. Such a shy boy in his youth, fearful of bullies who taunted him about his mother turning tricks to feed her coke habit; they beat him up when he dared resist. He'd remained a classic underachiever until he'd learned algebra, and then his fascination with the order and predictability of mathematics, which the bullies failed to grasp, gave him an edge. He'd also grown taller and stronger.

As the bullies discovered drugs, he'd applied the knowledge he'd gained watching his mother. And he'd learned his great secret—he could exploit anyone once he found the key, which was another way of saying "solving for x".

No, he wasn't going to retreat from it now. He would see this through, whatever steps he needed to take, whomever he had to eliminate, for his own good.

CHAPTER FORTY-THREE

Tuesday, March 7th, 11:03 AM

"Police yesterday morning arrested two men they believe were responsible for the mass shooting at the Cove in the Meatpacking District two weeks ago. The shooting killed nine people and wounded ten more..." Kim allowed herself a smile as she paid for her morning coffee and left Tal's.

Barlowe was waiting for her outside. "You don't look like someone who made the biggest collar of the year yesterday."

"Someone assaulted my boyfriend, Jake, yesterday." She decided not to say more. She'd left him in the hands of the Eight-Four, a good precinct. And he was to check in with her every hour.

"Oh, Kim. That's awful. I hope he's all right."

She thanked him. "I can't stay long. We're interrogating Cal Lewis at Rikers today."

Barlowe considered it. "Rings a bell, but I couldn't say why."

"And we've learned who was supplying Paredes..."

"Viper Kincaid." He grinned at her surprise. "Heard from one of my snitches. Kincaid's been ramping it up, trying to take Williams' place. Paredes was one of his guys. As I remember, Kincaid talks big. Wants everyone to think he's the next El Chapo."

"Duval says Kincaid's network is already bigger than Williams' was."

"I'd be careful about what I believe from Duval. He's..."

"Delusional?" Nolan had said the same thing.

Barlowe smiled at her. "No. But he does sometimes get carried away. So, now you're wondering if someone intended the shooting as a message to Kincaid. Logical conclusion. Another dealer wouldn't appreciate the competition. I'm working on identifying the dealer."

"Fine, George, but there's also the possibility Kincaid ordered the hit himself. Apparently, things were less than rosy between him and Paredes. I need to find Kincaid. You have his last known?"

"Yes, but he's no longer there. I'm meeting with a snitch later today who might know. I'll text you later if I find out. We can work out a meeting place."

.   .   .

Andy slid into the passenger seat of Joyce's car wearing a dark blue suit, white shirt and paisley tie.

Joyce snickered. "Not even a hint of mascara." She examined his hair. "Well, I'm relieved. At least you didn't have it cut."

"This is bad enough." He placed a small handbag in the back seat. "For the trip home."

"I kind of hoped you'd be..."

"Dressed? No. Alli begged me not to. She's on my side—at least I think she still is. But my two brothers? Forget it."

Joyce pulled out and turned onto Fifth Street, heading towards the Expressway. A white Camry made the turn right behind them. "Are you at least wearing your clear nail polish?"

"No. I'm keeping Leanne totally underground today and tomorrow." He glanced around. "Even wearing my one remaining pair of men's briefs." The Camry, two car lengths behind them, changed lanes when they changed.

"You okay?" Joyce asked. "You seem nervous."

"This'll be the first time I've seen my brothers since my father's funeral." The Camry couldn't be following them. A simple coincidence. He told her about the referral he'd gotten the day before from the Employee Assistance Program and the appointment he had for Thursday evening with a specialist in gender issues.

"Sounds great." But then Joyce caught him glancing back as they passed Glen Cove Road. "What are you looking for?"

"Nothing. Just looking around." He tried to stop, but as they passed South Oyster Bay Road, he couldn't help himself.

"All right," Joyce said. "What's going on? And don't tell me, 'nothing'."

It would be better to tell her. "I guess I'm a little paranoid these days, what with the case. A white car's been trailing us since we got on the Expressway."

"A lot of cars have been behind us since we got on the Expressway."

"I know. One more look." He craned his neck again. No sign of the white Camry. "Huh. Not there."

"See? Now please try to relax. Save the nervous breakdown for the funeral home."

· · ·

"Hey, Kim. Want one?" Jimmy Stephenson beamed as he offered a cigar. The twinkle in his eye went well with his light brown hair, green eyes, and the spattering of freckles across the bridge of his nose.

"Congratulations, Jimmy. But no, thanks. How's your wife doing?"

"She's fine. Kicked me out a day early. Said I was driving her crazy. Called me a 'helicopter husband'." He turned serious. "And congrats, yourself. I understand you're the lead on the Cove case. You must be in it up to your neck."

She grinned at him. "You're in it with me, partnering with Dobson. When the congratulations wind down, join me in Kiley's office and I'll bring you up to speed."

He glanced around. "Looks like they're done already."

Kiley had tucked his cigar in his shirt pocket. "Kim's got everything right here on the case board." He turned to her. "How's Jake?"

"Fine, thanks."

Stephenson took his time. "What's this about an FDNY bus?"

Kim explained the odd appearance outside Lewis' building. "Mike and I are heading to Rikers today to interview Lewis. I'd appreciate it if you and Dobson could check on what emergency calls the local FDNY ambulance battalion got early yesterday morning." She turned to Kiley. "It's the one source we didn't check yesterday."

CHAPTER FORTY-FOUR

Tuesday, March 7th, 12:07 PM

Yvette Driscoll met Kim and Mike outside same the building at Rikers in which they had interrogated Duval. Lewis and his Legal Aid attorney were already in the conference room.

"You've had a busy couple of weeks," Yvette said. "Stole a vehicle, used it in a drive-by shooting, killed nine people, tried to sink said vehicle in Jamaica Bay after redecorating the upholstery, and failed Nursing 101."

"Let's slow it down," the Legal Aid lawyer said. "All you can prove is he brought the alleged shooter to a clinic."

Kim liked Yvette a lot, but she wasn't about to give her the ball until Lewis gave Kim the information she needed. "He drove right past an eyewitness the night of the shooting." Kim looked him in the eye. "Didn't you?"

"Not a word," Legal Aid said to Lewis. "Nice try, Detective."

Kim maintained her eye contact. "We also have an eyewitness to the vehicle theft and forensic evidence connecting the vehicle to the shooting. A doctor at the urgent care center provided a nine-millimeter slug fired by one victim subsequently dug out of Jack Choo's knee."

"Ballistics says it's a perfect match," Mike added.

Legal Aid shrugged. "Mr. Choo could have driven himself and gotten shot, picking up my client afterward to take him to the clinic."

"Except," Kim said, "our eyewitness was specific—she saw Mr. Choo in the back seat with his weapon. And the slug entered the vehicle through the passenger side rear door. The Crime Lab people will testify no slug could have struck Mr. Choo had he been sitting anywhere other than the back seat on the passenger side."

Legal Aid was ready to rip off a sharp retort when Yvette stepped back in. "Even if I were to accept your interpretation, it's still accessory after the fact. And I don't accept it. So, let's try to agree on a viable middle ground option."

"And the middle ground would be...?"

"Who ordered the hit?"

Legal Aid heaved a sigh. "My client does not know of..."

Yvette cut him off. "Then he's a conspirator."

"Besides," Kim said, "your client called Pierre Duval ten minutes before the shooting to tell him to make sure no one left the Cove."

"Says who?" Lewis asked before his attorney could stop him.

"Duval. He rolled on you. Confirmed you came to his apartment to give him instructions and called him to tell him you were on the way and to keep everyone inside the bar. You were his initial contact when he first approached Viper Kincaid about doing business."

Lewis lost the sneer. "The fuck." Sure didn't take long.

The lawyer placed a hand on his arm. "So, the guy who admits he was inside—an accomplice—is trying to get out from under by giving up my client."

"Another accomplice," Yvette replied. "We're working our way up the chain. Your client is a little guy in this, like Duval. Whatever deal I give him depends on what he has to say, now."

Lewis was breathing hard through clenched teeth, his eyes burning. Kim had seen the look in other bit players in schemes gone bad. "You'll feel a lot better, Calvin." She leaned forward and looked into his eyes. "You're not a rotten guy. You could have left Jack Choo to bleed to death.

Or finished him and skipped town. But you didn't. And while you might be okay with offing some rival dealers, machine-gunning a crowded bar and killing six innocent bystanders doesn't sit well with you."

He stared at the table.

Yvette turned back to Legal Aid. "It's clear he was tight with Kincaid. Not a partner, but a trusted foot soldier, close enough to tell us who planned this shooting. If he gives us the information, and where to look for Kincaid's protection, he will buy the same deal Duval got—no charges, and witness protection."

The lawyer turned to Lewis and nodded.

Lewis took a deep breath. "Viper said his partner wanted a job done..."

"Who's his partner?" Kim asked.

"Don't know. But since Viper took over, we ain't never had trouble with nobody. Not cops, not other dealers. Viper told me Jack Choo would call me and to do whatever he said."

"When and where was this?" Kim asked.

"The Saturday before the shooting, at a house in Queens Viper uses to break down large shipments of girl for street sales."

Mike dropped a notepad and pencil on the table. "Address, please." He slid it over to Kim after Lewis finished. "Lindenwood. Near where they fished out the Blazer."

Kim gestured for Lewis to continue.

"Monday night before the job, Jack came to my place, said he'd off some punks. Told me I'd be driving. Duval would be inside to keep anyone from coming out, and he'd have the three punks out front. Duval was a pussy, but it was what security wanted."

"Security?" Kim asked. There was that term, again.

"What we all call Viper's partner. Even Viper uses it."

"So," Yvette continued, "you realized at this point this was a hit."

"Seemed obvious. I couldn't understand why anyone wanted to involve Duval."

Kim jumped back in. "So, about the job?" Enough about Duval. He was a pawn.

"Yeah. Choo gave me ten big ones. Said it was my share."

"For the job? Choo was paying you?" The money trail had to be clear.

"Yeah. Security paid him for both of us, Jack paid me my share."

"How could you be sure he was paying your full share?" Kim asked.

"Whatever he paid me was my full share."

Yvette's eyes met Kim's. "So, how much did he get?"

"I couldn't tell you. Just what I got."

Kim had to cover all possibilities. "So, it's possible he didn't get paid at all."

"Are you fucking kidding me? You think the driver gets paid but the shooter don't?"

It wasn't enough. "Approximately how much of the ten grand remains?" At least, she had to nail down Lewis' share.

"About a grand, or a little less. I owed some people. Most went to a garage for extensive car repairs. Seven grand. Got tail-ended on the BQE by a truck, and I have the minimum insurance. All but totaled the fucking thing. So, I took it to a guy I know."

Mike pointed to the notepad. "One of those places over in Willets Point?" When Lewis hesitated, he added, "We won't be checking VIN numbers."

Lewis wrote the name of the place and the address. "He won't have paperwork, you know."

"We need to verify your story," Kim said. "How big is Viper's network?"

"He's got guys slinging in four boroughs, and two other safe houses."

Well, that would help. She gestured toward the notepad. "Names and locations, please."

"I only have street names, and no other safe house locations."

"We'll take whatever information you can provide," Mike said.

Kim needed the details from Lewis' view. "What happened the day of the shooting?"

"Jack was in Washington Heights, watching Sylvia Walters' place. I met him late in the afternoon. We hot-wired this old Blazer, real piece of shit, and drove downtown. When we were close, I called Duval. I made the left from Washington onto Gansevoort; figured I'd see anyone on the street, but they wouldn't get a clear look at Jack."

"You passed a woman," Kim said. "She picked out Choo's mugshot."

"Shit. Anyway, one of Paredes' boys had a piece and fired, hitting the Blazer. Jack ripped off a burst, hitting all three punks. I heard a couple more shots—the kid, I guess—and Jack squeezed off a long burst, blowing out the door and front window of the bar."

"To keep everyone inside?" Kim asked.

"Fuck, no. That was Duval's job. Jack had this crazed look. I yelled for him to cool it and he started moaning about his knee. I hung a left onto Ninth. Figured I'd head for the Holland Tunnel and Jersey, but Jack's knee was all fucked up. Decided on Queens, instead. Figured I'd get Jack medical help, then ditch the Blazer."

Kim made notes. "Go on." Her cell buzzed. Text from Dobson. *Confirmed. No calls for a bus to any ambulance battalion in Northwest Queens Monday morning.*

Lewis took a deep breath. "We waited at my place a few hours, then I took him to a clinic. Paid the doc five hundred bucks to pull out the slug and not to report it. Told him I'd come back and kill him and his family if he did. Jack told him he had friends in the NYPD who'd make sure I never got caught."

Whoa. "What did Choo mean? What friends?"

"No clue. I figured Jack was fucking with him."

Kim locked her glare on him until he looked away. "No, you didn't. What friends? Who was Kincaid's 'security'?"

"Nobody ever mentioned any names. We used the term."

"Even Choo?"

"Yeah."

"Go on."

"I still had to ditch the Blazer. I figured the creek was good since the saltwater might fuck up any evidence. Got there around two in the morning. Dark as hell. Jack had bled all over the back seat, so I ripped out the upholstery. On my way out of the marshes, some homeless guys had a trash fire going. I threw the upholstery onto the fire. They were grateful for the extra fuel. Let me stand by the fire to dry out. I'd gotten soaked getting out of the Blazer and it was cold as fuck. Took a bus and two subways home."

One more detail. "We didn't find the AR-15 with the Blazer. What happened?"

"I heaved it into the Gowanus Canal on my way to ditch the Blazer. Jack got pissed when I told him. Said he'd converted it to automatic and could have gotten good money for it. I told him keeping both our asses out of jail was more important than ten grand."

How convenient. Lewis had to realize, as she did, no one would jump into toxic sludge to look for it. "What exit did you get off?"

He screwed up his face. "What, you don't believe me?"

She would not get played at this late stage. "Convince me I should. Details."

He threw up his hands. "Fuck. Took the BQE to Hamilton, swung back around to Huntington, drove to the end and chucked it in the fucking canal. Okay?"

The same route she'd have taken. "Just one more thing. Where did the ambulance come from? There were no 9-1-1 calls yesterday morning."

"What ambulance? The only ambulance I saw was the one you had for Jack."

"Then," Mike put in, "why did you pack a bag?"

"Shit, man, I always have a bag packed. No telling when I'm gonna need to move in a hurry."

"So," Legal Aid said, "do we have a deal?"

"We'll check out his story about the car repair first," Kim said. As soon as they were outside, she called Stephenson and asked him to head to Willets Point with Dobson.

CHAPTER FORTY-FIVE

Tuesday, March 7th, 2:05 PM

Andy's mother was in the first chapel as they entered the funeral home. Rod and Sean stood outside, talking. Their wives were chatting with Alli nearby.

Joyce whispered to him. "Your sister's the red-haired woman in the black dress? Beautiful. She looks a lot like you."

"Thanks. I needed that."

Alli saw them and approached. "Hi, Andy." She embraced him and held it. "Thank you so much for being here."

He introduced Joyce. "A wonderful friend from work. How're you managing?"

Alli took a deep breath. "I'm doing my best. You look great." She was staring at his suit.

A little joke might ease her anxiety. "I told you I wouldn't come dressed."

Her eyes sprang open with alarm. "Please don't say anything about that."

"Sorry, I was kidding."

Rod approached. "Andy. Good to see you." He made no move to embrace him or even shake hands. He turned to Alli. "I think we should go in now, unless you'd prefer to wait for Bart."

"No, now is okay." She linked her arm with Andy's. "Would you come with me?"

He didn't want to go view his mother, but he couldn't refuse Alli. "Sure."

Rod gestured for them to go first. When they got to the casket, Alli stood and gazed down. Her grip on his arm tightened. After a moment, she released it and knelt. Andy followed.

He studied his mother's face, now at peace, and tried to conjure up some sentiment for her. But with every article of Alli's clothing discovered in his room, their mother had regarded him with increasing irritation at the inconvenience. Her sole objection to his father's rages had been the neighbors might hear. He'd gone away to college, stopped coming home for holidays, and moved out for good, and all she'd ever said was, "Perhaps everything works out for the best, dear."

He waited, studying the material of Alli's dress and thinking she deserved so much better. She nodded, and they stood. As they turned away, a group of women approached.

"Excuse me," Alli said. "Friends from the Parents' Association at the kids' school."

Bart entered the chapel and intercepted Alli, shooting Andy a menacing glare. Andy led Joyce out to the lobby.

"She's lovely," Joyce said. "I can see you two are close. Is the man talking to her now her husband? He looked angry."

A heavy-set man in his mid-thirties with black hair thinning on top, wearing a maintenance uniform, entered the lobby, glanced at the names outside each chapel, and walked out.

Andy peered inside. Bart was berating Alli. Rod and Sean joined them and looked grim as Bart talked. Alli appeared ready to burst into tears.

"What's that all about, I wonder," Joyce said.

Bart pointed toward the lobby.

"I don't think it's about her not waiting for him." Andy led Joyce back outside, where the afternoon air was balmy for early March. "Alli couldn't have told him."

Bart rushed out. "Keep away from my family, you fucking degenerate freak. You hear me?"

Andy started to answer, but Bart grabbed him by the lapels and slammed him against the building, pinning him. "I'm warning you. Come near my kids, I'll kick your fucking homo ass."

Rod appeared in the doorway. "Let him go." Bart released him. "Go back inside." He waited until Bart had gone, then dropped his voice. "Are you serious about this sex change thing?"

"Did Alli tell you?"

"No, Bart did."

"How did Bart know? No way Alli told him."

"No, she didn't. He saw an e-mail you sent her."

"And you're angrier about me than Bart spying on Alli. Sickening."

"You don't have to tell me Bart's a piece of shit. But he saw what he saw." Rod glared at him. "You do this, you'll be turning your back on your family for the rest of your life."

"My family turned its back on me when I was five years old. All of you except Alli." He started walking away. "Let's go, Joyce."

Rod called after him. "Hey, where the hell are you going?"

He kept walking, with Joyce close behind. Once in her car, he turned to make sure Rod hadn't followed. "Sorry you had to see this."

"I'm glad I was here." She pulled out of the lot.

Andy flipped down the sun visor in front of him and opened the lighted mirror. He pulled eyeliner out of the handbag he'd left in the car.

She pulled over on Main Street. "I don't want you stabbing yourself in the eye if I hit a bump."

"Thanks." After the eyeliner, he pulled out the mascara. "At least it took my mind off my paranoia for a while." A few quick strokes of the mascara and he'd finished. "Okay, thanks. Go to the end of the block and turn right onto Vernon Valley Road."

As Joyce made the turn, she scowled. "Now you have me doing it."

His heart skipped a beat. "What?"

"A white car turned right behind me."

He turned in his seat, straining against the seat belt, and saw the same car he'd seen on the Expressway, earlier. It trailed a few car lengths behind them, with one car in between. He couldn't see the driver.

At the merge with Laurel Road, the light was yellow. They went through.

Both trailing cars followed.

"The next traffic light is Pulaski Road. Turn right and see if he follows."

Joyce made the right.

The Camry followed.

Panic rose in his throat. "Turn right, here." Joyce made the sudden turn on to a quiet side street.

This time the Camry didn't follow. "Okay, make two more rights and then continue south to the parkway."

"Sorry I spooked you," Joyce said with a nervous laugh.

"No problem." Every exit, he glanced around to check, but the white Camry did not return.

CHAPTER FORTY-SIX

Tuesday, March 7th, 4:06 PM
Meet me at the Irving Place gate to Gramercy Park.

"Excuse me," she said to Jimmy Stephenson. "Be right back."

Barlowe was waiting, his collar turned up against the brisk wind. He fell in step next to her as they continued to walk around the park, devoid of any visitors. "I have it." He slipped a note into her hand. "Kincaid's address. Don't take it out here. It's in Queens, near LaGuardia. My source says he rented it last week, so he isn't going anywhere for a while."

"How good is your source?"

"Outstanding."

"I need the snitch's name and his angle."

"I can't tell you. There's a reason they're called confidential informants."

"Confidentiality is not absolute. How can you be sure you're not being played? I can't take the chance my guys are being set up to walk into an ambush."

His face hardened. "I don't get played, Kim, not by anyone. And I'd never let you walk into anything." He broke into a warm smile. "You're growing on me."

"The name, please."

He glanced around. "Okay. Francisco Robles. A mid-level dealer who works for Kincaid and has a nasty grudge against him. Seems Viper's been making it with Robles' wife and not being very discreet about it."

"Any other motive? Like moving up?"

"Robles? Nah, doesn't have the chops for it."

She gave him a quizzical look.

"Doesn't possess the ability to attend to details or command respect. I mean, who stands by while another man uses his wife and carries on business as usual? And who could respect anyone like that? Believe me, respect and fear are how these guys keep people in line."

They turned off Gramercy Park West.

He grew reflective. "It's bad in the unit right now. Nolan's been nosing around, asking questions, looking for information he can sell to cover his ass."

"I thought you weren't making any accusations."

"No accusations. I'm reporting what I've observed. Get anything from him?"

"He claims he never left you out of the Williams case report. But I checked the file and your name doesn't appear in it."

Barlowe broke into a boyish grin but said nothing.

A sudden thought. "How did you discover he'd left you out? Your name isn't on the access list."

The grin vanished. "He told me, claiming he was doing me a favor."

"What kind of favor?"

A humorless laugh. "Beats the hell out of me. I told you, I decided not to pursue it."

She needed more. "What about bodyguards? Did your source mention how many guards Kincaid has with him?"

Barlowe shook his head. "None. He's keeping a low profile."

She stopped. "You're telling me a drug kingpin, a guy who sees himself as the next El Chapo, has no protection around him?"

He laughed. "I know. Crazy, right? I won't try to figure out the logic. I'm passing on the intel. Hey, I'd appreciate the chance to question him

after you're finished. Might help me connect some dots of my own."

"Sure. Why don't you come with us when we collar him?"

"Can't. I have something else going." He checked his watch. "Gotta run."

CHAPTER FORTY-SEVEN

Tuesday, March 7th, 8:21 PM

"Holy shit." Jimmy Stephenson ducked as an Airbus A-320 passed right over them on its way into LaGuardia. He and Dobson had followed Kim and Mike out from Manhattan.

Kim laughed. "Geez, Jimmy. They're still a few hundred feet up."

The lights of the next plane were already blazing southwest of them. "I can't believe these folks live here and put up with the noise. How do they sleep?"

A sergeant from the One-Fifteen laughed. "This is nothing. You should've seen it back when the old 727s used this runway. Deafening when they were taking off." He turned to Kim. "I've deployed my guys around the house. We're ready when you are."

She waited until the plane passed overhead. "Okay. Jimmy, circle to the rear in case he slips out the rear door. Kyle, you watch the south side of the house. The fence and high hedges on the north side should block him if he slips out a window. Mike, you and two uniforms are with me."

The light in the bay window in the single-story house appeared to be from a lamp. No other windows showed any light. Another plane passed over, louder than the others. She pulled her Glock and mounted the front steps and got her first surprise.

186

The front door was ajar.

She tried the storm door. Unlocked. She whispered to Mike, "Gloves."

He pulled on a pair and opened the door. Kim, also wearing gloves, stepped past him. "Kincaid? Police."

The smell of death.

There was an open door—panes of glass in a wood frame—between the small vestibule and the living room. She nudged it open with her foot and stepped into the living room.

Kincaid was lying on the floor, dead. She waved Mike and the uniforms in. "Check the rest of the house." She studied the body. Five shots, all to the chest and abdomen. Burns on Kincaid's shirt.

Mike returned from the bedroom and kitchen while the uniforms came up from the basement. "Place is empty."

Dobson and Stephenson came in.

"Gloves, both of you." Kim called to them. "And Jimmy, please call it in."

She pulled out a flashlight and walked back to the front door. No forced entry. Either Kincaid had let his attacker in, or the attacker had a key. The first blood spatter on the rug appeared inches inside the vestibule door. A second, larger spatter, appeared two feet further into the living room. Kincaid's body lay behind the large spatter.

Dobson stared down at the body.

"Don't touch him, Kyle," Kim said. "Wait for the ME and CSU to arrive." When Dobson wrinkled his nose and backed away, she added, "Yeah, he's starting to bloat. This happened several hours ago."

She returned to the front door and walked backwards into the living room, back to where the body lay.

"Talk to me," Mike said.

"He let the shooter into the house. The shooter pulled the gun upon entering, or it's possible he already had it out. Kincaid never had time to turn around."

"Or the killer shot him in the back," Dobson replied.

"No. The burns on the shirt show the killer shot from the front, and at close range. Those aren't exit wounds, although there should be five of them in his back. And look at the blood spatter. One shot, stagger, then the other shots." She paused while another plane flew overhead. "You and Jimmy, please go canvass the neighbors. Start with the houses on either side; they're the most likely ones with any information. Find out whatever you can about him."

She searched the floor. "No casings. Either he had a revolver, or he cleaned up after killing Kincaid." She stepped around the body and checked the far wall. She found four holes the killer had gouged. "Looks like he did a thorough cleanup job. Nothing in the wall." Another searching glance around. "No sign of the fifth slug."

Mike stepped through the kitchen and returned. "Someone left the back door unlocked."

Kim nodded. "The shooter's exit route."

Dobson and Stephenson returned after CSU arrived. None of the neighbors had seen or heard anything, and one couldn't believe anyone would have murdered the quiet guy who kept to himself.

"She gave us the old line, 'always the quiet ones'," Dobson said.

How would she know he was quiet? "Which one?"

"Next door, beyond the hedges."

Kim took Dobson with her. Several neighbors were gawking from beyond the yellow tape already put up by CSU. Dobson pointed out the woman in question, standing part way up her front stoop, leaning on the wrought-iron railing, watching.

Kim approached and identified herself. "Were you acquainted with your neighbor?"

"Not really. I didn't see him very much. When I did, I'd wave to him and he'd wave back, but we never talked or anything. The first time I saw him, I walked over and rang the bell. You know, to introduce myself and welcome him to the neighborhood. I'd seen him go in a short while before, but he didn't answer. Well, I can take a hint. Afterward, I contented myself with waving and sometimes saying hello."

Kim pulled out Kincaid's mug shot, pausing as another plane passed overhead. "How long have they been using this approach, today?"

"It's been nonstop since around eight this morning." She shook her head. "It's like that some days."

"Must be irritating." Kim showed her the photo. "Is this the man?"

The neighbor gasped. "Yes."

"When did you first see him?"

"Let's see. I'd say it was early last summer, late June or early July. But I'd go weeks, or even months, without seeing him at all."

Kim took out her cell and showed her mug shots of Pierre Duval, Cal Lewis, and Jack Choo. "Ever see any of these men here?"

The neighbor studied each photo. "No. Sorry." She cast a wistful glance in the house's direction. "He's a criminal?"

"Not anymore. Thanks for your time." She walked back to where Dobson and Stephenson were waiting. "Jimmy, Kyle, tomorrow I need you to find out who owns this house."

CHAPTER FORTY-EIGHT

Wednesday, March 8th, 8:55 AM

"I don't understand," Kiley said as Kim finished updating the case board, noting the ME had fixed the time of Kincaid's death between eight and nine Tuesday morning. CSU had found no prints and no fibers, and they were still searching for a fifth slug. "Now you think Kincaid wasn't in charge?"

"He was hiding by himself, no bodyguards. His killer was furious and wanted Kincaid to know it before he died. He backed Kincaid up from the front door into the living room, shot once, then a few moments later, fired the rest. But the killer wasn't in such a rage he failed to clean up the crime scene. This was a cold-blooded execution."

"Hell of a pink slip," Mike said. "How did Barlowe react to the news about Kincaid?"

"I haven't talked to him, yet." She turned back to Kiley. "Both Duval and Lewis talked about Kincaid having 'security'. Better than what Ice Williams had."

Kiley leaned forward. "So, what are you saying?"

"It's inside the department. I was hoping we'd get a lead good enough to turn it over to Internal Affairs. Maybe they upped the ante and

Kincaid refused to pay it, or decided they didn't need him to run the operation. Either way, we can't wait any longer, lead or no lead."

"You want to go to IAB now?" Kiley's tone made it clear he didn't.

Dobson and Stephenson both looked shocked.

Kim held firm. "Yes."

"And what's the complaint? Nolan didn't tell you everything you wanted to know?"

She gestured at the case board. "Everything I wanted? He hasn't given us anything."

Kiley threw his hands in the air. "Well, there's a felony for you. And how does IAB react if we report this with no evidence?"

"Whatever they say, it'll be worse the longer we wait. What's the matter, Lieutenant? Afraid of going to IAB?"

He bristled. "I'm surprised you're so anxious, given your family history."

Mike placed a hand on her leg, but she shoved it away. Enough sins-of-the-father bullshit. "You sure were anxious not to make waves when Sergeant Phillips from the Bronx complained our investigation was interfering with some burglary sting that may or may not have existed."

Kiley jumped up, seething, as the needle sank home.

"John." Mike, a voice of reason. "I think Kim's right. We have to call in IAB, now." He turned to her. "You suspected it was inside when we first talked to Nolan, didn't you?"

"Yes." She glared at Kiley. "He threw my father in my face."

Kiley settled back down. "Sorry, Brady. Mike, if we go to IAB now, we lose control of this case."

"Not likely," Kim replied. "They need us too much."

"I agree," Mike said.

Kiley stared at the case board. The facts bothering her had to be bothering him. "All right. I'll make the call."

CHAPTER FORTY-NINE

Wednesday, March 8th, 11:37 AM

Yvette Driscoll met Kim and Mike at Bellevue. "After some intense discussion, I got a judge to sign off on the search warrant for the Lindenwood house."

"You should've gone to Judge Castellano." Kim remembered Kiley's plan in the event Leanne hadn't come forward.

"I suspect he was afraid I would."

A woman in her mid-thirties, dressed in a black pantsuit and low heels and carrying a briefcase, emerged from Jack Choo's hospital room. "I'm Sharon Foster, representing Mr. Choo. My client requests you postpone your interrogation until he recovers from his serious injury."

Mike rolled his eyes. "Would he like some milk and cookies in the meantime?"

"Perhaps Mr. Choo should have sought follow-up care for his gunshot wound," Yvette replied, "instead of hiding out and allowing it to become infected. I'm told his fever is down and he is lucid. Unless you have medical documentation stating he's unable to respond to questions, we will proceed."

Ms. Foster pouted, as if she'd made a reasonable request. "Very well."

"Mr. Choo," Yvette said, "we have an eyewitness who establishes you as the gunman in the Cove shooting. We're looking at nine counts of murder-one and ten counts of attempted murder, and…"

Foster's head snapped up. "Whoa, wait a second. Where do you get murder-one?"

Kim stepped in. "Unless Mr. Choo is claiming, out of the blue, he went on a shooting spree, this is a murder for hire. The three victims outside the bar were dealing; we found drugs and cash in their possession. The victims inside the bar were witnesses."

"If he tells us who hired him," Yvette said, "I'm prepared to drop the murder-one counts to murder-two, and the attempted murder counts to assault-one."

Sharon Foster snorted. "So, you'll charge him with murder-one unless he admits to murder-one. You can make a better offer."

"Not unless he has something substantial to offer us," Yvette replied.

Choo stirred. "Fuck you, bitch."

"Did we hear the serious injury talking?" Kim asked. "Let me give you an update, Choo. Viper's dead. Gunned down sometime yesterday. So, even if he were running the show, which would be useful to know, he's not running it anymore. Which means he can't protect you anymore."

He looked down but said nothing.

Kim shrugged. "Whoever hired you will go free while you rot in jail for the rest of your life and they run a massive drug ring. You okay with that?"

"What do you want?" Foster asked.

"Detective Brady already told you," Yvette replied.

Foster shrugged. "Make my client a serious offer."

"Fuck their offers," Choo snapped.

"Rest up, Mr. Choo," Yvette said. "There's a trial in your future."

"Not until he's recovered, there isn't," Foster called out as Kim, Mike, and Yvette left the room.

"I need to give this to the grand jury as soon as possible," Yvette said once they were outside. "I need proof someone paid Choo if I'm to make Murder-one stick. All we have now is circumstantial."

"We have the warrant," Kim replied, "so we can take down the Lindenwood house. If it's under new management, we might catch a lead."

Yvette mulled it over. "All right. I'll go for Murder-One. At the very least, it'll give me room to make a deal I can stomach."

CHAPTER FIFTY

Wednesday, March 8th, 1:36 PM

Stephenson had checked on the house in which Kincaid had been killed. "Owned by a limited liability company. Newhouse, LLC. I checked with the New York Department of State, and their records show it has one member, a Richard Odessa. So far, we're not finding anything on him."

"Thanks, Jimmy," Kim said. "How did your wife react your first day back on the job?"

"Pissed I got home so late. When I offered to return home on leave, she decided it wasn't necessary. Oh, CSU called. They found the fifth slug from Kincaid's. Ricocheted off a radiator. Looks like a .44 magnum, but it's pretty banged up. They doubt Ballistics will do much with it."

Mike was on the phone with the One-Oh-Six, arranging for backup on busting the Lindenwood house. Dobson was pecking away at his laptop.

Kiley waved her into his office. "I spoke to Captain Forrest over at IAB. He and his team want to meet with us tomorrow. Nolan's lieutenant, DeMarco, might already be on their radar. After we see what the Lindenwood house has, I'd like you to press this Barlowe guy for more information. So far, the only hard information he's given you was Kincaid's location. I'd like to make sure we've got a solid grasp on this before we meet with Forrest. Make certain you don't tip him off about going to IAB."

She was about to answer when a clattering behind her made her start.

Mike was sitting at his desk, ashen faced, his cell on the desk in front of him. "I spoke to the desk sergeant at the One-Oh-Six. The Lindenwood house is burning as we speak. They have units on the scene, along with the FDNY."

.   .   .

Nothing remained of the Lindenwood house but its charred frame and two charred walls.

"Arson," the fire investigator said. "No doubt about it. Started a little before nine this morning. The entire place burned like cellophane. We got it out a while ago, so I'm going in. Stick around for a bit and I'll tell you what I find."

"Can we look?" Kim strained to peer past him.

"No point. Believe me, Detective, if we find anything useful to you, we'll let you know."

A police captain approached. "You two are Resnick and Brady? Captain Brian Emerson, Queens Special Narcotics Task Force. SpecNarcs for short. I just learned of your planned raid. Rather far afield for Manhattan Homicide detectives, isn't it?"

"This wasn't a simple drug bust." Kim needed to avoid a turf war, no matter what. "It's part of a murder investigation. How did you get wind of it? We got the warrant this morning."

Emerson looked surprised. "Someone from the One-Oh-Six said you called for backup. We often work with them. Look, if there's anything you're working we can help with, please let me know."

"Thanks," Kim said. "You guys have intel on this location?"

"No, I came over when I learned of the fire." He gave her his card. "But please call me if you need anything else."

The fire investigator approached holding a digital camera as the captain sauntered away. "Okay. If it wasn't still so hot in there, and if I wasn't so concerned the entire remaining structure might collapse any minute, I'd invite you in to see for yourselves. But this should suffice."

He turned the camera face down and clicked to bring up the most recent image. "See the dark, U-shaped burn pattern on the floor joists? We call that a 'saddle burn'. Someone poured an accelerant—gasoline, most likely—on the floor to set the fire. We'll wait for the lab results to make it official, but you can take this to the bank. It was arson." He turned back to the smoldering wreckage. "No insurance payoff on this one."

Mike chuckled without humor. "They were after a unique brand of insurance."

"We had reports of massive amounts of cocaine in there," Kim said. "Any chance the crime lab could analyze the residue?"

The investigator shook his head. "As hot as this fire got? No, nothing you could identify with certainty as cocaine. Sorry."

The team had only discussed the Lindenwood house within Kiley's office, and even then, only in general terms. The one specific mention of it had been by Cal Lewis. One answer remained: there'd been a wire in the consultation room at Rikers.

CHAPTER FIFTY-ONE

Wednesday, March 8th, 5:18 PM

He ended the call. At last, something done right. Although the loss wasn't negligible. The torched product carried a street value of seven million, six hundred and fifty thousand dollars, based on his most recent calculations. And there was the house itself, from which prudence now demanded that he walk away. In the current market, the value was somewhere north of six hundred thousand dollars.

The other safe houses remained undetected, proving it had been a wise decision to keep Lewis' knowledge confined to Queens. Still, he'd give almost anything to get his hands on the list of names he'd given to Brady.

•   •   •

Dobson was as white as a ghost when he met Kim outside of PBMS. "Chris Ryba is dead. When he didn't show for his tour again this morning, my lieutenant tried to reach him. No answer, so he asked if I'd check on him. I found Chris sprawled on his kitchen floor. I called for a bus. They pronounced him dead on the scene. Heart attack, they think. Sometime last night."

Ryba was in his mid-thirties, in good shape, worked out. Kim's radar was out. "Any sign of drugs?"

"Nothing. He'd fallen off a chair. The place was neat as a pin."

"And you're about to tell me Ryba was a slob at home?"

He nodded.

She led him inside, where she told Kiley. "It's our jurisdiction. I'd like to have Stephenson ride herd on the ME's office for cause of death. And a tox screen. And, Lieutenant, if you say anything about conspiracy theories, I promise you with all due respect I will totally lose it."

Kiley's phone rang. "Homicide." He listened, nodded, and said, "Yeah, okay. Hold on." He hit the hold button. "Yvette Driscoll. A nurse at the Rikers infirmary was taking Choo's blood pressure when she noticed a bruise on his arm. He says he got it when we arrested him."

Kim snorted. "Bullshit. He was delirious with fever when we collared him. Besides, it would've been on the admitting sheet at Bellevue."

"True," Kiley said. "As soon as Choo's attorney found out, she asked us to move him. Yvette's moving him up to Sullivan—it's max security and close enough to the city—but it'll take two or three hours to arrange. You want to take another run at him before he goes?"

Kim told Kiley her conclusion about the wire and Kiley took his phone off hold. "Yvette? Kim Brady. The Lindenwood house burned to the ground before we arrived. I'd suggest we not question him at Rikers. If his lawyer says he's ready to cooperate, I'll take a run up to Sullivan with you."

Stephenson came in as Kiley hung up. "I tracked down Richard Odessa. He's ninety-four, living in a nursing home in Bay Ridge. Alzheimer's."

"You sure it's the same guy?" Kim asked.

Stephenson shrugged. "The Social's a perfect match."

"Okay. Find out from the nursing home who has power of attorney, then alert them about the identity theft and the East Elmhurst house. Search for any other assets owned by the LLC, and any other activity with his identity."

CHAPTER FIFTY-TWO

Thursday, March 9th, 7:45 AM

"Early again?" Pat Holloran asked with a grin as she passed the front desk. "Don't forget, tournament selections are Sunday. We're doing a pre-tournament Seed Pool." He waved a form at her. "Four points for each correct first seed, three for each second seed, two for each third, one for each fourth. Winner takes all. If you're in, I need your entry by end-of-tour tomorrow."

Kim smiled and waved. "I'll let you know." The tournament was nowhere on her radar. Ryba's tox screen had showed a significant level of cocaine, suggesting the possibility he'd snorted it uncut. Kiley wasn't in, yet, and she was due over at Centre Street at nine to testify before the grand jury against Choo. She updated the case board.

"I think you'll need a bigger board," Stephenson said from behind her.

True, she was running out of room. "What brings you in so early? Did your wife kick you out again?"

"No, I caught another case last night. A jogger found a stiff up on the High Line trail. An FDNY emergency medical technician named Gustav Volnick. Single shot to the head. CSU says it looks like they killed him elsewhere and dumped him on the trail."

200

"Where on the trail?"

"Just north of the stairway on Twenty-Third."

"Inconvenient place to bring a body. Did he live or work nearby?"

"According to his driver's license, his residence is in Fort Greene, Brooklyn. I'm in early to check on where he worked. Why? You interested?"

"Three deaths with no clues within twenty-four hours makes my eyelids twitch."

"Yeah, you and the CompStat guys." He held up an entry form. "You think Duke will be a one-seed?"

"Nope. UNC will, and no conference is getting two this year. And please keep me posted on this Volnick guy."

She turned back to the case board. The note about Barlowe's name being removed from the Williams file caught her eye. Nolan had sworn he'd included him, and no one else had accessed the file. One-PP was a stone's throw from 80 Centre Street, where the grand jury was meeting. She had time.

. . .

When Kim had first met Vera Koshkin, she'd thought she looked like one of those trophy wives wealthy American men imported from Russia. The twenty-eight-year-old computer expert with shoulder-length blond hair was petite and curvaceous, leaving many men who dealt with her smitten. The rumors about Vera being ex-*Politsaya* made Kim laugh.

"Good morning, brilliant American detective lady," Vera said. "You look like you not getting enough sleep. Is not good for you."

"And yourself?"

Vera shrugged. "Is how I work. Is why I have no boyfriend. Unlike you. How is Jake?"

"He's fine. Wants to marry me."

"But you not want to? Still sad about your papa?"

Vera was direct. "I'm not sure if it's good for me right now. I'm in the middle of a big case."

"Yes. Cove shooting." Vera brightened. "I can help?"

"I hope so. What can you tell me about the workings of our file system? Is there any way a Member of Service can access a case file and not have it show on the access log?"

"*Nyet.* Cannot happen. Must have User ID to log in, and system records to access log from the login field."

Kim gave her Ice Williams' case file number. "Can you bring up the access log for this file?"

"*Da.*" A few strokes on the keyboard, and the log appeared on the screen.

Nolan's ID appeared five times, all within two weeks of the bust. Kim's recent login was next, and one more from Nolan the day she'd mentioned it. "Can you identify changes every individual made with every entry in the file?"

"*Da.* Give me a minute." Vera accessed a history file. "Which you want to see?"

"The first entry."

Vera brought it up on the screen. Kim read the arrest narrative with care. It mentioned an informant, but not whom he had informed. Barlowe's name appeared in three places. Svetlana Bolshoi's name appeared once. "What happens if someone alters a prior entry?"

"Is like WORD. Deleted text appears as strike-through and added text appears as underlined."

"Please check each subsequent entry." She glanced at her watch. She'd be a few minutes late, but Leanne Mallory was testifying first.

Each of the subsequent entries corresponded with one of Nolan's logins. His last login, like Kim's, did not include an entry of any kind. "Vera, can you log in to the case file itself, please?"

She did.

"None of the references to Detective Barlowe or Svetlana Bolshoi are there," Kim said. "And all the entries showed them still in the file. How is that possible?"

"Is not possible. Unless someone hacked the system. Will take time to find out."

.   .   .

"Thank you, Ms. Mallory," the young ADA said after Leanne had completed her testimony before the grand jury. "Are there questions members of the grand jury wish me to put to this witness?" He hadn't mentioned her running out, nor even any mention of her being trans.

The grand jury members had no questions. The ADA turned to her. "Thank you, Ms. Mallory. You're excused."

Detective Brady was waiting when she came out. "Hi, Leanne. You look lovely."

"Thanks. Do you have a minute?"

"Sure. Is anything wrong?"

The ADA emerged from the grand jury room. "Thanks again, Ms. Mallory. Detective, the grand jury will hear your testimony, now."

"I wanted to ask a question," Leanne said to the detective.

The ADA stirred. "Um, Detective? We're ready."

Leanne waved it away. "It's okay. I'll call you if I need to talk."

It was a beautiful day outside. She squinted a little against the bright sun as she made her way past the court buildings. When she reached the far side of the Municipal Building at One Centre Street, she paused, gazing at the trees budding over in City Hall Park. Out of the corner of her eye, she caught a flash of tan as someone ducked behind one of the immense concrete columns. She stopped and stared, waiting for it to reappear.

No, she was being paranoid again. She made for the stairs down to the Brooklyn Bridge station.

As she waited for the uptown Four train, a homeless man sat with his back against the wall. He was dirty, with tattered clothes, long tangled gray hair, filthy socks peeking through the splits in his old boots. She assumed he was sleeping, but his eyes opened, and he sat up and held out a dirty, crumbling Styrofoam cup. "Can you help me out, lady?"

Her first impulse was to turn away. But his eyes met hers. Pleading. Desperate. Alone.

She reached into her purse and pulled out a bill. "Here." She placed it in his cup.

His mouth fell open for a moment. He reached in with filthy fingers and fished out the bill, a twenty. "You're one fine lady. Thank you."

The speakers in the station crackled. "There is an uptown express train approaching the station."

"Good luck to you," she said and awaited the incoming train, its headlights growing in the tunnel's gloom, the rattle of steel wheels on steel rails growing louder.

A stout older woman sidled up next to her. "You have a good heart. God bless you."

Leanne thanked her. The train pulled into the station and she got on, finding a seat next to a door, smoothing her skirt as she sat and crossing her legs at the ankles.

As the train was turning into the Union Square stop, she glimpsed someone staring through the window of the door leading to the next car.

He turned away, sitting back and staring up at the advertising overhead. Wearing a tan windbreaker.

He was heavyset with a round face and wore a houndstooth snap-billed cap. He looked familiar.

She stood and walked to the rear of the car, glancing back to see if he noticed. But he didn't move. She sat on the opposite side of the car, and at Union Square, she got off and rushed to the next car back.

She checked for him again as she got on. No sign of him.

This car was more crowded, and few seats remained empty. Not good. She tried to stay out of the sight line of anyone looking through the windows between cars. A black man sitting near the end of one of the long benches moved a little and gestured for her to sit.

"Thank you," she said.

He nodded. He was wearing dark blue work pants and a dark blue work shirt. The train pulled out.

Blue pants. Blue shirt.

Like the maintenance worker at the funeral home.

She realized where she'd seen the guy in the cap and the windbreaker.

At Forty-Second, she got out and hurried downstairs to the Seven train. No sign of tan.

She glanced back when she was halfway down the long ramp. A glimpse of tan. She broke into a jog, furious with herself for having worn heels and fearful she might trip and fall.

She made the turn to the stairs to the platform, jammed with waiting passengers. Please, not a delay. Not now.

She edged up, staring back at the nearest stairway, then up and down the platform. He could be anywhere in the crowd.

The speaker system crackled. "There is a Flushing-bound local train approaching the station."

A steady stream of people was pouring down the stairs, and she caught a momentary flash of tan.

As soon as the train doors opened, she boarded and worked her way to the front end of the car. She grabbed a pole as the throng pushed onto the train. She wondered if the tan windbreaker had gotten on. The doors closed. She breathed more easily. One stop to go.

At Vernon-Jackson, she got off and rushed to the exit. No sign of him.

No, wait.

There. A few car lengths back.

She pushed through the turnstile and raced up the stairs, the first one to reach the sidewalk in front of P. J. Leahy's Pub. She rushed along Vernon, wishing she could run faster. At the corner of Fifty-First Avenue, she glanced back. The stalker in the tan windbreaker emerged from the subway steps and broke into a hard run.

She made it inside the heavy front door, but they kept the vestibule door locked. She fumbled with keys... Hands trembling... Key wouldn't slide into the lock... Deep breath. Out of the corner of her eye, through the vestibule window, she saw the stalker turning the corner and running straight for her building.

She slid the key into the lock, and the door opened. She slammed it shut behind her. The apartment door was easier. The stalker still hadn't made it inside the main door by the time she entered her apartment and locked the door.

She slipped off her heels and padded over to the living room window facing the street. Standing back, she peered between the slats of the blinds.

There he was, across the street. Houndstooth cap, tan windbreaker; without a doubt, it was the guy at the funeral home. Now he was watching her place.

Hand trembling, she took out Detective Brady's card and called her cell number. It rang three times.

"Brady."

Calm. She had to stay calm. Deep breath.

"Is this Leanne? Are you okay?"

She forced out the words. "Someone's following me."

"Are you sure?"

"He was at my mother's wake on Tuesday. A white Camry followed us out there. I saw him today after I left the grand jury. He followed me on the subway and chased me to my building."

"He chased you? Did you see him?" Detective Brady took the description. "Keep your door locked and stay away from the window. I'll be there as fast as I can. We'll arrange for police protection for you."

CHAPTER FIFTY-THREE

Thursday, March 9th, 11:27 AM

Kiley was livid. "What the fuck do you mean, postpone it? You're the one who asked for this meeting." Heads turned in the squad room.

Kim shoved her cell back in her purse. "Leanne's being stalked and today her stalker chased her on her way home from the grand jury." She turned to Mike, who looked like his mind was some place else. "If you drive, I'll call the One-Oh-Eight to arrange for protection."

He snapped out of it. "Huh?"

Come on, Mike. "Someone's stalking Leanne, and we need to hurry, remember?"

"Oh. Yeah, sorry. Let's go."

"Wait." Kiley held up a hand. "What am I supposed to tell IAB?"

"How about this? We have three stiffs with blank crime scenes, at least two of which we've connected to this case, and I wanted to make sure we don't add another."

"I'll see what I can do," Kiley replied.

Stephenson flagged them down on their way out the door. "The stiff from the High Line, Volnick, the EMT? Worked out of Northwest Queens. Astoria."

Astoria. Right next to Ravenswood, where they'd collared Choo and Lewis. The mysterious ambulance flashed in her mind. "Jimmy, check with the battalion and see if Volnick worked Sunday night or Monday morning. If he worked either shift, get the names of his crew."

· · ·

Two squad cars from the One-Oh-Eight sat parked in front of Leanne's building when they got there.

"Fast response." When Mike didn't answer, she remembered. "Hannah's surgery's today, isn't it?"

"Yeah. She went in at nine this morning. My sister and brother-in-law are at the hospital. Sloan-Kettering."

"Excellent hospital for the surgery she needs." She paused at Leanne's front door. "A lot of outstanding people are pulling for her and a lot of good professionals are doing their best. I bet she comes through okay." She buzzed Leanne's apartment.

"Hope so."

Leanne buzzed them in and had her apartment door open, waiting. "Nice to see you so calm," Kim said.

"I have to admit," Leanne replied, "I freaked out at first. But ten minutes after I called you, these guys were here."

"Officer Bridget Dubinsky." She extended her hand. She had blond hair tied back in a ponytail, large blue eyes, and an impish smile. "This is my partner, Officer Steve Larkin."

"Detective," he said as they shook hands. "Pleasure." He stood over six feet tall with broad shoulders, wearing an uncomfortable expression. "We'll be, er, Ms. Mallory's daytime protection, bringing her to and from work."

"She's also explained to us about her doctor's appointments," Dubinsky added, "and we'll do the OT on those nights."

Leanne blushed. "Transition. My first appointment's tonight."

Kim grinned at her. "Good for you."

208

"The instructions we got from our lieu made perfect sense once she filled in the blanks for us," Dubinsky said. "The other officers arrived before we did. They saw the guy in the tan windbreaker. He departed before anyone could question him." She patted the device attached to her uniform shirt. "But we've got the new body-cams. He shows up again, we'll bag him."

.   .   .

"I'm not happy, Harold. I told you to take out the tranny, and now you tell me he moseyed on down to Centre Street today. Meaning he testified before the grand jury."

"I followed her when she came out, and I tailed her home. I was waiting for her when the cops showed up. Besides, you said I had a week to…"

He had to fight to keep his temper. "Just because I gave you a week didn't mean it was okay for you to take the entire week."

"Please. I'm still sleeping in my car, and…"

"I hope you're moving around a lot."

"Sure."

No sense crying over… "All right. Get it done, and I'll pay you enough to get off the street. But this is your last chance."

CHAPTER FIFTY-FOUR

Thursday, March 9th, 1:28 PM

The text from Barlowe had asked her to meet him at the Union Square Greenmarket at one. Since the greenmarket wasn't there on Thursdays, there was nothing but open space.

He was leaning against a closed newsstand. "You're late." As ever, his clothes were perfect. Not even a smudge on his shoes.

"I've been busy. So have you, apparently."

"Sorry I wasn't able to answer you. Heard the news about Kincaid. I haven't been able to contact Robles, which has me worried. If he double-crossed me…" He shook his head. "Any leads on Kincaid's murder?"

"Not yet. Someone wiped the crime scene clean. No prints, no casings, no fibers. The shooter planned this, right down to the planes passing overheard, drowning out the sounds of the shots." And then she remembered. "One odd thing. A neighbor told us she'd seen Kincaid around for several months, on and off. I thought his move was recent."

Barlowe shrugged. "I told you what Robles told me. I had no reason to doubt him. If I find him, I'll give you the word." He paused, as if considering what to say next. "I believe Nolan was working him."

"Working him, how?" Kim grew wary.

Dad had described the two principal ways dirty cops "worked" guys in Narcotics. They took what they had in return for not arresting them, or they gave them what they needed in return for information.

"Supplying him from guys he'd ripped off." He took a step closer. "Don't get played at this stage of the game, Kim. Don't let Nolan get away with using 'Your dad and I were buddies, and he was such a wonderful guy' shit on you. He's as slimy as they come."

Sometimes, Dad had been, too. "So, now you are accusing Nolan?"

"I am. To you, not for the record, yet. I have to find Robles, first."

. . .

She was walking back along East Twenty-First Street when Vera Koshkin called. Whoever had altered the Williams case file hadn't done so by logging in and making entries. They'd hacked into the system and altered the master file. The department's IT Unit was now investigating.

Dobson flagged her down as soon as she entered the squad room. "ME is listing Chris' cause of death as 'cardiac arrest subsequent to insufflation of cocaine'. No way he was into coke, Kim. No way."

She smiled and patted his arm. "I understand. And you said there was no sign of coke anywhere in his apartment. So, someone was with him and cleaned it up afterward."

"Someone forced him to snort coke?"

She thought about it. "A definite possibility, or they might have cajoled him. If it was uncut, the heart attack would be a logical result."

"But why?"

She thought back to Kincaid's dead body. "Another pink slip?"

She sat down at her laptop. Time to see what she could learn about Francisco Robles. She checked him for priors—busted once for dealing, pled down to possession. Looked like he'd rolled on somebody. Which made him a suitable candidate to be a snitch.

She checked his case file to see who had collared him, although it had to be Barlowe.

But it wasn't.

It was Bob Nolan.

CHAPTER FIFTY-FIVE

Thursday, March 9th, 7:46 PM

Leanne felt far greater discomfort on her first visit to Dr. Helen Greene than if she hadn't arrived in a police car. Officers Larkin and Dubinsky waited outside.

The doctor put her at ease right away and conducted a thorough interview. After she finished making extensive notes, she looked Leanne up and down. "You realize you'll be entering an unfamiliar world?"

For the first time, Leanne could smile. "That's the whole point, isn't it?"

"It is, but I make a point of reminding my patients societal norms about beauty can make things difficult for trans women. And you may have already noticed how the working world treats women."

Leanne told her about Joyce and the harassment complaint.

"I see," Dr. Greene replied. "Well you've already had a taste of the worst." She looked her up and down. "You present very well, and you need not shed weight, which I always recommend before starting on hormones. You mentioned you've come out to your family and your friend. What about at work?"

"I've been to our Employee Assistance Program. At first, I thought I'd wait until I'd been on hormones for a while. But there's this case for which I'm a witness. Testifying might force my hand." She mentioned Joyce's comment about the harassment complaint making it an excellent time to come out.

The doctor sat back. "She's right. So, I'd recommend doing so whenever it feels right. In the meantime, I'll see you once each week for therapy. You control your voice, but a voice therapist will help you make it better. Once I'm convinced you're ready, I'll refer you to an endocrinologist. Fair enough?"

Leanne was walking on air as she emerged from the office building.

"Looks like somebody got pleasant news," Officer Dubinsky said with a teasing grin back in the patrol car.

Leanne's exhilaration lasted all the way home. But as Officer Larkin made the turn onto Fifty-First Avenue, a hunched over figure darted down the block toward Fifth Street, and all joy died.

"Okay, girl," Dubinsky said. "Out."

The patrol car pulled away even before the door closed, and tires screeched as it made the tight left turn at the corner onto Fifth Street. She watched for a moment from her front door before going inside, praying they'd get him.

As the minutes crawled by, worry mounted.

The buzzer sounded, and she opened the door for Officer Dubinsky.

"We chased him. He ran down Fifth toward Borden, and we lost him. Too many routes he could have chosen, or he might have hopped the fence into the train yard. We split up and looked around. Saw nothing. But don't you worry, the night crew is outside. You're safe." She patted the new body cam she wore. "Besides, we might get a pic."

After Dubinsky left, Leanne thought back on her session with Dr. Greene. It was official: she was on her way to transitioning.

Unless the thug out there stopped it.

.   .   .

Excellent timing for a night off. The Nets were near the end of a ten-game road trip and weren't playing again until tomorrow, so Jake was home. He'd prepared a pleasant dinner, and they'd shared a bottle of wine. Now she was curled up with him on the couch. The swelling around his eye had gone down and his bruises were fading.

Soft kisses were leading to caresses when the ringing of her cell jolted her. She popped up, ready to silence it, when she saw a number she didn't recognize.

The voice was robotic. "Good evening, Detective Brady, your days are numbered."

Jake stared at her. "What is it?"

She took a deep breath. I'm not faltering. Not now. Never. "Another problem." She opened the door and summoned a member of the protection detail. "I received a threatening phone call naming me. Please remain vigilant both with this building and with Jake."

CHAPTER FIFTY-SIX

Friday, March 10th, 9:02 AM

"They said nothing else?" Kiley absorbed the news of the phone threat with difficulty. "What the hell's the point?"

"The same as all the other shit. Misdirection. Distraction. Whoever this is, they don't need to threaten me if they plan to kill me. They can do it. And it's no coincidence Leanne's stalker was loitering outside her building last night. I got an e-mail this morning from Officer Dubinsky, who's on her detail. Her partner got an image of the guy on his body cam."

Kiley studied it. "Can't tell everything, but they got a significant amount of his face."

"Sheila Gregg is working up a sketch based on the photo, filling in some details. I should have it within the hour."

Kiley nodded. "Good. You can bring it to our meeting with IAB down at Hudson Street at eleven."

"Yep. Now, if you'll excuse me, Lieu, there's someone whose background I need to check."

•　　　•　　　•

Captain Jeremiah Forrest of IAB greeted Kim with warmth, then shook hands with Kiley and Mike and led them into a well-lit conference room. Most cops grew wary at the very mention of Internal Affairs. And most cops didn't have fathers with the checkered history hers did. But Captain Forrest, tall and thin, in his early forties, and his genial manner helped her relax a little. And she wasn't the one in trouble.

He introduced Lieutenant Steve Colangelo. "His unit will handle IAB's role in this case. He was in Narcotics before joining IAB. Lieutenant Kiley, since this is now a joint investigation, you and Lieutenant Colangelo will keep in regular contact."

Colangelo's olive complexion, cynical eyes and thick brows gave him a menacing appearance. Although he was anything but imposing in stature, Kim couldn't help but think he'd been tough on the street.

"I worked with your dad for a while," Colangelo said. "Very glad to have you working with us. Talk to me."

It didn't seem like a shot. Deep breath. They were on her side. She laid it all out, including Sylvia Walters' connection to Ice Williams and Kincaid. "I suspected Kincaid was operating with police protection. Some uniform from the Five-One was at the crib of one of the dead dealers—in the Four-Oh—the day after the shooting. He claimed he was investigating some burglary ring. Smelled like week-old fish, and when we tried to check his story, a sergeant named Phillips gave Lieutenant Kiley grief."

"It didn't strike me as troubling," Kiley said.

Colangelo nodded. "Understood. Proceed, Detective."

She recounted everything suspicious about the case, from destroyed evidence to their prime suspect being murdered. She concluded with Nolan's denials, Barlowe's suspicions and the tampering with the Ice Williams file.

Mike spoke up. "And don't forget the harassment, the assault on your boyfriend, and last night's death threat." He was better today. Hannah had survived the surgery and was recovering in ICU.

Colangelo was rock steady. "Anything else?"

"Yes. Someone has been stalking our lone eyewitness. Since Ryba learned about her from his time with us, I have to assume he passed the information on."

"And you want us to identify the recipient," Colangelo said.

"No. I know the recipient. The same person who was the impetus for taking down Ice Williams and propping up Viper Kincaid until he was ready to toss Kincaid aside; who tampered with the Ice Williams case file and left no signature. He's a former computer whiz-kid at Cornell University who could hack our case file system—George Barlowe."

CHAPTER FIFTY-SEVEN

Friday, March 10th, 1:30 PM

When Kim returned to PBMS, Stephenson had updated the case board: the ME had retrieved a nine-millimeter slug from Gustav Volnick's skull. Ballistics had examined the striations and declared a Glock 19 had fired it. And Sheila Gregg e-mailed her sketch based on Dubinsky's photo.

The four of them—Mike, Dobson, Stephenson and Kim—pored over the mugshot books but found no matches. She forwarded a copy to Colangelo to see if he was a current or former Member of Service. She also asked him to check to see which members of the Narcotics Unit carried Glock 19s.

Twenty minutes after she sent the e-mail, Cordell Washington, a member of Colangelo's team, called her. "I found one. Bob Nolan. We're putting him on Restricted Duty pending investigation based on his non-answers to your questions. He must surrender his piece, giving Ballistics a chance to check it."

"Thanks, Cord. I love how fast you guys work."

"Hey, you're one of us, now. Like our lieu said this morning. This is now a joint investigation. We're checking your sketch and bringing in DeMarco and Nolan for interviews on Monday."

"What about Barlowe? He's the guy."

218

Cord chuckled. "Sure looks like it. Problem is, you don't have hard evidence on him. Colangelo is hoping Nolan or DeMarco might tell us enough to implicate him."

·   ·   ·

"Sergeant Holloran asked me to give this to you." Dobson handed her a brown envelope.

"There's no stamp on it, and no postmark." The printing was the same as the ones she'd gotten at home. Her name and the address of PBMS, period. She donned gloves to open it, even though the crime lab had found nothing on the other envelopes.

"The sarge said a messenger delivered it a few minutes ago," Dobson said. "A teenager wearing jeans and a blue windbreaker."

A photo.

Not of her, or Jake.

Not of their building.

"It's Leanne." Kim's sense of dread intensified. "In front of her building. From the other side of Fifty-First."

Dobson laughed. "She's a guy? With those legs? No way." Her withering look snuffed any humor.

The photo included a date-and-time-stamp in the lower left corner. "They took this last night. About the same time as Dubinsky's body cam shot." Shit.

"So?"

"Leanne has two stalkers."

CHAPTER FIFTY-EIGHT

Friday, March 10th, 3:36 PM

Kim reviewed the images caught by the multidirectional video cameras standing watch over the primary entrance of PBMS. A young black male wearing jeans and a dark blue windbreaker had approached from the Second Avenue end of the block and entered the building through the main door. His jacket bore no insignia of any kind, so there was no way to tell if he worked for a delivery outfit. There was nothing in his demeanor to suggest he was nervous or angry. A moment later, he exited the same way and strolled back toward Second Avenue.

She had the technician scroll back to the best look at the messenger's face. "Enlarge and print, please. It might come in handy." She placed a copy on the case board close to the edge.

She received another e-mail from Cord Washington. The guy who'd been stalking Leanne Mallory was a former Member of Service named Harold Garner. Upon graduating from the Academy, they assigned him to the Five-One in the Bronx. He'd then moved to Nolan's unit until being terminated for drug abuse.

The Five-One. Sergeant Henry Phillips' precinct.

Cord had caught the connection, too. The e-mail had two attachments: a photo of Phillips and one of Garner. Kim e-mailed back, thanking him and asking to check into both Phillips' and Barlowe's backgrounds—Academy classes and assignments—to see what else popped up.

"I remember his name," Mike said. "If memory serves, he was Bob's partner for a while."

"We should talk to Bob tonight, before the IAB interview on Monday."

"We're too new at this IAB thing to go screwing around with procedure, Kim."

Her flip comment remained unspoken when she got a check-in from Jake. *Still breathing. Nothing ominous. Be home for dinner?*

She had nearly finished tapping out a noncommittal response when Mike leaned over and said, "You need a break. Go home on time. Relax. Be with Jake."

He was right. She needed Jake's arms around her, calming her nerves. She erased her incomplete response and replaced it with, *Yes.*

A moment later, his reply came back. *Glory be!*

But before she left, she forwarded the photos of Garner and Phillips to Officer Dubinsky in case Phillips was the second stalker.

CHAPTER FIFTY-NINE

Friday, March 10th, 5:02 PM

Andy waited until the office had emptied. It was the lull before the quarterly closing, and everyone left by five o'clock. Even Joyce had gone. All week, he'd been wearing women's tailored slacks and cotton blouses. He checked himself in the compact mirror now hanging from the side of his section of the bullpen—androgynous, as he wanted it. It was time to tell Mr. Goddard, the company controller.

Mr. Goddard started at the knock. "Andy. I've been meaning to talk to you all day. Close the door, will you?"

As Andy sat, Goddard jumped right in. "HR has concluded its investigation of your harassment complaint. Mr. Meagher has resigned rather than face termination, and Mr. Franco has accepted re-assignment to a non-managerial position in our Jersey City office."

"Thank you, Mr. Goddard. It's wonderful news." His anxiety drained away.

"Evelyn Gleason has done well so far as acting manager, and I like to promote from within. So, I'll have her continue on a trial basis. If she's as effective as I think she'll be, we'll make it permanent. You get on well with her, don't you?"

"Yes, I do." Moving the conversation to his transition would be difficult.

Goddard didn't pause. "Good. She'll need plenty of support. I'll need you to keep working like you have been, taking on a major suspense account project and getting it done. You're a resource I didn't realize we had. I want you to function as Evelyn's assistant. It's unofficial, for the time being. Show you can do the job, and we'll promote you to senior accountant when we promote Evelyn. Fair enough?"

It hit him like a boulder. "I... That's so kind of you."

"Kindness has nothing to do with it. You've earned it. Do you accept?"

The euphoria drained away. "Before I do, I should explain why I came in."

"Go on."

"I'm transgender. I've begun transitioning to a female identity. It's a lengthy process. But in the next few months, I'll start on hormone replacement therapy and then my appearance will change. At some point I'll be, um, dressing the part. Here at work."

Goddard sat back. "I see. Will you miss work?"

"Not in the near future. Any surgery wouldn't be for at least a year."

Goddard studied him. "My single metric is how well someone does the job. I don't understand this transgender business." He waved it away. "But you're an outstanding worker and you get along with people. If wearing skirts will make you more comfortable in your work, I don't care." He looked Andy up and down. "So, do you accept the senior accountant position?"

"Yes, with pleasure. Thanks for understanding."

"I don't understand."

"Accepting is even more important, so thank you."

He had trouble containing his excitement as he packed up and shut everything down for the weekend. But as he walked through the lobby, his euphoria evaporated. Officers Larkin and Dubinsky were waiting. The threat was still out there.

.　　.　　.

A wonderful dinner prepared by Jake awaited Kim when she arrived home. He refilled her wineglass until she'd drunk a little more than she could handle. He followed with affectionate nuzzling, pushing all her buttons, igniting her passions as they undressed each other. By the time she collapsed on top of him, everything else was background noise.

She kissed his cheek as she rolled off him, cuddling beside him.

He grinned. "Think it'll be even better when we're married?"

Everything rushed back. She couldn't say anything.

"Kim? Hello?"

She couldn't stand her work putting him in danger. She also couldn't stand to hurt him.

"You're having second thoughts, aren't you?" he asked.

"Not about marrying you. I love you. But…"

He turned away from her.

"Jake, please listen…"

"Not tonight."

.　　.　　.

To: <Leanne>
From: allimall@gmail.com <Alli>

Dear Leanne,

I'm so sorry for what happened at the wake. Bart breaking into my e-mail account is the lowest thing he's ever done. I set up this new e-mail address at the library. Please use it to e-mail me.

Your news shocked me a little. Coming when Mom was so sick, I guess I wasn't able to deal with it. Tbh, I'm still not totally okay with it, but it's your life and I respect it. I'll be there for you. I wish we'd had time to talk.

We should, soon.
Just us girls. Keep me posted about how you're doing. Love, Alli.

.　　　.　　　.

To: <Alli>
From: <Leanne>
Thanks, Alli. I'm well. Job is improving, might get a promotion. And I'm going to be a witness in a big criminal case. Sorry, can't tell you more about it.

The thing is, someone has been stalking me, and I now have police protection.

They even drive me to and from work and doctor's appointments. It's a little scary, but makes transitioning look easier. Love, Leanne.

P.S. Bart's a weasel. You deserve way better.

CHAPTER SIXTY

Saturday, March 11th, 7:22 AM

Kim's ringing cell jolted her out of a sound sleep. The same robotic voice said, "You can't win this. It's impossible. Perhaps taking the painless way out, like Daddy did, is the answer."

As with the call about her "numbered days", this one displayed no name. A burner phone for certain. Calls and mysterious photos from the same source. And he had to realize she'd connect the calls and photos to him. He wasn't stupid and had been anything but careless. She could only conclude he wanted her to connect them.

Jake sat up. "Who called?"

"He didn't say."

"Another threat?"

"Yes."

"Isn't there some way you can track him down?"

She sat by him on the bed. "You can't help me with this. Not brainstorming, check-listing, or being a sympathetic listener. He'll use whatever he can against me."

"So, why did you turn silent when I mentioned marriage last night?"

"You promised me we wouldn't talk about it until after this case is over."

He drew back, stunned. "I didn't plan anything. I was talking in general. Won't it be nice…"

She waved it away. "You don't get it. I have to be a fanatic if I'm to run this motherfucker to ground, because he is."

Jake stared at her, remaining silent.

"He's very smart, and very evil."

"You know who he is?"

"I know what he is." She drew back a little. "I should have moved out. I might have protected you. But it's too late, now." She got dressed.

"So, conversation over?" he asked.

"For now, yes. I'm sorry, Jake. I'm in a war and I need to keep you safe."

He said nothing else until she was almost ready to leave. "Fine. But I told you before, I'm staying with you. You go, I go."

"You can't go where I go. But I appreciate the sentiment."

"Okay. Let's at least make the promise. I don't care when it happens—sooner, later, doesn't bother me. Let's say we will."

She had to shove the doubts away. She would never meet anyone like Jake. Not in this life.

She leaned over and kissed him. "All right. Yes."

Her cell chimed. A text from Dubinsky. *Leanne OK. But urgent you meet us at 54th and Center, right by the river.*

CHAPTER SIXTY-ONE

Saturday, March 11th, 7:53 AM
"Fast trip from Brooklyn." Officer Dubinsky greeted Kim as she alighted from the Eight-Four's patrol car and thanked the officer at the wheel for the lift. "You need to see this." They crossed Center Boulevard to the plaza of Hunter's Point South Park and Dubinsky pointed to the reeds at water's edge below the walkway.

A dead body was lying face down on the rocks. Attendants from the Queens ME's Office lifted the body to the walkway. As soon as Kim saw the face, she recognized it. "Garner."

"Yep," Dubinsky replied. "A jogger saw him at about six this morning and called it in. Steve and I were in early, catching up on some paperwork. We responded to the call."

A technician from the ME's office approached. "He took one shot in the back of the head, no exit wound, and one clear through the neck. Given the tides in these parts, I'd say he floated in at high tide, caught on a rock, then stayed as the tide went out."

"Floated in?" Kim asked.

He pointed downriver. "He was already dead when he hit the water, somewhere down there. Incoming tide, these waters flow north. Tide's been coming in for about an hour, so high tide was about one o'clock this morning. I'd estimate time of death between ten and eleven last night. He hit the water downriver, floated on the tide for two or three hours."

Steve Larkin sidled up beside Kim. "I'd say somewhere in Greenpoint. I sail and fish these waters a lot. Tidal current along this stretch is less than two knots, and it slows at the mouth of Newtown Creek."

"Thanks." Kim turned back to the guy from the ME's office. "Please get the slug to Ballistics and have them get the results to me as soon as they can."

.   .   .

Kim rushed back to PBMS, opened her laptop, and checked the tower pings from both threatening calls she'd received. The first had been from near Battery Park, the second from Brooklyn Heights.

She updated the case board with information of Garner's death.

Mike walked in while she was adding the details of the threatening calls. "You got another one? So, you're adding it to the board?"

"Yes, to both. This morning's call originated and ended at the same cell tower. He was in my neighborhood. He might as well have taken out a full-page ad in the *New York Times*."

"You think this is Barlowe, or someone working for him?"

"It's Barlowe."

"You think he's trying to scare you? I'd think he's smarter than that."

"He's playing some sick mind game." She pointed to the entry taped to the wall she'd printed out from a hackers' site. It described Barlowe as a "genius" who'd gotten the nickname "Houdini" in college because "he could get into anything".

"I'm still not getting it," Mike said.

"He sent the photo of Leanne from the other night, figuring no one saw him. One of those computer geeks who believes he's smarter than the rest of us. I think he's taunting me."

Mike nodded. "So, I guess we keep her protection from the One-Oh-Eight in place."

"Not good enough." She returned to her laptop and banged out an e-mail to Yvette Driscoll requesting she place Leanne in protective custody as soon as possible.

Then, she checked the Master Roll Call. "Bob Nolan is designated for Restricted Duty. He's been out on leave since yesterday afternoon."

Mike sat across from her. "Rubber Gun Duty will drive him straight up a wall. I wish IAB hadn't scheduled his interview for Monday."

"Me, too." A single choice remained. "We have to talk to him. Today."

"But shouldn't we ask IAB…"

"Forrest said we're part of IAB, now, and this won't wait. I need to discover what Nolan had on Robles, and anything else he can tell us. And I need you to convince him to come clean to us and to IAB."

"At least call Forrest to…"

"No."

He stopped and stared at her. "What's eating you?"

She took a deep breath. "Barlowe played me, Mike. From the beginning. He found out Nolan was grumbling about our first meeting and used it to cement my notion pegging Nolan as the dirty guy. And it gave him a way to track our progress even after we kicked Ryba off the case. Shit, I told him everything."

"Calm down. Work the facts. Lately, you've been all emotion. It's hurting your game, clouding your judgment." He studied her. "What are you so eager to talk to Bob about?"

It spilled out. "How did Barlowe find out what killed my dad? His references have been too specific to be a mere lucky guess. Nolan seems to have known my dad pretty well, so he might have some idea." She took a deep breath. "And I need to apologize to him. I'm thinking Barlowe may have set him up, too."

"Well, the hardest thing for an excellent cop is admitting he, or she, was wrong."

"Like my dad used to say."

He gave her his big brother look, which she sometimes loved, sometimes resented. "Why don't you forgive him, already? Hold on to the helpful things he taught you and be an excellent cop?"

"I forgave him a long time ago."

"Well, something made you take it back. What did Shakespeare say? 'What's gone and what's past help should be past grief'."

It should be, but it wasn't. She would have to revisit it.

CHAPTER SIXTY-TWO

Saturday, March 11th, 1:28 PM

Kim tried calling Nolan twice on their way to Staten Island. No answer. Mike didn't hide his worry as they pulled up to Nolan's house.

"He may not be too friendly," Mike said. "Why not let me handle the preliminaries?"

But whatever Mike had in mind vanished when Bob answered the door. He looked like hell and smelled like a brewery.

"Come on in." Bob gestured with the beer can he was holding. "Would you care for one?"

They both declined.

Bob snorted. "Always on duty, both of you. Commendable." He drained the can. "They're putting me in the Rubber Gun Room. You convince them I'm involved with your shooting?"

"Are you?" Mike asked.

Bob stared at him. "*Et tu?*"

Mike sat next to Kim on the couch. "We graduated together from the Academy."

Bob focused on his beer can. "I know."

"Do you?" Mike asked. "Remember water rescue training, in the pool on freezing winter mornings? The impossible physical demands, steering

232

clear of the sixth floor, the discipline? We followed with foot tours in the same shitty neighborhood. Promoted to second grade the same year, first grade a year apart. You were an excellent cop, and I hope you still are."

"But you're not sure." Nolan sat back and took a long swig of beer.

"Let's start with that," Mike said. "You were sober for fifteen years."

"Fifteen years, two months and four days, to be exact. Last night seemed the perfect time to end it, although I'd been considering it for a while."

"When Kim and I first met with you at the bagel place?"

"Not then. When I told her someone whose name didn't appear on the access log had changed the Williams case file, she didn't believe me."

Kim considered making a comment but decided against it.

Bob turned a bleak smile on her. "You're a bulldog, like your old man was. Shit, Joe Brady scared off the entire old Internal Affairs Division. Then again, they scared easy—bunch of cheese-eating rats. But even IAB never brought him down, maybe because he was Dan Brady's son. Or maybe they realized he was an excellent cop."

It was time to take charge. "I believe you about the file, Bob. I admit I didn't, at first, and I'm sorry. But a technician at One-PP confirmed someone hacked in and altered the case file with direct entries to the master file. She explained it's why nothing showed on the access log."

Nolan cast a rueful glance at his beer can. "So, why am I on Rubber Gun duty?"

"IAB is looking at your unit." After considering whether it was against procedure, she added, "and a guy we're sure is connected to the case, an EMT named Volnick, was murdered the other night with a Glock 19..."

Nolan's face hardened again. "And you think I did it."

"No, I don't. But you're the one member of your unit with the same weapon. Ballistics will check and rule you out as a suspect." She tried a grin. "Unless you did it."

He relaxed. "I see you also have your dad's sense of humor. God, he was proud of you."

She turned serious. "How did you discover he died from an OxyContin overdose, and he'd been hoarding a large stash of it? The department never released any such information, and you didn't guess."

"Is IAB going to ask about this?"

Mike shot her a warning look, but she ignored it. "We're attached to IAB for this case, now. I don't think they'll ask, and I'm not asking as IAB. I'm asking as Joe Brady's daughter." She hoped he didn't catch her voice thickening.

"Okay. A few years back, I collared a street dealer named Robles..."

She started. "Francisco Robles?"

"Yeah. He agreed to become a snitch."

"A confidential informant?" Mike asked.

"Didn't want him in the system as a CI. I told your dad about him because he and I had done the same thing for years. We'd keep them out of the CI system because it was then a lot easier to squeeze them for information whenever they held back. I was telling him things hadn't changed much since he'd dropped his papers."

She gestured for him to continue.

"In early January, Robles came to me and told me someone had shaken him down twice, some old guy—his words, not mine—for OxyContin. His description fit your dad. He'd ripped him for a couple hundred pills. When I checked with your dad, he said it was bullshit. But Robles' description was too on-the-money for it to have been anyone else."

"Was Barlowe still your partner when you first collared Robles?" Kim asked.

"Yes."

So, she'd found the connection. "Thank you, Bob. I'm sorry I got it wrong about you. One other question. To your knowledge, did Robles have any connection with Viper Kincaid?"

"None he ever told me about. Once Barlowe and I split as partners, I got no information on Kincaid. We got a tip last fall about some operation in Queens, and I wondered if it involved Kincaid. But they passed it along to Queens and there was never any other news about it."

Kim and Mike exchanged glances. It could have been Lindenwood.

Nolan caught it. "What?"

She needed to press him. "Bob, I owe you a lot for what you've told me. More than you can know. But this is key. Who would have received the information?"

"Why?"

"I can't tell you. It might affect your statement on Monday, and I can't take the risk."

"I know who we should have notified. One of the Queens Special Narcotics units."

Kim had one last question. "Your original version of the case report mentioned Svetlana Bolshoi. Why did you tell me you didn't remember her?"

"Because, when you first mentioned the name, I didn't. I only recalled it when you put her in context. I also told you I'd written Hill's collar up as Barlowe's. You didn't believe that, either."

"I'm sorry, Bob. But suppose it had been you investigating? Suppose the individual claimed they'd written something not appearing in the file, and there was no record of it being altered? I don't think you'd have believed them, either. It always comes down to what we can prove."

"Where's DeMarco fit in all this?" Mike asked.

Nolan scoffed. "He's an asshole. Looks nervous these days. Like he knows the shit's about to fall on him and can't figure out where from or why."

"How the hell did he ever rate a command?" Mike asked in disgust.

"He has a rabbi somewhere. Couldn't say who." Nolan finished his beer and fetched another. "You sure you don't want any?" He looked right at Kim. "You look like you could use one."

"And you look like you've had more than enough," she replied.

He continued to the kitchen and returned with a fresh can. "You are your father's daughter. For sure. But come Monday morning, they'll say,

'Nolan, your police career is over.' Either I admit to illegal activity and lose my job or deny it and lose my job and get convicted." He popped the top. "I'm a dead man. This is my anesthesia."

"We'll both be there," Kim said. "And I'll be asking a lot of the questions. Just describe everything you know about DeMarco's command. Mike and I will both fight to make sure the cost to you is minimal."

Nolan stared at the beer can. "I have nothing else to help you. Can't even help myself."

Mike stood and clapped a hand on his friend's shoulder. "Yeah, you can. Get into a program. Get back off the sauce. You did it before, do it again. And Kim's right. Tell IAB everything you know. They're not the old IAD. No cheese-eaters there."

"Admit to ripping off dealers instead of collaring them? Using confiscated drugs to buy information?"

"I'll start off by asking something about the case," Kim replied. "Answer me straight, then bring out the other stuff without being asked. You told me once you were trying to uncover information related to the case. Give us the details, including what you've told us this afternoon. IAB will go easy on you. And if you can give us anything we can check out in advance, we'll use what we find to help."

Nolan considered it. "You might be right."

"I haven't mentioned who in your unit we're looking at." She had to be careful. She was edging close to coaching a subject of her own investigation. "But we both know."

Nolan's jaw dropped. "Holy shit. You *are* your father's daughter. All right. Look into the case of German Montero. Find him and talk to him."

She extended her hand, and he took it.

"We have to get back," Mike said. "But I'll call you in the morning to check in, okay?"

Nolan's eyes locked on his. "Brothers-in-arms, huh?"

"You got it, Bob. Brothers-in-arms."

CHAPTER SIXTY-THREE

Saturday, March 11th, 6:28 PM

Leanne clutched two enormous shopping bags in one hand and opened the door to her apartment with the other. Officers Dubinsky and Larkin helped her carry everything inside.

Dubinsky grinned at her. "Quite a haul."

"Sorry I took so much time," Leanne replied. "But I'm still building up my work wardrobe."

Dubinsky's grin widened. "You're not sorry. You loved every minute."

Larkin frowned. "Mistake being in here. I'll wait outside. Unless you need something else."

"No, thanks very much." She flashed a brief smile. "I still can't believe you guys took me shopping."

Dubinsky laughed, "Hey, it's the easiest overtime we've ever worked. Besides..."

Gunshots. The living room window blew apart.

Dubinsky shoved her to the floor and piled on top of her.

More shots.

The TV screen splintered. Sparks flew. A lamp bulb shattered.

"This is Dubinsky; shots fired; Send back up."

Hard to breathe...

"You okay?" Dubinsky cried.

.   .   .

Kim had spent the rest of the afternoon researching German Montero. Barlowe had busted him for possession and he'd gotten a one-year sentence. He was out in seven months. His parole officer had nothing but excellent things to say about him. Montero checked in every week, now living and working in Corona, in Queens, gave every sign of staying away from the drug world. She wondered what information he'd provide they could use.

She'd been ready to sign out when a call came in from the One-Oh-Eight about Leanne. Mike had a car warmed up when she jumped in, and they sped toward Hunters Point.

Not Leanne.

Stay in control. She called Yvette Driscoll. "I don't have details other than there were shots fired, and Leanne was unconscious when the call for backup came in. CSU is on the way. So is an FDNY bus. Now, can we get her into witness fucking protection?"

Yvette's voice remained steady. "I'll get there as soon as I can."

Mike hit the siren and grill lights as they entered the Midtown Tunnel. "Easy, kiddo."

She caught herself before snapping off a sharp reply. Deep breath. Yvette was doing her job. Nolan's comment about being her father's daughter rang in her ears. He'd had a point.

"So," Mike said. "A .44 magnum killed Garner?"

Good. Something on which to focus. She'd gotten the report an hour ago. "Yeah. Hollow point. Ballistics identified the weapon as a Ruger Redhawk."

Mike whistled. "Heavy duty and not department issued."

She already had Dobson checking on all RedHawks registered in New York, though she was certain he wouldn't find what they were looking for.

"Wasn't a Redhawk used killing Kincaid?" Mike asked.

"Caliber matches, but the slug was fucked up, so nothing for Ballistics."

Mike parked on Vernon. CSU already had the street blocked off.

Dubinsky approached Kim thirty yards from Leanne's building. "She's okay, she wasn't hit, she fainted. You'll find her in that ambulance, but she's okay."

A CSU officer passed by. "Don't fuck up my crime scene."

Kim checked. They were halfway between Vernon and the building. "This far down?"

"Yeah. The shooter fired from across the street. So far, no shell casings."

"What about slugs?"

"Found five inside, three of them too fucked up to be useful, two buried in the wall—plasterboard, so we might get something useful. We'll send them to Ballistics."

"What caliber?" The absence of shell casings suggested they had to be from a revolver. Like a Ruger Redhawk.

"Looks like a .44 magnum."

Larkin approached, white as a ghost. "My fault. I should never have gone inside." He explained about the packages. "I was leaving through the front hallway when the first shots were fired. The shooter ceased firing as I reached the door. Then he started firing again from behind that van. I couldn't see him, and I couldn't return fire. I ran across the street to get a better angle, but by then he'd fled."

"We can have the transit guys pull the video," Mike said, "in case they got something."

Leanne was sitting in the ambulance, shaken but alert, when Kim got to it. "Hi, Detective."

"Hey, you." Kim gave Leanne's arm a squeeze. "You okay?"

"I guess so. It's kind of unreal."

"Your feelings will change." She gestured toward the building. "You can't stay here. Even with protection, it's not safe. I'm working on getting you moved into witness protection." Which was not the complete truth. She needed Yvette's buy in. Best to kick start her thinking.

.   .   .

Leanne's head ached. Her living room window lay in shattered pieces of glass on the floor. Yellow tape blocked off the street.

Someone had just tried to kill her.

The paramedic who'd examined her kept his distance once he realized she was trans. But Officer Larkin paced back and forth, stopping by every few minutes to ask, "You sure you're okay?" That made her smile.

Ms. Driscoll from the DA's office ducked under the yellow tape and made her way over to the ambulance. "How're you feeling?"

"A little shaky."

"Just a little? Outstanding."

No one had ever called her outstanding. "Detective Brady said something about witness protection?"

Ms. Driscoll stared at the remains of the front window. "You can't stay here, for sure. You work over on West Street?"

"Yes. Between Murray and Vesey."

Ms. Driscoll turned to the paramedic. "She okay to go?"

He shrugged. "All, um, she did was faint."

The ADA turned back to her. "Please go inside with Officer Dubinsky and pack enough clothes for a week, work and casual. Be careful not to disturb anything with a yellow tab next to it or the tabs themselves. I'll make some calls."

Larkin planted himself at the front door. Inside, Leanne pulled out one suitcase and a duffel bag. She packed the new work outfits—tailored slacks and blouses—in the suitcase, along with a few skirts. She tossed everything else into the duffel.

"You got much nicer things than I do," Dubinsky said as she helped her shut the suitcase.

Broken glass crunched as Ms. Driscoll made her way to the bedroom. "Leanne, you are now in witness protection. You'll be staying at a hotel close to your office building. Do not tell anyone. Never use the hotel phone for outside calls, or your own cell. We'll provide you with throwaways. You'll get a stipend every week for meals, and police officers will take you to and from work and anywhere else you need to go."

Leanne turned to Dubinsky. "You guys?"

"They'll take you tonight," Ms. Driscoll said. "The First Precinct will provide protection unless you return here. Then Larkin and Dubinsky will bring you. Please keep those trips to a minimum and vary days and times."

"What about my doctor appointments?"

"We'll handle them, too." Dubinsky hugged her. "Come on, girl. We got work to do."

·   ·   ·

With Yvette standing beside her, Kim watched as Larkin pulled away with Dubinsky and Leanne in the back seat. "Whoever did this won't stop until he locates her. And he knows where she works."

"The First Precinct will assign a plainclothes detail to drive her to her office and back. They'll vary the cars used each trip and take roundabout routes. I'll arrange with the One-Oh-Eight to have Larkin and Dubinsky use an unmarked car for her appointments." Yvette dropped to a whisper. "We've never used this place before. So, anyone who knows our usual locations won't have a clue where she is."

Mike approached, tucking his cell back in his pocket. "I think we're done here for tonight."

Kim heaved a sigh of relief upon returning to the car. Mike glanced at her as he slid into the driver's seat. The first day they'd been partners, he'd given her the same look. It had several variations, but the message was always the same: girl first, cop second. Before long, he'd become her big brother.

She didn't want or need a protector, she wanted a fellow cop to watch her back while she watched his. He didn't try to "teach" her much these days, and he'd even taken a back seat on this case. He'd backed her up with Kiley more than once.

"Hey, you okay?" He snapped her back to the present.

"Fine. I'm glad Leanne is safe. Were you speaking with Nolan?"

"Earlier, while you were talking to Leanne. He said to tell you he decided you were right, and he'll see us Monday. But I was talking to my sister. Hannah's still in ICU and my sister's camped out at Sloan-Kettering. I would drive you home after we sign out, but..."

"Don't be silly. Drop me off at the Two train and I'll be fine. The Clark Street station is a block and a half from home. Nothing to worry about there."

CHAPTER SIXTY-FOUR

Sunday, March 12th, 12:15 AM

Although the subway car was about half full, no one else got off at Clark Street, and Kim stepped off the train onto a deserted platform. Halfway up the stairs to the elevator, she stopped. She could swear she'd heard footsteps.

She peered down toward the platform but saw no one. This pace was getting to her. Her legs ached as she finished the climb.

No one else was waiting. As always, the elevator took forever to drop to the lower level.

More steps, this time right behind her. She swung around.

"Kim Brady, as I live and breathe."

Barlowe.

Stay cool. Give nothing away. "Hello, George. Odd place to hang out on a Saturday night, isn't it?"

"I have a friend who lives nearby. Weird station. No stairs. I had no idea you lived around here." The elevator door opened, and he gestured inside. "After you, my dear."

She stepped inside.

He was right behind her. He stood by the panel, pressed a button and the door slid closed. The elevator started with an upward jolt. "You haven't called. I thought you were keeping me in the loop."

They were playing a chess game, and Barlowe had made the first move. "You said you'd get back to me when you had something on Robles." Aggressive defense struck her as the best policy. "Any news to report?"

"My lieu tells me IAB is calling him and Nolan on the carpet. I told you I wasn't ready."

She shrugged. "Guess not. But I am." Grandad's Chief's Special, tucked in the waistband of her slacks, nudged her lower back. She leaned back against the opposite side of the elevator to reach it. "And it's my investigation, remember?"

He flashed an icy grin. "You have all the evidence you need?"

"I have the correct questions to ask."

"They were smart to put you in charge." The elevator stopped, and the door opened. The lobby of the Hotel St. George was empty. Before she could react, he hit the "door close" button, then shoved a small block of wood on the floor into the door's path to keep it from closing.

Stay cool. "And several are for Robles. If you want to help, bring him in so I can question him."

His grin grew wider. "You're good."

"I've got a good opponent. Smart." Downstairs, another train rolled in. Their isolation wouldn't last much longer.

His grin vanished. "Oh, I think so. Very smart."

"A regular Houdini."

The flicker of concern across his face was infinitesimal. "Interesting analogy. What made you think of it?"

There were voices downstairs, waiting for the elevator. Time was growing short. "It just came to me. What about Robles?"

"I still can't find him. I told you, I think someone got to him."

"Nolan? Your issues with him date back to the Williams case, correct?"

"He's a possibility." The concern was no longer a flicker.

She tucked her hands behind her, resting on the bar at the rear of the elevator. Her right hand rested against the grip of the Chief's Special.

Pounding on the door below. "Hey! Who's holding up the fucking elevator?"

"And he was Nolan's snitch at the outset, right?" she asked. "I mean, Nolan's the one who first collared Robles."

"Is that what he told you? In between stories of him and your father in the good old days?"

"It's in Robles' case file. Which no one but Nolan and I have accessed. You keep bringing up Nolan being friends with my father. My father never mentioned him to me."

"He wouldn't have wanted his baby girl to learn about the things he was doing. Be careful, Kim. Squeeze Nolan too hard, and he might spill all sorts of filth about your father."

"My father has gone to his ultimate reward, as several parties keep reminding me. If Nolan tells anything about him, it'll be ancient history."

More pounding.

"I'm concerned for you, Kim. It must hurt, hearing all those things about him." He shook his head. "I hope you don't lead with what I've told you. Without evidence, it's mere hearsay."

"I know."

He hit the "door open" button. The lobby remained empty. "I should go." He made a sweeping gesture with his arm. "After you." He pressed the button for the station level.

She'd been stranded down in the station when someone held up the elevator, so she'd experienced what the guys down there were feeling right now. But Barlowe wasn't about to give in, so she couldn't, either. She stepped toward the lobby but stopped and turned around, taking a wide stance to block the door from closing. "When did Robles tell you Kincaid's location?"

245

"An hour before I told you. Why?"

"When you told me, he'd already been dead for four or five hours. So, he was already dead when Robles told you."

"You think Robles killed Kincaid?" He chuckled and shook his head. "Robles was a miserable little street mope."

"I thought you said he was a mid-level dealer."

"Some mid-level dealers are miserable little street mopes. Didn't your dad tell you how things work on the street?"

"I keep hearing about how good Kincaid's security was, but he was all alone..."

"Kincaid was controllable."

"... and whoever set up the Cove shooting did so up by convincing Paredes to operate in the open with no avenue of escape. If Robles was a street mope who was he working for? Who replaces Kincaid? Because he's the person who ordered the Cove shooting."

"My dear, you have nailed the question. I don't have a clue."

"You claimed you're on top of this."

"I am on top of it." He pressed the "door close" button, even though she was blocking it.

More pounding from downstairs. "Let's go, already."

She ignored it. "I still don't understand why Robles told you where to find Kincaid."

He turned hard. "Because I told him I'd cut his balls off if he didn't."

Time for a gambit. "Oh, I'm sure you threatened him. But what made you think he'd be able to tell you?"

"I deduced it from..."

"Wait. 'Deduced'?"

"Yes. Deduced. Inferred from logical reasoning; concluded from known facts or general principles. You know, like all brilliant detectives since Sherlock Holmes."

"Oh, of course."

"As I was saying, I deduced it from many comments he'd made to me. It's too complex to explain it to you, now." He gave an approving nod, as if she were a ninth grader who'd solved a tough algebra problem. "You have superb questions, and Robles should provide answers. Too bad for you, he's fled his last known."

"With his wife?"

"Not likely. She's reported to have returned to the Dominican Republic." Barlowe's eyes narrowed as he studied her. "You think you know. But you have no evidence. Nothing you can prove. Which means the killer—whoever he is—will remain at least one step ahead of you. We'll keep on it and I'll help however I can. We'll get him." He gestured toward the lobby, and she stepped back.

He remained on the elevator as the door slid shut.

CHAPTER SIXTY-FIVE

Sunday, March 12th, 7:42 AM

No one else was in. She updated the case board with the latest on Leanne and added a notation in red under Barlowe's name, "Familiar with Kincaid". She also called Colangelo and left a message to get back to her.

Her immediate concern was what to do with Barlowe next. For a moment, she chided herself for not taking him into custody right there in the Clark Street Station last night. But she'd had no basis for an arrest, no probable cause. He could explain away everything he'd said as conjecture. The intangible subtleties, the look in his eye, the tone of his voice, and his body language—all of which had taunted her—was not evidence.

She checked the Master Roll Call. There it was. Barlowe was out on leave.

For the next two weeks.

.   .   .

As soon as Dobson and Stephenson arrived, she asked them to track down Francisco Robles and, if he'd ever married, his wife. Kiley wasn't in, so when Mike arrived, she had him accompany her down to IAB. He looked like hell.

"Hannah making progress?"

"Serious but stable condition. They say they got it all." After he parked the car, he took a photo from his wallet—a teen girl in a gown with a guy. "Her first prom date, last spring."

"She's a beautiful girl." She grinned at him. "I can see the family resemblance."

"Not much. She sure as hell doesn't have my nose." He turned somber. "Kim, I couldn't stay in the ICU with her. All those tubes..."

"She'll be okay, Mike. I'll bet she has your fight in her, too."

He stared straight ahead. "I don't have much fight these days, I'm afraid."

"We'll see." She led the way inside where Colangelo and his team were waiting. Once in the conference room, Kim described her encounter with Barlowe in the elevator.

"So, he knows you know," Colangelo said.

"Yes. Which makes him both more cautious in his movements and more desperate to eliminate anyone who can give him away. His two weeks of leave will allow him more freedom of movement. He already tried to burn Leanne Mallory. Assume he'll try again and go after the other witnesses in protective custody if he can find them."

"Not likely," Colangelo said. "They keep all information restricted to an as-needed basis."

Not much comfort. "What about helpers?"

Brandon Hollis stood and turned a blank page on a flip chart, revealing a diagram. "I checked into your sergeant in the Bronx. Henry Phillips. Graduated the Academy four years before Barlowe, so no immediate connection. Assigned to the Seven-Four in Brooklyn, made sergeant after five years, the minimum, and transferred to the Five-One in the Bronx. But his last year in Brooklyn, guess who got assigned to the same precinct."

"Harold Garner," Kim said.

"Correct. They even did some street busts together."

"Establishing an early narcotics connection." Interesting. "What else in Sergeant Phillips' file might interest us?"

"Not much," Hollis replied. "Exemplary career, decorated three times. Even did a stint on some special mayor's task force back in the early 2000s. It's odd he got to sergeant and stopped. Never took the lieutenant's exam. Unusual for a go-getter. Also, he bought a house three years ago in the Country Club section of the Bronx, over by Eastchester Bay."

Mike whistled. "Pricey. Lots of McMansions."

"Yeah," Hollis said. "But he doesn't live in a McMansion. It's a modest, tidy house on a quiet street with a Hyundai in the driveway."

"Where did he live before his move?" Mike asked.

"Woodlawn."

Mike nodded. "So, a step up."

The youngest member of the team, Marisa Fuentes, who looked sixteen but was twenty-three and a recent graduate from the Academy, shifted in her seat. "Doesn't mean he's dirty, though."

"No," Colangelo said. "Not by itself. What does his wife do?"

Hollis broke into a slight grin. "Stay-at-home mom to their three kids. And, for the record, Kim, we found no record of any investigation into a burglary ring in the Bronx."

"Country Club section on a police sergeant's salary?" Mike shook his head. "Not happening."

Colangelo took charge. "We'll dig into his finances. It's possible a relative croaked and left him a bundle. If not, we'll call him in for an interview after we talk to Nolan and Lt. DeMarco tomorrow. Anything on the Ruger or Glock 19?"

Cord Washington spoke up. "The department has never issued Phillips a Glock 19. And he has neither a Glock nor a Ruger Redhawk registered in his name, nor in the name of anyone in his family."

"I'm sure he didn't acquire either weapon through proper channels," Kim said.

CHAPTER SIXTY-SIX

Sunday, March 12th, 1:46 PM

"Do you think she understood us?" Mike shouted over the loud music. They had ordered lunch at El Puerto de Acapulco, a Mexican restaurant and bar in Corona, Queens. German Montero worked there as a delivery man, according to his parole officer. The waitress had smiled and said, "*Gracias.*"

"If she hadn't, I'm sure she would have asked us to point to the menu." Kim glanced around, noting the tiny stage, empty except for two chairs and a microphone. "Looks like a fun place."

"Think you might bring Jake?"

"It's his kind of place." She checked her watch. "Montero comes on at two."

The waitress emerged from the kitchen with enchiladas for Kim and fajitas for Mike. As she was setting them on the table, Montero entered.

"Excuse us," Kim said to the waitress. "We'll be back in a moment."

The waitress blinked, not comprehending.

As Montero hung up his jacket, Kim struggled to remember her high school Spanish. "Um... *discúlpenos, volveremos en un momento.*"

The waitress smiled and nodded. "*Si, si.*"

Kim approached Montero and showed her badge without it being seen by anyone else. "My partner and I need to talk to you. You're not in trouble. Can we step outside?"

"I'm clean," he said as they stepped out to the sidewalk.

"We know," Kim said. "Your parole officer assured us you were a model parolee. We're from the department's Quality Control Unit, and we have some questions about your arrest and the disposition of your case. Okay?"

Montero was still nervous, but he nodded.

"A detective by the name of George Barlowe arrested you," she said. "What happened?"

"He busted me two years ago."

She softened her voice to relax him. "We know, but it would be a tremendous help if you could remember. Was it a buy-and-bust?"

"It wasn't your basic street-buy. He'd gone to one of my runners and said he wanted two ounces of girl. So, the runner steered him to me. I never seen him before, and I figured he wanted to sell some himself. But he looked like he was jonesing, so I sold him the two ounces. Then he busted me. I was lucky: my lawyer cut a deal with the DA. I got a year, and I was out after seven months."

"After you sold him two ounces?" Red flag. "Sounds like you had a miracle worker for a lawyer. One year is the minimum time for less than half an ounce. Give up a big name?"

"Didn't give up nobody. My lawyer told me they'd worked out the usual deal."

"Did Barlowe try to contact you after you got out?" Kim asked.

"Don't know. I got out of Manhattan. My parole officer set me up with this job, and it's a lot better than getting busted all the time. I ain't had nothing to do with any shit since I got out."

"Thank you," Kim said. "I'll see your parole officer receives a letter of appreciation for your file."

Mike was shaking his head as they returned to their table. "Two ounces?"

"According to the arrest report, it was one gram. Barlowe ripped off the other fifty-five grams." Oldest number on the crooked cop's playlist, Dad had said. But this was different. "He took that coke as part of a legal arrest. Which means he ripped off the city's evidence, not the dealer. I think we have sufficient probable cause for a search warrant."

CHAPTER SIXTY-SEVEN

Sunday, March 12th, 5:16 PM

If Kim had harbored any doubts George Barlowe was dirty, she banished them when she saw his one-bedroom fourteenth floor apartment on Leonard Street. The rent was over four thousand a month, and he'd had the entire apartment redecorated by a professional.

Mike whistled as he looked around. "Some place."

Yvette Driscoll had done a terrific job on the search warrant, specifying drugs, paper or computer records supporting a narcotics distribution operation, weapons, ammunition, and cash. A new desktop computer sat on an expansive mahogany desk. She donned latex gloves and powered it up but couldn't get past the login. "We'll need the techies."

She searched the desk. Nothing useful there. "When we get back, let's check his bank records." Mike didn't answer. She looked for him in the bedroom.

He was on his hands and knees, searching the floor of the walk-in closet. "Nothing else to speak of. Some expensive suits and shirts. The banks he'll be using for the money buying a place like this are offshore. I'm thinking he must have a cash stash."

254

"In the meantime, I'll check the kitchen." It was all white, and when she turned on the LED lighting it was so bright she shaded her eyes. Like the rest of the apartment, the kitchen was spotless. She checked the drawers—flatware arrayed in perfect order. In the cabinets, dishes and glasses were as neat as the flatware.

When she'd first met Barlowe at Tal Bagels, his appearance had been impeccable—more like a model than a detective. Even his hair had been perfect.

Mike walked into the kitchen. "Found it. Must be twenty thousand here, stuffed in the sleeve of an overcoat." He glanced around. "Does he have it sterilized by professionals?"

"No," she replied. "I'm sure he does it himself. He's compulsive." She grabbed a glass from the cabinet and filled it halfway with water. She spilled some on the gleaming counter-top and left the glass on the kitchen table. Then, she mixed the organized flatware into a jumble of knives, forks, and spoons. "Also, leave one of his shirts on the floor." Matching Barlowe in head games. "Let's bag the cash and have the tech guys grab his computer. I'll ask Colangelo to arrange for a detail to stake out this place in case Barlowe comes back."

A text came in from Jake. *We have the Knicks in tonight. You making it?*

She glanced at her watch. Already six. By the time they came for Barlowe's PC, even with Mike driving her home…

So sorry, Jake. I realize I promised. Couldn't help it. Stay safe.

CHAPTER SIXTY-EIGHT

Sunday, March 12th, 8:52 PM

She arrived home to find the apartment unlocked.

Jake never left the door unlocked. He was fanatical about security. She pulled her Glock and eased the door open, careful not to make a sound.

The apartment was unlit, except for a strange glow from the desktop monitor. She slipped inside and closed the door. Listening.

Not a sound.

The monitor should have gone into sleep mode hours ago.

Still no sound. She reached for the dining area light switch, ready to dive to the floor.

She flicked the switch and crouched. Nothing but silence as she studied the room, now bathed in light.

With her Glock at the ready, she searched each room, ignoring whatever was on the computer screen for now. The living room and dining area were clear. And the bedroom was clear.

In the kitchen the window was open, and a plant lay on the floor, its terra cotta pot in pieces, the soil spilled and scattered.

Back to the living room. The monitor was still aglow, but not with Jake's wallpaper image of Michael Jordan driving to the hoop. Instead, it was a photo of Jake leaving the house. Someone had photoshopped it so

256

his head was on the ground by his feet. Underneath, bold and italicized letters spelled out, "Next?"

· · ·

Kim waited until the game was over to text Jake about the break-in. By the time he arrived home with his escort, other units of the Eight-Four had been there for over two hours. Mike, Dobson, Brandon Hollis, and Cord Washington had arrived, and CSU had set up shop.

"We'll take the desktop," Hollis said. "We've got our own experts. Grab any files you need."

"I have a backup service." Jake clasped Kim's arm. "We need a video security system?"

"No." She shot a pointed glare at the sergeant. "The Eight-Four will keep a close watch on it."

The Sergeant nodded. "We will."

CSU had found no prints on the kitchen window, the keyboard, or anywhere around the main door to the apartment. The intruder had entered through the kitchen window and waltzed out the front door of the building.

The sergeant from the Eight-Four summed up the search. "We found two ways into your small courtyard in back: from one of the apartment buildings sharing it, or from the church on Pierrepont Street."

"There's one house on this block has a security camera," Dobson said. "I checked it, and five people walked toward Clark Street between 4:30 and 8:30; three of them were women pushing strollers and two were kids. Problem is, between 5:50 and 6:05, there was a UPS truck blocking the view of your side of the street."

"He could've gone the other way," Mike said. "Toward Pierrepont. There's a surveillance camera on the front of the courthouse."

"We'll grab the video tomorrow," Hollis replied. "But I ain't optimistic."

Jake emerged from their bedroom, white as a sheet. "Kim, what the hell was this doing in my sock drawer?" He held up an unspent round of ammunition.

"Holy shit," Dobson said. "A .44-caliber, full metal jacket bullet. Think it's a match for what they found at Kincaid's?"

Kim was still wearing latex gloves. She took the round from Jake. "Doesn't matter. No one has fired it."

"What does it mean?" Jake asked.

Dobson spoke up before Kim could stop him. "This guy is one sick fuck."

Jake's temper flared. "Who's Kincaid? You know who did this?"

"I have a strong suspicion." She shot a glare at Dobson, who shrank back.

"So, you can go get this Kincaid guy and end this?" Jake was growing livid.

"Will you guys excuse us for a minute?" She gestured toward the bedroom. Jake followed her, and she closed the door behind them. "I can't discuss an ongoing case with you."

"Since when?"

It was a fair question. She'd been open at the beginning. But then she'd misjudged Nolan, misjudged Barlowe, and she'd realized she had to keep it all locked down. "You need to trust me."

"But I'm now part of this ongoing case of yours. And I'll take a wild guess the assault last week was also part of it. And the weird threatening shit you've been getting."

"We're assuming it is."

"So, what's stopping you from nailing Kincaid?"

She had to give him something. "Not the guy. He's dead."

Jake was ready to explode. "Then who is it? Why don't you arrest him? Even if you're not positive, he'd be in custody."

Where was Barlowe hiding? What was he planning as they remained gathered in their apartment? This could all be a ruse.

First, settle Jake. Second, return to the street and discover what other developments had emerged. "We don't have enough evidence to hold him. If we tried, a lawyer would have him back on the street in an hour."

"I've been attacked and threatened, and the overriding concern is some killer's rights?"

She took his hands in hers and made him sit next to her on the bed. "This is my worst nightmare. My work has put you in danger. I trained for it, you didn't. I'm doing my best to protect you. You must trust me. I'll run this motherfucker to ground, but I have to do it right."

He pulled his hands away. "So, gotta do it by the book. Where does this leave us?"

This was so not the right time. But as she recalled, there had never been time for Mom and Dad's important talks, either. "You tell me, Jake. You said you were sticking with me and don't worry about statistics. But, for a lot of cops who get divorced, it's not because they screw around. It's because their spouses can't take the worry and the threats."

"So, we're back to you not wanting to get married."

"Please don't say that. I wanted to wait until after we close this case because it would be bad. And it's worse than I expected. My most pressing concern is keeping you safe. When we nail this bastard, you will be. As will a lot of other people."

He still looked doubtful.

"This is my life, Jake. It's who I am. I always wanted to be a cop, to protect people and to follow the law doing it. Few people understand how hard that is. You've gotten a tiny glimpse. Can you stomach the tension and pressure? If you can, and you still want me, then I'll marry you. After I solve this case."

Two sharp raps on the door.

It was Mike, holding her cell and looking grim. "We have a serious problem."

CHAPTER SIXTY-NINE

Monday, March 13th, 1:48 AM
The Sunset Motel in Suffolk County, Sylvia Walters' home-away-from-home while in protective custody, sat between a Family Dollar to the south and a strip mall to the north. Mike parked in the strip mall's lot, in front of Harry's Smoke Shop. Dobson, Brandon Hollis, and Cord Washington pulled in right behind them.

At first, Kim had focused on what Jake's answer would be, and she couldn't grasp what Mike was saying about the frantic call to her cell from Sylvia. She'd turned to stare at Jake.

He'd glared at her. "Go. I get it."

Mike had repeated the details of the phone call several times on their trip east. But she'd still struggled to grasp it all: Sylvia's desperate call warning someone was lurking in the wooded area behind the motel... Watching her... She recognized him...

But now, with flashing red lights everywhere, a gaggle of police cars and ambulances, she understood.

She found a Suffolk police lieutenant. "Detective Brady, New York City Police. How many down?"

"One of my men, shot in the head in the parking lot," he said, "and your witness, shot in her room. Both killed with a .44 magnum, judging by a slug we recovered. No one saw a thing."

"The other guard still here?" she asked.

"Yeah. He's pretty shaken up."

"I need to talk to him. And the desk clerk of the motel."

"Detective, this is our responsibility. I assure you we can handle..."

Kim's voice dropped to a low growl. "Lieutenant, these murders relate to a major ongoing investigation of ours. I expect full cooperation, including allowing our ballistics people to examine all slugs recovered from the victims." She turned and cast a meaningful glance at a local news van.

The lieutenant's eyes followed hers. "Shit. He's sitting in his patrol car."

She found the officer alone in the patrol car, staring straight ahead. "Can you tell me what happened?"

"He's dead."

"Your partner?"

His stare was still vacant. "Yeah, shot in the face. Tom. Why would anyone do that? His face... just gone."

She kept her voice soft. "Can you tell me what happened?"

"Heard glass shattering."

"Where were you?"

"In the hallway. How Tom and I worked it. I called to Sylvia to check on her. She didn't answer, so I opened the room with my key. She'd been shot... I called it in..."

"How many times was she shot?"

"Three. One head wound, two in the chest. Shame. She was nice."

"Where was your partner at the time?"

"Outside. That's how we always worked it. Me and Tom. One inside, one outside. He's dead. Shot in the face."

"Did you notice, tonight or any other nights, anyone lurking in the lot or the woods?"

"No. Sylvia complained about someone hanging around. We checked, but we never saw anybody."

"Okay, thanks." She took his hand, but he didn't clasp hers. "Very sorry about your partner."

Papers and assorted junk and old takeout containers strewn everywhere created a mess in the cramped motel office. An ancient seventeen-inch television was on with the sound off. A detective approached. "You Brady? I'm with the Suffolk County police. I've been expecting you. The motel has a video surveillance system."

She turned to Dobson, Hollis, and Washington. "Why don't you guys check it out? According to my cell, the call from Sylvia came in at 12:40. Work back from there."

"On it," Hollis replied.

"How's the desk clerk?" Kim asked the Suffolk County detective.

"Says he saw nothing."

Kim held his gaze. "But you don't believe him?"

"No."

"Can I speak with him?"

He shrugged. "Be my guest." He stepped outside. "Son, can you join us, please?"

The clerk stood six feet, gaunt, with a dreadful case of acne and stringy hair looking like he hadn't washed it in a month. As soon as he saw her, he brushed it back off his forehead, as if that made any difference.

"Hi," she said, extending a hand. She introduced herself before turning to the Suffolk County detective. "We'll take it from here, Detective. Thanks so much."

He didn't enjoy being dismissed, but he went. She closed the door. The desk clerk breathed a little easier.

"Okay," Kim said. "It's been a tough night and you've been through a lot already. I need to ask you a few questions. How long have you worked here?"

"Since May. I needed the money."

"Did you see or hear anything unusual before you heard the shots?" she asked.

"I didn't even hear shots being fired. I was sitting at the front desk, reading. The first I learned about it was when the officer—Merkle—ran down the service stairway yelling for his partner."

She kept her tone conversational. "See anyone hanging around the motel in the past week?"

"No." His voice was flat.

She walked over to him and looked into his eyes. "I think you're scared. I don't blame you. But if you've seen anyone, you need to tell me. Otherwise, it could be bad for you. You seem like a decent guy."

He gave a tight nod of the head, like he was bursting to unburden himself. "I've seen this guy. Tall, slim, not blonde, more like sandy hair. The kind of guy girls around here go nuts for. First time I saw him was about a week ago, hanging around outside. Walked past the place a few times. Then, Friday night, I went outside. Rest room wasn't working. Saw the tall guy in the parking lot."

"Did you tell the police?"

He was panicking. "I realize I should have..."

"I'm not concerned with 'should've'. Did you inform the police? Tell me the truth."

"I was afraid they'd tell the manager, and he'd fire me. I'm never supposed to leave the building when I'm working."

"So," Kim said, "you never told them."

"No."

She thanked him. Outside, it was getting light. She needed air.

Dobson stopped her. "I think we've got something."

CHAPTER SEVENTY

Monday, March 13th, 5:07 AM

Cord Washington guided Kim through the surveillance recording. "At 12:40, the camera covering the rear of the motel went dark. So, scanning back to 12:18... and..."

"There's the rear of the motel," Kim said.

"Right. Play forward and check out the closeup of the wall. A fixed-focused camera, so easy to approach and turn without being caught on screen." He switched to the camera covering the parking lot on the side of the building. At 12:48, a Ford Escort appeared, leaving the lot, pausing for a moment before turning onto the roadway. Cord froze it. "Previous vehicle left a half hour before, and nothing leaves after. I also scanned back to before 12:18. This vehicle enters at 12:13; no one else enters after 11:32."

So, this was their guy. She stared at the frozen image, able to see only the driver's light hair but no details. "Can we get a close-up?"

"Not here. Back at Hudson Street, or at One-PP, we might. But these aren't state-of-the-art cameras. The number of pixels won't change, so the effect will be to blow up a grainy image."

Once again, she knew who it was but couldn't prove it. But that Escort was a rental. "Okay. Brandon and Cord, please get what you can from video and tell me when you do. See if you can get the license plate either coming or going. Dobson, you canvas car rental places and see if anyone rented an Escort out on Sunday. I'll call Jimmy Stephenson and have him help you when he gets in. If Cord catches the license number, he'll get it to you."

Dobson gave her a blank stare. "Where do you suggest I start? How many rent-a-car places are there between Leonard Street and here?"

"Start in Brooklyn. We've established he was there late yesterday afternoon. Then the airports, JFK first." In answer to his quizzical look, she added, "Easier to get to by subway from my place."

But, without the plate number, it was a longshot.

CHAPTER SEVENTY-ONE

Monday, March 13th, 7:25 AM

"You want to tell me what the fuck is going on?" Kiley had Yvette Driscoll waiting in his office. She wasn't happy, either.

The ride back from Suffolk County hadn't helped Kim's mood at all. She had a shitload of work ahead, but first she needed to talk to Jake. "Give me a minute."

She ignored Kiley's reddening face, retreated to Room One, and called Jake.

Voicemail. She couldn't leave a message; Jake calling back while she was in with Kiley and Driscoll would be a disaster. She tried again. Still no answer.

She hated texting at a time like this, but she needed to connect with him. She couldn't leave it as they had. *I need to talk to you, but I can't right now. Please text me you're okay. Please.*

As she returned to Kiley's office, two other detectives were wrestling with a perp who was resisting being put into a holding cell. Sergeant Holloran provided reinforcement and the cell door clanged shut.

Yvette sat in one guest chair in Kiley's office, and Mike stood to give Kim the other. Kiley sat behind his desk with his arms crossed. "So, what's so terrible Mike won't even tell us?"

Oh, hell, Mike. You could've at least prepped them. She recapped the break-in and what had happened at the Sunset Motel.

"So," Kiley said with a growl, "I take it we're doubling down on Barlowe for this, too?"

"The motel clerk's description of the guy he saw loitering in the back fits Barlowe," Kim replied. "As did Sylvia's description of the guy who bribed and threatened her to go in the tank at Ice Williams' trial."

Kiley stared at her. "I thought her description was vague."

"Not the one she gave to me last night on the phone," Mike said. "Her exact words were, 'He's outside, the same guy from before the trial'. It was the last thing she said."

"So, what part makes up a description?" Kiley asked.

Yvette spoke up. "Nothing, but with the clerk's more specific one, her previous description is enough."

"Not to mention," Kim added, "someone removed all references to Sylvia in the Ice Williams file by hacking into the system. Nobody but Barlowe possesses the computer expertise and the motive to do so."

"Walters' death highlights another problem," Yvette said. "We had two non-accomplice witnesses, and Sylvia Walters was one of them."

"Leanne is the other," Kim said. "Yvette, are you sure she's safe? How could Barlowe have found Sylvia?"

"No one should've been able to find her. My office never releases protective custody information except on an as-needed basis. Barlowe must've somehow gotten a list of places we use. I'm making sure protection's increased for both Lewis and Duval. It's only a matter of time before he finds them."

Kim's cell buzzed, with a text from Jake. *I'm okay.* Okay, a little relief. "What about Leanne?"

"Her location doesn't appear on any listing. But I've alerted the First."

"What about the list?" Kim asked. "Who'd have access to it?"

"Someone in a command position, captain or higher," Yvette replied. "The thing is, to make Murder-one stick for Choo, I have to prove he was paid. Saying he paid Lewis is mere circumstantial evidence. Walters could have corroborated Duval's statements about Kincaid."

"Walters and Kincaid are dead." Kim spat her words.

Yvette nodded. "Correct. I'm considering going for an evidentiary hearing. Getting a judge to say, for Choo and his lawyer to hear, we've got sufficient evidence to go to trial on Murder-One might shake Choo loose."

Kiley stood. "Meanwhile, we're due down at Hudson Street. We'll be in touch, Yvette."

Kim excused herself. "Be back in a minute."

.   .   .

She ducked back into Room One and texted Jake. *I'm about to call you. Please answer it.*

When she did, he answered. "Hey."

"I'm sorry I never explained the dangers we faced. It wouldn't have compromised the investigation."

"Okay. What dangers do we face you haven't told me about?"

She told him about her encounter with Barlowe in the elevator, although she was careful not to mention him by name.

"You could have arrested him right there. Or even killed him."

"I'm sorry for not telling you, Jake, but I'm not sorry about anything else I said last night. I am who I am. If I'd killed him, we'd never learn who else is working with him." She hesitated before finishing the thought. "Destroying me and any relationship together, if you still want one."

A sharp knock rattled the two-way mirror. She held up one finger.

"You know I still want one," Jake said. There were several more knocks. "I know. You've got to go. And for a change, you check in with me. By text, every hour."

Mike, not Kiley, had been knocking. "Hollis has something for us. They're waiting."

CHAPTER SEVENTY-TWO

Monday, March 13th, 9:20 AM

"Jesus, Kim," Colangelo said, "when did you sleep last?"

"A few hours early yesterday morning. Where's Brandon?"

"Over here," Brandon called. There, on his twenty-nine-inch monitor, was a frozen grainy image from the motel's surveillance video of the white Ford Escort before it turned out of the lot. "The best shot we can get of the driver."

It wasn't clear at all. "Could be Barlowe. But it also could be plenty of other guys." She tried not to show her annoyance. "I thought you had something for us."

"I do." He advanced the image, frame by frame, showing the car moving forward and starting to turn. Then he froze it again and enlarged.

The license plate. "Looks like the first three letters are Victor, Tango, X-ray, followed by numbers I can't quite make out."

Brandon slapped the top of the desk. "Cord, what do we have for our winner?"

Cord appeared and handed Kim a printout of a data search from the Department of Motor Vehicles. "A list of all white Escorts with license numbers beginning with our sequence. There are three in the entire state: one in Syracuse, one in Plattsburgh, and one registered to Metropolitan Car Rentals, on Rockaway Boulevard, outside JFK."

Kim called Dobson and relayed the information. "Get over there and get the details on this rental, including the driver's license and counter photo of the renter. Take Stephenson with you."

"Okay, next." Brandon led them to an empty cubicle with Jake's desktop. "I checked this out. The wallpaper is a simple jpg file. Looks like the intruder took it with a cell. But this guy's got superb skills. Jake's security is tight. I tried getting past it and couldn't. I had to use the password Jake provided. No idea how our guy got past it. Good news is he doesn't seem to have disturbed anything else. No files copied to external drives or other security breeches."

"He wasn't after inside information on the Brooklyn Nets," Kim said. "Can you get this back to Jake?"

"Sure," Cord replied. "This afternoon."

"What about Barlowe's desktop?" Kim asked.

"Vera Koshkin down at One-PP is analyzing it."

Colangelo appeared. "Lieutenant Kiley updated me. Bob Nolan's on his way up. Captain Forrest is joining us. Brandon, please join us, too. Marisa will take notes. In the meantime, we have a detail staking out Barlowe's place."

.   .   .

Nolan's appearance had improved somewhat since Saturday. He'd showered and shaved. His shirt was clean if not well pressed. His tie hung loose at the neck and his sport jacket sagged. Kim smiled at him, and he acknowledged it with a nod. He faltered when they walked into the conference room and Captain Forrest was sitting at the table.

"Because of the scope of this investigation," Colangelo said after introducing everyone around the table, "Captain Forrest is sitting in, as he will when we interview Lieutenant DeMarco this afternoon. Let me begin by saying your..."

"Excuse me, Lieutenant," Kim said. "Before we begin, can we afford Detective Nolan the chance to volunteer any information he may have about wrongdoing in his unit?"

Colangelo raised his eyebrows and exchanged glances with Captain Forrest, who said, "We'll need him to explain why he hadn't already come forward. But if he explains, we'd take into consideration whatever information he provides."

All eyes were on Nolan. He stared at Kim, then at Mike, then back at Kim. "I'll start by saying I should have come forward before now. I accept my responsibility. I didn't, in part because my knowledge of what was going on in the unit was incomplete..." He froze.

"We've uncovered certain irregularities in one of your case files," Colangelo said after a nod from Captain Forrest. "Detective Brady has also advised us of your cooperation in the Cove Shooting case. Any information you provide on your own, and the frankness of your answers to questions we might have, will weigh in your favor."

Kim gave Nolan an almost imperceptible nod of encouragement.

He took a moment. "Okay, thanks. I guess I should start with this. On many occasions, I've confiscated drugs from runners and street dealers rather than arresting them and exchanged them with others for information. I realize this has long been against departmental policy, but it's still done because it's the easiest way for us to get the information we need. Not justifying the practice, but I'm explaining why it still happens. As does using non-registered informants, which I've also done." He stopped.

He accepted the glass of water Kim offered. "Thanks. One point is vital: I used confiscated drugs to get information, and no other purpose. Please understand I never diverted them to anyone else, never sold them, and never used them myself. Not trying to excuse what I did, but it's important to know."

Colangelo nodded. "Understood. Continue."

Nolan described the deterioration of his partnership with Barlowe following the Ice Williams collar. "We'd been trying to nail Williams for a

271

long time when Barlowe reported he'd gotten inside information from a snitch. It panned out, and we collared Williams and Jordy Hill, and a few others. It was almost like someone had set up Williams. And when I asked Barlowe about his source, he refused to tell me. I asked him point-blank if Viper Kincaid, the lone senior guy in Williams' setup we hadn't collared, had informed. Barlowe complained to our lieutenant and requested a new partner."

"Lieutenant DeMarco?" Colangelo asked.

"Yes. And DeMarco made the switch without even talking to me. When I asked him about it, all he said was, 'It's done'." Nolan took another drink. "Over the next year, I realized Barlowe had become DeMarco's 'go to' guy..."

"Which you resented," Colangelo said.

Nolan stopped and glared at him. "Yeah, I did. It's not like Barlowe was some choir boy. He had more unregistered informants than anyone, and he convinced one of my snitches not to cooperate with me. Francisco Robles came to me and said he couldn't work with me anymore because someone had threatened him. He wouldn't say who. But, this past January, he came back to me to complain a retired narc had ripped him off, twice, and he'd gone to Barlowe about it, but got nowhere. Barlowe was using information from Robles to shake down other dealers."

"Did Robles say who the retired narc was?" Colangelo asked.

Nolan looked away from Kim. "He did. It was Detective Joseph Brady."

Good. A relief bringing it into the open. "It explains how Barlowe had enough information about how my father died to harass me with it." She needed to change direction. "You say Barlowe became DeMarco's 'go to' guy. Can you give an example?"

"Whatever information came in, DeMarco consulted with Barlowe about it." Nolan told of the tip in Queens. "I reported it to DeMarco, and he huddled with Barlowe behind closed doors. Afterward, he said they referred it, but nothing further was ever said about it."

"Since the Williams collar, what information have you received about Kincaid?" Kim asked.

272

"Nothing except you guys found him dead last week."

"What about Harold Garner?" Kim asked.

"My partner before Barlowe. He was quite interested in Garner when he came into the unit. I could never figure out why. After we split, I sometimes overheard him questioning others about him. But I can't tell you anything else about it."

Colangelo broke in. "Overheard, how?"

"Barlowe sometimes talks louder than is necessary. He thinks it gives him an aura of command. It wasn't hard to hear when he was on his cell in the unit. I didn't glean much from these snippets, other than Garner was a sleazy guy, still using and hanging out in strip joints."

Kim took over. "Have you ever known a sergeant named Henry Phillips?"

"The name rings a bell, but I couldn't tell you who he is. Friend of DeMarco's, I think."

Kim softened. "What makes you think they're friends?"

"DeMarco's mentioned him a few times. To Barlowe. But I don't recall what about. Must've been something trivial." Another drink. "Check our unit's CompStat numbers over the past three years. Interesting stuff."

Captain Forrest waited for additional questions. There weren't any. "Thank you for coming in, Detective. We'll get back to you. For the time being, you'll remain on Restricted Duty."

CHAPTER SEVENTY-THREE

Monday, March 13th, 11:51 AM

"Ballistics got back to me," Kiley said. It had been a half hour since the interview with Nolan had ended and they were all digging for information before talking to DeMarco. "The slugs from Sylvia Walters and the Suffolk County officer were both .44 magnum hollow points, fired from a Ruger Redhawk."

"The same piece was used to kill Garner and shoot up Leanne Mallory's apartment." Use a revolver, leave no shell casings. "I'm certain Kincaid, too, although we'll never have proof. Volnick's murder with a Glock 19 is the lone one out of profile, so I suspect someone else killed him." She turned to Cord Washington. "Cord, please check the officers of the Five-One. See if any of them have a Glock 19 registered."

Cord gave a thumb-up gesture. "On it."

Brandon Hollis brandished a printout. "Nolan was right. CompStat numbers on their unit are down for total arrests, and almost all are penny-ante dealing. And those were all pled down to possession."

Mike chuckled. "Welcome to Eight Balls R Us."

Kim studied the chart. "Looks like lots of repeats of Montero."

Stephenson rushed in with Dobson close behind. "Hey, Kim. Lieu. Got the ID of the guy who rented our Escort, but it ain't Barlowe. He ain't even white. Dobson's got a pic on his phone."

Dobson brought up a photo of a driver's license with a black face and the name, Richard Odessa. Kim stared at the face, then showed it to Mike. "He rented it Saturday night, hasn't returned it, yet. Does he look familiar to you?"

Mike studied it. "I've seen him. But where?"

"The morning we checked out Paredes' apartment. He was the PO who got there ahead of us. From the Five-One." She pulled up her Notes App. "Ken Ames." She turned to Brandon. "Can you check the Master Roll Call for the Five-One today?" While Brandon typed, Kim stared at the image. "Mike, Richard Odessa. Same name they used for the ownership of the house where they killed Kincaid."

"Ames," Brandon said. "Yeah. He's working the eight-to-four."

She turned to Dobson and Stephenson. "Go pick him up."

"Under arrest?" Stephenson asked.

Kiley stepped in. "Tell him he's wanted for questioning by IAB in connection with a murder. If he resists, arrest him as an accessory."

"And bring him here," Colangelo added. "Cord, when they get back, put him in Room Two until we're ready for him."

"Will do. Oh, and Kim, I'm still checking on your question, but so far I have three officers in the Five-One with Glock 19s in their names, including Ken Ames."

"Lieutenant," Marisa Fuentes said, "the front desk called. Lieutenant DeMarco is here. Oh, and Kim, I checked on DeMarco and Phillips, like you asked. Here's the printout. I've highlighted the matches in yellow."

•   •   •

Lieutenant Nicholas DeMarco looked like he was in command. Wearing an impeccable suit, his styled silver mane without a hair out of place, he was the picture of self-assurance, serene in the belief all his decisions were correct.

Kim pictured DeMarco and Barlowe a matched set.

Unlike the session with Nolan, Captain Forrest spoke first. He reviewed the CompStat numbers from the past three years, noting the drop-off in arrests for dealing of significant amounts of narcotics. "One member of your unit has described the ongoing practice of confiscating drugs without reporting it and without turning them over as evidence. We've also documented a case in which one of your detectives arrested a dealer with two ounces in his possession but reported a single gram."

DeMarco pulled himself up straight, looking as dignified as possible. "May I assume the individual in both cases was Detective Nolan?"

Forrest turned cold. "You don't ask the questions. We do. Detective Brady, please continue."

She was glad to have the ball. "Where is Detective Barlowe at the moment?"

"On leave."

She glanced at a printout from the Master Roll Call. "Yes. Since yesterday. When did he request the leave?"

"Yesterday morning. He called me. Explained a personal matter had arisen, and he needed two weeks leave."

She feigned surprise. "He must have called early. Did he ask for the leave or did he tell you he was taking it?"

A little of his self-assurance slipped. "Well, he told me he had a problem and needed the time. I said it was all right."

"Did you ask him why he requested two weeks off on such brief notice?"

"It didn't strike me as relevant. He had the time coming."

Time to press harder. "And he told you he was taking it. Do you always give in to last-minute requests for leave without a specific reason? Or was Barlowe a special case?"

DeMarco squirmed. "I try to be accommodating. Detective Barlowe has an exemplary record."

"Does he?" She gestured to the CompStat report. "You mean he had nothing to do with the falloff in your unit's performance?" Before he could answer, she added, "Are you aware of the practice of shaking down dealers by detectives under your command? And Barlowe stands accused of having done so?"

DeMarco snorted. "By Nolan."

Heads snapped up around the table.

Kim closed in. "You were aware of suspicions against Barlowe?"

"No. No. But there's been bad blood between them."

"Why?" she asked.

For the first time, he looked helpless. "I don't know. A short time after they arrested Ice Williams, Barlowe came to me and said he couldn't work with Nolan anymore and asked me to assign him a new partner."

"Were you surprised?" Kim made sure he didn't miss the note of skepticism in her voice.

"Yes. I'd thought they worked well together."

"But you agreed to reassign them without talking to Nolan first."

"I thought it best. It was a command decision."

"Yes, but who was in command?" Before he could answer, she turned to Cord. "I believe you have some questions about this man's financial status?"

Cord referred to a printed report. "You live in Westchester, correct? Armonk?" DeMarco nodded. "In fact, you and your wife bought your house a year ago for a little over a million-and-a-half dollars. You also have invested assets, not counting 401Ks, of four-hundred-fifty thousand. And you own an Audi Q7." He passed the report to Kim.

She studied it. "All on a lieutenant's salary. I'd say you've accomplished quite a feat."

"My wife is in business, giving us two incomes. And we have no children."

She flipped a page. "In fact, she's vice president of marketing for a Yonkers furniture seller. Not what I'd call high finance."

"She inherited a sum from an aunt years ago. An investment fund…"

Kim rifled through several pages. "Nothing mentioned of it here under either of your names. What was the aunt's name?"

DeMarco blanched. "It's, er, an offshore investment, Tortuga Bank and Trust. It's in the Cayman Islands. My wife always referred to her as Aunt Julia."

"Find out her full name. We need to verify your story." Mike had said Barlowe had to be hiding money offshore. Time for another pivot move. "Are you acquainted with a Sergeant Henry Phillips?"

"Somewhat. We were in the same Academy class."

Kim pulled out the service records of both DeMarco and Phillips, which Cord had provided. "Yes, I see. You also both served on the Mayor's Narcotics Task Force back in 2002. Several of you attained command positions in Narcotics, but Phillips returned to a precinct in the Bronx. Why?"

"I don't know. You'd have to ask him."

She gave him an icy smile. "We intend to. One other thing. Do you recall receiving a tip last fall about a major operation in Queens?"

"Can't say I do."

"Imagine that. Your detectives recalled it well enough."

"Perhaps if you tell me your source, I can..."

She stood and leaned across the table. "You're in command. You got a report of major drug activity in another jurisdiction. My source is irrelevant."

DeMarco stood. "Detective Brady, Captain Forrest, I've done my best to answer your questions, but I object to the direction this is taking, smearing me by innuendo. I refuse to answer any further questions without counsel present. Unless you have grounds to arrest me, I'm leaving."

"We'll be in touch," Colangelo said.

After DeMarco had gone, Kim turned to Cord. "Can we get a list of everyone who served on that task force?"

"We'll get on it."

Kim's cell buzzed with a text from Vera Koshkin. *I got in.*

CHAPTER SEVENTY-FOUR

Monday, March 13th, 2:15 PM

"Is not much," Vera said. "Hard drive has usual programs—word processor, spreadsheet, whatever—but no files. Also, I have no trouble penetrating his password protection." She shook her head. "Was too easy. He not care if anyone sees what he has."

"Or, he figured his protection would be sufficient?" Kim asked.

Vera smiled. "*Nyet*. Lots of stories about Barlowe. He is hacker, and hackers are good at keeping others out."

It made no sense. "So, this computer is what? An ornament?"

"I think he uses for whatever he is doing but saves data files someplace else. I find text-to-speech program..."

"For his threatening phone calls."

"*Da*. He protects himself low-tech. Is one file listed in the text-to-speech program, lots of files listed in the spreadsheet program, and some in the word processor. All with innocent-looking names, and all saved to the 'I' drive. Here are printouts of file lists."

Kim scanned the lists. The date of the text-to-speech file was the same as the last threatening phone call. The dates of the spreadsheet files spanned three years. She turned to Mike. "Around the time they collared Ice Williams. Barlowe's flash drive could have the records of the entire operation on it."

"We searched his apartment," Mike said. "And the detail hasn't seen him since."

"But there was a gap between our search and when the detail began their surveillance. We still have the warrant, and the warrant includes any financial records connected with a drug operation. Barlowe's flash drive is the key. Let's see if there's a clue to where it is at his apartment."

.   .   .

The glass Kim had left on the counter at Barlowe's apartment now stood in perfect alignment with its mates in the cabinet. The flatware drawer reflected perfect order, not a single piece was mislaid. Barlowe's shirt, which Mike had left on the bedroom floor, had vanished.

"He realized we'd been here," Mike said, "saw we'd taken his computer, and he took time to tidy up?"

Kim crawled underneath the desk, searching for anything near it Barlowe might have dropped. "He's obsessive compulsive, Mike. Not surprising." A small bit of white caught her eye. She snatched it and stood.

"Find anything interesting?" Mike asked.

"The corner of an envelope. He opened his mail. You check the garbage. I'll check any trash cans."

Everything was clean in the apartment. The superintendent who'd let them in was waiting in the hallway.

"Where do tenants dispose of their garbage?" Kim asked him.

"There's a chute for dropping garbage down to the Compactor Room, and a bin for recycling." He pointed down the hall.

The bin was overflowing. "When was this last emptied?"

The super looked sheepish. "Saturday morning. One of my guys has been out sick and we're a little behind."

Kim dug down into the pile. Most of it lay in small, clear plastic bags. One such bag had an envelope with Barlowe's name and address pressed against it. She grabbed it and pawed through the pile, looking for others. There weren't any.

She sifted through the contents and found a bill for a safe deposit box from the Chelsea Community Bank.

CHAPTER SEVENTY-FIVE

Monday, March 13th, 5:24 PM

"Glad you're back," Colangelo said. "Ames has been cooling his heels for three hours and he's asked for a lawyer. The PBA is sending one over, now. Also, Yvette Driscoll called. The hearing is on for tomorrow morning."

"Great. I also need a search warrant for Barlowe's safe deposit box. We're looking for one or more flash drives, a notebook or laptop computer, a Glock 19, a Ruger Redhawk and any ammunition for either."

Colangelo stared. "Is that all?"

She broke into a grin. "Isn't it enough?" Ames was demanding they allow him to leave, but as soon as she walked in with Mike, Brandon, Marisa and Colangelo behind her, he froze. "Officer Ames, we meet again."

She sat down across the table from him and arrayed a notepad and her cell in front of her, just so. "I'm sure you remember our last encounter, in Diego Paredes' apartment in Mott Haven. You handed us some bullshit story about a joint investigation of a burglary ring. And when we checked into it, your sergeant went nuclear with our lieu."

Ames was about to argue, but she stopped him. "We found no burglary ring, and no joint investigation. But we'll get to your alleged investigation later. First, I need you to explain this." She slammed her fist on the table in front of him, holding the image of his phony driver's license.

Ames stammered. "I…"

"I'm waiting, Mr. Odessa. You rented a Ford Escort from Metropolitan Car Rentals in Queens yesterday. Someone used it while committing two murders last night—a witness and a Suffolk County police officer. Making you an accessory."

"I'm not saying anything until my lawyer gets here."

It was outstanding when they played right into her hand. "Then, you can listen. Suffolk County will want your ass out there to answer for this cop killing. But since it was our witness who got killed, we get first dibs. In both cases, you can help yourself plenty by telling us who asked you to rent that car. Also, who provided the phony ID, and who took possession of the car after you rented it?"

"Your police career is over," Colangelo said. "Leaving us to determine whether we will charge you with a crime."

Ames squirmed in his seat. "It ain't like you think."

"Sure, it ain't," Kim said. "But you invoked your right to counsel. And we're not going any further until either your lawyer gets here, or you provide a knowing and willing waiver of your right."

Several knocks, and Cord Washington poked his head in. "His PBA lawyer is here."

The attorney walked in. "May I confer with my client in private?"

•   •   •

Leanne got off the phone with Detective Brady, stunned. She'd been back in her room for a few minutes when the call came in, and she needed to steady herself. She texted Alli. *There's a hearing, sort of a trial before the trial. Must come out at work soon. Can't even.*

The minutes crawled by as she waited for the response. Maybe Bart was there. Four minutes. Then five. At last, a response. *I thought you wanted to come out. What am I missing?*

Relief. *The trial wasn't supposed to be for another five or six months. I haven't even started on hormone therapy, yet.* After sending it, she added the ultimate indignity. *As it is, I had to go clothes shopping with a cop.*

A moment later, the response came back. *ROFLMAO!!*

The response shocked Leanne, and she couldn't compose an answer. When Alli called a few minutes later, she answered with an accusation. "You're laughing at me?"

Alli didn't quite stifle a giggle. "Not at you. But the thought of a big, burly cop standing there while you pick out..." She started laughing again.

Leanne's anger evaporated. "It wasn't a guy." Imagine Officer Steve standing with her in Victoria's Secret... She had to laugh. "Officer Bridget Dubinsky. She and her partner take me to my appointments."

"But you're okay? I worry."

"At first, I was terrified. But it's not so bad, except I can't..." There was a knock at the door. "Gotta go."

It was one of the regular plainclothesmen in the hall. "I thought I heard you on the phone. I'm making sure you're using the cell they gave you and didn't tell anyone where you are."

An icy dread gripped her. "No, I was talking to my sister. She understands."

"Just want to make sure you do."

Yes, she understood.

Compared to someone shooting up her apartment, trying to kill her, announcing to her fellow employees who she was didn't seem so terrible. She'd already told her friends, and they even called her Leanne in private. Evelyn, her manager, too. Mr. Goddard had remained unfazed when she told him why she wouldn't be in tomorrow and would assume her new persona the following day. Ms. Donner in Human Resources would assure the records and systems reflected the changes, too.

Not so bad.

CHAPTER SEVENTY-SIX

Monday, March 13th, 6:02 PM

"First," the PBA attorney said as they returned to the conference room, "Officer Ames needs your assurance if he cooperates in full, you won't charge him with any crime."

"DA's decision." Colangelo scowled. "Not ours."

"But we will tell the DA how helpful he's been," Kim added.

"He may not tell everything you expect," the attorney replied. "I need an assurance you won't hold his incomplete knowledge against him."

"Then," Kim replied, "I guess we'll all have to see what he can tell us and what we can do about it."

The attorney nodded to Ames with obvious reluctance.

Ames took a deep breath. "No one told me why they wanted the car."

"Yeah, yeah, yeah," Kim said. "You always use a fake ID to rent cars for other people." She turned to the lawyer. "Did you explain to him how deep the shit is he's in?"

"No, I assumed you did. I told him what his options were."

"Then let's cut to the chase." She turned back to Ames. "Who asked you to rent it, who paid you and how much? Who took delivery?"

"My sergeant, Henry Phillips, approached me Saturday morning, said he needed me to rent a car near JFK. Gave me the fake ID and credit card.

Told me to leave the car on 148th Avenue off Rockaway Boulevard, next to the Springfield Gardens Motor Vehicles office. I left it there and I haven't seen it since. Took the ID and credit card home with me and shredded them."

"Did you see who picked it up?" Kim asked.

"No. I boarded the Q6 bus and rode it to the subway, then took the subway home."

"How much did Phillips pay you for this?" Kim hated having to ask twice.

"Nothing."

She leaned forward. "I don't believe you. And if I don't believe you on getting paid, I don't believe the rest of it."

Ames got flustered. "I meant he didn't pay me anything on Saturday. He pays me five hundred dollars a week for certain favors. He's kind of looked after me ever since I was a rookie in the Five-One."

"How big-hearted of him." There was more. "What started this largesse?"

Ames turned to his attorney, who nodded. "I'm an addict."

An oldie but a goodie. "Coke, smack, or pills?"

He shook his head. "Not drugs. I'm addicted to gambling. About six months into my posting at the Five-One, we busted a bookie. Sarge let him off easy and started betting through him. So, I started, too. But I ran into a string of rotten luck. Before too long, I was three months behind on the mortgage on our co-op, I'd maxed out all my credit cards, and my wife was threatening to divorce me."

"As wives will do," Mike said.

Ames relaxed a little. "I told Sarge I was considering declaring bankruptcy, and I had to know what the department would do. He told me not to and advanced me enough for the overdue mortgage payments and to lower the credit card balances. Then he said he'd pay me the five hundred each week if I did any favors he asked, and if I agreed to limit my gambling to the five hundred."

"And you're still receiving this allowance?" Kim asked. Ames nodded. "Okay, so what were you doing in Diego Paredes' apartment on the morning of February 24th?"

"Sarge had told me Paredes had been part of a fencing operation our precinct was working with others in the Bronx to bust. He told me to check his apartment for stolen goods and anything showing a connection to a drug ring. He needed to know if there might be police involvement with either. I was to remove any evidence I found."

"And you believed this?" Clearly, he wasn't brilliant. Then again, if criminals were bright, they wouldn't be criminals.

"It sounded weird, but this was the kind of thing he often asked me to do."

Colangelo pushed a notepad over to him. "I want a list of all the things he's asked you to do in the name of this allowance he paid you. Be specific. Dates, times, amounts."

The lawyer raised a hand. "Just a moment. Before he proceeds, I need assurances…"

"If he's forthcoming," Colangelo said, "and his information pans out, he won't…"

Kim interrupted. "Just one more thing before you write," Kim said. "Do you have, or have you ever used, a Glock 19?"

Ames looked wary. "Yeah, my primary piece is a Glock 19."

She held out her hand. "Please."

The PBA lawyer jumped up. "What's this all about?"

"Sit down, Counselor," Colangelo said. "He's headed for Restricted Duty, anyway, and he must turn it over then. Detective Brady is saving some time."

She gave the piece to Mike. "Ballistics, please."

"On my way."

Ames panicked. "Ballistics?"

Kim leaned forward again. "An EMT named Gustav Volnick turned up murdered with a Glock 19 and left on the side of the High Line trail last Thursday night. Ballistics will now check to see if your piece is a match for the slugs recovered from the body. Given your role as Phillips' go-fer, I suspect it will be. So, I'm giving you the chance right now to tell me whether you killed Gustav Volnick."

"Ken," the lawyer said, "not a single word unless you get a deal."

"If Ballistics comes back with a match, he's going down for Murder-One," Kim replied. "Since I doubt he has anything of value to tell us, I'm cool. And if it's not a match, then he already knows he's in the clear and shouldn't have a problem saying so."

"And," Colangelo added, "no specific promises until he says what he has to say. If I think it's helpful, I'll recommend leniency to the DA."

Ames stared at the table.

"Ballistics is lining up those striations as we speak," Kim said.

Ames gave the lawyer a look of disgust. "I killed Volnick. Sarge told me he'd put all of us in danger."

"Did he say who he meant by all of us?" Kim asked. "Then or ever?"

"No. Everything was always between him and me. He never mentioned any other names. He only ever referred to 'the task force'."

CHAPTER SEVENTY-SEVEN

Monday, March 13th, 8:32 PM

"Looks like we're getting close to the end of this thing," Mike said has he turned onto Monroe Place. "Even if we are spending the entire NYPD annual budget on it. Yvette got you the search warrant for Barlowe's safe deposit box, Colangelo's deployed a detail to bring in Phillips, and the Evidentiary Hearing is tomorrow morning."

"But Barlowe's still at large."

He pulled up in front of the magnolia tree. "Explains why I drove you. I'll pick you up in the morning, too."

"Thanks. We'll grab Barlowe's box after the hearing."

She mounted the steps to the apartment. The Nets had no game tonight, so lights blazed from the living room window while the guys from the Eight-Four maintained their vigil. Mike was right; between the overtime, the investigation, and the protection this was costing the city a bundle.

It felt like days rather than hours since her brief chat with Jake. She'd texted him every hour, on the hour, as he'd asked. He'd responded each time.

Now, she had to face him.

She stopped at the mailbox. Empty. Right, made sense. Jake would have grabbed the mail. She hesitated before opening the door. Please, no more jabs today.

"You look awful," he said as she walked in. He held her. "I'm sorry I freaked on you."

She'd been debating with herself all day whenever there'd been a lull. And she said it. "I was wrong not to tell you everything. My dad never told my mom; it came out in bits and pieces, and she imagined the worst on all fronts. Well, I'd never cheat on you, but I'm sure you'd worry about everything else. I used to think the best thing to do was to downplay it, so you wouldn't. But downplaying and minimizing would make it worse until it got so bad you'd stop believing anything I said. So, now I'll tell you everything I've had happen in this case."

CHAPTER SEVENTY-EIGHT

Tuesday, March 14th, 10:07 AM

Kim sat in the back row of the courtroom on Centre Street. Evidentiary hearings, though open to the public, were almost never major media events. But the courtroom today was almost full, and camera crews were panting in anticipation right outside.

Her testimony had been flawless, and she'd stared down Sharon Foster, whose cross-examination hadn't sullied a single point. Matt Berringer had followed, establishing Leanne had fled before the shooting. There had been no cross. Despite having learned Leanne's secret, he spoke of her with fondness. She hoped Leanne felt better about their encounter.

"Counselor," the judge said, "call your next witness."

Yvette stood at the prosecutor's table. "The people call Leanne Mallory."

This was it. If Leanne held together, they'd squeeze Choo. If not... It didn't bear thinking about.

Leanne stood a few rows in front of her, wearing a trim navy-blue skirt suit and heels. Nervous, but not terrified. Kim smiled to herself. *I'm an excellent judge of people. Most of the time.*

. . .

Even though Leanne expected what was coming, hearing her name called as a witness startled her. She walked toward the witness stand, her high heels clip-clopping on the polished floor.

They swore her in, and her voice remained soft but firm as she said, "I do." ADA Driscoll gave her a little encouraging smile as she began the questioning. "State your full name, please."

"Leanne Mallory."

"Is Leanne your given name?"

She swallowed hard. "No, my given name was Andrew. I'm transgender—a genetic male, but I identify as a female."

"Have you had gender reassignment surgery?"

"No, I'm beginning the transition process. Surgery won't be for at least another year."

"Why did you wait until now to change your gender identification?"

She took a deep breath. "It's such a hard decision. The public doesn't understand transgender people, and some make us targets for hate crimes. It can be terrifying."

"What made you take the step?"

"A woman in my office was being harassed, and I urged her to file a complaint. After hesitating, she did, and I supported her. When the company assured us it would protect us, and anyone else, from harassment, I realized I had much less to fear than I'd thought."

Ms. Driscoll turned to the night of the shooting and established Leanne's presence in the bar. "And did anything occur following you entering the bar?"

She had to smile. "Someone bought me a glass of wine and joined me at my table to talk."

"That would be Matt Berringer?"

"Yes. The bar got very crowded and loud, and we were shouting and straining to hear each other. He asked me if he could take me to dinner. I declined. I wasn't comfortable being with a guy for an entire evening."

"Did there come a time when you left the bar?"

Every eye in the courtroom focused on her. "Yes. Mr. Berringer was staring at my throat. I thought he'd seen something giving me away. I panicked and ran out."

"Did you have any difficulty leaving?"

"Yes. A man in a gray suit blocked the exit, and I had to force my way through. Then he groped me, which frightened me even more. So, I stomped on the top of his foot with my spike heel."

Chuckles rippled through the courtroom. The judge banged his gavel once for quiet.

"Now, can you please tell us what happened when you got outside?"

She repeated what she had told Detectives Brady and Resnick: three men arguing; walking as fast as she could toward Washington Street; a dark turquoise Blazer turning onto Gansevoort, slowing down, its rear passenger-side window rolling down as it passed her. She described the man inside holding an assault rifle. Panic rose in her, like it had that night. Someone had tried to kill her to prevent her from saying this. "I ran to the corner and saw a livery cab parked there. As I opened the door, I heard three single shots. Then a burst from the assault rifle. Two more single shots, then several long bursts. I closed the door, and the driver sped away."

Ms. Driscoll paused for effect. "Do you see the individual from the Blazer in court?"

Leanne sat up straight. "Yes. The defendant."

"Are you sure he's the one?"

"I'll remember his face until the day I die."

"Thank you, Ms. Mallory. No further questions."

Ms. Foster stood and hesitated before approaching the witness box, as if she didn't want to get too close. "Mr. Mallory..."

Ms. Driscoll jumped up. "Objection. The witness is a woman."

"Your honor," Ms. Foster replied, "the witness is not a woman. The witness pretends to be a woman. He has already admitted to not even having sex-change surgery."

The judge leaned forward. "How is her gender relevant to this case?"

"Goes to credibility, your honor. The witness is a genetic male. He lives a lie. It's not unreasonable to assume he might tell some."

"Your honor," Ms. Driscoll replied, "the New York City Human Rights Law in pertinent part prohibits discrimination based on gender identity. Transgender individuals have the right to be addressed according to their gender identity."

Foster didn't hesitate. "The people have placed in evidence this witness's testimony regarding his changing genders. But the defense seeks to test his testimony under cross-examination for legitimacy. He might've changed his identity for reasons connected to this crime, and it's possible he could be in league with the actual murderer. The defense may test for alternate theories of the crime and the credibility of the witness."

The judge considered it. "I will allow this line of questioning, Counselor, but you will address the witness according to her gender identity."

Leanne braced herself. They were about to shine a spotlight on her "otherness".

Foster gave a tight nod. "You testified earlier you 'identify as a female'. How long has that been the case?"

"I've always wished I'd been born a girl."

"Always?" Foster sneered. "Played with dolls, did you?"

"When I could without letting my father or brothers know. My father encouraged my brothers to 'toughen me up' as he called it. They'd beat me up or force me to do things they could do, and I couldn't, such as catching a baseball..."

Foster feigned shock. "Making a boy catch a baseball? What an outrage."

It was taking all her strength not to cry, not to flee. "It is when it's thrown full force at your face and you end up with a broken nose." She remembered the pain shooting across her face, the red stain on her shirt spreading, the baying laughter of Rod, Sean, and the neighborhood boys.

Ms. Driscoll jumped up. "Objection. None of this has any relevance to People v. Choo."

"Sustained. Move along, Counselor."

Foster shook off her annoyance. "Ms. Mallory, you said something about a harassment complaint. Were you a victim of sexual harassment, too?"

"Yes."

Foster approached the witness stand, a cat closing in on its prey. "You must have felt validated."

Ms. Driscoll stood. "Objection. Defense is badgering the witness."

"Sustained," the judge said. "Ms. Foster, you stated your intention was to probe for an alternative theory of the crime, but you've yet to provide even a coherent statement of one. Get there now or dismiss the witness."

Foster turned back to Leanne. "You testified when you tried to leave, you ran into a man in a gray suit. How tall are you without heels?"

"Five feet, six inches."

"And how much do you weigh?"

"A hundred and thirty-two pounds."

"Your honor, the police department's arrest report describes the man identified as standing at the exit the night of the shooting, Pierre Duval. He is listed as five feet, ten inches and weighs one hundred eighty-four pounds." Foster turned back to Leanne. "So, despite a disadvantage of four inches in height and fifty pounds in weight, you somehow forced yourself past this man after how long?"

"About half a minute."

"Sufficient to keep anyone else who wanted to get out of the bar inside before fleeing yourself?"

"My lone concern was getting out. I was terrified. I thought he'd seen something to cue him I'm not a cis girl."

Foster took a drink of water from a glass on the defense table. "When you arrived home, did you call the police?"

"No."

"In fact, you never contacted the police on your own, did you?"

"No, not true. I called Detective Brady to tell her I'd help."

"When did you call her?"

"March fifth."

"Two weeks after the shooting." Foster paused for effect. "Figured the trail had gone cold enough by then to pin the rap on someone else? Like my client?"

Ms. Driscoll rose again. "Objection. The witness has already testified she had never seen either Mr. Choo or Mr. Duval before February twenty-third. This is more badgering."

"Sustained. Do you have any relevant questions for this witness, Counselor?"

"No more questions," Foster said, sitting down.

Ms. Driscoll stood again. "Redirect, your honor. Ms. Mallory, following the night of February twenty-third on Gansevoort Street, where did you next see the defendant?"

"First, I saw his photo in a book of mugshots, then I saw him at a police lineup."

"Where you identified Mr. Choo as the defendant?"

"Yes. I recognized him as soon as I saw him."

Ms. Driscoll flashed her a warm smile. "Thank you, Ms. Mallory."

"You may step down now, Ms. Mallory," the judge said.

It was over. Leanne wanted to cry, to shout, to celebrate getting through it.

She stood and walked around the witness stand, then down the center aisle of the courtroom. Ms. Driscoll gave her a discreet thumb-up. But most stared as she passed. Curious, accusing, judging... Pitying? Was she another attraction in the city's never-ending freak show?

Joyce approached her at the back of the courtroom and hugged her. Leanne hadn't seen her when she'd arrived at the courthouse, but Joyce had announced the night before, "There's no way I'd ever let you face your ordeal alone."

"Thank you, Joyce," she said now. "Let's get out of here." She was desperate to escape, and for everything to return to normal.

She opened the door of the courtroom and faced flashes from dozens of cameras.

Normal would have to wait.

.　　　.　　　.

Kim slipped out of the courtroom as Leanne was embracing her friend. Larkin and Dubinsky, who had escorted Leanne to court, were waiting. But first Kim had to prevent the news cameras from catching Leanne with police protection. "I'll get her downstairs. It might take a while."

"We're parked on the corner of White and Centre," Dubinsky replied. "How'd she do?"

"Great." Kim glanced at the phalanx of media types. She couldn't sidestep all of them. No sign of Barlowe or any threat. Off to the side, she recognized a reporter from one of the local TV stations—Joanna Dunbar—and sidled up to her. "I need your help. No questions asked."

"And you help me?" Dunbar asked.

"That's a question. And I can't go on the record without DCPI approval."

"It's not you I want to talk to. Not today, anyway."

This would be tricky. She didn't want to frighten Leanne, and she didn't want the reporter to learn Leanne was still in danger. But she couldn't pull this off alone.

.　　　.　　　.

Leanne pressed through the door. A jumble of voices called from the throng closing in around her.

"Ms. Mallory?"

"Are you a fresh voice for Trans Rights?"

"Don't you feel guilty corrupting impressionable teens?"

296

The resolve she'd carried through her testimony crumbled and she grabbed Joyce's arm. "Get me out of here."

Detective Brady materialized out of the crowd. "Please come with me. Your friend, too." She herded them down the hall and into an empty courtroom.

The quiet was an instant relief. She hugged Detective Brady, choking down a sob.

"It's over," the detective said. "You did it. You were fantastic."

Leanne calmed herself as the detective flashed a reassuring smile.

A reporter slipped through the door. "I'm Joanna Dunbar. All I want is a moment. A friendly moment. I expect you don't want to give an interview. I don't blame you, after everything Foster put you through, the bitch. But you'll feel better if you do. Regardless of whether you give me an interview, I'll give you a fair deal in my report."

Joyce nodded encouragement, and the panic that had threatened to drown her receded. "All right."

"I'll get you out of the building after you're done. You're still under police protection." Detective Brady pointed a finger at Ms. Dunbar. "No mention of police involvement, or what I say to Leanne."

"Agreed."

Brady took her hand. "The stalker remains at large. When you and Ms. Dunbar finish your interview, she'll stay here while Joyce goes out the way we came. I'll escort you down the back stairs. Trust me on this."

It wasn't over.

CHAPTER SEVENTY-NINE

Tuesday, March 14th, 12:53 PM

"How'd it go?" Mike was waiting for her in front of the Chelsea Community Bank.

"Leanne was a rock. Choo must realize he's done. Got the warrant?"

He held it aloft. "One of Yvette's assistants delivered it this morning. Worded as you asked. Oh, and Dobson called in from the courthouse on Pierrepont Street. The video from Sunday shows nothing. Barlowe must've ducked behind the parked UPS truck."

The bank bustled with activity. When they approached the manager and showed him the warrant, he nodded and took them to the safe deposit vault. He placed the box on a small table and opened it.

It was empty, except for a black oblong object.

Mike regarded it with caution. "What the hell?"

Kim picked it up. "It's a battery for a notebook computer. Must be a spare. This confirms Barlowe has a notebook, and we've established the model: an HP Elitebook 8460p."

Mike rolled his eyes. "Don't tell me. You have one."

"No, but Jake does." She turned to the manager. "Can you tell us when this box was last accessed?"

He took down a binder with collected sign-in sheets and began paging through. "Monday, the sixth."

The day before Kincaid was killed. "Please show us the security video from last Monday."

Back in the manager's office, he started the run from March 6th at noon, twenty minutes before Barlowe had signed in. He appeared on screen, entering the bank at ten after.

"Enter our boy, stage left," Mike said.

"Freeze it." Kim studied the image for a minute.

"What are you looking for?" Mike asked.

"Don't know, yet." She signaled for the manager to continue. They watched while Barlowe waited to gain access to the vault area, then another ten minutes for him to come out.

"He's doing something in there," Mike said.

Kim waited until the image showed Barlowe exiting the vault. "Freeze it." The view was now from behind him. "Can we see a fresh angle? Perhaps from behind the teller whose window he's passing?"

"Give me a minute," the manager replied. The monitor's image split, with Barlowe frozen on the left and a jumble on the right, which froze when it reached the same moment.

She now had an unobstructed view of Barlowe from his right side. "Thought so." She turned to Mike. "You see it?"

"Yeah. The bulge. He's carrying. Right jacket pocket."

"He wasn't when he came in. He's also got something in his right hand. Looks like a paper bag." She turned to the manager. "We'll need the drive."

The manager rolled his eyes. "As I suspected."

•   •   •

Back at Hudson Street, Kim watched while Brandon Hollis recreated the sequence the bank manager had followed, and then printed out images of Barlowe coming in and leaving.

"Outstanding work, Kim," Colangelo said. "But aside from the battery, which tells us the make and model of his notebook but nothing else, I'm afraid it doesn't prove very much. The bulge and the bag prove nothing."

"Not for court," she replied, "but they establish the timeline. We arrested Choo and Lewis the morning of the sixth. They kill Kincaid the next day, and Garner two days after Kincaid. Then they shoot up Leanne's apartment and gun down Sylvia in a motel no one should even know about. All with the Ruger, which is what Barlowe's got tucked in his jacket, there. There's ammo in the bag."

"My guess, too," Colangelo said. "Meanwhile, Phillips vanished after we bagged Ames. They see the walls caving in."

"Ames said Phillips referred to 'the task force'." Kim pulled up her Notes app. "I wonder if their reference is to that Mayor's Task Force on which Phillips and DeMarco served."

"Could be," Brandon said. "I haven't been able to dig up anything on it. Seems it was such a bust, the mayor's office buried any record of it."

She grinned. "Maybe if we shake DeMarco's tree enough, he'll tell us."

"I'll bring him in tomorrow," Colangelo said. "Let's see."

Another idea. "How about if we get a search warrant for his home and car? For the missing notebook and flash drives?"

Colangelo looked askance. "With what we've got on him? Not likely."

"I bet Judge Castellano would listen," she replied.

CHAPTER EIGHTY

Tuesday, March 14th, 3:55 PM

Sharon Foster approached Yvette outside the courtroom. "Can we talk?" Cal Lewis had followed Leanne as a witness, and Duval had followed Lewis. The judge had ruled there was sufficient evidence to go to trial on Murder One.

"What about? Leanne Mallory buried your client this morning."

Foster's shoulders sagged. "Yeah. She was good. What can I say? He refuses to consider a deal."

"So, what is there to talk about?"

"I think he was counting on Mallory either not testifying or falling apart on the stand. Almost as if someone promised him something. I suspect he's figured out at last someone's been playing him. It's worth a shot."

Yvette had to agree, so she got hold of Kim Brady and Mike Resnick. They met Foster and Choo at the holding cell behind the courthouse. Choo was in an agitated state. "I need a new lawyer."

Yvette sat down and opened her briefcase. "Mr. Choo, your lawyer isn't responsible for your predicament, you are. She's done her best with the shitty cards you gave her to play. You can't bluster your way out of criminal court."

He crossed his arms and fell silent.

"I've got you cold on three murders-for-hire," Yvette said. "And I can make a powerful case for six felony murders, but I'd settle for depraved indifference. You're done. You have little to trade. But if you tell me who hired you and who ran Kincaid's 'security', I can make a sentencing recommendation. I can ask that you have a chance, if you're a model prisoner, of getting out in your seventies when you still have time to make something useful of yourself."

"Where would he do his time?" Foster asked. "It would have to be somewhere safe."

"Hey," Choo said. "I ain't agreed to..."

Foster wheeled around on him. "Shut your face and listen for a change."

"Have you had any problems at Sullivan?" Yvette asked. "Any incidents? Any threats?"

Choo re-crossed his arms. "No."

"Then, I'd be fine keeping you there. And if we learn of any threats, we can make other arrangements."

Choo remained silent.

"Going once... Going twice..."

Choo shook his head. "Fuck. All right."

CHAPTER EIGHTY-ONE

Tuesday, March 14th, 5:11 PM

Kim took charge. "Now or never. Who was Viper's 'security'? Who hired you to shoot Diego Paredes, Luke Wilson, and Malcolm Drake?"

Choo uncrossed his arms and slumped down in his chair, defeated. "A ring of cops protected Viper. Killed investigations. Fucked over any rivals. No idea how they worked it. Barlowe was the one I always dealt with. He called and said Viper had a problem, some PR run by Duval done gone rogue. Gave me fifty big ones and told me to take care of it."

"Fifty thousand?" All the pieces had to fit. "What did you do with it?"

"Gave ten of it to Cal Lewis to drive and to set it up with that shithead Duval. Barlowe insisted. Paid off debts with another ten. Gave two to my bitch. Still got the rest hidden."

Kim slid a notepad over. "Address. And where's it hidden?"

Choo scribbled. "Under a loose floorboard in the bedroom closet."

Kim checked the address. Morrisania in the South Bronx. "Where's Barlowe, now?"

"Don't know. We weren't friendly. I met him when I was working for Ice Williams."

"You mean before Viper Kincaid sold Ice out?" She held her breath.

Choo stared at the table. "Shit."

Another piece of the puzzle. "Yeah, we know. So, fill in the blanks for us."

"Viper fed Barlowe everything on Ice's operation," Choo said, "including where and when they could bust him with lots of girl."

"And you know this, how?"

"I was Viper's bodyguard. Anyway, when Jordy Hill's bitch, a pole dancer called herself Svetlana, gave him an alibi, they told me to deliver a bribe and threaten her at the same time. But some police captain—never found out his name—told me at the last minute Barlowe would take care of it. They figured no one would notice a detective talking to a witness."

"Did you ever talk to this police captain?"

"A few times. He called me to ask if I'd set up the hit. I said yeah, at the Cove. Three punks and make sure no witnesses."

Accomplice testimony needed corroborating evidence. "Got proof of the call?"

"When you find the money, you'll see a cell phone with it. Not a burner. Name on the account is Thomas Lee. I used it for all my contacts with Viper's Security. The captain's number is the only one starting with 347-319 ever called my phone. I can't tell you more about Viper's 'security', other than he had cops in Manhattan, Brooklyn, Queens, and the Bronx on the take."

Foster exhaled. "Deal?"

But Kim had one more detail to nail down. "After you killed Paredes, Wilson and Drake, you continued to fire. You killed six more people, paralyzed three, wounded seven. Why?"

Choo stared at the table. "Didn't mean for it to happen. Tried to keep everyone else inside. Figured people inside would panic and Duval wouldn't do his job. But somebody shot back at us, and one slug hit me in the knee. Didn't feel it at first, but when I turned, the pain was horrible. Hand clenched; couldn't let go of the trigger."

Yvette stood. "If we recover the money and the phone, and if his leads pan out, we have a deal."

CHAPTER EIGHTY-TWO

Tuesday, March 14th, 5:47 PM

Leanne entered the hotel room exhausted. Larkin and Dubinsky had brought her home to check her mail and pick up some different clothes. The adrenaline rush of testifying, followed by the media circus and the thrill of being interviewed, and the terrifying news someone was still out to kill her, had tapered off. Detective Brady was proving to be a wonderful friend.

But now, she was crashing, and all she wanted was a long, hot bath, followed by curling up in her nightgown with a cup of tea and a wonderful movie. At least her landlord had already replaced her living room window and had planned to clean up the mess from that awful night. And she rather liked the hotel room.

"Mind if I turn on the TV?" Officer Dubinsky asked. "You sure looked good, today. Very classy."

When this was over, she'd need to buy a new TV for her apartment. "Thanks. Go ahead."

A Eurasian anchor led with the trial story. "The prosecution team for accused hit-man Jack Choo took the unusual step of requesting a pre-trial hearing. A key witness was a transgender woman who testified she saw

Choo in the Blazer with an assault rifle on Gansevoort Street moments before the shooting."

Joanna Dunbar appeared. "Leanne Mallory's testimony was unshakable, withstanding a hellish cross-examination by the defense, who tried to impeach her credibility because she's transgender."

And there she was, answering Joanna's question. "I don't think there was anything heroic about it..."

Dubinsky came over and rubbed her back. "You okay?"

"Yeah." And she was. She'd been honest with the reporter—she didn't see it as heroic.

Dubinsky turned serious. "They told us you're still in protection."

Maybe she was a little heroic. She tried not to think about it.

CHAPTER EIGHTY-THREE

Tuesday, March 14th, 9:19 PM

They located the box in Choo's closet. Back at PBMS, Kim donned latex gloves and emptied the contents onto her desk. Twenty-eight thousand dollars in cash and the cell phone. Mike bagged the cash. They'd check it in to the Property Clerk's office in the morning.

She used a link on her laptop to check the phone's account and noted the mysterious captain's number listed among the call history—three calls over the course of a year.

According to the clock on her computer screen, it was after nine. Tal Bagels was closed. No decent coffee available. She checked the refrigerator downstairs. No Red Bull. Besides, it smelled like someone had a science project going in there. Coke Zero, available in the vending machine, would have to do.

She called Jake. "It looks like another all-nighter."

"So, you'll check in with me every hour?"

"I will if you want me to." She didn't want the limitations hourly check-ins would impose. "But I won't be anywhere but here or Hudson Street, in which case Mike would drive me."

"No, it's okay. Try to get some sleep."

"I'll try." But she had to follow the breadcrumbs, first to the captain's phone, then wherever they led.

307

CHAPTER EIGHTY-FOUR

Wednesday, March 15th, 7:32 AM

"Cheer up, Miss," the counterman at Tal Bagels said. "It's a beautiful morning, and the coffee's fresh."

Kim managed a smile. "Thanks." Closing this case would cheer her up. She race-walked the one block back to PBMS.

Mike came in as she was unlocking the file drawer in her desk. "I deposited the cash with the Property clerk." He gave her the receipt for the case file. "Any word from Ballistics, yet?"

"Not yet."

She got a text from Jake. *Still inhaling and exhaling. Get any sleep?*

She shot off an immediate reply. *Yes, from three to six.*

Well, that's something, anyway.

She showed Mike the diagram she'd worked up during the night. "Most calls to the mysterious captain originate in the Bronx—no doubt Phillips. Outgoing traffic includes the Bronx number, one in Queens and another in Manhattan. Queens was the Lindenwood house, and I expect Manhattan is Barlowe, although it's a different number than the ones he used to harass me."

"Meaning?"

"Barlowe's been changing off burner phones. I wouldn't bet he's still using any of the three I've logged. The weird thing is the 347 number doesn't appear to be the hub; the Bronx number is."

"You mean, this captain is taking orders from a sergeant?" Mike shook his head. "Doesn't sound right."

"I know. But the pattern is there. Calls from the Bronx cell to the 347 number always lead to calls from the 347 number to someone else in the network. And catch this—a call to the 347 number from yet another number on March seventh pinged off the tower near Rikers Island."

"The warning we'd learned of the Lindenwood house. Let me guess. Another burner?"

She checked on the other phone number. "Yes." She studied the screen. "But no call going out in response. So, someone delivered the order to torch the place up close and personal." Yesterday's hearing had been all over the news. Barlowe had to be figuring Choo had cut a deal. "We need to wrap this up."

Mike agreed. "Evidence may be disappearing at this moment."

Kiley wasn't in yet, so Kim led Mike into his office to study the case board. "The captain who showed at the Lindenwood fire, do you remember his name? Some guy from SpecNarc." She searched for the note. "Emerson. Captain Brian Emerson."

She returned to her laptop and brought up Emerson's file, using the login IAB had provided. "There it is. He served on that mayor's task force with DeMarco and Phillips." She clicked on the link to his current command. "Queens SpecNarc rents space right near JFK and the tower pinged by the call from Rikers on March seventh."

Kiley caught it as he walked in. "Excellent work, Brady. And pleasant news. Judge Castellano bought your argument. Here's your search warrant for DeMarco's 'home and any neighboring structures owned or controlled by him.' Hollis is on his way; Colangelo and I agreed he should join you so he can speak for IAB. Take Stephenson and Dobson with you, too."

Mike laughed. "This is DeMarco we're talking about, not Al Capone."

But Kiley remained serious. "We've already had too much shit go down on this case. We're not taking any chances. Go in strong and squeeze DeMarco for all he's worth. Emerson can't know we know, so he can wait. I want Barlowe, fucking maniac, off the street before he takes out anyone else."

CHAPTER EIGHTY-FIVE

Wednesday, March 15th, 10:15 AM

Even home on leave, waiting for an investigation to take him down, DeMarco appeared dressed in dark gabardine slacks and checkered Eton shirt, with not a hair out of place. But lines of worry creased his face as he studied the search warrant. "This is ridiculous."

Kim pushed past him into the central foyer of his massive home. Mike and the others followed. "Okay. Mike, Jimmy, Kyle, please get started on the search. Brandon and I will chat with the lieutenant." She recapped what Choo had told them about help from the inside, and what they had learned about the network of burner phones.

"I have no burner phones." DeMarco's tone suggested such things were beneath him. "Search anywhere you want for anything. With or without a warrant. You won't find a thing."

Kim made a note. "An excellent start, Lieutenant. Now, what can you tell us about George Barlowe? His current whereabouts?"

"He's on leave, as you know."

"I didn't ask his status, I asked about his whereabouts. He hasn't been to his apartment since early Sunday morning."

"What makes you think I'd be able to tell you anything about him?"

"Because," Kim said, "he's been running your unit."

DeMarco spluttered. "Don't be absurd. I…"

She cut him off. "Detective Hollis has made some inquiries."

Brandon pulled out a small notepad. "Your 'offshore investment', the Tortuga Bank and Trust, is on the FBI's list of money laundering operations."

"You're familiar with the term 'money laundering', aren't you?" Kim asked. "Where criminals try to make the income from their illegal activities look legitimate, like, oh, inheritances from old aunts."

"I also did a little background check on your wife," Brandon said. "She had one aunt, who died fifteen years ago in a nursing home, intestate and with no significant assets."

Kim took over. "You and Phillips served on the mayor's anti-drug task force back in 2002, an effort so ineffective they buried most of the records. Captain Brian Emerson served on it, too. Do you recall him?"

"Slightly." DeMarco turned sullen.

Kim jumped on it. "You mean, as the head of a Narcotics Unit in Manhattan, you have no contact with the head of a task force in Queens? Tell me, when we met on Monday, you claimed ignorance about a tip your unit had received about an operation in Queens. But suppose you had known. Who would you have notified?"

"Depends on the circumstances…"

She pressed him. "Isn't Captain Emerson's unit near JFK? Why would there be any question?"

Brandon jumped in. "Don't play dumb, Lieutenant. Let's have a reality check on your status. Your police career is over, unless you were unaware of everything going on under your very nose, meaning you were dumber than dog shit. But if you are—and you will have to demonstrate that beyond all doubt—then you can forget any meaningful command assignment. Ever. So, please answer Detective Brady's question."

Mike walked in carrying a notebook computer. "This the gizmo we want?"

It was an HP Elitebook 8460p. She turned it over. The battery was the same as the one they'd recovered from Barlowe's safe deposit box. "Looks like it."

"That belongs to my wife," DeMarco said. "She uses it to work from home."

"Dobson grabbed a bunch of those flash drives," Mike said. "Must be half a dozen."

"Those are my wife's work records," DeMarco cried.

"Bag them all." Kim turned back to DeMarco. "If we don't find the files we're looking for, we'll return the notebook and the flash drives as soon as we're finished with them. Now, about your tip…"

DeMarco plopped onto the spotless sofa. "I remember, now. We got a tip. I asked Detective Barlowe to refer it to the Queens Special Narcotics Task Force. Captain Emerson's unit. As far as I know, he did."

So, DeMarco was ready to throw the others under the bus. "You mean you didn't follow up?"

"No."

"Because Barlowe was such an exemplary detective?" Grab the ball. "Or because he was the one controlling the cash being fed into your offshore account?"

DeMarco froze.

Almost there. "The sooner you tell us, the easier it'll be for you. And your wife."

His voice was a whisper. "I never found out who paid me. The deal was I would do my job in normal fashion, but I'd ask no questions and say nothing to anyone about their practices."

"Where do Phillips and Emerson fit in with Barlowe's setup?" Kim asked.

"Phillips is Barlowe's second-in-command. Barlowe calls him his 'aide-de-camp'. Emerson is a lackey. I don't know what Barlowe and Phillips have on him."

"Does Emerson have access to the list of locations used for keeping people in protective custody?" Kim asked.

"I believe so, yes."

So there it was. "Lieutenant, we're taking you into custody, now. We'll give you a minute to call your wife and your attorney. Detective Hollis will get the seized items back to you as soon as they're cleared by our experts.

I have one other question for you. To your knowledge, does Detective Barlowe, or Sergeant Phillips, or Captain Emerson, own a Ruger Redhawk?"

DeMarco stood. "I don't know."

CHAPTER EIGHTY-SIX

Wednesday, March 15th, 3:36 PM

According to Vera Koshkin, the notebook and flash drives were, as DeMarco had said, used by his wife in her work. Kim repeated the news to her cohorts at IAB.

"So," Colangelo said, "time for our next move."

Yvette had already secured arrest warrants for Phillips and Emerson. But Phillips, like Barlowe, was avoiding his home, leaving Emerson as the one member of the trio they could grab.

"Let's leave him for the moment," Kim said. "The 347 cell shows no activity in the last twenty-four hours."

"Think he's switched phones?" Colangelo asked.

"Not likely." Kim pulled out her chart. "These phones have remained consistent, except for Barlowe. And I suspect he switches off more to show everyone how clever he is rather than out of a deep concern about security."

"Because you've analyzed him so well?" Brandon asked with a grin.

The confrontation in the subway elevator flashed through her mind. "I've got him pretty well pegged. He's already shown he thinks he can outsmart all of us, for example using the Ruger as his calling card. But he's also shown he has limits, and despite being skilled at evading

315

detection, he'll need help soon. Ditto for Phillips. I'd say one of them will reach out to Emerson before long."

Colangelo considered her summary. "Okay, Kim. Why don't you go home and get some sleep? Our folks will keep an eye out for both Barlowe and Phillips. We'll call you if we get a lead on either of them."

Sleep. Now, there was an idea.

CHAPTER EIGHTY-SEVEN

Wednesday, March 15th, 4:52 PM

Leanne powered down her desktop and tidied her workstation as her first workday as Leanne ended. On the advice of both Dr. Greene and Ms. Donner, she hadn't altered her appearance in any significant way. She still wore tailored slacks and blouses, now with dress flats.

Mr. Goddard had met with all the managers and laid down the law, saying the company would not tolerate any harassment. She'd found congratulations cards from Evelyn Gleason, Celia Coravos, and Joyce on her desk in the bullpen when she'd arrived, and the rest of the women had been cordial.

"How's everything going?" It was Frank Casio, who shared space in the bullpen with her and Joyce. "Anyone giving you a hard time?"

Microaggression. Little comments sounding supportive but pointing up her "otherness". Dr. Greene had warned her about it. Frank wasn't the only one, but he was the easiest to deal with. "I'm fine, Frank. Did you get those entries posted, yet?"

"Um… I'm doing it now."

"It's almost five. Please finish them up."

She finished putting everything away. She called her police detail. "I'll be down in five minutes." She checked herself in the compact mirror now hanging from the wall of her end of the bullpen.

"An—I mean, Leanne," Frank said, "I've finished the postings."

"At last." She picked her purse out of the bottom drawer. "Thank you, Frank. Have a nice evening."

Her cell rang. It was a number she didn't recognize. "Andy," a robotic voice said, "the police can't protect you. You're about to die." The call dropped.

She called her protection detail and told them.

"I'll meet you in the lobby," the officer replied.

CHAPTER EIGHTY-EIGHT

Wednesday, March 15th, 5:09 PM

Kim's legs felt like lead as she climbed the stairs to the elevator in the Clark Street station. It was her first time on those stairs since her encounter with Barlowe and she scanned her surroundings with each step. Receiving the call from Mike about the threat to Leanne as she stepped off the train didn't relax her. She'd asked him to check the cell tower from which the call originated and promised to call him as soon as she got to the apartment.

Unlike the night of her encounter with Barlowe, there were plenty of commuters on the stairs and in the elevator trying to beat the rush home. But crowds also made it easier for him to hide.

It was a relief to reach the street. The detail in front of the apartment reassured her.

"You okay?" Jake asked as she rushed in. "You don't look it."

"Leanne's received a threat." She gave him a quick hug and kiss. "I have to call Mike back."

Mike answered the phone with, "The call originated in the Bronx."

"Country Club section?" It was worth a shot.

"Close, but no cigar. Crosby Avenue in the Pelham Bay section, across the Bruckner from Country Club. Maybe it's Phillips this time."

"No way. The head games are Barlowe's department. He might have wanted to hide out at Phillips' place, but spotted the detail staking it out. The call is a misdirection play."

"You think he wants us to drop everything and run to the Bronx?"

For the first time, she was inside the sick bastard's head. "No. He knows we'll track his call to Leanne. He wants to pull the detail away from Phillips' house to look for him. Plus, it has to gall him he wasn't able to prevent her from testifying."

"How the hell did he even get her cell?"

Good question. "I don't know, Mike. We gave her a burner so he couldn't..." She stopped. "How fucking stupid of me. I called her cell on Monday to tell her about the hearing. The bastard must have pulled my LUDs."

Mike put Colangelo on, and she repeated the information.

"Did you call Leanne during the day or in the evening?" Colangelo asked.

"During the day. But if Barlowe checked the tower hits on her burner phone, he knows she's staying downtown. It's vital every member of Leanne's protection team knows what he looks like and is aware he's an active threat."

"I'll take care of it. I'll also get a BOLO out to every precinct in Manhattan. As soon as you locate him, make your move."

No. He'd have them chasing his shadow all over the city. "We have to wait him out. I'll keep watch on Emerson's burner cell because Barlowe has no other place left to go. By forcing Barlowe and Phillips underground, we've made Emerson the hub of the network."

Kim grabbed sleep in short snippets, tracking Barlowe's most recent burner and Emerson's cell on and off all night. Neither registered a single incoming or outgoing call.

CHAPTER EIGHTY-NINE

Thursday, March 16th, 9:04 AM

Leanne waved away the suggestion. The previous evening's threat hung over her like a thunderhead, and she had no tolerance for this. But Joyce and Celia were serious.

"You should," Joyce said. "You're already out, no one had a heart attack, and you so want to."

Leanne glanced around as the office buzzed with chatter. "I'm not comfortable wearing skirts to the office."

"You looked ready in court," Joyce said. "So corporate."

Celia lowered her voice. "And everyone saw you on the news." She and Joyce giggled.

Evelyn poked her head over the side of the bullpen. Leanne braced herself for her to add to the teasing. But Evelyn looked serious, even pale. "Leanne, can you join me in Mr. Goddard's office for a minute?"

The giggling stopped.

"Something wrong?" Leanne asked.

Evelyn's expression grew pained. "We need you, now. Bring your purse."

Joyce became indignant. "Hey, what…"

Evelyn cut her off. "None of our concern, Joyce. Please get back to work. Celia, please return to your section."

Leanne took her purse and followed Evelyn. They couldn't be firing her; everything was going so well.

Mr. Goddard was already standing, looking grave, flanked by a man and a younger woman. Goddard had Evelyn stay and close the door.

The woman, appearing young enough to be in high school, smiled and extended her hand. "I'm Police Officer Marisa Fuentes. Detective Kim Brady has told me so much about you. This is Detective Cordell Washington."

Leanne shook hands with them.

Detective Washington took over. "A short while ago, your protection detail spotted the man we suspect of trying to shoot you. He was attempting to enter this building through the service entrance. We're uncertain where he went. He might have circled back and made it inside. We've deployed detectives all around the outside of the building and we'll be conducting a thorough search. In the meantime, we want you to shelter in place. We'll stay with you."

"Ms. Donner has an interior office available down in Human Resources," Goddard said. "You'll be comfortable there."

"You'll be safe with us," Officer Fuentes said. "Promise."

Leanne thought back to the night someone shot up her apartment, with bullets blasting her television screen to pieces. Somehow, this felt worse.

CHAPTER NINETY

Thursday, March 16th, 10:08 AM

Kim had already been at Hudson Street for two hours when the call came in from Leanne's protection detail about Barlowe. An enormous map of the financial district hung on the wall of the conference room.

Colangelo was studying it. "It'd be a bitch to seal off the entire area around West Street. Where was Barlowe when they spotted him?"

Kim placed a pushpin on the map. "Right here. The service entrance to Leanne's company's building, on Murray Street. He tried to tailgate his way into the building behind a delivery man when someone from the detail spotted him and called out. He was last seen running here…" She placed another pushpin at the corner of Murray and North End Avenue. "From there, he could have circled south to Vesey and then back to Church Street and the subway stops for the 2, 3, E, and R."

"Or," Colangelo said, "he also could have circled north to Chambers and the 1, 2, 3, A, and C. Or even further north to his place on Leonard Street."

Kim gave a cynical laugh. "Except he knows we've got a detail there."

Colangelo threw his hands in the air. "Fuck. No sense in sealing anything off. He's long gone by now."

Kim turned to Hollis. "Can you check to see if Emerson is on the Master Roll Call today?"

A moment later, he said, "Yep. On duty." He checked again. "They have Phillips listed as on leave since yesterday."

She turned to Colangelo. "He'll get a jump on us in any event. If Mike and I are already mobile, outside of Manhattan, we'll be able to respond."

"What if he comes back for Leanne?" Colangelo asked.

"He won't. His lone concern, now, is getting away. Keep her sheltered in place, but he threw us another feint."

Colangelo was still mulling matters over when Hollis yelled, "Whoa. Hey, Kim, Barlowe's cell he used yesterday made a call to Phillips' home number in the Bronx."

"From what tower?"

"Give me a minute." Hollis's fingers flew over the keyboard. "TriBeCa. Tower on Sixth and West Broadway."

Kim checked the map. "Canal Street station for the A, C, and E. Duration?"

Hollis returned to the prior screen and refreshed. "Still connected. Six minutes so far."

"It could be Phillips is there, or else Barlowe wants us to think he is. Lieutenant, why not give us a little time to get mobile, then have the Bronx detail search Phillips' house? They've got the arrest warrant. Let Barlowe think we've taken the bait."

Colangelo agreed. "Queens SpecNarc is based in a small dump of a building stuck in with the hotels along the Belt Parkway. Stake Emerson out. We'll keep you posted. When he leaves, arrest him even if you still haven't seen Barlowe." When Kim scowled, he added, "Lackey or not, we can't afford to let him slip away. Maybe you're right and we'll catch a break and nail them both. But don't wait for Barlowe."

She nodded and got ready to leave.

Colangelo stopped her. "Wear armor and don't argue. ESU will contact you. Coordinate with them. I'll send Dobson and Stephenson out as soon as they come in, and I'll have the One-Oh-Six provide two detectives. Hollis will stay here to monitor cell activity."

As soon as she got her vest on, she called Jake. "Just checking in."

"You checked in twenty minutes ago. You okay?"

All at once, she wished with all her heart she'd already married him. "Sure. Just wanted to say I love you."

CHAPTER NINETY-ONE

Thursday, March 16th, 12:58 PM

Kim was second-guessing her own plan, wondering if they'd made a mistake planting themselves a scant ten yards beyond the Queens SpecNarc unit's headquarters. They could have cruised the Cross Island Parkway, so they'd be in a better position to react when Barlowe made his move.

No. He'd never bring himself to walk away. So, he had one move remaining. Here.

The radio crackled and squawked. "E-base to Unit One." It was ESU.

Mike responded. "Unit One, acknowledging."

"We have ground and air support ready when you need it. Over."

Kim signaled she wanted the mic. "E-base, this is Unit One. Please provide a cell number we can use if needed."

The operator at the other end gave it and Kim entered it into her cell's directory.

"Why?" Mike asked.

"I thought it might come in handy." She waited until Mike had signed off. "What's the latest on Hannah?"

For the first time since he'd first told her of his niece's condition, Mike looked relaxed. "She's out of ICU, regaining her strength, a little each day. She'll be getting a newly developed treatment called proton therapy and then, in two months, she'll start chemo. The doctors express cautious optimism."

The radio crackled. "Unit One, this is Unit Two." Stephenson's voice. "Dobson and I are turning off South Conduit onto Rockaway. Where do you want us?"

Kim grabbed the mic. "This is Unit One. We're at the SpecNarc parking lot entrance at 159th Street. One-Oh-Six team is at the other end, on 160th. Take a position on Rockaway and stay ready to give chase or provide backup."

"We copy, Kim. Out."

Hollis called. "Update, Kim. The detail busted in on Phillips' house about half an hour ago. They searched the place from top to bottom, including the garage. He ain't there and his wife has no clue where he is. No sign of the notebook, either. But when they got inside, the phone was off the hook and Barlowe's cell was still on the other end, still at Canal Street station. A detail from the Fourth searched the station and bagged the phone but no sign of Barlowe. Looks like your guess was right on the money."

"Thanks, Brandon." She ended the call. "We'll wait for baby to come to mama."

CHAPTER NINETY-TWO

Thursday, March 16th, 3:44 PM

The buzzing of her cell phone gave Kim a slight start. It was Hollis. "Hey, Kim. We just logged a call into Emerson's 347 number. From a number we haven't seen before. It originated and ended at the same tower, right by you. Weird."

She turned to Mike. "He's here."

Mike craned his neck to scan the parking lot. "Where?"

"Thanks, Brandon. Tell the lieu we're on it and contacting ESU." She ended the call. "You want to search car by car for him?"

Mike laughed.

She called the cell number ESU had provided earlier. "Subject Barlowe is in the vicinity. Not sure of his exact location."

"Okay," ESU replied. "What's your plan?"

"Expect Subject Barlowe and Subject Emerson to leave together. Will follow and wait until we have them in a location where pulling them over is an option. Will keep you posted."

CHAPTER NINETY-THREE

Thursday, March 16th, 4:42 PM

"There's Emerson," Kim said. She and Mike watched as he walked to the middle of the parking lot and got into an old, decaying unmarked Crown Victoria.

"A relic," Mike said. "Even for the NYPD fleet. I'd bet he has a Jag in the garage at home."

"If we don't see Barlowe, it means he's already in the car or somewhere close by and Emerson will pick him up." She called her ESU contact and reported in.

The Crown Vic pulled out of the parking lot. Mike pulled away from the curb and followed at a discreet distance. Emerson turned onto North Conduit, heading west, and merged into the traffic.

"Barlowe's already in the car." Kim said.

•   •   •

Mike tightened his grip on the steering wheel. Leave too much space and he risked losing him. Close the gap and he'd give it away for sure. "Stephenson and Dobson are a few cars behind us, and the One-Oh-Six guys are somewhere behind them." They were approaching the 150th

Street intersection, beyond which lay the entrance to the Belt parkway. Decision time.

He peered ahead. "I don't see Barlowe." Mike closed to within a car length of the Crown Vic to get a better look. Emerson made a sudden right onto 150th without signaling.

"Shit." Mike picked up the microphone. "This is Unit One. Subject Emerson is alerted to our presence. Tailing him north on 150th Street from the Belt Parkway."

"Roger, Unit One," ESU replied. "Expected route?"

He keyed the mic to respond.

.   .   .

Kim stopped him. "Stay off the radio. He might pick it up. I'll call on the cell."

"Okay. Tell them our best guess is he'll loop around the bottom of Baisley Pond Park trying to get some open space."

Kim connected to Bluetooth and hit the number she'd gotten for ESU and repeated what Mike had said.

"Okay, Detective. Let's stay on the call."

Emerson took a fast right at Rockaway Boulevard.

"Ha," Mike muttered under his breath as he followed.

"Our units heading for Baisley Boulevard," ESU said.

But Emerson stayed on Rockaway.

Mike pounded the steering wheel. "Shit."

Kim passed the news on to ESU. "Quick, Mike. Where's he going?"

"Eastbound Belt's already a parking lot. But he might make the turn onto South Conduit." Traffic coming in the opposite direction had the left turn lane at South Conduit backed up. They sped past the Belt. "Next chance to turn off is Farmer's Boulevard."

"Where are you, Kim?" ESU asked. "The chopper's airborne."

"Approaching Farmers," Kim replied. "Will advise."

The traffic light at Farmer's Boulevard turned yellow.

330

"If he runs it," Mike said, "we're fucked."

Emerson picked up speed. Mike closed on him.

The light turned red.

Traffic coming out of the airport moved into the intersection.

Emerson sped through.

Mike followed.

Blare of horns. Screeching brakes.

Impact on the rear quarter panel jolted Kim in her seat. Mike regained control of the car after it fishtailed. "Had it all the way." He glanced in the rearview. "Lost our backup, though. Jimmy had the excellent sense not to try."

"Where next, Mike?"

"Can't stay on Rockaway forever," he said. "Takes him into the Five Towns."

"Chopper should be over you any minute," ESU said.

Mike gave a grim smile. "At least they'll keep tabs on him if we lose him."

The Crown Vic leaped away as the road opened. Mike floored it to close the distance. "Damn thing won't do over 105."

She peered ahead. A brief glimpse of a head in the passenger front seat. "I see Barlowe."

Emerson pulled into the opposite lane to get past a cluster of trucks. Mike followed, the two cars weaving through the pack.

She needed to think further ahead. "What's in front of him?"

"Two miles of airport on the right and marshland with a freight company's transshipment facility in the middle of it on the left. At Brookville Boulevard, he'll have two choices—left on Brookville and into Rosedale, or straight into Meadowmere. Once in Meadowmere, traffic slows to a crawl."

"Hey, Kim," ESU said, "you want a roadblock?"

Not much time. But if they blocked Brookville, and Emerson stayed on Rockaway, traffic would give them time to recover. "Brookville." She was getting the hang of Queens geography.

"As close to the head of the marsh as they can manage," Mike added.

"We copy," ESU replied.

Maybe they could force Emerson's hand and improve the odds. "Think you can goose him?"

Mike broke into a grin. "I love this woman." Brookville Boulevard was less than a half mile ahead. Mike hit the siren and grille lights.

When they reached the intersection, Emerson careened around a sickening left onto Brookville.

Mike camped on his tail. "Got to stop him before he gets into Rosedale."

Emerson skidded through the narrow road's left curve. Mike closed the gap.

A car approached from the opposite direction. Emerson lurched to his right to avoid hitting it and clipped a telephone pole. Mike hit the brakes but still slammed into Emerson's rear.

Emerson's right rear tire slipped off the asphalt, spinning in the mud for a moment.

Mike hit him again, coming to a bone-jarring halt and propelling the Crown Vic off the road and into the marsh.

Kim and Mike slipped out and crouched down. The car's body provided ample cover for Mike, but Kim had only the passenger's door. She drew her Glock.

The passenger door on the Crown Vic swung open. Barlowe.

She needed a better angle. A telephone pole stood about five feet ahead of the car where the road curved back to the right. It had two metal signs nailed to it.

Not enough cover. It would have to do.

"Captain Emerson," Mike called. "Exit the vehicle with your hands up."

Emerson did not move.

The ESU chopper circled overhead. Sirens wailed in the distance.

"Captain Emerson," Mike called. "Do you need medical help?"

No answer.

Mike started out of his crouch.

"No, stay down." Kim made her move for the telephone pole.

Two shots. Shock to her left arm, below the shoulder, knocking her backward.

Searing pain.

She grabbed her injured arm, dropping the Glock. A fistful of blood.

Too much blood.

"Kim, you okay?" Mike's voice. Wonderful man. Excellent partner.

She took a deep breath. Keep control.

A glint of light off stainless steel. The Ruger.

Couldn't give herself away.

"Kim?"

Peering between the two metal signs, she could see Barlowe.

Away from the car.

She'd have a moment or two, and one functioning arm.

Starting to feel lightheaded. Losing blood.

She couldn't find the Glock. She wiped the blood from her functioning hand on her slacks and pulled out the lighter Chief's Special from her waistband.

Tried to steady it.

Talk to me, Dad.

The ESU chopper swooped in. Barlowe jumped, startled.

Center mass, Kim.

Now.

She slid to the right, lifted her right arm, willing it to remain steady; squeezed off two shots. Center mass.

Heard a cry.

The surrounding marsh started to spin.

Light fading.

Should have married… Jake…

CHAPTER NINETY-FOUR

Thursday, March 16th, 5:14 PM

Mike could see Emerson still sitting in the Crown Vic. "Kim?"

No answer. If anything happened to her...

He grabbed the radio microphone. "Unit One. 10-13. Shots fired, officer down."

The ESU chopper circled over the marsh before setting down. Mike took aim at the Crown Vic. "Out of the fucking car, Emerson, or you die."

The driver's side door opened.

"Toss your piece out first." He needed to hurry, so Kim could get help, but he needed to take the time to do it right.

A Smith and Wesson thirty-eight landed on the asphalt.

"Exit the vehicle, showing your hands."

Emerson got out and began walking toward Mike. A shot rang out and Emerson crumpled to the pavement. ESU closed on Barlowe.

Sirens from approaching ambulances.

"We've got him, Detective," a voice called from the marsh.

Mike approached Emerson. He was lying on the ground, blood from the wound in his side turning the dirt dark. Mike holstered his piece as an ambulance pulled up. "Brian Emerson, you are under arrest for murder, conspiracy to commit murder, drug trafficking and obstruction of justice. You know your fucking rights, don't you?"

Emerson stared at him but said nothing.

Mike kicked him in the back. "Answer me."

Emerson groaned. "Yeah."

Several patrol cars from the One-Oh-Six and four ambulances swarmed in, choking off Brookville Boulevard. Mike recognized one of the police officers. "Hey, Bucky, make sure no one touches their Crown Vic. I'll be back. My partner's been shot."

Two EMTs got Emerson onto a stretcher and into an ambulance. Mike rushed across the road. Kim was lying in the mud, unconscious, deathly pale. He waved and cried out to an ambulance crew. "Over here! Now!"

They rushed over with a stretcher.

"Gunshot wound, upper arm," one EMT said. "Get a tourniquet on her. Might've hit the brachial artery." He yelled over his shoulder. "Get ready to crossmatch two pints."

Another crew picked up Barlowe, deeper into the marsh.

The EMT continued to give instructions. "Pressure's low, but pulse is steady. Get her into the ambulance."

For a moment, Mike felt seized by murderous thoughts about Barlowe and Emerson, but then his training kicked in. Bucky was still standing guard over the Crown Vic. Mike donned a pair of latex gloves and opened the driver's-side door to the back seat, spying an HP Elitebook.

"Hey, Bucky, give me an evidence bag." Mike bagged the notebook. "Got another?" He combed both the front seat and the back. Nothing. He checked the glove compartment. Still nothing.

He found Barlowe, unconscious in an ambulance. He patted down Barlowe's trouser pockets.

"Sorry," an EMT said, "we can't have you here."

"Just be a second." Lumps on the right-hand side. He reached in. Three flash drives.

CHAPTER NINETY-FIVE

Thursday, March 16th, 5:36 PM

Kim woke up in an ambulance, an IV running into her right arm and a tourniquet on her left. Where was the Chief's Special?

A handsome EMT in his twenties leaned over. "How are you doing, Detective?"

The trembling she'd fought off at the roadside now overtook her. "You... tell me."

"Bullet passed clean through. Excellent. Didn't hit any bones or joints. Also excellent. Nicked an artery. Bad, but could be much worse. You're getting blood, so you'll feel a little more alert before long. You'll have a scar. Bad, but only slightly."

She relaxed a little. He was nice. Funny. Comforting. Like Jake.

"We'll clean and dress the wound here, but you'll need some surgery on the artery at the hospital. Shouldn't be anything major."

Surgery on an artery sounded major to her.

· · ·

Mike appeared. "You okay?"

Her left arm now had a pressure dressing on it. Must've dozed off. "Bastard got my arm." Her voice shook. "Just below... the shoulder."

"And you still brought him down?"

She tried to smile, but it was more of a happy grimace. "Grandad's piece. Think one missed."

"Three shots?"

"Two."

He grinned. "You didn't miss."

She glanced down at her arm. "Going to have a scar. No sleeveless tops in summer."

"Hey, not the worst tragedy."

"Jake will freak."

An ESU lieutenant appeared. "Detective Brady? Switching from radio to cell phone was brilliant."

"She's a great cop," Mike said. "She gets Barlowe's collar."

"You must be Detective Resnick. You're both great cops." He and Mike shook hands. "I think your lieutenant has arrived."

Colangelo and Kiley appeared.

"Barlowe took one in the chest, one in the collarbone," Mike said. "Kim shot two-for-two. Barlowe shot Emerson in the side. Also..." Mike held up the two evidence bags.

Kim couldn't believe it. "You got them?"

Mike grinned at her. "Make that three-for-three."

The EMT checked the dressing. "You rest, now, Detective. We'll get you to the hospital as fast as we can."

Not yet. "Mike, please call Jake. Tell him I'm okay. Then Yvette... Leanne can go home."

"You got it, kiddo. I'll see you later at the hospital."

"Before you go, Mike," Kiley said, "I need your pieces. Yours, too, Kim."

Mike handed his over.

Right arm getting blood. Left arm immobilized.

The EMT held up the Chief's Special. "Got it right here. Even when she was unconscious, I had a hard time getting her to let go of it."

Colangelo hefted it. "Very nice. A classic."

Kim was getting drowsy again. "Ask ESU... Dropped Glock... in the marsh."

Colangelo broke into a grin. "Just until the shooting's cleared. ESU already recovered the Glock." He held up an evidence bag. "This, too." It was the Ruger. He patted her shoulder. "You're one damned fine cop, Kim."

"Thanks."

We did it, Dad.

The fog of sleep closed in.

CHAPTER NINETY-SIX

Saturday, March 18th, 11:10 AM

Kim brightened the moment Mike, Colangelo and Yvette walked into her room at the Queens Hospital Center. Mike had visited her twice already, but not the others.

"How's the arm?" Yvette asked.

First things first. "Leanne's settled back home?"

"Ask her, yourself."

Leanne walked in. "I heard you'd gotten hurt. Detective Resnick told me you were here. Are you okay?"

"The arm's fine. They repaired an artery and I should go home tomorrow. With rest and some physical therapy, I'll be ready to return. You're back home?"

"Officers Larkin and Dubinsky drove me home Thursday night, stopping first for a new television. It's on the wall and the apartment is back to normal." She hesitated. "Thank you for everything."

Kim took her hand. "Thank you, Leanne. You cracked the case."

"You did much more for me." She kissed Kim on the cheek. "Must run. I'm meeting my friend Joyce for lunch."

"Thanks for coming by," Kim said.

"Did you tell her your news?" Mike asked once Leanne had gone.

"No, I've never even mentioned Jake to her."

Yvette brightened. "What news?"

Mike nudged Kim. "Go on."

She blushed. "Jake said he wouldn't give me a hard time about returning to full duty if I marry him, first."

Yvette hugged her. "So, when's the day?"

"Two weeks from Monday at Brooklyn Borough Hall. Lieutenant, have we collared Phillips, yet?"

"Not yet. We're questioning Emerson and Barlowe in a little while."

"I'm hoping to motivate Emerson to tell us where he is," Mike added.

Mike's use of the first person got her attention. "But you're on Administrative Leave, like me, until they clear the shooting. Or did you figure you'd keep me company while Yvette and the lieu interrogated them?"

"As of nine o'clock this morning," Colangelo said, "IAB has declared Thursday's incident a righteous shoot. The entire ESU team from Thursday's operation offered to give statements on your behalf. Mike will join us."

"You'll be the first one I tell afterwards," Mike added.

Oh, no. "Yvette, please help me with my pink robe." She slid out of bed and slipped her right arm in the robe's sleeve. Yvette draped the robe over Kim's left shoulder.

Colangelo held up a hand. "Hold it, Kim. You're off Administrative Leave, but you're now on Sick Leave. You…"

"I'm on my time, like any other off-duty cop. Nowhere does the Patrol Guide say I can't be an observer." She stepped into a pair of slippers.

"I like it," Yvette said. "Emerson first."

CHAPTER NINETY-SEVEN

Saturday, March 18th, 11:30 AM

Mike fixed Emerson with a malignant glare as they entered. The other bed was empty, so they didn't have to throw anyone out.

"My client suffered a gunshot wound destroying his right kidney on Thursday..." the attorney began.

"You mean when his own accomplice tried to kill him," Mike said. "My heart bleeds."

The attorney frowned. "I'm not sure 'accomplice' is the appropriate word."

Mike scoffed. "I am. We tracked cell phone calls between him and Barlowe. And they were in the same car together when my partner and I were in pursuit."

"So," Yvette added, "unless you give me convincing evidence to the contrary, 'accomplice' is the term of choice."

Emerson stirred. "He was hiding in my car. He threatened to kill me if I didn't do what he said."

"Accomplices turn on one another all the time," Yvette said.

Mike jumped back in. "Let's recap what we already know. You killed an investigation of the Lindenwood safe house. When you later received a warning about an impending raid of it, you had it torched to destroy evidence, then had the balls to turn up at the scene. You functioned as the hub of a network of burner phones linking three safe houses used for distribution and four groups of police who protected drug dealing operations. And you used your position to protect dealers and crooked cops. This network functioned as the 'security' for a drug ring headed by one Thomas 'Viper' Kincaid, now deceased. Your ring ordered the shooting carried out by Jack Choo. It bugged a conference room at Rikers Island and executed Kincaid, a witness, two accomplices, and a Suffolk County police officer while stalking and attempting to kill another witness."

"That was Barlowe," Emerson said, his voice a mere croak. "Jesus Christ, I never would have ordered a drive-by shooting. All Barlowe had to do was have Kincaid cut off their supply."

Yvette took over. "You called Choo on February twenty-second, instructing him to kill Paredes, Wilson, and Drake, and to leave no witnesses. We have proof of the call."

"Barlowe forced me to cooperate."

Yvette ignored him. "So, Counselor, my first question for your client: who else in the NYPD of equal or superior rank to his own took part in this drug ring? Or even knew of it?"

The attorney gestured to wait. "What's your offer?"

"Nothing. He's going down as the leader unless he can give me someone higher."

"What if it isn't so clear cut?" the attorney asked.

Yvette shrugged. "What do you mean?"

"Off the record, what if my client started out as the titular head of the operation you described, but another took over the enforcement responsibilities? And the individual in question slipped away from his control?"

Yvette considered it. "I'd need convincing hard evidence."

"In the back seat of the car I was driving Thursday," Emerson said, "there is a notebook computer. It contains several files—records of shipments and payments, a contact sheet, even an org chart with names and commands. It's not the most recent. Barlowe was carrying some flash drives on Thursday with the most recent versions of the files. If he didn't ditch them in the marsh."

"We have the notebook and the flash drives," Colangelo said. "But we can't get past Barlowe's PIN. What is it?"

"Snowfall!9X4."

Mike had him repeat it. "What was Phillips' role in all this?"

"He and I had contacts in the department all over the city from when we served on a mayor's task force back in '02. They're all listed in the files. He protected Kincaid's distribution system. About a year ago, Barlowe decided he was better at organization, so he took over Kincaid's operation."

Yvette cut in. "Just for the sake of credibility. If Barlowe 'got away' from you, why couldn't you use your position in the department to bring him back into line? And why did you agree to make a phone call incriminating you for something you claim he did? What did he have on you? Everything must be a perfect fit."

Emerson's shoulders sagged. "He discovered a girlfriend I had. He threatened to expose the details. His method. Finds your weakness and stomps on it."

"Must have been cringeworthy." Mike leaned closer. "How old was she?"

Emerson paled. "Fifteen."

Yvette sat back. "Tell me everything."

"I supplied her and her school friends with free coke."

"We're done for now," Yvette said.

CHAPTER NINETY-EIGHT

Saturday, March 18th, 11:50 PM

Kim wouldn't let him slide. "Where's Phillips?" Colangelo shot her a glare, but she pressed it. "You know where he's hiding and don't hand me any bullshit."

"She's right," Yvette said. "You must know, and there's no deal unless you tell us."

"His cousin—well, step-cousin, actually—has a cabin on Lake George. The address is in one of Barlowe's files. He fled right after Ames took a deal. He realized you'd be coming for him next."

Next question. "And what was Detective Chris Ryba's connection? He didn't decide to snort coke in the middle of an investigation."

"Barlowe had met him on a case he'd worked early in his time with Narcotics. Saw him as a weak link. He never told me how. Barlowe planned the Cove shooting for a night when the Master Roll Call showed Ryba would be on duty, since the Cove is in the Sixth. Told Ryba beforehand to be ready for action at the Cove..."

"So, Ryba was Barlowe's mole," Kim said.

"Yeah. And he called me to tell me they'd assigned you and your partner to the case. From then on, he reported to me everything happening on the case until he got taken off. Then Phillips paid him a visit."

·　　　·　　　·

Kim couldn't help but feel satisfied seeing Barlowe, whom she'd hit in the chest, was in far worse shape than she was. He was still on oxygen.

Barlowe's attorney did a double take. "What's she doing here? She's under investigation for shooting my client."

Colangelo informed the attorney of the decision to clear the shooting.

She tried being coy. "I'm doing my best to aid an investigation."

"Guess we came out even," Barlowe said.

Mike laughed. "Not on the best day you ever had." He turned to the lawyer and recounted everything they'd learned. "We recovered the Ruger Redhawk from him in the marsh, the weapon he used to kill four people and tried to kill three others. Also, Jack Choo has told us he paid him fifty thousand for the Cove shooting."

"And," Colangelo said, "a fellow conspirator has fingered him as the ringleader of the police protection Viper Kincaid enjoyed."

Yvette continued. "Can your client tell me now of any other high-ranking police officers who were part of his ring and whose names don't appear in the files we recovered from his notebook and flash drives?"

Barlowe responded with a blank stare.

Yvette pressed on. "If so, I might consider allowing him the chance to leave prison before he goes to the Great Beyond. Otherwise, we go to trial on eleven counts of murder-one, two counts of murder-two, three counts of attempted murder—Detective Brady, Captain Emerson, Leanne Mallory—conspiracy to commit murder, drug trafficking, and multiple counts of obstruction of justice. So, Mr. Barlowe, anything you want to tell me?"

"Emerson was the leader."

Kim broke her silence. "You are so full of shit. He wasn't even number two. Phillips was. A team will be arresting him shortly at Lake George, if they haven't already."

Barlowe turned red, straining against the handcuffs keeping him chained to the bed.

Kim grinned and leaned closer. "You can't stand it. You believe you're a genius. Houdini, the hacker king. It must kill you to realize you weren't smart enough. Even worse, it was a woman who bettered you." She pointed to her shoulder. "I'll recover in a few weeks, and you'll be rotting in prison when I'm a great-grandmother."

Barlowe yanked hard against his constraints. "Get her out. Get her the fuck out. Fucking bitch."

Yvette picked up her briefcase. "We're done."

Barlowe hollered after them. "Who did you suck off to get your gold badge, Brady?"

Barlowe's attorney rushed out after them. "Detective, I'm filing an official complaint against you…"

Kim turned on him. "For what? Telling the truth?"

"He'll never agree to a plea deal, now," the lawyer said to Yvette.

But it was Kim who answered. "Excellent. No deals. I want to testify against him in court, to hit your piece of shit with everything we've got. He doesn't deserve just to spend the rest of his life in prison, but if he's reincarnated, his next life, too."

CHAPTER NINETY-NINE

Monday, March 20th, 12:18 PM

"Hey, there, Sarge," Mike called out as they entered the conference room at Rikers. "Fouled any crime scenes today?"

Phillips' attorney held out both arms. "You want to keep it down? You trying to get my client killed?"

Mike sat down across from Phillips, feigning shock. "I'd want a dirty cop killed?"

"How about innocent until proven guilty?" the attorney replied.

Mike recapped everything they had, including the swelling of Phillips' bank accounts over time with no additional source of legitimate income.

Phillips dropped his head into his hands. His attorney slumped in his chair. The lawyer variation of the "oh, shit" look.

"You should know," Yvette said, "I've already told Barlowe's attorney I'm not interested in a plea deal. I've already got everything I need to convict him. I'm not sure I'm interested in a deal for your client, either. This city despises dirty cops."

The attorney straightened. "He wasn't the boss. You already have Barlowe."

Mike refused to budge. "He should have cooperated instead of hiding. If he'd helped us run Barlowe down three weeks ago, he would've saved some lives."

Phillips raised his head. "I was against the shooting at the Cove, but Barlowe insisted."

"Easy to say, now you're in here," Mike replied.

"It's true. I told Barlowe if he thought Paredes was such a problem, there were much better ways to deal with it. But George had decided Kincaid screwed up when he agreed to let Paredes, Duval and Walters back into the business. He'd been looking for an excuse to force Kincaid out, so he figured having Paredes gunned down and making it look like Kincaid was responsible would solve everything. It was stupid, and I told him so."

"And yet," Mike said, "you planted Chris Ryba as a mole. How did you accomplish it?"

"The Master Roll Call showed Ryba was on the four-to-one for February twenty-third, so I called him and told him we needed cover. Paid him five grand, promised him twenty more if the case remained unsolved. Wasn't the first time he'd helped us out, but it was the first time we'd used him for something like this."

"He already had learned what to do?" Mike asked.

"No. I had to coach him. Barlowe decided he wasn't helping, so he had me provide him some girl to show there were no hard feelings. Turned out to be uncut. No wonder he keeled over. When I told Barlowe, he laughed."

"And you will so testify?" Yvette asked.

Phillips nodded.

CHAPTER ONE HUNDRED

Monday, May 15th, 7:45 AM

On the subway ride in, Kim glanced down every five minutes at her left hand, the engagement ring and wedding band together. If she closed her eyes, she could almost hear the cries of herons diving for their dinner in Magen's Bay in St. Thomas. She'd found the bay and its surroundings exquisite for the five days she and Jake had spent there on their honeymoon, the one they'd put on hold for too long.

Now she was back, and full recovery wasn't far off. She'd already promised Jake she wouldn't push it. And Kiley had promised he'd assign her to light duty.

Sergeant Holloran stood at the front desk as soon as she entered PBMS and began the applause that rippled across the entire first floor. She smiled and waved at everyone, glad to be back. As soon as she put her purse down, Kiley waved her into his office. "Welcome back, Kim. How's the arm?"

"I'm getting physical therapy. Coming along quite well, thank you."

He gestured for her to sit. "I have news for you. The commissioner has approved recommendations for you for a Purple Shield and a medal for Meritorious Police Duty—Honorable Mention."

She caught her breath. "Honorable Mention?" The highest level of the MPD medal.

"Captain Forrest recommended you. You made quite an impression on him. Lieutenant Colangelo and I provided the additional endorsements. Congratulations."

"Thank you, Lieutenant." The commendation holder she wore with her dress uniform would only hold four bars; with two fresh bars plus her Community Service Commendation, her Firearms Badge, and, at the top, the American Flag bar, she now needed a larger holder.

"Also, the department has promoted you to Detective, Second Grade. Your work on this case was exemplary, and you've shown you have what it takes to be a lead detective. You've garnered a lot of attention. A raft of opportunities will open up for you in the department."

"Thank you, but I'm thrilled right here." She couldn't believe a little over two months earlier, she'd been ready to transfer out.

Kiley sat back. "I'm flattered, but Internal Affairs wants you."

She wasn't sure she'd heard right. "What?"

"IAB rotates with a few other commands in getting first crack at the best people. It's their turn, and they've tabbed you."

What about Mike? "But I want to stay here."

"And I would love to keep you. But IAB isn't a voluntary post. When they select, it's a conscription, like it or not, for a two-year hitch. I hope you'll come to like it. Most do. It's also a tremendous boost to your career, whatever direction you want to take."

Mike knocked on the window and waved. She waved back.

"You've made an impressive pair of partners," Kiley said. "You've dragged him into the technology era of policing, and he's refined your already well-developed gut instincts. But you'll both thrive on the change."

"Does he know?"

"About IAB? Yes, I told him. He wasn't surprised. Forrest and Colangelo were effusive in their praise of you." He pulled out a file. "Vera Koshkin over at One-PP broke into Barlowe's files. They pieced together

350

how Barlowe had conspired with Kincaid to bring down Ice Williams. Barlowe had started by listing everyone in Williams' operation loyal to him and everyone he could count upon to stick with Kincaid. He'd spotted Sylvia Walters as a weak link early on. Your new colleagues collared all the cops on his lists, and they all took deals. They gave up the dealers who Barlowe had organized, and we've taken down the entire network. Even their guys in Corrections. The commissioner has relieved six commanding officers of command in four boroughs. He fired DeMarco, who's also facing federal charges for money laundering."

It had been an excellent bit of police work from start to finish.

Kiley gestured to the file. "Emerson pled out. Three counts of accessory after the fact. Also, drug trafficking, conspiracy, taking bribes, and obstruction. Phillips pled to the same, plus an additional accessory count for Ryba's death. Driscoll respected your wishes not to give Barlowe a deal. He'll go to trial. Captain Forrest will give you time off to testify."

"It'll be a pleasure. When do I report to IAB?"

"Tomorrow. Your physical restrictions will be less of a hindrance there than here."

"What happened to the rest of my open cases?"

"All re-assigned. Kyle Dobson transferred in. He appeared disappointed to learn he was replacing you, rather than joining you. And although you didn't think much of him at the outset..."

"No, he did well."

"A bit of an eager beaver, but Mike will tone him down, now he's gotten his mojo back."

One more question to ask. "What happened with Bob Nolan?"

"IAB recommended against any charges being filed against him or any disciplinary action by the department. He's transferred out of Narcotics. Not sure where to." He stood and extended his right hand. "Good luck, Detective... Still Brady?"

She took it. "Still Brady."

"I expected no less."

.   .   .

Half past four, and traffic on the Brooklyn-bound side of the Manhattan Bridge had slowed to a crawl. Kim gazed over at Mike, who'd insisted on driving her home one last time. "How's Hannah doing?"

"She's started chemo. They say she's got an excellent chance of remaining cancer-free. The family's relaxing a bit."

"I'll bet the dog helped."

Mike blushed. "Sonny is the friendliest dog. Hannah loves him."

"As does her uncle."

He cleared his throat and changed the subject. "I'll sure miss you, kiddo. Who'll teach me how to use Bluetooth?"

"Your new partner. Kiley told me about Bob Nolan. I'm glad. Any word on where he went?"

"Brooklyn North Homicide. Once I got the news about you going to Internal Affairs, I was kind of hoping he'd land here." He shrugged. "No such luck."

She turned serious. "Mike, thanks for coming to get me that night in Brownsville. Thanks for being the best partner, ever."

He didn't take his eye off the road. "Thanks for being the best cop I've ever worked with." His voice caught. "Ever."

She stared out the passenger side window. Traffic on the nearby Brooklyn Bridge was no better. Beyond it, ferries churned the river from lower Manhattan to Staten Island, Jersey City, and Weehawken. A cruise ship stood at the Bayonne terminal, ready to sail for sunnier climes. She thought of St. Thomas.

She thought of Dad. His little monologues about police work had been his way of connecting with her. Police work and basketball.

In her teen years, his stories changed, focusing on street life, rough and often disgusting. Perhaps he'd been trying to derail her growing interest in police work. Or prepare her for it. They'd cemented her desire to become a cop. An excellent cop. The kind of cop he'd once been before he'd succumbed to the slippery notions of street justice.

Back at the Academy, one of her instructors had pounded a simple message into their heads: "The Law: know it, love it, live it and breathe it." But she'd always understood. She thought Dad had, too.

She still didn't understand how he could have straightened out and avoided disgrace and yet felt the need to kill himself. Why he couldn't have forgiven himself. But then, she hadn't forgiven him, either. Not until this case.

How had Mike put it? "What's gone and what's past help should be past grief." The only time he'd ever quoted Shakespeare to her. Must've been the one time he'd stayed awake in Lit class.

She turned now to smile at him. He smiled back.

Mike had been right.

ACKNOWLEDGEMENTS

Writing this novel has been quite a journey, with several unexpected twists and turns, and I owe a debt of thanks to several who helped along the way. While I did vast amounts of the research and background reading, not everything is in books or on the internet. Lt. John Grimpel of the NYPD's office of the Deputy Commissioner of Public Information (DCPI) was an enormous help, always patient no matter how many questions I asked. I'd also be remiss if I didn't tip my hat to my late stepdad, Sgt. George Ofenloch, Badge #169 of the Nassau County Police Department, whose stories gave me some background in the politics of police departments and some details about "the job".

I received an enormous amount of help to work the story into publishable shape from authors Susan Breen and David Rich. I can't thank them enough for their advice and encouragement. And thanks to Reagan Rothe and his crew at Black Rose Writing for having faith in my story and bringing the ultimate product to the public.

I also found brilliant and thoughtful beta readers, all of whom offered excellent suggestions and insights: Linda Davies, Jan Foley, Ray Lodato, and Sydney Young. Most of all, I want to thank my wife of 44 years, Cindy Leahy. She read through the manuscript twice (making insightful points along the way). She also tolerated being dragged to several locations in the book, including the block on which Leanne lived and the block on which I set the Cove. I compensated her by taking her to dinner at Tournesol. We also had breakfast at Dorian Cafe. Her encouragement and support never flagged. She is the love of my life.

ABOUT THE AUTHOR

Edward J. Leahy was a finalist for the 2018 Freddie Award for Excellence. He is a member of the Mystery Writers of America and the International Thriller Writers and has been published by New York Teacher Magazine. He's a retired International Issue Specialist for the IRS with investigative experience and holds a B. A. and M. A. from St. John's University in Government & Politics. He serves on the Board of Directors of AHRC-NYC.

NOTE FROM THE AUTHOR

Word-of-mouth is crucial for any author to succeed. If you enjoyed *Past Grief*, please leave a review online—anywhere you are able. Even if it's just a sentence or two. It would make all the difference and would be very much appreciated.

Thanks!
Edward J. Leahy

Thank you so much for reading one of our **Mystery** novels.

If you enjoyed our book, please check out our recommendation for your next great read!

K-Town Confidential by Brad Chisholm and Claire Kim

"An enjoyable zigzagging plot."

–Kirkus Reviews

"If you are a fan of crime stories and legal dramas that have a noir flavor, you won't be disappointed with *K-Town Confidential*."

–Authors Reading

View other Black Rose Writing titles at www.blackrosewriting.com/books and use promo code **PRINT** to receive a **20% discount** when purchasing.

Made in the USA
Middletown, DE
28 August 2024

59908260R00205